Dear Dad,

OUT OF HER LEAGUE

Happy reading.
Best wishes
and
all my love,

Del
xx

May 2007

OUT OF HER LEAGUE

A Novel

Delores Airey

iUniverse, Inc.
New York Lincoln Shanghai

OUT OF HER LEAGUE

iUniverse books may be ordered through booksellers or by contacting:

iUniverse
2021 Pine Lake Road, Suite 100
Lincoln, NE 68512
www.iuniverse.com
1-800-Authors (1-800-288-4677)

This is a work of fiction. All of the characters, names, incidents, organizations, and dialogue in this novel are either the products of the author's imagination or are used fictitiously.

ISBN: 978-0-595-42199-2 (pbk)
ISBN: 978-0-595-86537-6 (ebk)

Printed in the United States of America

For my father and my mother

Faith is the substance of things hoped for, the evidence of things not seen.
Hebrews 11 :1

Acknowledgements

Thanks and praises be to God, the creator of the Word.

Much gratitude goes to Michelle Lambert for her valuable support during wonderful discussions over many Sunday lunches. Thank you to Gemma Lee for her genuine support. ~~To gratitude goes to Michelle Lambert for her valu-~~ ~~able support during wonderful discussions over many Sunday lunches. Thank~~ ~~you to Gemma Lee for her genuine support.~~ To "Susie," a great big and hearty thank you. My thanks to Nancy Berry for her kind support, encouragement and for listening to my entire recitation of the book during our hike up San Jacinto Mountain in Palm Springs, California. Thank you to my babe, Germany Andrade in Manhattan, New York for her genuine interest, waiting patiently for the book's publication with much belief.

I owe a great many thanks to the publishers, iUniverse for their expertise and advice. A special mention and thank you to my heroine, Rachele Walter, for coming to my rescue and taking me under your wing, providing genuine support, patience, feedback and kindness. Much appreciation to Blair Wyant for his expediency and genuine help sorting out my teething problems at the crucial initial stage when I needed a helping hand. You were great Blair, immediately returning my calls and helping me out.

CHAPTER 1

When Amy Scott walked into the Montague room, she didn't quite know what to expect.

"Ah. Good morning," said the course instructor, Petra Kindell.

"Good morning." Amy sat down and looked round about her. Someone was opening the door. He entered the room, smiled confidently at the delegates and walked coolly over to Petra. A couple of women ogled him. Amy delighted at the sight of him.

"Ah. Hello. And you are?" said Petra, working busily at her desk on the final paperwork prior to the commencement of the workshop.

"Mike. Mike Brandleton," he oozed.

"Thank you." Petra made a quick stroke on the sheet of paper in front of her. "We're about to begin. However, there is one other gentleman who should be arriving shortly, hopefully within the next two minutes. Please, make yourself comfortable, Mike."

"Thank you," said Mike, strutting over to a seat situated at the back of the room.

Amy's eyes followed him, as he took each stride with manly elegance. She eyed the immaculateness of his attire. Bedecked in a silver gray suit, exquisitely cut by a bespoke Savile Row tailor, gray shirt, gray tie and, smart black Bellucci shoes. His highly polished black leather Italian briefcase swung stylishly from one hand. Sheer elegance, quality and sophistication, Amy thought. Nonchalantly staring straight ahead, no-one had noticed Amy's roving eyes following Mike, admiring his tall, lean and athletic build. His jet black hair, cut neatly, was slicked back smoothly behind his ears. Closely shaved, his skin was smooth and slightly bronzed. Just over six feet tall and absolutely gorgeous, Amy

...med up. She imagined that, if anyone had been watching her, she'd proba-bly resembled a ventriloquist's doll from the roving of her eyes and the non-movement of her head. On the point of that thought, Amy casually reposi-tioned herself in her seat, turned to face the front of the room and scrutinized the fixtures and fittings as a distraction. There were no portraits, object d'arts, hanging or otherwise to distract one's attention or cause one's mind to wander from the subject matter. Amy approved of the décor. To her standards, the business institute's Montague room in Bishopsgate, London, the heartbeat of the financial centre, was quite cleverly put together, ergonomically. The color scheme was a mixture of soft, warm shades of pink, blue, yellow and green, complemented by a glow of subtle lighting. Solid pine tables and chairs were arranged in a horseshoe style. A stage was set at the front of the room where hi-tech, state-of-the-art audio visual equipment stood strategically appointed. Amy did a quick head count. Overall, there was a total complement of eleven delegates out of an expected total of twelve. Most were women. Six in total. Nobody spoke. Amy fidgeted.

"He hasn't arrived. I'll have to begin without him," Petra announced, pop-ping her head around the door, peering over her bifocals down the corridor. "Nope. He doesn't appear to be arriving. Therefore, I'll begin the workshop. We'll start with simple introductions. Please state your name, organization and position, the nature of your business and length of service. I'll kick-off by introducing myself." Petra closed the door, proceeded to the front of the room and faced the delegates. "Welcome. My name is Petra Kindell, founder and director of Antenna Associates. I've been in the business of successfully provid-ing bespoke executive services and training packages to private individuals, groups, corporations and numerous institutions for over eighteen years now," she proudly enthused. "Please introduce yourselves in this fashion, or else we'll be here all day should one choose to go off on a tangent. I'm certain that a number of you may have longer introductions than others and would want to air all your attainments. There'll be ample opportunity to do so over the course of the next three days." Petra reassured. "We'll begin, leading from this lady seated here in the front and work our way around." Petra gestured Amy to come forward.

Amy rose gracefully out of her chair and faced the delegates. Petra sat in Amy's seat. Elegantly poised, dressed in a smart navy blue pants suit, a light blue blouse and navy blue court shoes, Amy delivered her introduction. "Good morning. My name is Amy Scott. I represent Planet Management, a firm of global management consultants. Our headquarters are based here in Bishopsgate. I've held the position of portfolio account executive for a period of two years now." Making eye contact with each person in the room, taking a few paces to the left and then to the right, like a moving target, Amy staged her introduction in true Planet Management style. She believed that Planet Management cloned their staff commensurate to the company's ethos. Planet Management reputedly employed only the very best individuals. Focused, astute, professional and intelligent individuals possessing outstanding credentials and proven unique business acumen. The company ensured that all business deals were approached and met by each individual in Planet Management style by demonstration and exercise of the four key words of the vision and mission statement, creativity, confidence, courage and control. "Planet Management 4C's The Way Forward." The founder and chairman, Victor Laidlaw, had the habit of presciently using the slogan in almost every internal meeting. And each time, Amy was convinced that he'd meant every word, hypnotically. He'd also had the slogan printed on almost all the company's internal stationery, much to Amy's annoyance. At the end of her introduction, Amy had notably observed that most of the women delegates had glanced at Mike surreptitiously and, Amy wanted to forget his presence, for the moment, at least until the coffee break, where she'd decided to spark up a conversation with him. "We pride ourselves on being the leaders in this field. We have the proven edge. We provide expert consultancy and management services to our clients and have successfully transitioned their operations on a global scale," Amy concluded, deviously advertising the company's products and services. Pleased with her delivery, Amy walked gracefully back to her seat, listened to the remainder of introductions and waited patiently to hear the most important introduction of all.

"Mike Brandleton, managing director of the Cortland Group," Mike announced, calmly.

An adrenalin rush, Amy drew a deep breath. With that deep and delectable voice, I'd be more than happy to have him whisper in my ears any time, Amy thought. Delirious, closing her eyes, Amy drifted into fantasies, imagining Mike whispering sweet sentiments to her, picturing them both standing, face to face, Mike drawing her body close to him, his strong hands gripping her tightly round her waist.

"… in my capacity as the head of food and beverage for the UK and European regions," Mike concluded.

Amy opened her eyes as Mike walked back to his seat. Oh yes, she thought, confident that she'd succeed in learning much, much more about him by the end of the workshop but, during the coffee break, Mike was engaged in conversation with Belinda Mitchell, who'd introduced herself as partner of the Omega Company, distributing agents of health and beauty products to prestigious health spas and beauty salons. Belinda hadn't wasted any time. As soon as Petra had announced the morning coffee break, Amy had watched as Belinda scooted across the room to Mike in a shot, initiated a conversation and walked alongside him to the coffee lounge. Amy didn't stand a chance, nor did anyone else for that matter as Belinda deliberately held Mike's attention.

"What are your thoughts on the workshop so far, Mike?" Belinda leaned across the table and poured herself a glass of mineral water.

"Not much has happened yet, but so far so good," said Mike. "I'm looking forward to the more beefy bits coming up later this afternoon."

"Tomorrow's role-plays on board room negotiations look pretty good and could be interesting." Pertly raising her eyebrows at Mike, her chest steadily rising, revealing an already exposed cleavage of her large, firm, shapely breasts, Belinda advanced one step closer to him.

"Yes, could be," said Mike, flicking through the pages of the course material, arriving at the role-plays section and skimming through the information.

From a discreet distance, Amy observed their body language. To her relief, Mike hadn't shown any signs that he was in any way, slightly or even remotely attracted to the tall, slim, beautifully blond Belinda flaunting her recently tanned bust at him, exposed through her white laced, low cut blouse, looking much better than her by all accounts. In self-mustered confidence, Amy felt that she hadn't lost her chance on Mike, not for the moment at least. As Mike wasn't responding to or showing any signs of interest in Belinda's cleavage, Amy concluded that, whilst he continued to politely and professionally act non-reactionary to the exposure, that thrusting one's cleavage in Mike's face was unlikely to impress him and felt there was a good chance of getting him interested in her later, much later.

Mike was the first to leave. He swiftly tossed his course notes into his briefcase, slammed it shut and made a quick exit without saying goodbye to anyone. Perplexed, Amy wondered why Mike had left in such haste. Speculating that he probably had to attend to a pressing engagement of some sort or, better still, perhaps avoid being caught up in another one of Belinda's cleavage scenarios, Amy decided to work on making her approach the following day.

Belinda, too busily lapping up the lustful attention of the investment banker, Robert Clark, didn't seem to notice Mike's quick exit.

"It's early. Only six o'clock. Would you care to join me at the bar for a quick drink?"

"I'd love to, Robert," cooed Belinda, seductively.

Amy hoped that Belinda's newly diverted attention to the investment banker would remain permanently so for the duration of the workshop.

Before leaving, Amy approached Petra and thanked her for an interesting day.

"Oh, that's very kind of you, Amy. I'm glad that you've found the day interesting. Believe it or not, thank you's are becoming a rare thing nowadays," Petra went on, "the majority of delegates are only too preoccupied in amassing great fortunes, colossal sums of money, wealth, exercising an overzealous exertion of power."

Amy turned and waved at the remainder of the course delegates bidding their farewells in unison. 'See you tomorrow," she said as she proceeded to the door. "Good night, Petra."

"Have a good evening, Amy. And, thank you, too."

Amy caught sight of Mike as she walked down the steps on her way out of the building. He was standing in the doorway of the main entrance, talking on his cell-phone. Amy's heartbeat quickened with excitement due to the unexpected encounter. She managed to shoot a sweet smile and motioned a quick wave. Reciprocating, Mike smiled, waved and returned to his cell-phone conversation saying, "I'll be there in two minutes, honey."

Amy's heart sank. Oh heck, he's spoken for. That explains things, she thought, as she continued down the steps disappointed and tormented by what she'd overheard, Mike's words torturously replaying over and over in her mind as she walked along the street. *"I'll be there in two minutes, honey,"*

Late at night, back at her apartment, Amy tossed and turned in her bed. She ran through the day's events notably, Mike and Belinda, trying to make sense of it all. She figured that Mike wasn't interested in Belinda or any other woman for that matter. It was plain and simple. He was already spoken for. She felt that she'd been foolish to believe that Mike could have been a potentially good catch. Resting on the belief that the ratio of appealing men out there with good looks and stature such as Mike were normally unavailable, Amy decided that it would serve in her best interests not to lose any further sleep over Mike, give up the pointless task of pursuing him and put the matter to rest. It was easier said than done. She was finding him too irresistible to shake off and she had no idea why. Could this be love at first sight? she wondered.

"I'd like to get you all into three groups, please?" said Petra, maneuvering the delegates. It was ten o'clock, day two of the workshop. "Now let's see. I'll have a group of four over there, with this group of four here and the final group of three situated here to my right. The moment you've all been waiting for. Each person has been allocated five minutes to demonstrate their effective communication skills in a boardroom scenario. Think about the ways in which you would successfully negotiate and arrive at clinching a deal, worth millions in long term revenue and profits, whilst tackling an awkward, incongruously opposing and argumentative key member of the board who continuously disrupts negotiations." Petra paused. "Before we begin, are there any questions, please?" A handful of delegates shook their heads. "No? Good. For the first round, please decide among yourselves who is playing what role. You'll all get an opportunity to play each role." In Mike's group were Amy, Belinda and Katie. 'Don't forget that the aim is to arrive at a win-win solution. Start the board level discussions at the sound of the bell and stop at the sound of the buzzer." The delegates spoke simultaneously at the sound of the bell. Amy observed Mike who played the lead role. Controlled, he demonstrated a calm and positive demeanor towards Belinda, who exaggeratedly played the disruptive one, disagreeing with every conceivable discussion point Mike raised. Not impressed with Belinda, Amy felt that she wasn't making a good job of it, shouting her demands, swearing and punching the table. Mike continued to handle the role as lead negotiator expertly and hadn't raised his voice to be heard. Petra sat in on each group, observing their style, content, expressional delivery of statements, and body language. Finding the whole thing quite hilariously entertaining, Amy looked forward to her role-play with Mike. Petra sounded the buzzer and the voices died down to an eventual silence. A minute later, Petra rang the bell.

"I totally disagree with all your ideas," Amy addressed Mike, almost distracted by his beautiful hazel eyes. "It's evident that you haven't thoroughly researched or even studied the key figures projected for next year's profit margins and budget forecasts!"

"OK," said Mike. "Would you care to provide me ..." he looked at each person seated at the table and continued saying, "pardon me. Allow me to correct myself. Would you care to provide the board members with evidence of your learned knowledge, views, findings and perceived concepts on the way forward on this?"

He's so calm, controlled, non-reactionary, so delightful, so delicious, Amy thought. Taking a deep breath, attempting to mirror Mike's composure, Amy said, "Yes, most certainly. Let's arrange another meeting. I'll be armed with documentation to serve as back-up for my rationale."

"Shall we agree on scheduling another meeting for the purpose of giving Amy the opportunity to present her rationale to this debate?" Mike asked.

The group reached a unanimous decision in Amy's favor to reconvene at the next meeting.

"Splendid. Excellent," Petra remarked, applauding Mike and Amy.

"I believe you would have liked my line better. You sounded the buzzer before I'd a chance to voice my win-win line!" Belinda protested.

Amy sensed that the acridity of Belinda's protest was brewing an unpleasant atmosphere. The room fell into an uncomfortable silence. Amy worked on ideas to defuse the situation should Belinda get too out of hand.

"You were all given a fair five minutes each and you all did perfectly well in that time. Belinda, you'll get another opportunity, as we've not quite yet completed all the rounds."

In sheer annoyance, Amy turned her back to Belinda. She also felt a little embarrassed for Belinda, belittling herself with such petty antics, outbursts and protestations. Amy felt Belinda's eyes piercing the back of her neck, seething with envy from the success of her role-play with Mike and Petra's public commendation. How could Belinda have missed the point? Amy wondered as she reflected on the events of the previous day. Day one, the cleavage thrust and now into day two, the unnecessary prima-donna antics and a pointless protestation. Amy questioned what other antics Belinda could possibly have hidden in store … possibly a grand finale antic with all the trimmings on top on the last day of the workshop? She glanced over at Mike. He'd remained his calm and composed self. Ambivalent, no longer seeing the need to spark up a conversation with Mike after all, Amy opted to avoid him for the remainder of the course. Losing interest in her pursuit, wanting to avoid a potential cat fight, for the remainder of the workshop, Amy made no effort to gain or attract Mike's attention and kept her distance from Belinda. But, she secretly fumed at Mike and Belinda, happily engaged in their chatter during the coffee breaks. She reminded herself of her objective to come away with the right impression of the course content as she had to produce a report of her findings to Vincent, who'd planned to send his executives on the next available course on the basis of her report. Applying total focus on getting the best out of the workshop, Amy soaked up as much knowledge as she could, circulated among the delegates, swapped ideas and compared notes.

"Prior to leaving," said Petra, "I wish to inform you all that, firstly, we finish at the earlier time of five o'clock tomorrow and secondly, the main thing is that, Antenna Associates would like to extend an invitation to you all to attend a social gathering to be held at the exclusive and highly prestigious Je La Buena champagne house from six o'clock onwards." The room filled with gasps, cheers and applause. "For the benefit of those who are not aware of the location, it's a ten minute walk from here and easy to find. Ask anyone for directions, everyone knows Je La Buena, you can't miss the building. It's the blue tinted glass building at the end of the street, situated on your right. I do hope that you can all make it. In the morning, I'll distribute invitations to serve as admission. I urge you not to misplace them. The management is very strict and won't grant entry to anyone who is not in possession of an invitation. Be warned." There were more cheers from Belinda and Robert. The Je La Buena was renowned for its enviable selection of champagne and wine. City lawyers, bankers, CEO's, the odd dignitary and celebrity, influential people, frequented the private members only venue. Pleasantly surprised by the invite, Amy was also pleased with the aspect of socializing at the prestigious venue. Je La Buena. What an expensive and luxurious place to be seen, the perfect venue. Maybe, just maybe, this'll be the time to find out more about Mike over a few glasses of champagne. Maybe. Perhaps, she thought, relapsing indecisively. She welcomed the prospect of socializing with the course delegates she'd connected with, mainly, Katie Morgan. They'd met during one of the coffee breaks and, somehow managed to remain together throughout the remainder of the workshop. Katie worked in the music and film entertainment industry for Panache Limited and had recently been promoted to an assistant director. At the age of twenty five, Katie was the youngest person to be appointed to director level and was blatantly thrilled with the new appointment. Amy enjoyed Katie's jolly soul. No airs or graces, a cuddly type, short in height, a bit on the plump side, Katie wore her auburn colored hair styled in an attractive French plait. Throughout the workshop, Katie made people laugh, cracking the odd well timed joke and generally amusing everyone that Amy hoped they'd remain in contact after the workshop and perhaps, become regularly acquainted. She wondered whether Mike would be attending Je La Buena and self-admitting that it would prove to be horrible without him, decided that she'd make the most of the evening, regardless. Day three, the final day loomed ahead and

Amy had no idea of knowing whether she would ever see Mike again once the workshop was over. Within the next second, she was dismissing the whole idea of wanting to see him and willing herself to stop fretting.

Katie nudged Amy, bringing her daydreaming to an abrupt end. "What a cracker this workshop has turned out to be," she blurted. Thank God for Katie, Amy thought, pleased that she'd been nudged out of her hapless thoughts. Waving her clenched fists in the air, Katie shook her body and swayed her hips from side to side. "I'm taking away a lot of ammunition with me so, look out guys, here I come!" she said.

Giggling, Amy thought that Katie looked like a drunken belly dancer. "Cino's?"

"Why not? Thanks, Amy. That's not a bad idea."

"Let's go."

"Please leave your contact details with me on your way out. A compiled list will be distributed tomorrow. Thank you and, see you all tomorrow," said Petra.

Amy and Katie arrived at Cino's coffee bar ahead of the crowds. Amy headed straight to her favorite table situated at the front of the bar near the window where she often sat, leafed through documents, read a few pages of a novel or simply people watched over delicious cups of decaffeinated cappuccino. Cino's, the only waiter service coffee venue in town, was a popular place, frequented mostly by city professionals who could easily afford the extortionate price charged for a cup of coffee. It was an ideal venue to conduct informal meetings between people who wished to *discuss matters over a cup of coffee.* The interior design had an Italian influence. Mosaic flooring. Tastefully marble and wood paneled walls. Each wooden table had a lamp that shone an ambient orange glow. Old, authentic and lively Italian folk music played softly in the background, giving the atmosphere a warm, homely and cozy Italian feel with a professional edge. Freshly ground coffee constantly wafted through the air that Amy found the strong aroma never failed to have an aphrodisiacal affect on her. The waiters were mainly all young, sporting fit, Italian men in their early twenties. They swiftly sped around serving tables smartly attired in crisp white shirts with rich, ruby red silk bow ties, black ankle length aprons worn with rich, ruby red pleated cummerbunds.

"Phew, we're just in time. It can get quite packed in here most evenings, leaving no available seats but standing room against the service counters. Not very comfortable, I must say, not when you've been on your feet all day long. After all the role-playing, we deserve this table."

"It's a pleasant spot," said Katie, peering out of the window, at the smart office buildings, designer shops and office workers rushing along the streets.

"Yes. My favorite coffee haunt," said Amy settling comfortably, wasting no time in launching into her preoccupying subject. "That Belinda! She was ridiculous. Hilarious. She'd gotten completely carried away and had taken things a bit too far for my liking. I thought she was going to cause injury to her wrists, repeatedly thumping the desk, or the make belief boardroom table, or whatever one described it as."

"I agree. Mike appeared to have had a strange affect on her. I thought she was going to whack him across the face," said Katie.

"She's dangerous." Pausing, not wanting to give away the fact that Mike seemed to be having that same strange affect on her too, Amy put a lot of effort into the delivery of her question. "What are your thoughts on Mike?"

"Ah!" exclaimed Katie, smirking, looking up at the ceiling deliberatively. "It depends on what you mean. Should you be referring to his character or personality? On first impression, I think he's OK, but a little on the quiet side. Anyway, why are you asking me about Mike? You haven't got the hots for him or anything like that have you?"

Without flinching, Amy cleverly concealed that Katie had caught her off guard.

"Can I help you, ladies?" said the head waiter, Franco, who spoke with a beautiful Italian accent partnered with a beautiful Italian smile.

Amy smiled up at Franco and thought, good timing. "Oh, yes please, Franco. I'll have my usual large decaffeinated cappuccino, without sugar and, let me get yours, Katie. What are you having?"

"A café con leche with loads of sugar, please?"

"Right away, ladies." Franco keyed their order into his small, hand held electronic device and sped off to the adjacent table.

"No, I do not have the hots for Mike. And besides, like you, I think he's a bit too much on the quiet side."

Katie winked at Amy. "Should you change your mind, I'll lend you a hand. Put a good word in for you."

Discretely impressed, Amy noted that Katie had a razor sharp intuition. Whether Katie was merely using her womanly wile or playing a guessing game, Amy was slowly realizing that Katie was not one of the most straightforward of people to get to know, suspecting that the true meanings behind a number of

Katie's statements were being disguised as jokes and comical gestures. "I'm sorry to disappoint you but, there won't be any need for you to do anything of the sort, not on my behalf, thank you." Amy assured Katie.

"Really? What a shame," Katie teased.

"A shame? Why?" Amy grappled Katie.

"Well, I could do with getting involved in something sexy and juicy like arranging dates, you know, getting you two to get it together. That would be fun."

Amy laughed. "Are you some kind of a relationship wizard or practitioner in the field of matchmaking?"

"Let's just say, I've been successful in that area so far. I know what signs to look for, you see."

Amy read that as a warning or a possible threat.

"I've arranged dates. In fact, there is a couple based at my office I'm currently working quite closely with. They're still dating after three months of having met one another," Katie stated proudly.

Franco delivered their coffees. Amy peered absently at the bubbly foam mounted at the top of her cup. She's just digging around, Amy thought, not prepared at this early stage, to let Katie in on any of her thoughts and feelings regarding Mike. Nothing had happened between her and Mike, therefore, there wasn't really anything to divulge, not yet, anyway. There was also the bugging issue of Mike and Belinda requiring clarification.

"What are you thinking about? You seem so far away. You won't find any solutions in that cup. You won't find tea leaves at the bottom of your cup providing you with an accurate reading, you see," Katie remarked, jokingly.

Astonished at Katie's unrelenting style, Amy looked at her queerly and laughed.

Katie's nervous giggle progressed to her throwing her arms in the air and bursting into a roar of laughter. "What's so funny, why are we laughing?" enquired Katie, patting her stomach.

"You tell me, you started it," said Amy, gasping for air in between her chuckles.

Guffawing, Katie pulled a tissue out of her handbag and dabbed at the tears streaming down her cheeks.

"It's you, talking about tea leaves in a coffee cup. You'd caught me by surprise. That was the last thing I was expecting to hear you say."

"Oh well," said Katie, getting her breath back, "it's good to laugh."

"You're right."

Another hour of shared jokes around the workshop events, more laughter, pleasant conversation and two more rounds of coffee, at seven forty-five, Amy called an end to the evening. "I'd better be heading off home, now. I'm working on a report tonight for my boss."

"Crikey, it's a quarter to eight!" Katie checked the clock on the wall against her watch. "We've spent a long time here. I've really enjoyed the evening. We must do this again."

"Gladly. I'm certain we will. We've got Je La Buena tomorrow night," Amy reminded Katie.

"Lovely. Free champagne all night."

"Would you care to share a taxi home?"

"Good idea. I don't fancy taking the subway tonight." Katie scrunched her tissue into a ball and tossed it in her empty cup.

Amy spotted Franco and beckoned him over.

"Same again?"

"No. Not this time. I'd like to settle the bill and my account, please. And would you order a car for me?"

"Sure," said Franco. "Your destinations, please?"

"I'm going to Maida Vale and my colleague is ..."

"Bayswater," Katie broke in.

"Right away, madam." Franco dashed off to do everything as quickly as possible.

Cino's, renowned for providing quick and efficient service, won the annual award for Best Coffee Bar Venue of the Year, organized by the UK exclusive venues association, a subscription only monthly magazine featuring an array of highly rated luxury venues, covering coffee bars, pubs, restaurants and wine bars to casinos, hotels and country clubs. Proud of the award, Cino's, in business for eighteen months, achieved their aim of attracting a more prestigious clientele, by introducing a number of initiatives to assist in successfully raising their profile. One such initiative was to be the only coffee venue in town to provide an executive company car service with the option to settle in cash or account. Amy regularly practiced frequenting fashionable, up-market venues. She wouldn't dream of being seen anywhere other than establishments that carried some form of prestige, luxury, credibility and exclusivity to their names.

"Your car has arrived, ladies," Franco announced, passing Amy a slip.

Amy whipped her platinum Mont Blanc pen out of her handbag and signed the slip.

"I'll escort you to your waiting car, ladies. It's the silver gray, seven series BMW parked out front."

"Thank you, Franco," said Amy.

CHAPTER 2

Amy arrived an hour earlier, at eight o'clock. Armed with her laptop, Amy sat alone in the desired peace of the quiet Montague room. She reflected on the previous two days and worked on the draft report from where she'd left off the previous night. The report was specifically worded, designed and structured in keeping with company requirements. Checking and reading through, Amy was admittedly impressed with the style, content and delivery of her views and findings, pleased overall with the report. One more day to go and, after that, a full and final report will be ready for submission to Vincent, on the dot, as promised, Amy thought. She'd worked quite closely with Vincent, during the latter part of the previous year. In that time she'd studied Vincent's personality and character traits like a book, thus enabling her to gain an apt awareness of his likes and dislikes, his habits, good, bad or indifferent and, his expectations of others. In his late fifties, Vincent managed to maintain his wonderfully youthful looks and fitness. Short, stout, of stocky build, fastidiously impeccable about his appearance, Vincent consistently dressed smart. He wore his thinning silver-gray hair boasting a subtly perfect quiff. He cocked his proud aloft chin in the air high and rigid. There was a look of profundity in his brilliant blue eyes, intellectualized, learned, experienced eyes, eyes that had seen it all, everything and more. In Amy's estimations, Vincent wasn't a difficult man to please. It was quite simple really. He liked things done his way and cloned his executives to perform to his Planet Management style. In five years, Vincent had successfully built his company from nothing to a multi-million pound global concern. He's obviously doing something right, Amy thought, recalling her first meeting with him on the day she'd joined the company. "I'm going to be instrumental in making you a very successful young lady, Amy, although, it's entirely up to you, mind. We can certainly do with more people like you, people with the ability to demonstrate their unique individuality and business acumen with flair, drive, skill, determination, not forgetting charm, of course." Vincent expected only the best on his payroll that he'd hired a team of head-hunters to scout the globe for talented individuals. Amy was head-hunted by that team whilst she served as an associate investments negotiator for The Welling Investment Corporation, also known as "Wellings." Busily giving her all, Amy worked her tail off in order to achieve her long awaited goal to directorship. The move up was long overdue. Seven years with Wellings, she'd joined as a young, keen and impressionable administrative assistant at the age of twenty. In those seven years, Amy had worked her way up the corporate ladder, notching an impressively enviable reputation making her mark in the financial world, successfully clinching a number of lucrative investment deals with conglomerations and mergers and acquisitions, deals worth millions of pounds in profits and assets to Wellings, ranking them at number five of the top ten investment company deal earners in the UK. Pragmatic, Amy had gained the necessary qualifications hands on and by earning the necessary certification, religiously attending the selective three year private equity, wealth and asset management course, at the expensive private investments business school, paid for, on a monthly basis off her own back, dedicating two evenings per week, giving up every other weekend. Nothing came easy for Amy. She grew up in what was categorized as a working class background, and toiled hard for everything she wanted. Each day at four o'clock, Amy would finish her comprehensive secondary school education and rush home with her two younger sisters, Helen and Emily. There was no such thing as going out with friends after school. It was school homework and straight into the family owned grocery store. They'd re-stock shelves, stick price labels on products, weigh and package fresh fruits, nuts and vegetables and mop the shop floor just before the closing time of eight o'clock. Amy's mother, a loving wife, doted on her daughters. Patriarchal, her father was overprotective of his girls, keeping them indoors, living together as a close-knit family, allowing them the occasionally rare privilege of going out with their school and neighborhood friends once, maybe twice a month on the odd weekend. "A father must take care of his family," he'd say. By his strict upbringing, Amy's father ensured, "my princesses," as he'd so often referred to them as, were not influenced by the, "advanced girls," who'd run the gauntlet, indulged in under-aged sex, cigarettes, drugs and petty crime. The comprehensive secondary school suffered a few cases of teenaged pregnancies in its time. Precocious thirteen and fourteen year olds, proud of their early motherhood, would show off their bulges or exhibit their babies outside the school gates. It wasn't long before the head mistress enforced a court ruling, banning the teenaged mothers from coming within half a mile of the school gates. "Babies having babies," Amy's father would say. A sheepish request to attend the school disco, watch the latest movie at the local cinema or take a trip to the local park would invariably be met with a loud, stern and adamant NO. A painfully long and boring lecture would occasionally ensue. Amy and her sisters would retreat to their bedrooms, slam their doors, throw themselves on their beds and sob for England. They didn't fully grasp or understand the well intentioned meanings behind half of their father's patriarchal attitude and painfully long and boring lectures that seldom provided them lucidity.

"Birds of a feather flock together."

"What does that mean, Daddy?"

"Show me your friends and I'll tell you what you are."

"Huh?"

"When you're older, you'll understand."

They were convinced he was being deliberately cruel and old fashioned.

"Do well, educate yourselves and study hard as much as you can. Push your own buttons, or else you'll be pushing buttons in factories where no-one of a decent standing would look at you, want to know you, let alone acknowledge your existence and, you stand the chance of not knowing who you are your-selves. You'll become brain dead, earning very little money, pushing ill-fated buttons in some cheap factory somewhere. When you're older and inevitably leave home, I want you pushing your own buttons. Don't wait or expect any-one to give you anything. In this life you've got to go out and create your dreams yourself. Mark my words, you'll think back and thank me one day."

"Create dreams?"

"What does that mean, Daddy?" Amy had asked.

"But, Daddy, I dream when I'm asleep." Helen had said.

"When you're older, you'll understand. You'll remember everything I've taught you."

"You're always saying that, Dad. When you're older. When you're older." Amy was older now and her father's words were fully noted and understood. His words thankfully reverberated whilst she sat her final exam at the private investments business school to acquire the certification, the paper that would open doors for her, grant her the access and mandate to command a higher position in almost any corporation, acquire the directorship she'd hankered for and lastly, push her own buttons. Dedicated, skilful and a hard worker, Amy wanted the recognition from Wellings she knew she quite rightly deserved. Vincent extended to Amy a very attractive offer with very attractive benefits. The offer came at the right time and at the right price. Amy accepted immediately that the beautifully timed move to Planet Management proved to be a great loss to Wellings who weren't prepared for the loss. Wellings not willing to match Vincent's offer, preferred to play the game of corporate politics. During her discussions at the quarterly personal management program conducted by an ineffective human resource director, Amy enquired an update on the company's plans in the specific area of appointment awards.

"At present, our top tier band of appointed officials is sufficiently complemented. We promise that should an opportunity arise, we'd like you to bear in mind that you'd be considered as our first choice. In another year, maybe sooner, the prospective appointment could be realized."

Promises are a comfort to a fool, Amy thought. The fact of the matter was that Amy was fully conscious that her successes posed as a constant threat to a couple of insecure individuals up there in the top tier reign in fear of being outpaced. She'd rightly suspected that every effort was being made to block her from making too rapid a rise to the higher echelons. The appointment to portfolio account executive at Planet Management was more than Amy had bargained for. She believed, that now, in an ironic sense, she'd finally earned the long awaited recognition, and calculated that she could become an executive director in two years. A point she'd made emphatically clear to Wellings when she'd declined to take part in an exit interview. Resigning on the spot, on the acceptance and strength of Vincent's offer, Amy didn't see the need to go through the motions of a pointlessly insignificant and time consuming exit interview process. Her precious time and energy were now being poured into achieving her dreams of climbing the corporate ladder to the very top at Planet Management. Vincent's offer had an irresistible array of benefits. An optional top of the range company car, quarterly bonuses, high percentage rated annualized commission, paid on secured deals, a selection of stocks, shares and bond options, all subject to delivery of targets, targets that Amy was determined to meet. Vincent had the reputation of rewarding very generous sums and equally generous gifts and perks to those who excelled. Many aspects fueled Amy's determination to succeed.

"Good morning, Amy," said Petra. It was eight thirty. "You're early this morning."

"Morning, Petra. I'm producing a draft report and workshop notes."

"I understand. There won't be much more to add to your notes from today's session as, we'll be summing up for most of the day."

"Great," said Amy, skimming through the report whilst Petra, assuming the stance of a cat burglar, tip-toed quietly around the room, placing course materials on the desks.

"Hi. Good morning," chirped Belinda, bursting through the door.

"Morning," Amy whispered, deciding that, now would be the perfect time to save and close the draft report, log off and head to the coffee lounge. On entering, Amy spotted Mike seated alone at a table with a cup of black coffee. He appeared to be totally engrossed in the *Financial Times* newspaper and didn't look up. Amy's heartbeat thumped rapidly. She took long, deep breaths to calm the tremor of sensations that flowed swiftly through her body and pondered on the idea of whether to join him or not. In her reluctance to interrupt him, Amy casually strolled over to the buffet area and poured herself a cup of fresh decaffeinated coffee.

Amy inhaled the floral scents of spring from the mid-April breeze that floated in the coffee lounge and, coaxed by the season's soft sun and the refreshingly crisp spring air, Amy opted to drink her coffee on the patio. A handful of clay pots filled with rich, yellow and white daffodils were evenly spaced on the balcony wall. Baskets hanging resplendently above the patio doors displayed their own profusion of yellow and white daffodils. Amy sipped her coffee to the hummed sound of the traffic below and smiled. Settling back against the cushion on the olive green wrought iron chair, Amy closed her eyes and, with her head slightly reclined, stretched her legs and sighed.

"Hi, Amy."

Positioning her hands like a sun-visor above her neatly plucked eyebrows, Amy raised her head and squinted at Katie. "How are we today?"

"Didn't get very much sleep last night, I kept waking up. Drank far too much coffee at Cino's last night so, I'm very wide awake. Feeling a bit hyper and very tired too, if that makes any sense to you." Katie yawned. "Bought this herbal tea to balance my mood and enhance my well being. Well, that's what the label states it'll do for me."

Amy sat up straight and sipped her coffee. "Gosh. You're certainly hyper this morning," she said, rising out of her seat. "Look, if it's any consolation to you, today's going to be easy. Petra informed me that we're mostly summing-up."

Blowing into her cup and slurping loudly, Katie turned to follow A
just go with the flow. If anything great comes out of it, then it would be an
added bonus," she muttered, unenthusiastically.

Petra had commenced addressing the delegates when Amy and Katie arrived.

"I'd like you all to get into your groups again for part two of the boardroom
discussions, please. And I do hope that you're all readily furnished with strategies to finalize on your chosen topical debates," Petra enthused. "I'll be studying each group and, at the end of each role-play, to those who are interested,
I'll be conducting one-to-one discussions on the areas of effectiveness, body
language, voice tonalities and strategies applied in reaching the desired results.
Mike's group will kick-off first."

Mike's group assumed their previous seating positions and, on Petra's signal, Mike reconvened as lead speaker.

"Discussions were postponed to allow Amy the opportunity to present the
evidence of her argument to the board, evidence that would serve as the rationale, justifying her opposition to the suggestions I'd put forward on the profit
margins, budget forecasts and sales projections for the coming year, which
would also purport to prove that my suggestions were indeed not completely
accurate. Finally, the aim is to conclude that Amy had been, in fact, absolutely
right all along."

"May I interrupt for a moment?" cried Belinda.

"Yes, please do," said Amy obligingly, pretentiously unperturbed.

Belinda slid off her chair and walked slowly over to Mike. All eyes were
focused on Belinda now parked behind Mike, ~~the palm of~~ her hands firmly
placed on his shoulders.

Amy, on the edge of her seat, waited for Belinda's stunt. What an attention
seeker, Amy thought, searching Mike's eyes in a senseless hope of mustering
clues on his thoughts. But, with no obvious signs, Amy became increasingly
furious and confused over the whole charade. She took her eyes off Mike for a
moment and her mind off the whole thing of Belinda touching him, experiencing the feel of him. Finding it hard to ignore, Amy wondered what Belinda
felt and imagined Mike's shoulders to be strong, firm and solid.

"This'll only take me a minute," Belinda purred. "You may or may not recall
that I hadn't been given a fair opportunity to complete my say yesterday? The
point that I wanted to make was that, I thought it would've been a good idea to
conduct a feasibility study. In the next three to six months we would be able to
identify our cost leverages and realize our future profit gains."

"Agreed. And thank you for your valid analogy that could prove to be workable from a speculative standpoint, Belinda. May I further state that it is paramount we immediately take appropriate action on this. We do not have sufficient time to conduct a feasibility study. Time spent on a feasibility study would result in the loss of revenue and profits. We couldn't possibly consider purchasing a new operational plant next year, we'd have to delay our plans another three to six months and prices would increase to …"

"I'm a true proponent of your ideas, Amy," Katie interjected.

"How would you know whether something is going to work well or not without giving it a trial run?" Belinda argued, lifting her hands, freeing Mike's shoulders, moving around to his right, lowering her head and gazing into his eyes. Transfixed, the delegates watched in suspended silence. Amy counted the painfully excruciating seconds.

"We ought to put things to the test. Do you agree, Mike?" Belinda said suggestively. Suggested

Well groomed, Amy couldn't take anything away from Belinda. Her peachy skin glowed healthily, her thin pert lips pouted to perfection, her breasts, voluptuous. Clients showering Belinda with free beauty products, complimentary head to toe beauty treatments, all expenses paid weekend breaks to the most luxurious health farms around UK and Europe, made her a walking beauty. What a drama queen, Amy thought, gasping silently, momentarily looking away, clenching her fists under the table. She couldn't believe that Belinda was putting on such a performance in a play for Mike, full of innuendos and in full view of everyone. Put things to the test? What things? And to what test? Amy thought, flashing a discreet glare at Mike watching him gazing into Belinda's eyes. The game's not lost yet. Nothing is definite until it's definite, Amy thought. "For ease of reference, please allow me to present my findings as shown in this diagram I'd prepared earlier," said Amy, reassuming the lead, distributing a single paged handouts Mike passed a copy to Belinda. She snatched it out of his hand. "From the financial position, as depicted on the flow chart, we can see that there would be tremendous savings should we opt for diagram number one. Therefore, our profit margins could be greater than we originally envisaged from discussions held yesterday."

"This is most impressive," said Mike. "It presents a clearer picture. I have every confidence in taking this route, as shown in diagram number one, as the way forward unless, of course, anyone has any further reservations or alternative suggestions to air?" Mike waited. "No? Good. I believe I can safely state that we are all agreed."

"Thirty five seconds remaining," Petra whispered discreetly.

"Agreed," said Katie.

Belinda slowly walked back to her seat. "Agreed," ~~she said, nonchalantly~~.

"Agreed," said Amy, smiling nervously.

"Agreed," said Mike, nodding to the applauding delegates.

"Well done, Belinda," Robert shouted.

"You may return to your seats, ~~now~~," said Petra, raising her voice above the applause, Robert repeatedly cheering Belinda and the second group busily making preparations to take the stage after the coffee break.

"That was very good. It had all the required ingredients with the aim to arrive at a win-win solution to a difficult debate," Petra addressed the delegates. Fixing her gaze on Belinda, Petra continued to expand on her summing up. "Belinda, I must say that I have not seen this form of physical contact conducted in a boardroom which could be misconstrued as a form of coercion. I found it rather unusual although, I'm not opposing, ruling out or objecting to your chosen style.

Amy sensed that Petra was neither enthralled nor convinced that Belinda's input was indeed appropriate. Petra then transferred an admirable stance to Amy. "And Amy, the fact that you'd produced a handout as a visual aid was most impressive. Board members had something to clearly follow, to assist in focusing on the picture. Very professional."

Not accustomed to receiving compliments so publicly, Amy blushed and nodded, ~~coyly~~ coyly.

Belinda, not sharing the same opinions as Petra, still hankering for the main spotlight, launched into further protestations. "Who set the rules on formats to be used in meetings? I believe meetings can be conducted in whatever format or style one chooses, provided all are party to it. Mike wasn't objectionable to my chosen style and, I mean, everyone applauded me, which meant I was enjoyed, I mean, it was enjoyed by all. And you wanted someone to play the disruptive role, did you not? I don't see anything wrong with me touching anyone. Provided I'm not hurting anyone, why should it matter?"

Petra breathed. "You're absolutely correct in stating that one had to play the role of the disruptive board member and you'd played that role rather well. Let me reiterate that I don't oppose to your choice of style or format and I'm not objectionable about it in any way. I'd merely stated that I'd found it most unusual. Belinda, we must get on or we won't finish the workshop on time."

Belinda waved her right hand in the air haltingly at Petra. "OK. Fine. I get your point. Fine."

Amy discreetly glanced over at Katie who was engaged in a private titter.

"Now would be a perfect time to break for refreshments everyone. Delegates wishing to have one-to-one sessions are to remain here," said Petra.

Katie and Amy strolled out of the room together. "Fancy the patio, again?"

"No. I'd love to but, I've got to pop out quickly," said Amy.

"No worries. See you later then."

"I'll be a few minutes."

Amy needed time alone, away from the building to shed some light on the whole Belinda and Mike saga, certain that they'd somehow built up a closer rapport. Pangs of nauseating guilt stabbed at Amy's conscience. Her lover, Jenson hadn't a clue or inkling that she'd been secretly entertaining an attraction for another man at the workshop. Jenson dutifully called Amy every day. As always, he'd expressed his genuine interest in all her activities and had enquired about the workshop. "Like all courses, as courses go, Jenson. This particular course involves demonstrating mechanisms of business psychology know-how. Practicing and developing the art of putting coercive techniques into action. Winning for you, achieving your personal best as opposed to competing with others or wanting to beat the other guy, that sort of thing. Let's just say, that the end result is to make me more of an effective communicator, team builder, net-worker, forger of influential contacts, hopefully. Well, that's the idea behind it all."

"Pretty heavy stuff," Jenson had said.

Amy had met Jenson at a children's charity event in London's Hyde Park in August of the previous year after Amy had accepted an invitation to the event by acquaintances of hers. The event was aired across London, live on radio, and Jenson was the main radio host. Amy remembered when she'd first laid eyes on Jenson. She'd spotted him inside the VIP marquee conversing with one of the event organizers. Alluringly handsome, Jenson exuded charm, energy and radiance. Their eyes met and, in an instant, they'd stemmed a potently mutual liking for each other. Their eyes did most of the talking saying, "*I want you.*" Amy walked over to Jenson and discreetly slipped him a handwritten note. It had read, "*call me, tonight on 555 6387. Amy xx.*" Bypassing the usual games of pre-ambling, initiating, the small talk and dinner dates, they'd made love, at her apartment, that night consummating their casual affair.

Amy struggled with the irony of it all, attracted to Jenson and Mike, two entirely different men. Jenson had the gift of the gab, the height, over six foot tall, rugged male model looks, playboy image and a fantastic body. He was irresistibly attractive, knew it and played on it. Mike, on the other hand, was mys-

terious. Handsome. Reserved. Sophisticated. Eloquent. Tall and athletically built. A gentlemanly type, he was charming, classy, although a bit on the quiet side, that Amy couldn't ignore that she was growing more and more intrigued by the mystery of Mike. Captivating him would take careful planning, she thought. She'd have to devise a new and different game plan. Jenson was a doddle. Mike would be a challenge. Not only a challenge that Amy was now beginning to accept, but she'd never dated a man of Mike's caliber, who was the complete opposite of all the men she'd dated.

Amy approached the House of Fraser department store, peered through the glass doors and, as there weren't many shoppers in the store, Amy thought she'd take full advantage of using the undivided attention of the young beauty therapist. Entering the store, Amy walked over to the cosmetics counter, tested a range of lip colors, eye make-up and perfumery, treated herself to a 50ml bottle of So Pretty De Cartier parfum and hurried back to the workshop.

Returning five minutes late, Amy quietly opened the door of the Montague Room. The lights were out. She crept in and perched on the chair nearest the door. The delegates watched the role-plays on a wide plasma screen suspended from the ceiling. Stunned, Amy hadn't recollected that any filming had actually taken place. Then, frowningly thinking back, she'd recalled having read notes on the course content section that aspects of the workshop were going to be filmed and filming would take place unnoticeably by hidden camera lens. Amy's image appeared on the wide plasma screen. She both looked and sounded quite professional. Good diction, clearly spoken, great facial bone structure, high cheek bones, chiseled, accentuated. The camera loved her. Belinda, on the other hand, was a knock-out beauty, although her screen appearance with Mike bordered on the pornographic. Amy now had it all figured out. Belinda had deliberately staged the boardroom escapade in the hope that it'd all be captured on camera. Sniggering delegates lapped up Belinda's screen action and Robert lightly applauded. At the end of the final scene, Petra switched off the equipment via the remote control. "You all deserve a round of applause, pats on the backs." The delegates applauded and cheered loudly. "Now that you've viewed yourselves on screen, I do hope you've all observed the potency and power in the use of body language and the choice of words used in reaching a win-win solution during negotiations. Please refer to the notes on this subject. Please also note that we have image consultants with years of experience who've worked with the crème de la crème of a varied array of personalities from dignitaries, politicians, celebrities to chief executive officers. It would be an idea to book one or two sessions, if at any time you felt you were in need of additional professional know how in areas such as voice coaching or indeed public speaking. Come and see me at the end should you be interested in taking this up, or indeed, any of our other courses featured in our program. The role-plays are available on DVD. Please come and see me if you'd like a copy." Petra checked her watch. "Lunchtime. It's approaching one o'clock and we're concluding earlier than expected. You have the remainder of the afternoon free. Please browse through the materials on offer. Are there any further questions?" No-one uttered a word. "No? Then it's time for champagne."

CHAPTER 3

Amy, Katie and Petra arrived at Je La Buena together. Smiling slightly, Amy warmed to the small mingling crowds. Waiters served champagne from their trays. Jazz music played in the background. Mellowed tones of the saxophone resonated soft blends of rhythmic tunes from speakers concealed in the ceiling. The guest services management team bestowed upon them their first class services usually reserved for VIP guests, briskly escorting them to the private functions area to their lavishly decorated champagne suite.

Je La Buena enjoyed earning considerable sums from companies such as Antenna Associates regularly hosting their events at the venue, that management felt they were duly eligible to receive the special guest services. Reveling in VIP status, flanked by two heavily tanned burly stewards, that one could be forgiven for easily mistaking them as heavyweight boxers, Amy walked elegantly by, flaunting a discretionary pout, head held high, revealing her stunningly chiseled profile.

"Who is she?" Amy overheard an inquiring female voice in the crowd say.

"Obviously a money-spinner. Look at her, she stinks of money."

Amy sensed a note of envy in the female's voice. Wishing she'd stunk of money, Amy stopped herself from smirking at the ostensibly flattering remark, although she couldn't help but feel sympathy for the female for making such an inaccurate judgment.

Their cabana styled private suite was cordoned-off with a banner that read, "*Private Function—Reserved for Antenna Associates.*" Black and gold brocade tastefully draped either side of the main entrance of the suite, smartly coordinated in a chromed, hi-tech theme. Fashionable designer furniture with matching fixtures and fittings complemented the decor. The walls and floors were covered with black reinforced glass tiles. A starry, subtle glow of speckled multi-colored lights illuminated through the floor tiles. Minute twinkling star lights, simulating the midnight sky, shone from the ceiling like perfect pieces of priceless cut diamonds. Je La Buena was renowned for its lavish décor including their stock of an enviable range of champagnes from Krug Grande, Louis Roederer's Cristal Rose, Bollinger Special Cuvee, Veuve Clicquot Ponsardin Le Grand Dane, Krug, Moet & Chandon, Mumm de Cramant to Don Perignon, brands from the well known, not so well known, unknown, to their own house brand. On occasions, a selection of champagnes would be specially flown in from almost anywhere in the world on behalf of clients willingly paying the price.

Antenna Associates had arranged an unlimited flow of Bollinger Special Cuvee to be served to their guests for the entire evening. How generous, Amy thought. Champagne glass in her hand, Amy looked round about her. The scene is set, she schemed. Her confidence renewed, Amy looked forward to the prospect of finally making her move on Mike, confident her claim would be made that evening. Her mixed feelings and emotions ran high from the excitement of it all. The effects of three days of yearning were driving her crazy, ecstatically conjuring, stirring and arousing her, taking over her mind and body.

Amy observed a small group of middle aged business men standing closely huddled together in the main bar area of the private suite. All had lucrative interests in Antenna Associates, Petra had informed her. They guzzled bottles of champagne at a rapid rate. Incessant laughter bellowed from their manly chests. Mike was among them. He appeared to be very comfortable, wrapped up, immersed in it all, like one of the lads, a real man's man, smartly clad in a pair of blue tailored slacks, contrasted with a blue cashmere sweater that Amy couldn't resist taking sneaky peeks.

Belinda and Robert sat closely together, conveniently tucked away in a dark and cozy corner, totally lost in their peculiar world, in a display of intimacy, canoodling and kissing. Amy was very pleased to note that Belinda had finally succumbed to Robert's unrelenting gestures, very pleased indeed and, couldn't help but wonder whether Belinda had decided to settle for Robert as second best. After all, Mike was proving to be a bit of a slippery fish that was difficult to catch. Amy hoped this meant that she'd be the better bait, and figured that in a little while, she'd pluck up the courage, choose her moment to stroll over to the main bar area and join the group of men, as soon as Katie ceased talking to her and Petra although, she hadn't been paying full attention to a single word of Katie's since their arrival.

Amy cut in quickly when Katie eventually paused for air, "If you'll excuse me, I'm going over to the main bar area to circulate."

"You do that. Always a good idea to circulate," said Petra.

Katie looked over at the bar and raised her eyebrows. "It's all men over there. Have an interesting time with them, won't you," she teased, accusatively.

"Thank you, Katie. I intend to do just that," said Amy. "Please feel free to join me later, won't you?"

"No worries. I'll be over later. Now, where was I?" said Katie.

Amy left Katie and Petra in their chosen topical debate on whether champagne and wine bars were becoming more popular than pubs. Yeah. Right! Amy thought, detouring to the ladies room, wondering what had gotten into them both, whether the ~~effects of the~~ champagne had gone to their heads. After applying the finishing touches of lip-gloss, Amy playfully pouted her full bodied lips in the mirror, swept her fingers through her hair and dabbed So Pretty De Cartier parfum behind each ear. Facing the full length mirror, Amy performed a final head to toe, back and front appearance check. Satisfied, she left the ladies room, ready to conquer.

A passing barman stopped suddenly in his tracks at the sight of Amy. Visibly captivated, the barman invited Amy to take a glass from his loaded tray of twelve, all brimming with champagne, just poured. Amy admired the barman's skill, the way he cleverly balanced the tray, on one hand, at an angle, in the air, walking at a fast pace without spilling a drop.

"*Vous voulez prendre quelque champagne, madam?*" said the barman, his eyes filled with desire.

Heeding gracefully, Amy plucked a glass from the tray. "*Merci, monsieur,*" she said, smiling pleasantly at him then heading off to the main bar.

"Ah. Hello. You've come to join us at last. Apologies, we haven't had a chance to introduce ourselves or get fully acquainted over these past three days. You're already aware that I'm David White?" David cooed, extending his hand, blocking Amy from advancing any further, during their handshake.

"Yes, I am aware. It'd all got a bit hectic to finally get around to speaking to everyone. I'm happy to meet you, albeit at the end of it all." Amy glanced in Mike's direction during the eternal handshake. "Excuse me, David," she said, jerking her hand free and inching herself over to Mike. She felt so good standing so close to him.

"Enjoying the evening?" Mike enquired.

"Yes. Very much," Amy responded brightly.

"I'm courting," said Mike, dispassionately.

Amy wasn't certain whether she'd heard Mike correctly or not. To be sure, she thought she'd ask him to repeat himself but decided against it. She'd heard him loud and clear, as clearly as she'd heard him say *"I'll be there in two minutes, honey,"* on his cell-phone on the first day of the workshop. "Great," she said, putting on a brave face.

"In fact, our engagement is imminent," Mike went on.

Mike's words cut like a knife. Amy wondered why he was torturing her, telling her this, and now. She was relieved that no-one had heard snippets of their exchange, conveniently drowned out by the combinational noise levels that emanated from sober conversations, music, laughter and the clatter of bottles and glasses. Her perplexity growing, Amy wondered how long Mike had detected her attraction towards him. She'd been cautiously diplomatic and had held back from revealing anything to anyone, including Katie. Gathering her thoughts, Amy searched for some form of distraction. She looked over at Katie, hoping for some form of eye contact or a signal that Katie would shortly be coming over to join her. No joy. Katie was still locked in conversation with Petra. Impressed with Mike's supposed perceptiveness of her on the one hand, Amy was exacerbated by the news of the imminent engagement on the other. Her mind raced. Why? Three days. Three days of a helter-skelter ride. She convinced herself that she had to put on an act, pretend to be undeterred by it all. David inched his way over to Amy and was now standing quite close to her.

"We've elected Mike as chairman to organize a social event we're in the middle of planning," said David. "You joined us at the point where we were brainstorming on where to go and what to do."

"Thank you for the information."

"People have come up with some very interesting ideas ranging from a day out at the zoo, a theatre night out, a comedy show," David informed Amy.

"Would you be interested in coming along?" Mike casually asked Amy.

"Yes. Of course. I'd love to." Amy smiled willingly, doing her utmost best to appear as keen on the idea as everyone else around her appeared to be doing.

"I'm in possession of your number. It's on the contact list Petra had provided. I intend to call everyone sometime next week. Would that be alright with you?"

'Sure," said Amy. Devastated, Amy put on a brave face and spent the rest of the evening effortlessly circulating, acting as sociably as she possibly could with everyone. A large consumption of champagne helped her along tremendously.

Katie came up trumps again, proving to be the life and soul, cracking a number of silly, but equally hilarious jokes. "OK," said Katie. "This is a clean one. How do you tell the sex of a fly?"

"I've no idea," David shouted.

"OK. A woman walked into the kitchen to find her husband stalking around with a fly swatter. "What are you doing?" she asked. "Hunting flies," her husband said. "Killed any?" the woman asked. "Yep. Three male, two female," her husband said. Baffled, the woman asked. "How can you tell the male from the female?" Her husband replied, "Three were on a beer can and two were on the telephone." The cabana filled with an eruption of laughter.

Amy swung her head around and caught sight of David ogling her. He'd spent the best part of the evening staring at her intermittently. David turned and looked the other way. It wasn't the first time she'd caught his eyes on her. Amy thought that David was a cute, blond guy who was, she recalled, in retrospect, David proudly stating during the workshop introductions that he was married with three children and, her then viewing him as forbidden fruit. But Mike, in all honesty, was the man of the moment. He'd everything going for him, on all fronts. Amid the cacophony of laughter, Amy turned to face Mike to try her hand at conjuring a real fun and pleasant conversation with him only to discover that he'd disappeared.

David had been chatting away and Amy hadn't listened to a word he'd said. She turned to David, who was looking at her quizzically awaiting her response. "Sorry, David, I didn't quite catch any of that. I'm going to have to ask you to repeat it all."

"Not at all, Amy. It is a bit noisy in here."

"Yes, it is."

"I was asking …" Does he have to? Amy thought, agonizingly. "What are your favorite hobbies or pastimes?"

Leaving Mike's whereabouts for the moment, Amy dragged her attention span back into the flow of things.

"My favorite hobbies? Pastimes? You are joking, David?"

"No. I'm serious," he said, groaning and smiling suggestively at her.

Pitying David, Amy almost laughed out loud at his abysmal groan that totally lacked the desired outcome, finding his flirtatious behavior grotesque and unbecoming. In an attempt to quell any fantasies David might have been secretly entertaining in his wild imagination about her, Amy deliberately appeared dull and boring in her response. "I'm very busy most of the time. However, I enjoy reading and word puzzles."

"That's surprising. You'd struck me as the type who'd enjoy fun, vibrant and energetic hobbies."

"You've made the wrong strike, David. Sorry! One can imagine things that are otherwise untrue about one."

Amy noticed that David had begun to show signs of disinterest. He suddenly jerked forward. Katie had slapped him playfully on his back. "Hello, David. How are you?"

"Steady on, woman," he said, turning around swiftly to face Katie.

Katie winked at him. "Come on. It wasn't that forceful was it? I have a powerful pair of hands but that wasn't nearly as powerful as I can get."

"I was merely caught by surprise not having seen or heard you coming, Katie."

"Seen or heard? What do you mean, seen or heard?" Kate blurted.

"Exactly what I've just stated. You're always making some form of an entrance visually or auditory."

Amy sniggered convinced something was going on between Katie and David that only they understood. She spotted Mike at the far end of the bar talking to the bar staff and wondered whether he'd return to his previous spot and, in the same breath, re-directed her attentions to Katie and David.

"Feeding ducks," said Katie.

"Now, that sounds like fun."

"And you?" Katie asked.

"I construct and fly miniature model aircraft," replied David.

"Interesting. Are they motorized?"

"Yes, they are."

"Where do you fly them?"

"In Richmond, Hyde or Regent's parks. Wimbledon Common. Wherever, really."

"So, do any of these parks have ponds with ducks in?" Katie asked.

Amy listened on intently, switching her gaze from Katie to David and vice versa.

"I'd much prefer to stay away from ponds not wanting the aircraft to land in water."

"I see your point. Have you ever thought about constructing an aircraft that takes off and land on water?"

David looked at Katie, thoughtfully and lingeringly. "A seaplane?" he gasped. "The thought hadn't crossed my mind. Sounds like a great idea. It's worth bearing in mind." Surprisingly taken by Katie's show of keen and genuine interest in his hobby, David instantly turned his back to Amy. Observing the evident signs of a possible romance forming on the horizon, Katie and David too engrossed with each other, left Amy fully aware that they were no longer acknowledging her presence.

Katie coughed a little before delivering her next line saying, "I like parks and feeding ducks and you like flying model aircraft in parks. I see a common thread developing here."

"Do you? Let me guess," said David, raising his eyebrows, pausing longer than necessary, deliberately keeping Katie in suspense. "Aha! Grass," he shouted. David and Katie erupted into cackles of laughter. Amy joined them. Intrigued, not certain what they were leading up to, waited around for the end.

"No! Well. Yes. Grass. As in parks. Lawns. That sort of grass. Not the other sort. Parks are what we have in common," Katie spluttered.

"Yes, I know, parks with ponds," David affirmed, chuckling and nodding in agreement.

Giggling, Amy was managing to enjoy their exchange of nonsensical banter. In the meantime, Mike remained at the other end of the bar in conversation with the bar staff. Curious, Amy wished she was a fly on the wall. Their laughter hadn't appeared to distract Mike's attention and there was no indication as to whether he'd be re-joining the group.

"I'd love to see your aircraft in action, in the air and on water."

"You've actually given me the incentive to construct a seaplane. Tell you what. I'll construct one and invite you along as the first person to witness its initial take off. How does that sound?"

Yes, she's done it. It's a date, Amy thought, experiencing the bitter sweet moment of joy and excitement for Katie but, at the same time battling with the daunting knowledge that David was, in fact, a married man and father to three children. Amy urgently felt the need to pull Katie aside and talk some sense into her. Unsure of how much of Katie's behavior was attributed to being under the influence of champagne or whether Katie was just being herself, Amy felt she had to make Katie aware of the fact that David was effectively unavailable, untouchable.

Mike quietly and inconspicuously made his way back, eased himself into a comfortable position, propped up at the bar and resettled with the group.

"We were just discussing hobbies. What are yours, Mike?" Amy had asked as soon as she'd spotted him.

"Wine tasting," he replied.

s one of the things you do for a living. Am I right?" queried

so a hobby."

"Right," Amy said. "Along with wine tasting, would you have any other hobbies or pastimes?" Probing, Amy was endeavoring to learn something more about Mike, something that would turn her off him completely, change her mind about pursuing him, put her out of her misery, something that would bring an end to her pining for the man.

"There are a number but, I'd rather not go into them right now."

The ever elusive Mike, Amy thought. "I'm baffled that you're able to donate time to a number of hobbies, let alone one," she said, feeling a strange tingle of tense excitement as Mike stared long, hard and searchingly at her.

"One can always find the time to dedicate themselves to the things they have a passion and love for," he replied.

From the sensitivity of his response, Amy believed that she'd finally pressed the button, penetrated Mike's wall of defense and was interested to note that he'd allowed himself to use emotive words such as passion and love.

An enchanting sound of wind chimes suddenly filled the cabana, signifying that the bar was about to close in fifteen minutes. Like Pavlov's dogs, in a collective act of respondent conditioning, people set about gathering their personal belongings. It was one-fifty in the morning. The time had flown by very quickly that Amy hadn't noticed its encroachment marking the sad reality that the evening had come to an ominous end. Bad timing, she thought, convinced she was close to getting somewhere with Mike, that she'd successfully tapped into his sensitive side, which she'd enjoyed doing. Her hopes for another opportunity were now dashed... *delete one elipse*

Katie snapped her fingers at Amy.

"I'd drifted away for a moment," said Amy, re-alerting.

"I'd noticed," ~~responded~~ Katie, ~~draining~~ her ~~glass of~~ champagne and slamming ~~her it~~ down on the bar. *20 finished*

"Well done, Katie. With only ten minute to spare, you hadn't enough time left to continue sipping graciously as you'd been doing all evening," said David, sardonically.

"Well, I couldn't possibly have wasted it!" Katie justified.

"Agreed," David said.

Dead on their feet and desperate to get home after working the long Friday night shift, the bar staff busily hovered around, providing assistance, keeping their fingers crossed that there wouldn't be any last minute requests or hitches.

Je La Buena practiced a strict work ethic on the provision of customer care. Staff expectations were high and rules had to be adhered to at all times, which sometimes meant that they had to work the occasional overtime, catering for the needs of clients who were charged nearly double the going rate for services rendered outside of the normal operating hours. Amy, Katie, Mike, David, Belinda, Robert and a handful of clientele said their hurried goodbyes and set off on their journeys home. Everything was happening far too quickly for Amy, perched on a high stool at the bar, observing the activities, bar staff painstakingly organizing taxis, fetching coats from the cloakroom, retrieving misplaced items, returning them to their rightful owners. Briefcases, Blackberry handheld devices, laptops, iPods, cigarette lighters, a Gucci handbag left under a table, and a black leather purse left on the bar. It was approaching five past two in the morning. Amy and Katie opted to share a taxi. Robert and Belinda, who hadn't socialized with anyone, save for the entire evening, strolled out together arm in arm. Mike and David boarded separate taxis. Amy stood on the edge of the curb and waved goodbye to Mike as his taxi sped off to an unknown destination.

CHAPTER 4

Amy hurriedly unlocked the main door of her apartment. She hoped to enter in time to answer the telephone before it had stopped ringing. She tossed her briefcase on the chair in the hallway, raced into the lounge and dived athletically on the couch reaching for the telephone. Kicking off her black patent, four inch stilettos, Amy spoke, trying not to sound out of breath. It was Petra inviting Amy to take part in an independent telephone survey on Antenna Associates. Amy obliged and arranged a convenient date and time.

"Thank you. I knew I could count on you, Amy. Your input will be most invaluable in ensuring that my company maintains its exposure and a firm foothold in the industry. Let me add that I hope to be of assistance to you in the not too distant future."

"Oh no!" exclaimed Amy, slouching on the couch. "It's my pleasure to be of assistance to you, Petra."

It was the second Wednesday since the workshop concluded and Amy had not had any contact with the delegates, not even Katie. Hanging up, Amy immediately called Katie.

"Hi. How are you? You were a bit low in spirits when we'd left the champagne bar. Don't know what it was but, are you OK now?"

Remembering the stark events at Je La Buena, Amy refrained from giving away any clues on how she'd really felt that night.

"Oh. Sorry to have given you that impression. It was not intentional. All was well with me, I can assure you," said Amy casually. "Any news on the social front?"

"Nada. Nothing. Zilch" Katie replied. "I'd found that mo⟨ ⟩ were quite cheesy that I'm not in a hurry to go trundling off to som⟨ ⟩ event with that lot."

"You could've fooled me, you were the light and soul, entertaining, amusing us cheesy people."

"Amy, don't be silly. You're not cheesy. I had to do something. They were all so stiff and proper, sipping champagne with their little fingers stuck up in the air. I thought they needed to let their hair down a little, loosen up a bit. Just watching them trying to unwind and let go amused me more than anything else," Katie went on. "As I owe you a coffee, we could make our own arrangements, you and I, that is."

Amy sighed. "You don't owe me a thing. Coffee was my treat. By the way, has Petra called you?"

"Yes. She went on about some market research thing."

"Then, I don't need to pre-warn you about taking part in an independent telephone survey?"

"No."

Amy sought to progress their conversation that wasn't exactly picking up or going anywhere and, to avoid simple small talk, she inquisitively moved swiftly on to the subject of David.

"Apart from myself, there is another exception to your cheesy rule, Katie."

"And what would that be?"

"David?" Amy fidgeted on the couch.

"David?" echoed Katie.

"Do you view David as cheesy, too?"

Katie laughed.

Gasping for a hot drink, Amy rose from the couch and wandered into the kitchen to make a cup of Chinese organic green tea.

"Yes, you're right, David is an exception," said Katie. "In fact, he'd called me one afternoon this week and mentioned that he'd bought the materials to build the seaplane."

Amy poured natural mineral bottled water into her kettle and switched it on. "Oh, I see," said Amy in a concerned tone of voice.

"What is it that you'd really like to say, Amy?"

Amy hesitated then thought it best to just spit it out. "I'd noticed the friendly rapport between you and David at the champagne bar and wondered whether there was anything going on because he is married, after all." Wary, Amy expected a retributively explosive response but, Katie remained silent for what seemed an eternity. Amy went on, "with three siblings, or at least I think there are three." She hoped she didn't sound as awkward and as stupid as she was now beginning to feel.

"I know. Don't worry. I know exactly what I'm doing. David and I get on very well and that's basically it. There is nothing going on between us. We're purely platonic."

"OK." Amy had heard words used along those lines so many times before only to see it all end in tears and feared that Katie may be going down the same route. Amy bit her lip. "Have you an agreed date to launch the model seaplane?"

"Sounds like a worrying question to me, if ever there was one. Don't worry Amy. It's only a walk in the park. No. He's not set a firm date yet. David's only just bought the materials and hasn't started building the seaplane."

The kettle hissed to boiling point. "Call me after your walk in the park. I'm keen to learn everything about the events," Amy enthused.

"I was just thinking," said Katie.

"Yes?" Amy listened attentively.

Katie sighed blissfully. "What a sight that's going to be. I can just picture it now. Me, feeding ducks, fascinated by David's seaplane performing a splash dunk in the pond, skittering along the water, upsetting the ducks, sending them into a panic, flapping and quacking themselves into a frenzy." Katie roared with laughter and Amy laughed along infectiously. "I wonder what color the finished product's going to be. Maybe a bright red or, whether a trail of smoke will be billowing from the rear on take-off?" Katie said, laughing convulsively.

"Promise you'll fill me in on all the details when you get back," said Amy, wiping away tears of laughter streaming down her cheeks.

"I promise," said Katie. "It's a deal."

"Great. Do remember to give me a call should you get any news on the social evening?" Amy hoped Katie would remember and not delay in relaying the news.

"As I've already stated, I'm not particularly keen to attend the social evening. We can do our own thing, you and I but yes, I promise to keep you informed," said Katie, ending the call.

Speculatively pondering aspects of the telephone conversation, Amy placed a tea bag into her cup and filled it with hot water. In her view, Katie and David  weren't entirely compatible, but opposites in many respects. Katie was loud, boisterous and unreserved. David had gone quite unnoticed during the workshop that Amy believed he had a reserved disposition until the night at Je La Buena had revealed otherwise. The telephone started ringing, interrupting her thoughts. Amy figured it would be Jenson and, avoiding a conversation, she asked him to call her back later on. She sipped her tea, brought her cup into the lounge, glanced at the workshop contact list attached to her notice board and thought it would be a good idea to call Mike at home. Setting her cup on the desk, Amy nervously dialed Mike's number. Her mind went blank. She hadn't given a rehearsed thought of what she was going to say to him and, after one ring, Amy hung up the telephone. Horrified at her behavior, Amy told herself to stop acting silly and resigned herself to practice the wise virtue of patience. Amy jumped at the telephone ringing again. Convinced it was Mike, that he'd traced her number as the last caller, with a huge guilt complex, she composed herself, cleared her throat, lifted the cordless telephone out of its cage and pressed it against her ear.

"Amy, I'd dearly love to see you tonight." It was Jenson again. Amy blew a deep sigh of relief. "No need to answer that, darling. You sound very tired, very weary," said Jenson apologetically.

Due to Jenson's misinterpretation of her blown sigh of relief as a sign of weariness, Amy was on the verge of bursting into laughter listening to Jenson's apologetics, being ever so very understanding. He had the art of persuasion, a way of making her give in to him, change her mind from a no to a yes, even when she'd been genuinely dead, dog tired after a hectic week at the office. But, Amy was adamant on this occasion. "Thanks for being so understanding, darling. I'll call you tomorrow night," she said, yawning.

"OK, darling," said Jenson, acquiescently.

For the remainder of the night, Amy spent a quiet and lazy time in. Before retiring to bed, she switched the telephone ring tone to the silent position and diverted all calls to voicemail.

It was Friday night and Amy still hadn't heard from a single workshop delegate. Continuing with the wait, Amy opted to end the night reading a quality suspense crime thriller in a steaming hot bubble bath. She heard the faint sound of the telephone ringing as she poured a few drops of Patchouli aromatherapy scented oil into her bath of steaming hot, running water. Damn, she thought, turning the taps off, dashing out of the bathroom and into the lounge to answer the telephone.

"It's David, here."

"Oh!" said Amy startlingly. "It's great to hear from you, David. How are you?"

"Good. Can't hang around," said David. "Just called to find out whether you'd like to meet with members of the group. We plan to have a Chinese meal at Yo Yo's in Soho Square next week Saturday. We aim to meet at around seven-thirty in Leicester Square, at a landmark yet to be decided."

"It all sounds great to me. Mike not making the calls, I take it?"

"No. He couldn't. He'd got tied up. Had to fly to France on unexpected business and asked me to take over for him."

"Oh!" said Amy, stumped, not knowing what to make of it nor did she want to appear pushy by asking David further questions about Mike.

"If there's nothing else, I'll contact you mid-week with news of final arrangements?"

"No. There's nothing else, thanks."

David quickly said his goodbyes and hung up.

Amy walked somberly into the kitchen and poured herself a glass of chilled Californian Chardonnay.

The remainder of the weekend was exhausting. It all began when Jenson arrived at eight on Saturday morning. He'd silently entered Amy's bedroom, undressed and slowly crawled into her bed. She knew when he'd arrived. She'd heard the sound of the key as he turned it quietly in the lock. It'd been three months since Amy had handed Jenson a spare key to her apartment, relieving her of the hassle of getting out of bed to let him in. Lain on her back, Amy pretended to be asleep. Jenson nestled closely to her and swept his fingers up and down her inner thighs. Amy opened her eyes slowly.

"Good morning, beautiful," Jenson whispered softly. He gazed into her eyes, excited, fully aware that most mornings her libido peaked. Speechless, highly aroused by now to say anything that would make an ounce of verbal sense, surrendering, Amy gripped Jenson's arms tightly as she received the power of his force and ecstatic energy renting through his body. She groaned in sheer excruciating pleasure, immersed in the sensations of extreme joy and painful pleasure. A few minutes after her climax, slumberous, Amy drifted off, awakening forty-five minutes later, making love to Jenson, repeatedly. It was two thirty in the afternoon when Amy eventually clambered out of bed. She took a shower, prepared a late lunch of prawn salad on toasted rye, followed by a finely chopped fresh fruit salad, black coffee and fresh orange juice. Jenson showered, ate and dashed off to his apartment to prepare and dress for the evening's event. He was hosting an after party in the ballroom of the prestigious Dorchester Hotel in London's Park Lane for a popular American rock band, JJ and the Crew currently celebrating their top ten hit in the UK music charts. Amy was never short of entertainment. Jenson invited her to practically all the events. For ease of entry, he'd placed her name on guest lists, VIP lists and, whenever possible, provided her with stage door and press passes. Guests were due to start arriving from eleven o'clock onwards. Jenson arranged for a luxury car to collect Amy from her apartment at ten-thirty to ensure her comfort and timely arrival. Amy booked an appointment at Etiquette, the late night hair, nail and beauty salon. Robbie Black, the proud and openly gay proprietor, a former celebrity make-up artist, always looked forward to seeing Amy.

"Yes *darrrliiiing*, a French manicure at eight, followed by hair and make-up *darrrliiiing*. Hope you've got lots to tell me. See you later at eight. *Moi. Moi.*," said Robbie. He dowsed himself in all the latest gossip related to his clients. And scandal thrown in for good measure really made his day. The more extremely outrageous, the better. Most of the gossip Amy found amusing, although she hadn't met half the clients Robbie blurted scourging news about, all closely guarded secrets, of course. Finical, Amy divulged very little about herself. But having Etiquette was a God-send. The late night beauty salon was a great idea saving her time, energy and effort in having to apply her make-up herself. Before attending her appointment, Amy took a two hour beauty nap. Hair, nails and make-up expertly done and home by ten o'clock, Amy slipped into a cream Oscar de la Renta, ankle length dress adorned with sequins. The luxury car arrived at ten-thirty sharp. Perfect, Amy thought.

People partied on the marble floor of the hotel's palatial ballroom. They pranced, pouted and posed to the loud, bass-thumping beat of the music Jenson played. Amy walked along casually, returning the revelers' smiles and greetings. Some beckoned her to join them. Jenson clearly knew how to get a crowd moving, Amy observed. She shouted in the left ear of one of the security stewards, asking him for guidance on where to hang her coat. The security steward had a tiny earpiece attached to his right ear. "Wait here whilst I drop your coat off in the cloakroom," he shouted.

"Will do," Amy shouted back. She tapped the security steward on his shoulder before he'd set off with her coat. "Do you know Jenson?" she shouted.

"Yeah," he shouted.

"Could you take me to him before handing my coat in, please?"

"Yeah. This way," he shouted, taking hold of Amy's arm, escorting her through the crowd to Jenson dancing in the DJ booth. Parked outside of the DJ booth, Amy enjoyed the intense party atmosphere; she tapped her feet and nodded her head to the music. Jenson, smartly dressed in a black Giorgio Armani suit, suddenly looked down and, by chance, caught sight of Amy. He rushed out of the DJ booth and physically lifted her off her feet.

"How long have you been standing here?" shouted Jenson.

"About ten minutes," Amy shouted.

Jenson dashed back into the DJ booth, stood masterfully over the impressive computerized equipment and spoke colloquialisms into the microphone. The revelers responded conformingly. Jenson handed the headphones to his young apprentice, Ben and instructed him to take over for a while. "I want to spend some time with my lady." Jenson lead Amy to the Crystal room which served as a VIP lounge and proceeded to introduce her to members of JJ and the Crew.

"You an entertainer?" asked JJ, the lead singer, flicking his shoulder-length, jet black, dyed hair, an attribute adored by his female fans.

"No, I'm not. Quite the opposite really, worlds apart from what you do."

"You sure you not no entertainer, 'cos you look like one o dem entertainer women."

Amy smiled sweetly at JJ and refrained from saying another word. She'd noticed that JJ's eyes were out of focus, sensed his slight incoherency, suspected that he was probably under the influence of drink, drugs or a cocktail of both and realized she'd not get an ounce of sense out of him. Jenson had observed enough.

"I need a drink. See you later guys," he said, taking Amy by the hand and swiftly leading her out of the VIP lounge.

Relieved, Amy smiled thankfully at Jenson. "Ah, this is my favorite song," she said, singing aloud, pulling Jenson onto the dance floor. They danced all night and pranced, pouted and posed with the revelers. Jenson never left Amy's side. Ben remained in the DJ booth, dutifully taking charge, providing first class entertainment. Amy was duly impressed.

The luxury car pulled up outside Amy's apartment. "Darling, we're home," said Jenson, gently nudging Amy. Five minutes after clambering into the car for the journey home after the party, Amy snuggled her head on Jenson's chest and slept all the way home. "Amy?" Jenson whispered, nudging her again.

Half asleep and quite comfortable in that position, Amy didn't want to move an inch. She lifted her swimming head, groaned and climbed clumsily out of the car. Planting her feet unsteadily on the ground, ears hissing from the after effects of loud music pumped directly into her eardrums for an entire night, Amy walked unsteadily to the main door of her apartment. "I'm going to have to stop doing this," she groaned as Jenson unlocked the door.

"Not too soon, I hope. You looked dazzling tonight in that dress. As always, I loved your dancing and your sexy moves," Jenson commended.

Amy couldn't wait to get out of her figure hugging dress. They both undressed, leaving a trail of clothing on the floor along the hallway. Naked, Amy collapsed on her bed. Jenson, on his knees, mesmerized by the sheer beauty of Amy's nudity, began to kiss her all over her body, working his way up from the tips of her toes. Fantasizing, allowing her imagination to run free, fighting off thoughts of Mike invading her mind, confusing her special moment with Jenson, Amy smiled. "Any moment now," she said, breathlessly, "any moment now." Her husky voice sent Jenson into heightened sexual delirium.

"I love it when you're drunk." Jenson whispered.

Amy arched her spine and cried out as Jenson entered her with manly force.

Jenson left at seven o'clock on Sunday evening. Declining his further invites, Amy was centering her thoughts worryingly on Mike.

"Got another soiree next weekend," Jenson enthused. Amy said nothing. "I'll give you a call when I've got all the details at hand," said Jenson.

"Sorry, Jenson. I've plans for next weekend, so I don't think I'll be able to join you on this one."

"Well, should there be any changes, let me know, won't you, darling?" Jenson pecked Amy on her lips then, turned to head out of the apartment.

"Will do," she said, waving as Jenson closed the apartment door behind him. To replenish her sapped energy, Amy strolled into the kitchen and poured herself a multi-vitamin health drink. She estimated that by Thursday, she'd have made a full recovery, be fit for purpose again. David hadn't called her back, as he'd promised, Amy thought in unfounded impatience, deliberating on whether this would be the perfect time, better still, the perfect excuse to call Mike. This time, she'd make her rationale a valid one. She wandered into her lounge and relaxing on her couch, Amy read through various briefs in preparation of a conference call scheduled to be held at eight o'clock that evening between top company heads of Planet Management based in New York, Paris and London to discuss high level strategic measures on the new, multi-million US dollar, Del Mar casino project, spearheaded by Vincent. Vincent had summoned Amy to participate, which she opted to do from the comfort of her home. Vincent conceded. At five minutes to eight, Amy answered the telephone wondering why the call was commencing five minutes earlier than planned, suspecting that Vincent could have been calling to conduct a preamble with her. "Amy Scott entering from London," she announced.

"Hi, Amy." It was Mike. An exhilaratingly sensational rush rocketing through her, Amy closed her eyes tightly, crossed her legs and clenched her fist. She remembered how handsome and comely he'd looked the last time she'd laid eyes on him at Je La Buena. "Are you busy?"

"No, no." Amy responded in urgency, desperately disappointed in Mike's timing. "I'd meant to say, yes. We've got five minutes," she said, quickly.

"Is everything alright?" Mike asked, concernedly.

"I'm sorry, Mike. Only, I've a conference call due to start any minute now."

"I understand. I'll call back in an hour."

"Please do. Thank you, Mike," Amy said gratefully. Mike hung up. Holding the telephone in mid air, Amy hoped that Mike would call back as there was always something obstructing them from having some form of a liaison. Amy replaced the telephone on its cage and waited for it to ring again. She desperately wanted to speak to Mike, to have the conversation she'd longed for, some form of dialogue with him. She wondered whether anything at all would ever happen between them, whether there was any possibility of them ever becoming an item and couldn't quite put her finger on why she was not willing to drop it, suppress her feelings, stick with Jenson, the devil she knows; the one she was sociologically on par with. Amy picked up the ringing telephone. "Amy Scott entering from London," she announced, re-assuming her official tone. Throughout the first ten minutes, Amy lacked concentration, daydreaming on what she'd say to Mike later on. Vincent had repeated a couple of questions directed at Amy. Her mind rested on Mike, Amy told herself that she had to snap out of her trance-like state and give her full attention to the call if she wanted to remain a key player on the new project, more importantly with the company. Moreover, she'd sooner avoid facing Vincent in a wrathful showdown the following day. In an instant Amy transformed into dynamism, powerfully exerting intelligent concepts, providing information on the transactional structure, backed by proven knowledge to her arguments, arguments that were vital in taking Planet Management considerably forward on the project with the potential to secure high percentage, pre-tax earnings on

the deal. Vincent, happy with the agreements, ended the con~~f~~
throat parched from the long, hard, consistent negotiations,
entire contents of a bottle of mineral water she'd taken out of her mini-bar
cooler. She'd given her best performance yet and had detected signs that Vincent was genuinely pleased with her input. Comfortable with that thought, not
wanting to call Vincent to recap or go over any important aspects before the
following morning, Amy read through her rough notes, finalizing her analyses.
By ten o'clock, Amy crawled into bed waiting for Mike to call.

The lamp toppled onto the bedroom floor as Amy, half asleep, accidentally
knocked it off the bedside table as she reached for the ringing telephone.

"It's me, calling back, as promised," said Mike. "Sorry. Am I disturbing you
again? Were you asleep?"

To wake herself up, Amy briskly kicked the bedcovers off, hurled herself out
of bed, placed the lamp back on the bedside table, and paced around the room
with the cordless telephone pressed firmly on her right ear. "No. Not at all," she
replied, stifling a yawn.

"It's late. Eleven-thirty," Mike pointed out.

Amy didn't care whether it was eleven-thirty or three in the morning, she
was enjoying him now, albeit not under the most perfect of situations. "Don't
worry, Mike. I'm pleased to hear from you. How are you?"

"Very busy and very well." Mike coughed awkwardly. "And how are you?"

"*Como siempre,* busy and functioning well," said Amy.

"Principally, I've called to inform you that the social event has been cancelled."

"Oh." Amy was determined to keep Mike on the line. "Why?"

"People were crying off like flies for various reasons. Neither was there
much interest nor much commitment shown and because of this, David and I
decided to call it off."

"How many people in total had actually committed?" asked Amy.

"Zero, practically. The evening would have consisted of David, me and possibly you, if you were still willing to attend."

"Of course. Absolutely. I've remained fully committed," said Amy overzealously.

"It's cancelled, I'm afraid, Amy."

Amy wasn't prepared to let go that easily. "I've an idea. Let's go ahead with
it, you, me and David" she suggested daringly, testing the water, waiting in
dread for Mike's response.

"There was very little enthusiasm from David when we spoke earlier this evening, so I don't think he'd commit to joining us both."

"Well, what would you say to the idea of just the two of us going along instead?" Amy asked. "I've every confidence that we'll have a most enjoyable evening," she added, desperately throwing anything in as an influential measure. She shuddered as the painful seconds ticked by, mentally pleading, please, say yes, yes, yes, wondering what she'd say or do should he decline.

"Sounds like a splendid idea."

Shell-shocked, it took Amy a few seconds to register Mike's response. "Brill. We, we could start with a change of venue."

"You can choose, Amy. I'll leave the decision entirely up to you."

Silent, Amy beamed with elation, entertaining the thought that she'd finally, at long last, broken ground. "There's a French restaurant based in Covent Garden, Beaujolais, I quite like. We could meet there at eight, if you like. I'll reserve a table."

"It's a done deal. We'll meet this Saturday, at eight, in the Beaujolais restaurant. I'll look it up and see you there."

"Great. See you then," Amy replied relieved.

"Well, I must be off now," said Mike.

"Yes. Me too. Well, good night, Mike." Pleased, her fleeting efforts had paid off, Amy hung up, yawned, crawled back into bed and slept like a baby.

CHAPTER 5

Amy performed her role as portfolio account executive remarkably well. She smiled radiantly at everyone she came into contact with at the office and walked with a spring in her step all day.

"I'm most impressed with your valid input and outstanding delivery on the work you've dedicated this week on the Del Mar casino project, Amy." Vincent had commended her during his summing-up at their weekly, Friday one-to-one session.

Amy smiled modestly. "Thank you, Vincent," she said, genuinely moved to have received such an accolade from Vincent, pleased her hard work hadn't gone unnoticed.

Vincent religiously held one-to-one meetings with account executives working on his key projects. He kept a rigid, ruthless and tentative eye on the progression of all projects. He possesses an astute business acumen which he applied with mastery, instinctively maintaining regular, if not, constant con-tact with key clients and account executives in his keeping abreast of activities. Inspired and in awe of Vincent, Amy observed him habitually. She admired his professionalism, unrelenting tenacity, working knowledge, business ethics, energy and drive, his insistency on achieving the highest results, which he invariably succeeded in doing. Individualized entelechy was an attribute Vincent expected to see driving his account executives, proven at each weekly session he'd conclude with a new set of results to be achieved and met within a set time-frame for presentation at a next session. On this occasion, Amy had excelled in the area of due diligence, remaining one step ahead on all aspects of the processes and procedures relating to the Del Mar casino project. She proactively researched the latest accounting trends, applied an investigative mind

"Crème de Menthe with plenty of ice, thanks?"

"Certainly, madam."

Soon after taking her first sip, Amy began to wind down. Happy with her choice of venue, she was imbued with Beaujolais' ambience and warmth. Apart from the observance of an odd looking couple, diners were mostly engaged in quietly muffled conversations over their delectable dishes. The aroma of French cuisine wafting through the air awakened her appetite. The waitress lead Mike over to Amy, casually browsing the range of liquors on the drinks list, her sultry crossed legs were adorned in shimmering silk black stockings. "Madam, your guest has arrived and your table is ready."

Mike leaned forward and pecked Amy on her cheek. His hazel eyes smiled into her soul. The smoothness of his skin, freshly shaved, gently brushing her cheek and the warmth of his firm lips aroused her. She loved the look of his clean, fresh and spruced-up stature. He smelt so good she was convinced he'd not long got out of the shower. "It's great to see you again," she said holding out her hand.

Mike's eyes moved over her aesthetically. "You look great." Amy smiled at him and sighed. The waitress hovered attentively around them.

"My name is Giselle and I am your waitress for the evening. This way please," she said, beckoning them to follow her.

Knees trembling, Amy stepped off the stool and followed Mike and the waitress into the main dining area. A couple of women glanced at Mike. His attractiveness turned heads. One particular woman Amy had spotted earlier on, dining with a bald, ashen faced, frail, old man, definitely old enough to be her grandfather, stabbed Amy an envious glance. Amy figured the old man to be in his mid-seventies, the woman, in her late twenties, possible early thirties. An odd couple, they clearly had a mutual, if not, intimate liking for one another, candidly stroking hands at the table. Suspicious, Amy felt that they were demonstrating the lascivious hallmarks of a clandestine affair. Could it be an estranged secretary and her boss, maybe? Amy speculated, coming to the conclusion that money had to be playing a huge factor somewhere along the line. Amy swished passed the woman's table, raised her eyebrows contemptibly at her with an expressional, "sorry to disappoint you but, he's all mine, thank you," proud to be in Mike's company again, at long last. The woman briskly looked the other way, viciously cutting her eyes at Amy in the process. Mike and Amy were ushered to their table situated in a semi secluded spot, conveniently tucked away from the marauding eyes of the woman. Antique Mahogany French doors with intricate paneled carvings, opened out to an elegant courtyard, hand paved in Chateau Terra Cotta tiles.

"Your table," said the waitress, gesturing them to take their seats, placing French and English menus on their table. "Anything you require, please ask and I'll do my utmost best to assist you," she said.

Mike and Amy thanked the waitress in unison.

"You look rather enchanting this evening," commented Mike.

Enormously flattered by the unexpected secondary compliment, Amy smiled nervously. "You look quite nice yourself, Mike."

"You're too kind. Thank you," Mike responded.

They'd both made personal efforts. Attired in smart casual dress, Mike wore a light weight, camel jacket over an open-necked, black shirt and a pair of black slacks. Amy opted for a classic keyhole design, Ardeche burgundy silk dress.

Mike glanced around the restaurant. "Good spot. So far so good," he said approvingly.

"Thank you. I'd hoped you'd like it. The cuisine and service are exceptional. I'd entertained clients here a few months ago. It's closely becoming one of my favorite venues."

"In that case, let's order," said Mike eagerly, flicking through the French menu, volunteering to order a five course meal, selecting an array of mouth watering dishes. "I'll place the order, if you like," he said.

"My pleasure," said Amy, happy that Mike elected to take care of things, ordering their dishes, fully conversant in French, discussing the nine stars Michelin chef's recipes, methods and cooking techniques with the waitress. Perusing the wine list, Mike looked questioningly at Amy.

"Wine?" he said. "I would recommend the Château Clos Fourtet 1961. It's a vintage from the St Emilion region in Bordeaux."

"Go ahead, that's fine by me," Amy responded. "Nothing but the best" she joked, noting the wine's category and cost.

"Exactly," said Mike. *"Je voudrais une bouteille de Château Clos Fourtet 1961, sil vous plait?"*

"I'm impressed," said Amy.

"Impressed? What with? The choice of wine?"

"No. Your fluency in spoken French."

Mike chuckled. "Oh, that. It's useful. Spoken familiarly helps to speed up the process, it's an advantage having a French waitress. She knows exactly what our standards and expectations are, that a good service is guaranteed," he commented confidently with an air of authoritative presence.

"Do you intend to exercise your authority a little?" enquired Amy.

"Authority? What exactly do you mean?"

"You are a connoisseur of food and wine by profession?"

"Yes. You could say that," Mike replied, leaning back comfortably in his chair.

"What I'm getting at is, your authority shows. I mean, I'm guessing here. You know exactly how things ought to be, right down to the cooking techniques, they won't dare to compromise on their services to you."

Mike raised his eyebrows. "I would be inclined to construe your statement as another compliment," he said. "Am I right or wrong?"

"Wrong. It was merely an observation," said Amy frolicking, disguising her inferiority complex.

Mike blinked. Amy smiled, relieved that the evening had kicked-off to a good start and hoped it would progress well. She also wanted to move things along a little, her way. The waitress presented the wine, and poured two glasses after Mike had sampled it. Mike announced a toast, which Amy viewed as a commendable gesture on his part.

"Let's salute," he said, raising his glass of wine in the air.

"Cheers," said Amy, clinking Mike's glass.

"To us," he said.

Mike's salutation caught Amy by surprise that she'd almost choked after she'd taken a sip. To us? she thought.

"Just the two of us," said Mike, fixing Amy an affirmative gaze.

Almost hypnotized by Mike's captivating eyes, Amy drew on everything in her power to stop herself from being sucked into his enigmatic presence. Maintaining her poise, Amy said nothing.

"Well, there are only the two of us here," Mike continued." As you are aware, David and I worked on getting a good number together for a good night out which has now resulted in just the two of us."

Amy wouldn't have wanted things any other way, she thought. "They've missed the opportunity to enjoy Beaujolais' exquisite cuisine. I'm sure they'd all had their valid reasons for dropping out, of course. Hopefully, there'll be a better turn out at the next event," said Amy

"Ah. Food is about to be served," said Mike. "I'm famished. I'd skipped lunch after I'd read first class reviews on Beaujolais."

"Smells divine," commented Amy on the French Onion soup the waitress had placed in front of her. "Yes, just the two of us this time around at least," she murmured, wishing that the statement carried more than its literal meaning.

"I'll give it a final joint effort shot with David in getting a bunch together. You never know, it may result in just the two of us again," returned Mike.

"Exactly. On the other hand, you may succeed in getting a good bunch together next time around." Amy had had enough of the ping pong and moved the conversation along to break up its stagnancy. It was beginning to make her nervous. "Tell me," she said, "on the subject of hobbies, can we continue from where we'd left off at Je La Buena?"

"Where exactly had we left off? You'll have to refresh my memory. I vaguely remember what we'd discussed that night. I'd had a lot to drink," said Mike.

Amy admired Mike's graceful table manners as he savored his snail and seaweed soup. She inconspicuously mirrored his movements. "You'd stated that you had a number of hobbies and your passion and love for those hobbies. Wine tasting was the only hobby you'd cared to mention." Amy enjoyed the succulence of a crouton melting on her tongue.

Mike nodded. "Yes. It's all coming back to me now. I love the aroma, texture, temperatures and taste of top quality wines, not to mention the palatable pleasures of an exquisitely rare vintage wine. I often attend vintage tasting events as far afield as California and South Africa to France and here in the UK."

"It all sounds very involved."

"It most certainly is very involved and serious business too."

"Oh, I can certainly believe that and I'm immensely enjoying the taste of this particular wine. It's delicious," Amy commented, adding, "And what are your other interests?"

"Steady on, you haven't shared any of your hobbies with me, yet!" said Mike.

"I thought you'd never ask."

"I'm interested," said Mike, urging Amy along.

"Hang-gliding."

"A dare devil at heart," said Mike. "You're an adventurous spirit. I've not met a hang-glider."

"Let's just say that I thrive on elements of excitement and danger. Like you, I stake great measures of passion and love into my hobbies."

"You too have more than one hobby?"

"Yes, I do," said Amy, daintily nibbling finely chopped celery, from her chef's special, French green salad with vegetable puree, blended with herbs and organic spices. "And since hang-gliding, whilst vacationing in Brazil, I'd made up my mind to take it up as a serious hobby, if you like."

"That must have been quite exhilarating, hang-gliding in Brazil." Mike's eyes glowed with a glint of adventure. "Please, elaborate on that experience, would you?" he said.

"I holidayed in Rio de Janeiro last year December with Rochelle, a holiday buddy of mine. I wanted to experience something different, unusual, exciting, something outside of the norm. I'd spotted a hang-glider from my hotel window. It was such a breathtaking sight that I called the concierge desk right away and enquired about hang-gliding for tourists. The concierge made all the necessary arrangements with a local travel agent situated within close proximity of the hotel."

"Excellent concierge services," Mike commented.

Amy nodded. "Yes, they were all very good. I can remember Rochelle and me returning to our hotel room for a nap after having spent practically the entire day sunbathing on Copacabana beach. Leaflets and brochures were left on the reception desk for me, packed with a wealth of information on the sport. I didn't waste any time reading, conducting a little bit of research of my own on safety measures, vetting of companies and so on prior to making a definitive decision." Amy glanced at Mike. He appeared to be alert, fascinated and genuinely interested in her hang-gliding story, although, Amy hoped she hadn't appeared too raconteur, talking too incessantly, boring his socks off.

"Good idea to have taken precautionary measures."

"Precisely. So many tragic accidents have occurred in various countries. It's amazing that some governments aren't seriously viewing safety as a basic requirement that shoddy companies are effectively getting away with murder."

"I agree," Mike said.

"A number of companies stipulate that tourists who are about to hang-glide should sign a disclaimer beforehand. This way, the companies forfeit their responsibilities, thereby freeing themselves of the probable eventualities of lawsuits being served against them and, consequently don't suffer the prospect of going out of business due to any fatalities. They've got a nerve. What a cheek," said Amy, waving her arms in the air in significant distaste.

"It works both ways, really. Perhaps more would be clients could spare a few minutes in research, you know," Mike shrugged, "conduct their own investigations prior to going ahead with any high risk fleets. The idea could culminate in fewer fatalities."

"Yes, you're absolutely right," said Amy, fully welcoming Mike's comment.

"Do go on," Mike insisted.

Ecstatic that Mike was showing genuine interest, Amy chatted on excitedly. "I was harnessed to a professional pilot who had a well documented ten years experience. The flight was absolutely exhilarating. Blew me away, if you'll excuse the pun." Amy giggled, sipped her wine and smiled effervescently at Mike. Mike smiled amusingly at Amy. "The ocean created an ideal up-wind for the sport. The pilot's gliding techniques were magnificent against the winds. We flew over unforgettable scenery, the shorelines of Copacabana and Ipanema beaches, the landscapes, hills, mountains, the Rio neighborhoods, Favelas, the splendor of the statue of Cristo—that's Jesus in English I think—on Corcorvado mountain, were all in clear view." Amy sighed. "Unforgettable. We climbed to an altitude of approximately ten thousand feet. All in all, the gliding was quite awesome and well worth it."

'Sounds like you had a lot of fun," said Mike. "I can tell that hang-gliding in Brazil is a treasured memory of yours." Mike beckoned the waitress over with a regal wave of his right hand. "A bottle of Bollinger, please."

"Certainly, monsieur," said the waitress.

Amy sighed, suppressing her secret thoughts of wanting to know what it would feel like being physically close to Mike. "Yes, it is a fond memory. I've taken up the sport here in the UK. I've a club membership and joined the British hang-gliding association."

"Well done. I commend you. Becoming a member of regulatory bodies, recognized associations, societies and the like could prove to be a wise move in most instances. Where do you hang-glide in England?"

"I may go to Oxford, Wales, Surrey or Cornwall, wherever the wind blows, really. Sorry, Mike! Another inadvertent pun, there."

"No. Not at all. Be my guest."

"Whenever I've free time to take a weekend break, I make a real meal of it then, hang-gliding for hours, weather conditions permitting, of course."

"What are your other hobbies?"

Not caught off the mark that easily, Amy looked at Mike for a few seconds, brought the Ivory linen napkin to her lips. "Steady on, you haven't told me about all of your hobbies yet!"

"Touché."

They erupted into simultaneous laughter with Amy curiously wondering when they'd actually make love. He's so cool, calm and collected, she thought. She'd not dated or made love to a man of Mike's caliber, exceptionally eloquent and well spoken, immaculately groomed, dignified, wealthy and expensively attired. By her estimations, Mike's background was one of obvious culture, educated, possibly at Eton. Wealthy, privileged, accustomed to the finer things in life, including finer women than her. On the other hand, Amy's matchless background was placed well over the other side of the spectrum. It was a hard and grafting climb up the corporate ladder in pursuit of a respectable career and a dreamed lifestyle. Amy was accustomed to the Jensons of this world, the ordinary every day, same old thing, gift of the gab with lots of money but no wealth, class, or culture types. She was growing tired of it, the snazzy dressing, gorgeous body, good looking and knows it, player types. She suddenly thought about Katie and David, how imminently close their date in the park and successful a time they'd spend together. The fact that David was married with children, the affect it would have on Katie later on, should their platonic friendship become one of intimacy, concerned Amy. Not ruling out Mike's fiancée to be, Amy imagined that she could be the one to come between them, ruining things for all concerned. With the reality of Mike's unavailability hitting home hard, Amy had to face up to the fact that she was chasing the wrong man and that she had to take a serious morality check. Amy couldn't easily envisage the ultimate outcome of her and Mike, even if he was unattached, for obvious reasons, she didn't believe that they'd ever become an item. Determined, she was hopeful that all she had to do was visualize the desired outcome and work on her dreams to fruition. Clinching Mike would take incredible focus. She didn't want to think about it any longer, contending with such unreasonably far-fetched concepts, not in this sweet moment, where things were going so well between them, where she was having so much fun. Stifled, it was becoming increasingly difficult keeping her thoughts and emotions about Mike to herself, ruthless thoughts about wanting him she hadn't shared with anyone. A confidant was needed as soon as, or she'd drive herself crazy. Erupt. Explode. Within a few days, she'd confide in Katie.

The waitress had arrived and was standing tentatively at their table. "Desserts?" Mike gently patted his stomach, indicating that he'd eaten enough and Amy followed suit. "Please let me know when you would like to use the after dinner lounge," said the waitress.

The after dinner lounge was made up of six partitions all fitted with deep leather couches organized in living room style layout for uttermost comfort.

The clientele sampled the finest liquors, ports and brandies. There was also the option for smokers to take advantage of a customized smoking room where they could enjoy fine cigars, pipes and cigarettes from around the world.

Mike deliberated. "We'll be ready in approximately ten minutes, after we've finished our champagne. Does that suit you, Amy?"

"Certainly, suits me just fine," Amy responded keenly.

"*C'est parfait,* I'll return in ten minutes."

"Giselle, before you leave, I'd like to state that I had a wonderful meal. I'd also like to thank you for your excellent service."

"*Merci, monsieur.* You're too kind."

Amy looked at the waitress blushing pathetically girlishly at Mike each time she'd approached their table and, wondered whether he'd noticed.

"I normally cast a critical eye on the standards of cuisine and services. I've no complaints. My compliments to the chef. The Gigot d'iagneau was absolutely delicious and succulently divine."

"*Merci, monsieur.* I will inform the management."

"Mike, I'm pleased you've found things in such favorable light and, to your satisfaction. Perhaps we could do this again?" said Amy presumptuously, crossing her fingers, toes and legs under the table.

"I'd be delighted. Tonight, a poor turnout however, proved to be a rich event. I'll most certainly be more than happy to dine with you again. I've enjoyed this evening immensely. Thank you, Amy, for your efforts."

"Not at all," said Amy pleasingly. Amazed at Mike's casual response, she hoped he wasn't just being ostensibly kind to her, agreeing to show up for dinner at Beaujolais tonight and that she hadn't shown any embarrassingly tell tale signs of desperately wanting to be with him. Amy didn't want the evening to end, not just yet. It felt good. It felt right, immersed in his presence. She had to remain with him for a few minutes more. He excited her. He was excellent company, intriguingly different. She had to keep him there, seated at the table, opposite her in all his handsomeness, for her to enjoy for just a few minutes longer, fully aware that she had to pull herself together, stop acting like a preposterously love-sick teenager. Before the end of the night, there was just one other thing Amy would seek to clarify. She knocked back her champagne, leaned back in her seat and spoke boldly. "Tell me, Mike. What thoughts were running through your mind when Belinda had her hands all over you during the role-play?" she said, the inducement of wine and champagne assisting her.

Visibly stunned, Mike answered clearly without hesitation. "Nothing particularly really came to mind to be honest with you. I considered it was her way of expressing herself. The end result could have worked out quite embarrassingly or disastrously different perhaps for someone who wasn't ably equipped to demonstrate a cool head. I'd imagined that, that was Belinda's aim. She'd cunningly put us all on the spot, tested our reactions, to see how successfully or unsuccessfully we'd all cope with, respond to or handle her individual style."

Not totally convinced, Amy, nevertheless, admired Mike's diplomatic stance, choosing to play it safe rather than expose his truth. "Oh, come on! After having gone through that experience, what man wouldn't have enjoyed Belinda or at least fantasized about her?" Amy reasoned flippantly.

"OK, there is something I can tell you," said Mike. "Belinda propositioned me during one of the coffee breaks. I don't remember which coffee break. I'd declined, of course. Actually, it was the day you'd sat out on the patio."

Now, that's more like it, Amy thought. She took her mind back to the coffee break in question, where Mike had had his head buried in the *Financial Times* newspaper. "I wasn't aware that you'd even noticed me. You were reading the FT, I recall," said Amy.

"Ah, yes. I was fully engrossed in an article," said Mike.

"I'd no idea she'd propositioned you. What was the reason behind your decline?"

"A personal date with Belinda, or anyone else for that matter, wasn't a notion I'd cared to provide focus to. You're already aware that I'm courting."

Amy hoped she hadn't ruined the evening quizzing him about Belinda. The waitress arrived to escort them to the after dinner lounge. Ready, they vacated their table, followed the waitress to the elevator and rode it to the first floor. The elevator doors opened and they stepped straight into the lounge. As Mike wanted to smoke a cigar, the waitress showed them to the smoking room. Cleverly appointed candles flickered golden, orange and yellow flames that danced their silhouettes on the stone washed walls. The layout of furniture paid every attention to comfort, giving the smoking room a distinctively homely feel. Mike sank in the red leather, brass studded antique wing smokers' chair. "A Chartreuse green liqueur for the lady, and I'll have the cognac, L'Esprit de Courvoisier and a Romeo y Julieta deluxe cigar, please?"

"Oui, monsieur."

Mike sunk deeper in his chair. "Tell me more about your vacation in Brazil."

"Oh! The list goes on! What would you like to know?"

"What did you enjoy most? What stood out for you?" It was the extra time Amy had craved for. Amy sank comfortably in the adjacent chair identical to Mike's. "Many things come to mind, like hang-gliding for instance which I'd mentioned earlier." She thought of something that would engage him for a considerable time. "The flower ritual on the beach on New Year's Eve was wonderful. Festa de Lemanja—that's the name of the ritual, if my memory serves me well," she said, hoping she'd gotten the name right. The waitress returned and served Mike the cigar on a tray. Amy was pleased with the liqueur. One sip sent her head spinning in seconds. Standing poised and ready, holding a silver cigar lighter, the waitress waited for Mike's cue. Mike popped the cigar in his mouth, wetted it and the waitress leaned forward and lit it. Mike sucked and blew out circles of aromatic smoke. Amy waved the circles of smoke away from her. "On New Year's Eve, people from all over Brazil, all over the world, in fact, flock to Copacabana beach to celebrate. There's music, live band performances, food stalls and an unforgettable fire works display. Those who come to celebrate Festa de Lemanja are dressed in white. Each person holds a lit candle and offers flowers to the sea in honor of Lemanja, the goddess of water, to thank her for favors of the past year and the years to come in whatever form, good luck, good fortune, fertility or whatever." Amy sipped her liqueur carefully. "This is going to take some time," she said, warning Mike.

"Go ahead. I'm enthralled."

Amy sank deeper in her seat. "Flowers are tossed into the sea. One makes a wish, stands back and watches their flower drift out to sea. Imagine the scene."

"Ummm, yes, yes," Mike quietly mumbled behind a haze of cigar smoke.

It's working, Amy thought. "Standing ankle deep in water, a soft Atlantic breeze stroking your entire being, with midnight closely approaching, hundreds of exotic flowers floating out on the silvery sea, colored by the moon in the night sky." Amy breathed, "Whisking waves, in shades of indigo blue and white reflecting the moonlight, gently ebbing and flowing along the beach. People celebrated by singing folk songs dancing energetically to Samba and Bosa Nova music, beating drums to the pulse of the heartbeat. I distinctly remember there were Brazilian women, known as Baina do Acarage, who practiced the Candomble.—That's a religion, by the way.—They cooked a tasty delicacy, sandwiches stuffed with shrimp and sold them from their food stalls. The celebrations are all steeped in old cultural beliefs, religions, trances and rites, you name it," said Amy, tirelessly.

Mike chewed on his cigar. "Did you make a wish?"

"Yes," said Amy, looking at Mike, her wish staring straight at her. "A returned flower signified a bad year ahead. You had a good year ahead if your flower hadn't got washed up on the beach."

Mike raised his eyebrows. "And your flower?"

"I stood there for ages and my beautiful white lily never returned."

"Then, good fortune befalls you in the year ahead. What a fascinating highlight, you'd taken part in an exotic ritual."

"Surreal. Fascinating, is it not?"

"Yes, quite. I could do with some fresh air and a stroll around Covent Garden," said Mike, stubbing out his cigar in the silver ashtray. "I'll settle the bill."

Amy uncrossed her legs, placed her glass on the table, reached into her handbag and fished out her purse.

Mike dashed a subtle glance of disapproval at her. "No, no, no. Please, put that away," he said sternly. He'd whipped his wallet out of his breast pocket, pulled out an American Express Centurion black credit card and discreetly waved it at the waitress who dutifully and blushingly launched herself into action. Mike settled the bill and tipped the waitress very generously in cash.

Amy welcomed Mike's strong, firm and protective grip of her arm, scuttling her across the busy Drury Lane, making his way to the centre of Covent Garden. A variety of music boomed loudly out of pubs, wine bars, clubs and shops. Strolling together aimlessly, blending with the diversity of the crowds, Mike and Amy observed the spectacles in the cool night air. They pointed things out to one another, shared jokes, laughed at the funny things they saw and steered away from the uglier scenes, the street brawls, staggering drunkards, listless drug users, dealers distributing provisions and prospecting game, street-wise teenagers, wide-eyed and confused runaways, rent boys and rent girls, bleary-eyed pub crawlers. The streets were bustling with a medley of activities, from a variety of street entertainers, a queue of mind boggled cinema enthusiasts, spoilt for choice, struggling indecisively selecting movies from the multi-screen cinemas, avid theatre goers forming orderly queues outside box offices, women of vice touting for business, die-hard late night shoppers excessively over-spending their store and credit cards; under-cover police mostly hoping for a virtually trouble free shift; some eagerly itching to pounce into action, flocks of oblivious tourists wandering aimlessly, energetic club goers, the in-crowd, the out-crowd, the wealthy stepping out of limos and prestige cars into the numerous fashionable and exclusive establishments, private members only clubs, and casinos, chic restaurants packed with chic diners. Mike kept Amy protectively close at hand and treated her like a lady. We're so good together, Amy thought.

"It's getting late. We've been on our feet for over an hour now. We'd better be heading off to our respective homes, don't you think?" suggested Mike,

ing into the road, hailing a taxi. A black cab braked sharply on the edge of the curb. Mike swung the door open and Amy got in without him.

Slightly disorientated, Amy soon figured out the fact that she was about to embark on a taxi journey home, alone." Thank you for a pleasant evening," she said, composedly.

Mike nodded, smiled at her and shut the door. Amy urgently sought Mike's intentions before the taxi ~~had taken off.~~ Crouching down, she leaned forward and opened the window.

"I will call you during the week," said Mike.

"Where to, guvner?" shouted the taxi driver.

"As directed, by the passenger," said Mike, waving at Amy as the taxi was pulling away.

Amy waved at Mike and leaned back in her seat. Speechless, she removed her shoes, leaned forward and began massaging the balls of her feet.

"Where to, me luv?" said the taxi driver.

CHAPTER 6

Katie glanced groggily at her bedside digital clock radio. "Heck, Amy it's a bit early. It's bloody eight o'clock!" she said, yawning loudly down the telephone.

"Sorry, I know. I know. I didn't get much sleep last night and ..."

"Is everything OK?" blurted Katie, sounding a little concerned.

Amy paced up and down her bedroom. "Mike and I had ..."

"SEX?" screamed Katie.

Wincing, Amy held the telephone a safe distance away from her ear. "No, not that, silly," she said.

"No? I bet you're looking forward to when you do, eh?"

"We had dinner last night. Just Mike and I, as everyone had cried off."

"Then it was meant to be, just the two of you in tow. You're calling to give me the low down, right? Then let's hear it."

Amy admired Katie's drive and energy, her consistent brashness, mischievousness and cocky, up-front style. "I had a wonderful time. I think Mike enjoyed himself, too. He's such a gentleman, generous, courteous and kind. What's really bugging me is ... well ... he's engaged, more or less or about to be and, armed with this knowledge, it's not deterring me from wanting him and that's not ethically right, is it? I'm so lost and confused about it all," said Amy, frustratingly.

"You want the man. Good stuff. I wondered how long you were going to hold back on me. I totally understand why you're calling me now, so early on a Sunday morning."

Damn! Amy thought, feeling ridiculously vulnerable, caught out and weak in character. "Sorry, I owe you one, Katie."

"Don't worry about it. Of course it's not ethically right. But that's the stuff that makes life just that little more exciting, interesting and challenging, attacking the boredom of our daily drudgery. Do you want my opinion?"

Amy thought Katie would never ask. "Fire away."

"Go for it. If he loves this chic and plans to marry her, don't waste any further time on it. Move on to some other guy. Goodness knows, there are so many of them out there to choose from."

"It won't be that easy …"

"Why? What's stopping you? Look, you can make your move on Mike now or forget the whole shenanigans. I'm willingly yours, ready and waiting to render my matchmaking services to you although, I would require full details of all your activities in order to get it right, if you know what I mean?"

"Lending me your learned ear would more than suffice for now."

"Fine," said Katie, reservedly. "What else have you called to say?"

"I need to work out the engagement issue. That's the main thing on my mind at the moment."

"How much do you know about his chic? What has he told you?"

"Nothing. He's told me nothing. I know nothing about her."

"Do you have a name, at least?"

"No."

"Then how did you find out about it?"

"He'd mentioned it fleetingly at Je La Buena."

"That far back, eh! Well, that's where you start. When you speak to him next, draft the fiancée bit into the conversation. Do it naturally. Draft her in naturally."

"How am I going to do that?"

"Effective communication skills, remember! It's always you're next move that counts."

Amy chuckled at the idea, knowing, in her heart of hearts, that Katie was right. It was worth a try, she thought. "I suppose so. I'll give it a go and keep you posted," said Amy unenthusiastically.

"Now it's my turn," said Katie.

"Your turn?"

"Yep. I'm meeting David this afternoon, at half past one, in Regent's Park. He's finished building his seaplane."

Surprised by the news, Amy realized that David was the culprit behind Katie's bright and bubbly mood. "Great," said Amy nonchalantly.

"At least sound excited for me, will you? I'm intent on having p[ ]terated fun with him."

Amy read Katie's statement as one laced with undertones filled with ulterior motives. "Let me know what happens, will you? Now, I'm going to get some sleep as I'm feeling much better now, thanks to you, Katie. You've helped me a great deal in shedding some light on my situation."

"Don't mention it. I'm here whenever you need me."

"Thanks a million. You're a star, Katie." Amy found comfort in Katie's willingness to be there for her. That's what friends are for, Amy thought. With the makings of a promising and trusting friendship developing on the horizon, Amy hung up, slid back into bed and slept until latter part of Sunday afternoon.

One fifteen in Regent's Park, amid the resplendent blooms of the flowering beds, standing at the edge of the duck pond, Katie waited for David to arrive.

"Spotted any ducks?"

Shrieking, Katie turned sharply to David. "You scared the living daylights out of me," she said, landing a playful slap on David's right arm.

"Careful, careful or you'll knock the equipment out of my hands."

"Oops! Sorry, David." Katie made a face like a scolded child and covered her mouth with both hands.

David knelt at the edge of the pond, opened the highly polished wooden box, lifted the model seaplane out and placed it gently on the grass verge.

"I can't wait to see that marvelous looking thing take off," said Katie, gasping incredulously. "You actually put this whole thing together yourself?"

"Single-handedly," said David, nodding proudly. "It's an electric, Lambert Compact, radio controlled model seaplane by the way."

"You are clever."

"Not really, it's quite easy when you get the hang of it." David stood back a few paces. "I now begin the launch," he announced.

"Good stuff," said Katie, taking a step back, landing in the right spot, a safe distance away from David as he started the seaplane's motor using a black remote control boxed object. He steered, the metallic blue and white seaplane towards the centre of the pond, taxiing it in preparation for takeoff.

"Aren't you naming it?" asked Katie urgently.

"That's a good idea."

"Let's inaugurate this event," suggested Katie.

"That's ludicrous, I wouldn't go that far."

"Oh, come on, you've put this thing, assembled the compact, oh … I don't remember the name. You've erected this marvelous seaplane, you could, at least, give it a name."

"Alright, you win. I'll name her … Freedom."

"Freedom," Katie repeated ceremoniously, sniggering saying, "What a pity we couldn't smash a bottle of champers against her. On second thoughts, she'd probably fall apart, I guess."

David ignored Katie and fiddled with the controls on the black box. "Freedom will take off on the count of three," David announced.

"One … two … three," they counted together shouting, "Freedom." The seaplane progressively accelerated and skittered along the water before take off.

Katie gawked in fascination as David intricately maneuvered the controls, steering the seaplane left and right as it soared in the clear, bright blue sky. The engine emitted a low buzzing sound as the seaplane ascended—its spectacular metallic blue and white wings radiated the sky, attracting a few onlookers, gathering close to the vicinity of David and Katie.

"Nice bit of gear you've got there," said a man, flanked by a boisterously energetic boy, jumping up and down, pointing frenetically at the seaplane.

"Thanks," said David, performing acrobatic swirls.

"Dad, I want one of those," the boy demanded.

"Promise me you'll be a good boy for a week son, and I'll buy one for you."

"I promise, Dad."

David performed a series of somersaults to the applause and gasps of the onlookers.

"Dad, can you go to the shop and buy one now, Dad?" the boy tugged at the man's shirt sleeve.

"No, son. Not just yet. Stop pulling my shirt. Stand still."

David sensed the man's irritability. There were applause, whistles and cheers as the seaplane landed impressively on the water. David took one step forward, bowed and thanked the onlookers. His sporadic display of humor pleased Katie. David handed the control box to Katie and he fished the seaplane out of the water. Katie held the control box with her arms outstretched in front of her.

"It won't bite," said David, carefully putting the seaplane back in its box.

"Very funny," said Katie, smiling wryly, slowly drawing the control box closer to her.

"I'll take that now, thank you," said David.

With the spectacle over, the crowd of onlookers began to disperse, except the man and the boy. The man sheepishly approached David saying, "Excuse me mate, where can I buy one of those?" The boy jumped up and down excitedly around the man's feet.

"This particular make and model, imported from the United States, can be purchased through a specialized dealer based in central London," said David, carefully laying the box on the grass at his feet, reaching for a pen in his breast pocket and whipping an unwanted piece of paper out of his wallet. "Here, I'll jot down a few details for you."

"Oh! Cheers mate," said the man, gratefully. "How easy is it to learn to fly one of these?"

"Dead easy really, once you've practiced regularly."

"What can you tell me about this particularly make and model?"

"Its wingspan measures fifty five inches and it's about fifty three ounces flying weight. The rudder …" Katie discreetly walked away to avoid listening to the technical jargon. "… the white fiberglass fuselage …"

She stood at the edge of the pond and gazed at her reflection rippling gently on the water. She rummaged through her handbag to retrieve the breadcrumbs she'd brought along with her to feed the ducks only to discover that, not only were there no sightings of ducks wading in the water but that she'd also forgotten the breadcrumbs. She smirked at the irony of it all, retraced her steps and recalled that she'd left the breadcrumbs on the kitchen table.

"Boo! A penny for your thoughts," said David, suddenly appearing behind Katie.

"Ah, not again," said Katie, flinching. "That's twice you've crept up on me today!"

"Is that so!" said David, chuckling. "I'm getting thirsty. Fancy a drink?"

"Thought you'd never ask," said Katie.

"I know of a great pub close by. The Regency. It's only two minutes away."

"Take me there," said Katie, strolling leisurely along the concrete path. "That was quite an impressive display."

"Thanks. Luckily there were no ducks to scare off," said David.

"I don't think the park authorities would have allowed the take off and landing if there were any ducks in the water," said Katie, logically.

"I suppose you're right," agreed David. "It's turned out to be my lucky day, flying the seaplane free of hitches."

The Regency pub was set in lavished surroundings, the décor and furnishings influenced by the Elizabethan era. Katie headed for a couch tucked away in a convenient spot. She thought the seating area was irresistibly inviting, housing attractive pieces of Elizabethan reproduction furniture. Dimly lit lamps hung elegantly from the four corners of the ceiling, couches stacked with Burgundy cushions.

David slid his box under the table. "What are you drinking?"

"Red wine, please," said Katie, nestling on the couch. David wandered casually over to the bar. This looks interesting, Katie thought as David returned five minutes later with two, bottles of Cabernet Savignon and two glasses. He poured the wine, handed a glass to Katie and raised his glass saying, "To the successful launch of Freedom. Thanks to you, Katie, I now have a seaplane to add to my collection."

"Cheers," said Katie. "How many model aircraft do you have in total?"

"Twenty-seven."

"Twenty-seven! You're kidding me, right?"

"No."

"That's quite a number."

"Keeps me out of trouble, I suppose. I derive enormous benefits, flying model airplanes."

"What benefits are these?" Katie noticed that she'd already guzzled away more than half a glass of wine and made a conscious effort to slow down in her attempt to display a little etiquette.

"Can I be totally frank and honest with you, Katie?" David's whole persona changed before her eyes.

"Sure you can."

"I don't know how much attention you'd paid to my mentioning at the workshop, during my intro, that I'm married," he said, looking at her searchingly.

"Yes, I do remember. I'm aware of that, with kids."

"Yes, I'd mentioned that also. What you're not aware of is that my wife and I have been separated for six months now. Taking up the hobby of making model aircraft has kept me from going insane. I miss the children and ..." David slowly put his wine glass down, clenched his fists and laid them on the table. "I deeply apologize. You don't need to know any of this. It's very insensitive of me."

Katie became receptive to his inner pain. "Please, don't apologize. You can talk to me, David. I'd be more than happy to listen," said Katie empathically, laying her hand reassuringly on his fists. For the want of intrigue, David's unanticipated mention of the true state of his marriage had Katie furtively brewing in excitement. "What on earth happened?"

David sighed. "We'd been having marital problems for Zowie—my wife, attributes or blames our problems on th time I spend away from home on business overseas."

"How much time are we talking about?"

"A week. Three to four at the most."

"Three to four weeks is quite a long time, David."

"I know. And when I'm back in London, she complains about the long hours I spend in the office or in my study at home."

"Maybe she has a point. Has it not occurred to you that your wife may want you to spend more quality time with her and the children?"

"You don't know Zowie. She's a greedy, conceited and an impossible woman to please let alone live with. She wants me to spend more time with her and the children but, she also insists on me providing her with all the material things she constantly craves," said David morosely.

Katie knocked back her half glass of wine, poured herself another and topped up David's glass. "What things?"

David sighed frustratingly. "Katie, I put in long, hard hours to earn the money to maintain the lifestyle she craves. Our house is a palatial, six bed-roomed detach in Richmond, Surrey overlooking fantastic views of the park." David counted each finger. "Number one. Zowie upgrades the Benz every six months. She hasn't used the brand, spanking, new SUV, customized to her personal taste and specifications, parked up in the garage at her disposal for God knows how many weeks. Two. She has a private nanny. Three. The kids attend private Montessori schools. Four. Every conceivable state-of-the-art, domestic gadgetry you can think of for the home, Zowie's got it. Money flits away on designer clothes, shoes, handbags, perfumery, and jewels. Her cut diamonds are worth no less than twenty five thousand pounds a piece. And there are the prestigious holidays to the Maldives, Martinique, Tahiti, the Fijian islands with no expense spared. We own a small villa in St Vincent. The list goes on and on. I've tried to make life better for her, but it's been no use. She complains that she has to cope with the kids on her own when they are sick or playing up and wants me to share in the burdens associated with rearing them, suggesting that I should go into semi retirement as I've made more than enough money. What finally broke the Donkey's back is that I'd missed one of the kid's birthday parties. That was the ultimate, the last straw in Zowie's books. The birthday party sadly, coincided with an urgent and potentially risky disaster recovery incident my company faced at the time, due to the computer main frame blipping and almost going out of action." Katie watched, uninterruptedly as David sighed, shook his head from side to side. A grieved expression riddled his face. "Unforgettable. I hate thinking about it. Two disasters taking place in my life simultaneously. There was no getting out of it. It was critically imperative that I attended to the problem of the main frame in person. I'd stood to potentially lose my company, Zowie and children. I was totally unprepared for it. Totally. Zowie threatened to ring all the guests and party organizers and cancel the party, which she eventually went ahead and had done, as threatened." David gulped a full glass of wine in one shot. Katie swiftly finished her wine and refilled their glasses. "I returned home at midnight to an empty house. Zowie had left and had taken the kids. She left a handwritten note in the kitchen on the Welsh Dresser. It stated that she'd gone to her mother's house in Falmouth, Cornwall to think things through, that she needed time.

"How awful," whispered Katie, moving closer to David.

David placed his elbows on the table and held his head in his hands. "I called her mother's place immediately, of course, and that's when she'd asked me for a divorce. That was all the time she needed. The time it took to pack and clear off to Cornwall. Not very much time, was it?"

"No, it wasn't," said Katie supportively, patting David gently on his back.

David reached for Katie's hands and cupped them in his. Katie warmed in his strong hands, hands that had seen labor. "Within a week, a letter arrived from her solicitor filing for divorce on the grounds of irreconcilable differences." David sighed. "She'd accuse me of having affairs which were unfounded and certainly not true. There was never another woman. Thinking back, perhaps I should have had the odd fling here and there. I'm completely innocent of any philandering. Productivity and flight of the model aircrafts, among other activities, have filled the gaps in my life and has kept my mind off things in between work and having the children over for the weekends, whenever I'm available that is."

This must be tough for him, Katie thought, gently easing her hands free. Her mind went into overdrive, recalling the fun night she'd had with David at Je Le Buena and, unable to hold off a manipulative streak, Katie devised a plan to become one of the gap fillers in David's life. "What are your views on affairs now that you're separated?"

"Well ... I ... I ... I confess I have thought about it several times, having an affair, when I've found myself dejected and alone in that big house in Richmond. But, fearing the hassles and problems associated with affairs adding more confusion to my already confused life, I've sooner shunned the idea at the drop of a hat."

I'll soon change that, Katie thought. "I'm hungry," she said, inebriating progressively, half way through the second bottle of wine.

"Me too. I could eat a horse."

Katie checked her watch. "It's four thirty. Time flies when you're having fun!" she said, eyeing the intricate craftsmanship on the antique wall clock, hating herself for quoting such a boring and out of date cliché. "Do you like watching movies?"

"Yes, who doesn't, although I seldom get the time," said David.

"Why don't you join me, at my place? I've got a wide selection to choose from, that is, if you've got no plans later today."

"Are you sure? I wouldn't want to intrude," said David, taken aback.

"Shut up, stop all that proper stuff and accept my invitation," said Katie humorously, slurring her speech, frivolously attempting to rid the unpleasantness of David's marital plight now plaguing the atmosphere.

David managed a painfully contorted smile. "Alright, I'll accept. Have you got The Instigation among your collection, the mobster, murder, mystery film? I've not seen it and it's had great reviews. There's also a sequel, right?" said David visibly fazed by Katie's invite.

"Correct. You're in luck, I have them both."

"Good," said David, switching on his cell-phone, scrolling through a long list of numbers. "What cuisine do you fancy as I'd like to invite you to a meal? I'm not fussy. I can call a restaurant and have a table booked for, say, in thirty to forty five minutes?"

"I have a better idea," said Katie. "How about a bite to eat at my place, a takeaway, perhaps?"

"That's fine by me."

"A Chinese would go down a treat," said Katie, polishing off the remainder of wine.

David reached under the table and slid the box out from under it with his foot. "Yes, I'll settle for that. The Golden Lilly is two blocks from here, we can place an order and arrange delivery if you like."

"Great stuff," said Katie.

David leaned forward, picked up the box and rose unsteadily on his feet. 'Ready?" he said, offering Katie a helping hand.

Katie glanced at the clock on the kitchen window ledge. "It's nearly five fifteen. We've half an hour before the food gets here," she said, filling two glasses with red wine. "Come on. Let's go next door. I need to sit down." Katie handed

David followed Katie out of the kitchen, into the lounge, ...at at the opposite end away from her. Katie observed the .... "We can watch the movie now and I'll stop it when the ... here."

"Whatever you say, I'm flexible," said David.

Katie put her wine glass on the coffee table, slithered off the couch and crawled over to the TV. She sat crossed legged with her back to David and waded through her DVD collection in search of The Instigation. "How many kids do you have?" she asked.

David shifted on the couch. "Three. Two girls and a boy. Five, three and eighteen months. Luke's the middle infant."

"Um. Nice. And the girls, what are their names?"

"Lilly and Lucy."

"Nice."

"Have you noticed any similarities in their names?" asked David.

Katie hadn't really taken much notice.

"Sorry. Er … no … I haven't. You tell me," she said, skimming through the back cover of a new DVD she'd not watched.

"Their names all begin with the letter L to denote the word love."

"That's really, really lovely," said Katie, turning around in time to catch the sad look in David's eyes.

"I know," he said, forlornly. "And now I'm losing them. All that love, lost."

We are not going there, Katie thought. She slotted The Instigation movie in the DVD player. "I'm sorry," she said.

"How can one woman cause so much pain and destruction?"

"I'm not able to answer that question. It's difficult. Who knows why! Let's face it, David. Life is full of challenges. We can't run away from them. They're here regardless of how we choose to deal with them or ignore them or whatever. Challenges and problems exist and are here to be dealt with as best we can. You'll get through it, David. I know you will." Katie got up, walked over to the couch and, without any reservations sat closely to David and cupped his hands in hers.

David sighed. "Thank you. I appreciate you inviting me round and all that," he said, drawing her closer, staring penetratingly into her eyes.

"Anytime. Glad to have you as my guest. And thanks for the takeaway. Should be here soon," she said, inclining her head, settling her eyes on his strong hands cupped comfortably in hers.

"I'm no longer famished, I'm absolutely starving now," said David, freeing his hands. He rose from the couch, removed his denim jacket and slung it on the back of the couch. "I can't wait to get into that movie."

Katie pressed the remote control, starting the movie. They watched fifteen minutes of it in silence and were interrupted by the intercom.

"That'll be the food. I'll leave the DVD running," said Katie, getting up.

David got up and followed Katie out of the lounge. "Here, let me help you," he said

"Sure." Katie returned to the lounge, picked up the remote control and pressed paused.

David obligingly assisted Katie in serving the meal, picnic style, on a Hessian mat on the lounge floor. They returned to the movie both sitting, crossed legged, on the floor, sampling the assortment of dishes. Katie spontaneously offered to pop a morsel of aromatic duck into David's mouth which he readily accepted. David popped a sweet and sour pork ball into Katie's mouth. A few moments later, Katie held a morsel of beef between her teeth, luring David to bite off a piece without touching her lips, keeping his hands behind his back. Visibly and fiercely in growing excitement, David eagerly obliged. Katie gripped the morsel of beef firmly between her teeth. David had trouble pulling it away from her without making full contact with her lips. Eventually, Katie released her grip, slipped the beef teasingly into David's mouth and kissed him. David chewed the beef hungrily and nibbled at Katie's lips. He brought his hands from behind his back, cupped and squeezed her breasts. Katie groaned. David assisted her to lie back on the floor. He pecked her nipples teasingly and stroked her tenderly. Katie groaned as David raised her skirt and kissed her thighs. They rolled on the floor, overturning the dishes, crushing, smudging and smearing food on the floor, Hessian mat, their clothes and bodies, making animalistic love, climaxing, long hard, loud and noisily. Panting breathlessly, David rolled over onto his back.

"It's been a long time, Katie," he said, his chest rising and falling.

Katie laid flat on her back blissfully exhausted, wanting more. The theme music, a car chase and the sound of gun shots from The Instigation movie played in the background. David took a deep breath, raised himself and reached down, kissing Katie's feet, her ankles, working his way up, parting her legs, devouring her hungrily, greedily and demandingly. They made love several times into the early hours of the morning, taking cat naps in between. There is no stopping him, Katie thought, marveling in sheer disbelief at David's sexual prowess, stamina and virility. Sharing the same amount of sexual appetite and drive, Katie had no trouble keeping up with David, gripping his shoulders tightly, enraptured in multiple orgasms. Her back ached, having taken a pounding making love on the floor. The smell of sex and Chinese food mingled in the air. Her body caked in food, Katie wanted to take a shower. What a mess, she thought, inspecting the floor as she stood up. She shook David awake.

"What? Where am I? What time is it?" David muttered nonsensically.

"Go take a shower. You're covered in bamboo shoots, soy sauce, duck you name it," said Katie. Standing naked and partially coherent, they flicked and peeled food off their bodies, stepped over the crockery and food strewn all over the floor and, staggered out of the lounge and into the bathroom. They held each other close as they stood motionless in the shower cubicle, under gushing, lukewarm water. They massaged each other sensually with lathering shower gel. Rinsed and, wrapped in bathrobes, they staggered out of the bathroom to the bedroom and clambered into bed. Exhausted, they rolled over and immediately fell asleep.

The clock alarmed at six thirty on Monday morning. Katie awoke and hit the alarm button hard. David stirred as Katie got out of bed. Katie groaned. Her head spun a mild hangover. David got out of the bed and stumbled clumsily towards her. He leaned naked against the bedroom door and scratched his head. "What time is it?" he asked, squinting, shielding his eyes from the bright morning sun bursting through Katie's bedroom window.

"Six thirty," she said, pulling down the Roman blinds, completely blocking out the dazzling sunlight.

"Come here you vixen," said David sexily.

Katie walked over slowly and into David's outstretched arms. He hugged her tenderly, stroked her hair away from her eyes and pecked her forehead. Katie's knees buckled at the warmth of his nude body pressing against her. He motioned his head towards the bed, guided Katie over and lay kingly on his back. Katie mounted and squatted on David, leaned forward and let her breasts dangle and fall onto his chest. David breathed, moaned and drew Katie closer to him. Their lips engaged in a long and lingering kiss, they made passionate love again. Climaxing together, David's eyes rolled to the back of his head and Katie's mind sailed to new and heightened pleasures. They slept, enwrapped in each others arms.

Later, Katie awoke and smiled blissfully, screening the ruggedness of David's face, as he lay sound asleep, cradled in her arms. She glanced wearily at the clock. "Oh shit, shit, shit, shit," she squealed. Unraveling herself, Katie jumped out of bed and raced around the apartment, gathering her laptop, Blackberry and whatever else she could muster.

David queasily raised his head. "What's up, Katie? What time is it?"

"It's late. I'll be late for a twelve-thirty meeting and if I don't get my ass out of here by eleven thirty, I'm history," said Katie, yanking a plain navy blue skirt suit out of the closet.

"What time is it?" asked David, stumbling out of bed.

"It's nearly eleven o'clock. I'm taking a shower."

"I'm right behind you," said David.

They showered together in cold silence. Katie was the first to emerge from the shower. She towel dried quickly and tried to throw her suit on. "Shit, what a way to start a Monday morning," she said, cursing under her breath, unsteadily on her feet, tripping over in a clumsy haste trying to step into her skirt. David picked up his clothes scattered around the lounge and precariously slung them on. Katie dashed out of the apartment and into the street with David in hot pursuit, clutching his box under one arm whilst putting the other arm in the sleeve of his denim jacket.

"When will I see you again?" he muttered, walking briskly behind Katie.

"I don't know. Call me tonight between nine and nine-thirtyish," said Katie, breaking into a wearisome jog for the oncoming bus.

David watched as Katie safely boarded the bus. "Thank you for a fantastic time," shouted David, as the doors closed. He walked a couple of minutes before flagging a taxi. "Princes Court Villas in Regent's Park then onto Pall Mall, please," he said.

At eight fifteen on Monday evening, Katie exhaustingly closed the door of her apartment. Not fully recovered from having David over, taking a deep breath, Katie dropped her bags on the floor and leaned on the door. She inhaled the refreshing scent of a drifting, floral fragrance that filled the apartment, instantly raising her mood to a pleasing state. Katie gathered the bags and walked into the lounge. The cleaner, Peggy had done a grand job of cleaning the apartment, applying her usual finishing touches. Katie's longest serving cleaner, all of six months, left no trace or evidence of the previous night. There were no food bits lying around. Everywhere was pristine clean. Previous cleaners had the habit of leaving dust in various places and got up Katie's nose by doing annoying things like not refilling the toilet roll holder or not leaving fresh bath towels in the bathroom. But not Peggy. Katie prayed she'd remain with her long term. Her cell-phone rang as she made her way into the kitchen.

"I've called to thank you for Sunday and this morning," said David, in a low, slow and sexy tone of voice.

"Don't mention it, David. It was my pleasure."

"I won't be coming over tonight to catch the end of The Instigation," said David. Katie was relieved. She'd planned to take an early night. "How about lunch, this week?" David asked.

Katie checked the calendar on her Blackberry. "I can do Friday at twelve thirty, that's the only afternoon I've got spare this week."

"Great. I can make that. I'll have my assistant book a table at Skate's the fish restaurant in Piccadilly. Do you know it?"

"Sounds perfect. I'll meet you there at twelve thirty."

"Dubai, to complete a signing agreement." David washed down the Beluga caviar with a sip of iced vodka.

"How long for?"

"Five days."

"When do you leave?"

"Monday morning." Katie burst the Beluga eggs with the tip of her tongue releasing its flavor. She took a sip of champagne which proved to be too sweet and distracted the taste of the Beluga caviar but, she didn't care for vodka.

"I'll be going over the prototype wall to wall simulations of a newly built shopping complex due to be completed and opened in six months near Dubai's main airport," said David, biting a piece of light toast, filmed with butter.

"How impressive," Katie enthused. "Had you envisioned that your company would have taken off on such a great scale as this?"

"Yes," replied David, confidently. "You don't go into something like this without visualizing success, growth and expansion."

"There's hope for me yet," said Katie, light heartedly, reflecting on her recent thoughts on trying her hand at running her own business.

"My eyes are on the US companies, once this has pulled off, out of the way and getting favorable publicity in the simulations world. I've got the leading edge, the upper hand using the best expertise in the business."

"I'm proud of you, David." Katie shivered as David gave her a long, hard and cold stare.

"No one, I mean, not anyone has ever said anything like that to me. My parents, not even Zowie."

Katie hadn't intended to hit such a sore chord. "Oh?"

"Zowie would scream and shout at the kids whenever they'd done anything wrong. She'd scream and shout at me also in front of them, it is no wonder they don't respect me. They're already taking me for granted, but I'll soon change that," said David remorsefully, checking his watch.

"I'll be here, eagerly awaiting your return. We could celebrate or have a quiet night in," said Katie soothingly.

David sighed. "Katie. We need to get something straight here."

Bracing herself, Katie had a suspicious inkling that, somehow she wasn't going to enjoy this. "Fire away."

"We have to come to an agreement, an understanding, here, now, in Skates."

Katie shifted around at the table preparing to block the blows. "Is everything OK?" she asked.

"I couldn't possibly conduct an affair with you, Katie. I don't regret what we did the other day as two consenting adults." Katie felt a sharp jabbing pain stab through her heart like a knife. "I don't want to give you any ideas about us having a relationship. I've intimated to you my aversion to having an affair and …" David reached across the table for Katie's hand. "I just don't want any of us getting the wrong impressions, giving off the wrong signals. There are my children to consider …"

You fucking bastard, Katie thought, bravely smiling stoically and sweetly at him saying, "I understand. You don't need to explain, David. Rest assured, you've nothing to worry about. I'm the least of your problems, quite happy to be mates with you, David." She squeezed his hand gently and reassuringly, mentally nursing her jostled feelings.

"You're a great girl, Katie. Fun bright and bubbly. I could easily be smitten by you. I trust you with my private life and glad you understand my position," said David, releasing her hand, checking his watch again. "The bill, please?" he said to a passing waitress. "I'll escort you back to your office."

"There'll be no need," said Katie, vacating the table. She leaned forward and pecked David on the top of his head whilst he scrawled his signature on the bill. "Hope the signing agreement goes well," she said, turning on her heels, leaving David sitting at the table.

"I'll contact you on my return from Dubai," he shouted.

Katie had already walked out of Skates.

CHAPTER 7

Friday night Mike called Amy. "Would you accept my invitation to a party to be held on a Saturday night, two weeks from now?"

Ecstatically pleased, Amy couldn't believe her ears, that Mike was literally extending a personal invitation to her. "Of course!" she said.

"Splendid. Pollkadots are staging their summer party at Candies, a venue based in the Monument, London. You'd be coming along as a guest on my private membership."

"That's very kind of you, Mike. Yes, I'll gladly come along." Amy was stunned that events were moving along nicely.

"Good. That's settled. Don't forget to browse the websites."

"I'll get on to it as soon as," said Amy promisingly. Amy casually hung up and typed the name of the first website address, *www.rubbba.com* on her laptop. Male models dressed in exotic leather and PVC clothing appeared on her screen, erotically posed on scarlet red Ducati motorbikes, red leather chaiselongues and goatskin rugs, slung on the back of red leather Chesterfield suites. Amy gasped at the images. Her pulses raced at the sight of their oiled, seminude, generously endowed physiques, dressed in tiny leather thongs from the rubbba.com underwear and beachwear ranges. Uncertain of what to make of things, Amy delved speculatively into the depths of her mind in search of clues, hints, anything that would give her an idea of what Mike was trying to tell her here. He's got to be kinky or something, she thought. Fathomless, Amy bookmarked the website and anticipatively typed the name of the other website Mike had mentioned, *www.pollkadots.com*. Images of women seductively modeling leather and PVC garments appeared. Amy immersed herself in the display of eroticism. Welcome to Mike's world, she thought. The seductive images on both websites appealed to Amy, awakening her appetite for things differently sensual, that she'd spent virtually all night surfing the net, gaining as much information as she possibly could about the companies, from their product ranges to their annual report and accounts. Amy leaned back in her chair visualizing herself wearing the tiniest black leather thong bikini, seductively spread-eagled on a gleaming Harley Davidson with Mike, adorned in black leather thongs seated behind her, his hands strategically placed on her thighs. Mike expected feedback on the websites and Amy thought carefully about her approach. Candies were based a few blocks away from Je La Buena and, as Amy saw no harm in checking out the venue beforehand, she endeavored to pay them a midweek visit on her way home from the office.

Candies were tucked away in a small, Tudor styled building on an Old England, pretty cobbled street. The main door opened to a spacious reception area. Huge, gilt framed mirrors hung on the glistening black walls.

An attractive hostess with jet black shoulder length hair and penetrating blue eyes sat behind a marble reception desk. "Good evening. Can I help you?" said the hostess, with a rigidly fixed smile.

Impeccably dressed in a pastel pink Chanel two piece skirt suit, stylishly clutching a Chanel hand bag at her side, Amy demonstrated her natural air of elegance with ease. She'd specially selected the head turning suit for the all important chief executive officers' meeting she'd attended with Vincent earlier, that afternoon. "Good evening, to you. I'd like to view the premises, if I may?"

"Sure," said the hostess, rising from the reception desk, revealing a pair of long, slender legs, gracing a pair of deep purple leather shorts, riding up the crevice of her firmly shaped, perked buttocks and a deep purple leather skimpy bra, barely cradling her large breasts. Wow! Amy thought, diplomatically looking the other way as the hostess walked on ahead of her.

"Go straight down the corridor, it's the first door on your right. Someone will be there to meet you," said the hostess, pointing her forefinger in the direction of where Amy should be heading, unaccompanied.

"Thank you," said Amy. She walked on slowly down the corridor to the first door on the right and tapped lightly on the charcoal black door. No-one surfaced for a number of minutes. Amy patiently waited. Suddenly, she heard the sound of quick footsteps coming closer to the door. A tall, thin, pale skinned, waif looking young man, looked in his mid twenties, entirely dressed in black, opened the door and stood stiffly. Amy peered over his head. It was dark in the room. The air conditioning blew its uninvitingly chilly breeze around the room. The young man stood back allowing Amy to enter. Her eyes and senses adjusted to the blackened room, floor, ceiling, walls, tables, chairs, fixtures and fittings, comprised of a dance floor, restaurant and a bar that stretched the full length of the sixty foot room. "Can I help you?" said the young man in a peculiar tone of voice.

"I'd like to take a quick look around, please?" said Amy. "This is my first visit here. I'll be attending a private function to be thrown here by Pollkadots in a fortnight." Amy treaded the blackened floor cautiously.

An ashen faced, thinner and younger man, appearing to be in his early twenties, suddenly popped his head up from behind the bar. "Pollkadots?" he asked.

"Yes. That's right," said Amy.

"They've hired the entire building. Should be a great do. They're known to have great parties. This way," he said, leading Amy to the back of the bar, commencing the tour. He ran through the logistics of the bar, restaurant, hospitality areas and fire escapes. "The unisex washrooms are this way," he said, leading Amy into corridors of deeper darkness.

"It's so dark in here," commented Amy.

"There's a reason for that. You'll know what I mean by this fact once you've seen the lighting on the night. Trust me. It's amazing when it's all lit up in here." Amy had seen enough already and cut short the tour, opting to save what she hadn't seen for the night of the party.

"Viewing the washrooms won't be necessary. I'm running late. I've got another appointment, sorry," said Amy pressingly, squinting at her watch-face in the dark.

"In that case, I'll see you to the main door," said the young man obligingly.

"Thanks," said Amy, leaving the building with puzzling thoughts on what to expect on the night of the party.

Lounging on her couch, snuggled between two large cushions, Amy picked up the telephone and called Mike. She thought it would be better to hold back on immediately launching into talk about the websites.

"Have you had a moment to browse through any of the websites by any chance?" asked Mike.

So much for holding back, Amy thought. "Yes, I have. Both websites."

"And what are your views?"

Amy clutched her cushion. "I'd found the clothing quite raunchy," she said. "I'd no idea you were into that sort of thing," she continued, testing the water.

"I wanted you to see the clothes I don at the weekend ever
into if you like. None of my close associates are aware that I attend these
let alone possess such items of clothing."

Hoping Mike wasn't harboring any dark secrets or living a double life,
stunned and speechless, Amy remained silent and struggled with the meaning
behind what Mike turned into as he hadn't exactly specified what exactly. She
felt an awe of privilege that he chose to share such personal information with
her, information he said his associates weren't privy to. "Would you dare to
wear any of the outfits?" asked Mike.

Amy pictured herself clothed in a long, black leather coat, nude under-
neath. "Yes. I would," she said casually, holding back on elaborating.

"Splendid. I'd hoped you'd say that. The majority of women at Candies
come dressed in Pollkadots's gear and the men in Rubbba's."

"Sounds great to me," Amy said.

"Would you be making a personal purchase or would you be hiring an outfit for the evening? I can assist you with full names and addresses of suppliers
in London to save you purchasing from the websites."

Amy deliberated.. "As I wouldn't have any further use for the clothing, I
think it would be best that I hired something," she said, philosophically.

"If you've a pen and paper handy, I'll give you the contact details of two hir-
ers that I use. They run out of stock pretty sharpish, so you'll need to get onto
them as soon as. It's useful to note that they both carry out on the spot alterations on their premises," Mike informed Amy.

"That's handy," she said.

Mike quoted the addresses and contact details which Amy jotted down on a
notepad. "Let me know how you get on. Sorry, I've gotta dash. Bye now," said
Mike, abruptly ending the call.

Amy held the telephone to her ear and listened to the dull drone of the dial-
ing tone for a few seconds. Hanging up, she read the notes she'd jotted down.
"Well, woman, what are you waiting for? Do as you're told, get down to the
suppliers as soon as, and hire the most exquisitely, tasteful and sexiest outfit
ever," she said out loud, mentally preparing to set off first thing in the morning.

"Miss Scott, Jenny of Flamboyance of Chelsea calling on Tuesday at three. Your
costume is ready for collection from our Kings Road shop. We look forward to
seeing you. Thank you."

Amy was disappointed that Mike wasn't among the number of people who'd left messages on her cell-phone when she returned to her desk after her presentation to new clients. There were only four days to go before the party at Candies and she had to speak to Mike regarding meeting arrangements. As there were no further engagements, Amy left the office at four to collect the costume. Before packing the costume neatly away in her closet, to be doubly sure she was totally happy with it the alterations and adjustments, Amy tried on the pieces again. The radio played chart music in the background whilst Amy pulled on the chic, blond bob styled wig, a pair of black leather thongs, which she'd purchased to wear under the high collared, black leather cat-suit she'd hired. The cat-suit was fastened by a two-way zipper that started from the high collar at the front of the neck and traveled under her crotch, up her spine, to the nape of her neck. Four inch stiletto, black leather thigh high boots and a miniature black leather whip worn around her wrist completed the ensemble. Amy prowled around her bedroom, flashing the whip in the air from left to right to the beat of the music. She was shocked at her reflection in the full length mirror. What a transformation. This is not me. My whole persona changed in an outfit. Just like that. Hell, I like it, she thought, excitedly. Her telephone rang. Amy lowered the volume of music and picked up her cordless telephone. "Hallo?"

"Quite a party you're having, I'm almost tempted to come over to join you," said Jenson, hinting threateningly.

"The music is to unwind to after a grueling day at the office." Amy hadn't any further plans for evening and thought it wouldn't be a bad idea to have Jenson over. "What time did you have in mind?"

"Around eight?"

"That suits me fine," she said, glancing at herself in the mirror, nodding in approval, happy there weren't any last minute alterations to be made.

"OK, honey," said Jenson.

Amy undressed and packed the clothing away in her closet. No news from Mike, Amy's agitation grew and, taking a deep breath, she dialed his cell-phone and was connected to his voicemail.. "I've hired an outfit from Flamboyance. Thank you for that. When you've got a moment, please call me back regarding final meeting arrangements. Thanks." Left with no other option but to wait for Mike to return her call, Amy diverted her attention to Jenson, guiltily and daringly gearing her, mind, body and soul, anticipatively visualizing the usually steamy, feisty, playful, indulgent and energetic night with him.

34

Lacking considerable concentration, inordinately worrying about whether or not Mike would be calling her back, Amy spent the best part of Friday in almost total oblivion that the inevitable tell-tell signs of stress were becoming increasingly apparent.

"Are you alright? Can I get you anything?" said her assistant, Richard Watkins, managing the Del Mar casino project. "You look sheepish. Rather pale, I'd say."

"I'm OK, Richard. Just a little tired that's all. It's been a long week. Thank you for asking," Amy responded sullenly. She felt irritable and touchy. Her stomach grumbled due to low food consumption owed to her loss of appetite. Her complexion lacked its usual glow due to catching only a couple of hours sleep the night before. This was not what she wanted, not an ideal situation to be in. Her work colleagues should never have to see her this way. She felt vulnerable in their presence, but more vulnerable without news from Mike. She had to shake-off the feelings that were doing her no good and, much to her chagrin, an about turn was required, otherwise she wasn't going to be in a fit state for anyone, more importantly, herself. Back at the apartment that evening, Amy checked her voicemail messages. Mike still hadn't called her back. A slight panic setting in, Amy began speculating on whether the date was still going ahead, if Mike was having second thoughts or whether she ought to call him again. Realizing how pointless it was working herself up into a frenzied state, Amy waited for the latter part of Saturday afternoon to return the items to Flamboyance if Mike proved to be a no show.

Saturday morning, Amy awoke early, showered, ate Muesli for breakfast and paced around her apartment. Pondering, Amy waited, hoped, stamped her feet, cursed and willed Mike to call. By midday, she grabbed the bag out of her closet housing the costume neatly packed inside and marched, in a huff, over to her apartment's main door. Indecisiveness played havoc on Amy's mind on whether to return the costume or give it another hour. Pull yourself together. What's gotten into you? Activity is the key. Occupy yourself. Get busy, she told herself, retreating to the lounge, tossing the bag and herself on the couch. I'll watch movies, read a book, listen to a CD, she thought, inserting a comedy DVD into the player which bored her to sleep. The telephone rang, awakening her. She checked her watch and rubbed her eyes. It was three twenty. Three hours and twenty minutes later and a comedy DVD she had no recollection of having watched, Amy reached for the telephone.

"I've just flown in from France and leaving Heathrow airport now," said Mike, from his car-phone.

Heathrow! I'm so glad you're safe! At long last, Amy thought, holding her breath, anticipating that Mike was about to break disappointing news to her canceling their date. "What are your plans for tonight?" queried Amy.

"Sorry, I hadn't given it that much thought whilst in France. By the way, I've received your voicemail message. I had to take an urgent flight out to France for a couple of days. Our Paris hotel had urgent issues that had to be resolved. The head chef threatened to walk, among other things. I caught the last flight out of Charles de Gaule to get me back in London at a reasonable time," said Mike plausibly. "I'm heading towards your place now," he added.

Amy heard Mike starting the engine. Her hopes of seeing Mike in full leather gear were dashed. "What will you wear?"

"My clothes are in the boot. Requesting permission to get dressed at your place?"

"By all means, yes."

"You're address?"

Amy provided Mike with her address and directions.

"See you in about an hour," said Mike, clicking off.

The date still going ahead, Amy rippled with excitement on the prospect of having him in her apartment and prior to taking her shower, she urgently sprung into action, dashing around the apartment tidying up, hiding every conceivable evidence of Jenson, making everything appealingly ship-shape. It suddenly dawned on her that the main door had to be secured into the permanent locking position, purely for the purpose of preventing Jenson from making one of his unexpected entries. They'd agreed not to meet this weekend when they'd left the apartment together on Wednesday morning but, with Jenson having a spare key, there was the constant and probable threat that Jenson would unexpectedly turn up at any given moment. Her emotions dulled as she envisaged the potentiality of an ugly, violent scene, Jenson erupting into an angry rage finding her with another man. She couldn't bare thinking about the inevitable pain, betrayal and subsequent embarrassment that would be suffered by all involved. Wasting no further time pondering the unpleasantness, Amy took a quick warm shower, pulled on the hired outfit and sat in front of the mirror deciding her make-up. She applied techniques that Robbie had taught her, techniques he'd claimed were top secret, known only by an elite handful of professional make-up artists. True or false, Amy sculptured her face beautifully, accentuating her lips, eyes and high cheekbones. Thank goodness for Robbie, she thought, on final inspection. The intercom sounded. Amy cautiously checked that it was Mike's image appearing on her security camera. Performing a final twirl in front of the mirror, Amy pressed the entry button and strolled out of her apartment to the main hallway to greet Mike. "You've finally made it," she said.

Mike, transfixed to the spot, gazed at Amy, his eyes filled with adoration. "You look … fantastic!"

"Thanks," whispered Amy, blushing slightly. "How was your journey? You got here rather quickly!"

"Quite straightforward," said Mike, taking a step closer to Amy. "Turn around. Let me look at you!" he said.

Overwhelmed by Mike's overt adulation, Amy gladly obliged, placing her hands firmly on her hips and performing a gracious twirl before walking into her apartment. Mike followed and Amy locked the door behind him. She turned to Mike. They looked at each other in silence.

"You look fantastic," whispered Mike.

Never any good at accepting compliments, Amy felt incredibly shy for a moment. "Thank you," she said, tingling in nervous apprehension. Taking a step back, Amy suspected that things could get out of control, measuring that she would have to be the one to take the initiative to quell them both. "Can I offer you a drink?"

"No thanks. But I know what I'd really like," said Mike teasingly, raising his eyebrows at her.

Oh no, Amy thought. "And what would that be?"

"I'm dying to get out of these clothes and could use a shower," said Mike.

"This way." Amy showed Mike to the bathroom. "There is a dressing room next door to your right that you could use after your shower."

Mike looked quizzically at the shower controls.

"Here, allow me," said Amy, turning on the shower. Hot, steamy water gushed out of the power jet at full force.

"Brilliant," said Mike, loosening his tie.

Amy made a quick exit saying, "Yell, if you need anything further." Mike's continuous compliments had left Amy overawed. She battled to recall an instant where she'd received so many compliments in such a short space of time. Basking in flattery, she continued preparing for the evening, filling her handbag with the necessities of cash, credit cards, keys, Bvlgari perfume, make-up bag, a Mont Blanc pen and her cell-phone. Yanking on the boots, it suddenly dawned on Amy that Mike hadn't mentioned how they were getting to Candies. She hoped he wouldn't drive. She heard movement confirming that Mike had completed his shower. Fifteen minutes later, Amy slowly and quietly made her way to the dressing room. Her mouth dropped open. She was lost for words, as Mike looked stunning, standing in front of the full length mirror, smartly attired in a black leather suit worn over an open necked red shirt. Mike administered the final adjustments to his outfit. He's truly an astoundingly handsome man, Amy thought. "Very, very nice."

"Glad you like it," said Mike.

"You look great. It's clearly evident why you like to wear this style of clothing," said Amy, dispelling the morbid suspicions she'd previously held about him. The open necked shirt beckoned Amy to run her fingertips up and down his smooth, broad chest.

"Yes, the clothes are fun to wear and I love the feel and the smell of leather," said Mike, inhaling deeply.

"I was wondering," said Amy.

"Yes?"

"How are we getting there?"

"Good timing," said Mike. "I was on the verge of asking you to call a cab."

"Sure. We can wait in here for the cab to arrive. They normally take five minutes to get here," said Amy, showing Mike to the lounge.

The cab driver looked at Amy with drooling eyes as she slid into the back seat. "What's happening at Candies tonight?" said the cab driver, breathing heavily, suffering from the effects influenced by Amy's mode of dress.

"A fancy dress party," said Amy, cold and dismissively.

"What's the latest football score?" asked Mike, butting-in diplomatically.

Impressed with Mike's receptiveness, his skillful mirroring and matching, Amy was quite happy to leave the cab driver and Mike to talk about football, which Mike ensured for the duration of the journey.

"We're here," said the cab driver as he pulled up outside the main entrance. Mike paid the fare along with a generous tip. The cab driver handed Mike his personal business card and counted the cash. He beamed like a Cheshire cat from ear to ear, "Cheers mate. Call me on this number when you're ready to be collected. I'll be waiting close by for you."

"Thank you. I will. That's most kind of you," said Mike, slipping the card in his top pocket. Mike ushered Amy to the members' only area. They were greeted by semi-nude hostesses serving free glasses of champagne on arrival whilst escorting them to the black room that Amy had previously visited, unbeknownst to Mike. Both the young lads she'd met were managing the door. Neither of them recognized her. Mike and Amy entered the room and were dazzled by a sudden flash of lighting. He was right, the lighting is truly amazing, Amy thought. Her eyes darted around the room at the state-of-the-art, futuristic lighting. Multi-colored strobes, laser beams and special effects filled the room. The dance floor was packed with people gyrating, dancing, jumping, singing, doing anything and everything to loud Techno music, all dressed in leather and PVC gear, from the outrageously hideous, outlandish, chic and stylish, to the most stunningly erotic. Mike took Amy by the hand and led her to another room. It was gloomy and dark, eerie was the first thing that came to Amy's mind on entering. Heavy metal, rock music played. Amy watched a few men, on their hands and knees, in an array of bondage, hand-cuffs, shackles, and chains. Their facial expressions were a mixture of twisted contortion of pain as well as immensely ugly enjoyment, deriving pleasures, being severely whipped, beaten, kicked and abused by petite women who screamed, spat and shouted extremely degrading expletives directly at them. Disgusted, Amy had difficulty taking it all in. This is most Bizarre. I've never seen anything like it, she thought, turning her face away in a bid to conceal her shock and prudishness from Mike.

"That man over there," said Mike, nudging Amy to look over to her immediate left at a man in a black leather cloak, his face covered in a full white mask.

"Yes, what about him?" she asked, from the corner of her mouth.

"He's chairman of the National Investment Bank,"

"You're not serious!"

"And the one on your right, wearing the mask and baby's diaper, he's a circuit judge."

"How on earth … no!" said Amy, shaking her head. "How could you possibly recognize them, behind their masks? How can you tell who's who?"

"Let's put it this way. Codes."

"Oh!" said Amy. "Do they belong to a lodge or some secret macabre society, perhaps?"

"Sharing her?" asked a woman in a German accent.

"No. Sorry. She's all mine," said Mike politely, quickly whisking Amy away to the bar at the back of the room.

"Sharing? What had she meant by that?" Amy quizzed.

"She's a lesbian and she wants to sleep with you. Don't worry she's backed-off now. She'll find someone to team up with shortly," said Mike casually. Moving away from the bar, they approached another man on his knees. His wrists and ankles were shackled in chains and a petite woman repeatedly kicked and punched him. "This, I'm finding a bit too gruesome," said Mike, stepping out of their way.

"I agree. It is hell in here," said Amy, curious about Mike's fantasies in fetishism and sadomasochism, whether he was entertaining any thoughts on getting her to perform lurid acts. Mike halted in an adjoining room where the DJ played eighties disco music. The room was considerably livelier and friendlier and Amy instantly started to feel better.

Mike sat in a low chair and motioned Amy to sit on his lap. "Please, sit here," he said. Facing Mike, Amy gripped his shoulders and squatted on his lap. She felt his firm, strong legs managing her weight.

"Hey, Mike, good to see you," a man shouted. "And who is this?"

"My wife."

"Very pretty," said the man, disappearing into the crowd.

Amy loved the essence of the short exchange of words and raised her eyebrows. "Who was that?" she asked.

"Oh, someone from the club. No-one of great importance," said Mike, shrugging his shoulders. "What are you drinking?"

"I'll stick with the champagne thanks, Mike," said Amy.

Mike ordered their drinks from a passing topless hostess parading in a white leather teddy. "Let's dance," said Mike, leading Amy to the dance floor.

Amy was in her element as they touched, laughed, frolicked, made use of the mini whip, taking turns to whip one another playfully. Mike had to fend off people who tried to take part in their private fun and games. "Let's sit, I'm beat," said Mike, after forty five minutes on the dance floor.

Amy found the whole scenario unbelievable as they nestled together in a much quieter room, gazing at each other, not uttering a word. Breaking the silence, Mike shocked Amy, driving her absolutely and deliriously crazy with the least expected request she'd ever thought would utter from his lips. "Let's make love," he suggested, calmly.

"What?" she exclaimed alarmingly.

"Now, here," Mike continued calmly, smiling at her.

Amy looked around the room. "Here? Where?"

"Come this way," Mike gestured.

Light headed, legs wobbling like jelly, blurry-eyed, filled with a confusion of apprehension, self-doubt and ecstatic yearning, under the influence of champagne on an empty stomach, Amy followed Mike to what appeared to be a lounge suite opposite the unisex bathroom. It was dark and crowded. People danced to loud rock music. Mike found a low chair and sat down. Amy spontaneously squatted on his lap again, facing him. Rubbing his fingers along Amy's leather cat-suit, Mike pulled the zipper working his way down from the front of her neck. He buried his face in her cleavage and fondled her breasts. Her world, as she had known it, was altering its course. Everything was about to change. Writhing, Amy fought apprehension. She held Mike in a completely different light now as everything she thought, believed and conceived about him had remarkably altered. Mike slowly pulled the zipper down further and Amy raised herself to assist him in pulling the zipper under her crotch. His tongue traveled up and down her cleavage and meeting her lips he kissed her tenderly. A surge of ecstasy shot through her as Mike fondled, raised her up and expertly entered her. Her eyes tightly shut, Amy felt like she was going completely out of her mind as she writhed in exceeding pleasure. Mike clenched Amy's buttocks. She moved up and down. Locked in the pleasure of Mike inside her, Amy hadn't noticed whether anyone in the crowd watched as they made love in the open—she didn't care, she couldn't stop herself, even if she wanted to, she wouldn't, Mike felt too good. Amy ran her fingers along his soft, smooth, slicked back hair and inhaled his manly scent mingled with his expensive aftershave. "Mike," Amy murmured, running her fingers up and down the smooth hairs of his chest, sensing an enormous orgasm emerging, gripping his shoulders tightly. Amy screamed at the sound of Mike's groans making her erupt in a long and lingering climax. He held her tightly and rocked her gently to a calm state. He kept his arms securely wrapped round her as she nestled her head on his shoulder. The session had left her completely and utterly drained of energy. Groggy, Amy turned her head slightly to observe the partying crowd dancing, singing, jumping, and gyrating to the loud rock music and noticed that no-one had actually taken a blind bit of notice of her and Mike. She tingled at the warmth of his breath blowing in her ear, arousing her again. Re-zipping her cat-suit Mike said, "Let's go home."

The cab driver pulled up outside Amy's apartment at three in the morning. Unlocking the door, Amy's heartbeat thumped as she nervously considered the possibility of finding Jenson asleep in her bed. She quietly closed the main door, locked it securely behind her, crept into the apartment and surreptitiously popped her head around the bedroom door. Thankfully, her bed was empty as Mike entered her bedroom following closely behind her. He took Amy into his arms and drew her close. "I love the feel of leathers rubbing," he said. "Don't undress. Let's make love fully clothed." Mike turned Amy's back to him. He nibbled the nape of her neck, unzipped her cat-suit as far as her crotch.

Amy gasped, "Let's," she said.

Amy awoke to the cheerful chorus of the birds perched on the tree outside her bedroom window. She ran her feet against the cold Egyptian cotton sheets to feel the touch of Mike's warm legs. Amy felt nothing. She turned around. The space that Mike had occupied was empty. She smiled sleepily and got out of bed to investigate his whereabouts. She listened out for him, but was met with silence. She tiptoed to the kitchen, lounge, bathroom, dressing room and the spare bedroom to discover that Mike, along with his clothes, shoes, car keys, travel case, toiletries, everything, had gone. She looked out of the window where he'd parked his company car the night before. The car had also gone. Amy looked around the apartment hoping that Mike may have left a note, something, anything. Mike had left nothing. Maybe he'll call, she told herself, returning to her bedroom, slumping on her bed, defeated. The cat-suit lay crumpled on the floor. Amy smiled as she recalled the memory of how ludicrously clumsy Mike had appeared, pulling the boots off her feet, falling flat on his back and bumping the back of his head on the wall. She reminisced on the fun time they'd had in Candies. She got exactly what she wanted, they'd finally had sex. Great! But yet, she felt emotionally confused, disorientated and yearned for more. The past events had taken their acquaintanceship to a new level. Mike was no longer the, reserved and sophisticated gentleman who'd graced the eyes of her soul on that memorable day one of the workshop. He meant more to her now, mysteriously, intriguingly and intensely more. She felt a discomforting change in her character, in that she'd made a spectacle of herself, wore a strange outfit, watched lewd acts, completely crossed the line by having sex in open view, she didn't know whether to feel ashamed or proud. The certainties were that she was no longer the same person and Mike had returned to his fiancé. Amy fought back the tears that stung her eyes. She was beginning to miss him, desperately. Insecurity kicked-in overtaking her rationality. Tears flowed down her cheeks. I've allowed him to use me, make a fool out of me. I've been such a stupid, stupid fool, she thought.

CHAPTER 8

Richard spent the morning, in great difficulty, staving his eyes from looking at Amy with intense desire, as she strolled majestically into the office at eight o'clock, swept past his desk and intoxicated his senses with the sweet aroma of her perfume that lingered in the air. The epitome of beauty, radiant as usual, there was something different about her today and Richard couldn't quite put his finger on it. Whatever it was, he liked it. He'd watched her beaver away at her desk, so impressed by her success on the Del Mar casino project. "Good, morning Amy. Good weekend?"

"Great thanks. And yours?"

"Good. I won a prize in a raffle at my local Cricket club."

"Ah. Good for you, Richard. Well done," said Amy, genuinely pleased for Richard.

"The bash was good but, I'm not so sure about the prize."

"Why? What have you won?" Amy enquired, scanning her emails.

Richard fumbled around his desk. "An all expenses paid, weekend trip for two to Amsterdam."

Astonished, Amy ceased scanning her emails and made immediate eye contact with Richard. "And what could possibly be wrong with that?"

"Amsterdam has never appealed to me. It's not my kind of place," he said disdainfully, dismissive of anything that wasn't quintessentially British. "As you're a seasoned traveler, I'd be quite happy to offer the prize to you," he said, placing an unsealed A5 manila envelope on her desk.

"That's very kind of you, Richard. But I couldn't possibly accept. There must be a family member, a friend or an associate you could extend the offer to!"

"I'd rather you had them. Anyway, I love listening to the tales of your travel exploits."

"Thank you, Richard." Amy reached for her Gucci handbag in the bottom right hand drawer of her desk and fished out her check book and pen. "What can I offer you for them, at least?" she said, screening the contents of the envelope.

"Nothing. Please. They're a gift. I don't mind giving them away," said Richard, objectionably waving his right hand in the air.

"I couldn't possibly take … do you have a favorite charity, church or an organization I could send a donation to, perhaps?" Amy opened her check book, preparing to write.

"No. Please," Richard pleaded. "I'd like you to have them. Feel free to give them away should you change your mind."

"Well, thanks again," said Amy, staring at the ceiling wondering whom to invite.

"There is a validity of three months on them, I hasten to add. So don't delay on your booking arrangements."

"Thank you for alerting me of that fact." Amy had suspected that Richard's preferential treatment of her wasn't of a wholly professional nature. She'd inadvertently caught him sneaking the occasional glance at her, but was grateful his glances weren't of a lecherous nature. He just wasn't her type. He'd bend over backwards in his will to please her and, she'd found his overbearing friendliness quite nauseating and tactless at times. But, she was gratefully fortunate to have such a reliable, efficient, helpful and conscientious managing assistant in Richard. Without further utterance, Amy dropped her check book and pen in her handbag and returned to screening her emails, virtually all requiring action.

Amy loved the hectic pace of the office, telephones incessantly ringing, fax machines constantly beeping, personnel milling around the photocopier, some flirting around the coffee vending machines, Vincent's middle-aged personal assistant rushing around, in a flap, hot, bothered and flustered, doing a bad job of supervising three, young junior secretaries under her jurisdiction, who were constantly scheming and running circles around her, window cleaners peeping through the tinted smoky-gray, reinforced windows. Whilst scrutinizing two burly men delivering the stationery order, Amy entertained the irresistible idea to invite Mike to Amsterdam. As a preparatory measure, Amy displayed Mike's office number on her Blackberry and waited for Richard to disappear to lunch, out of earshot, before she embarked on calling Mike. Bridled to her desk, Amy busily sent, received, deleted and archived a constant flow of emails, patched into a couple of conference calls, conversed with various belly aching clients, nervous and insecure about their deals and investments—she much preferred to do business with clients who were high achievers, results driven who thrived on taking high risks.

"I'm popping out for a quick bite. Can I get you anything on my way back?" said Richard.

"No thanks. I'm having a late lunch today. Enjoy," said Amy, waving him off as he headed to the elevator. With Richard now safely out of the way for the best part of twenty minutes or less, Amy hurriedly called Mike.

"Hello. Mike Brandleton," Mike bellowed gruffly.

Amy almost hung up. Why am I doing this? she thought. "Hi Mike. How are you? It's Amy." She was met with a cold silence. Ignoring the fact that she was quite perturbed by him, disappearing from her bed on Sunday morning, that he hadn't called her or left a note and, although nervous, she refused to allow herself to be put off by his now curt telephone manner. "I've not called you at the office, so I'm not surprised that you're surprised to hear from me," she said, disguising her nervousness. Mike said nothing. The silence was unbearable. The palms of her hands moistening and her ears hissing, Amy was suffering under the prolonged silence. Seething, her blood boiled. And yet she wouldn't consider having anyone along with her on the trip apart from Mike. Breaking the silence Amy said, "This won't take five minutes."

"What can I do for you?" Mike enquired coldly.

"I've called to invite you as my guest to an all expenses paid weekend trip for two to Amsterdam."

"Thank you for thinking about me," he responded sullenly.

"I take it that you'd like to come along?"

"But, of course. Yes. Indeed."

"The trip is valid for three months from now so, let me know what weekends work for you and I'll book accordingly."

"Wait a second, would you?"

"Sure," said Amy, one eye looking out for Richard.

"I've a few dates here I can provide you with now."

"Great."

"Let's see … ah, the last weekend in May is free and … the second and third weekends in June. Need any further dates?"

"No, these are fine. I'll get back to you," said Amy, jotting down the dates.

"Once you've finalized on the booking arrangements, give me another call at the office with the details and I'll meet you at the airport."

"Fine, I'll do that," said Amy. Clicking off, Amy retrieved the envelope and dialed the telephone number that appeared at the top, right-hand corner of the winning competition document. Amy lingered on the busy line for an agonizing eight minutes, painfully enduring the ghastly music, interrupted by periodic bursts of the repeated announcement, *"you're being held in a queue and will be answered shortly."* Her patience gradually diminishing, Amy worked up a huge appetite outweighing the need to remain on the line a moment longer. She hung up with the decision to make another attempt first thing in the morning, in private, tucked away in a conference room.

"House Services department, Juanita speaking. How can I help you?"

"Juanita, Amy Scott here, I need a small conference room booked tomorrow morning from, say …" Amy quickly checked her diary and the opening and closing times on the voucher, "eight o'clock please, for about an hour."

"Certainly, Miss Scott, one moment please … Room A on the third floor's available."

"That'll do. Thanks."

"Your meeting room booking reference number is A308T."

"I've got it. Thanks, Juanita," said Amy, scribbling the reference number on a Post-it note. She slipped the voucher back in the envelope and tossed it in her top, right-hand drawer. Logging off her computer, Amy grabbed her Gucci purse and proceeded to the elevator. In the salad bar, over a plate of fresh green salad in the cool Atrium styled staff restaurant, Amy deliberated on things to do in Amsterdam and Jenson. Things were simple concerning Jenson but a lot less concerning Mike.

CHAPTER 9

"Hey, it's great to hear from you," said Katie. She welcomed the sound of David's voice over the telephone, early on a Sunday morning. She thought he'd indirectly dumped her after having made his views on not wanting to have an affair with her adamantly clear over lunch at Skates. "When did you get back?"

"Flew in late last night."

Katie wished he'd called her then. "How did the signing go?"

"Fantastic. A success. We've signed a five year contract. I won't go any further than that, material breach and all that. Everything's left in the capable hands of the lawyers."

"I understand well and good. And how was Dubai?"

"I hardly saw the place, too busy going over contracts, service level agreements, architectural plans, attending meeting after meeting, inspection sites, lunches, dinners."

Katie sniggered perkily. "I like the sound of the latter two."

David laughed. "I missed the end of The Instigation. We didn't get a chance to watch the entire movie, did we?" he pitched.

Grappling with astonishment and gladness, Katie was also a little wary of David's motives. Too early in the morning to figure it all out, throwing her cares to the wind, Katie responded obligingly. "What are you waiting for? The DVD is still in the player. Come on over, I won't be venturing out today."

"Well, how about now?"

Katie needed time to prepare as she'd just rolled out of bed. "In an hour would be better," she said, setting a mental stop watch.

"In an hour, it is," said David.

Katie wanted to keep David coming back to her again and again and, she solemnly promised herself that she'd not display, say or do anything that would warrant him feeling cornered by her in any way whenever they were together. It wasn't going to be easy holding back on the growing feelings now coming to the fore but, she was going to give it a damned good try not to jeopardize things between them, not now, now that the fun seemed to be reconvening. Her belly full of sex, banter and fun had to be kept well fed. Sauntering into the kitchen, Katie checked her wine selection stocked on the wine rack, fetched two wine glasses from the shelf and left them on the breakfast bar. She speculated on whether David had changed his mind about having an affair, flagrantly using the movie as an excuse to see her again, but she knew, in her heart of hearts, that the movie wasn't that high on his agenda, guaranteed. Whatever David's motives, Katie, at least knew what she wanted and, at ten minutes past eight, with the hour of David's emergence soon approaching, she had to look more appealing than at present, slumming around in an old baggy, gray jogging suit. After a cup of sweet, hot, milky coffee and a shower, Katie swapped the jogging suit for a pretty, flowing, white cotton halter-neck, summer dress that fitted nicely around her fully rounded hips, thighs and buttocks. The front pearl buttoning and intricate ribbon and lace design of the low cut bodice alluringly cupped her large, shapely breasts. Her auburn hair remained in its usual elegantly styled French plait and, a dainty pair of gold Indian slippers completed the outfit. Fortunately, she was dressed and ready by the time David had cheatingly arrived under the hour, within forty minutes of hanging up the telephone, standing in the main doorway, grinning from ear to ear with his hands behind his back.

"Are you going to stand out there all day or what? Come on, get inside," said Katie playfully. David whipped out a bouquet of thirteen red roses. Stunned, Katie froze on the spot. "Oh, David!" she cooed appreciatively, bringing the roses to the tip of her nose, inhaling their sweet fragrance. "I don't believe this … thanks."

"Come on, get inside. Are we going to stand out here all day?" said David, mimicking Katie, gently shoving her into the apartment. They entered the kitchen chuckling loudly. Katie removed a vase from the shelf and began to prepare the roses. David interrupted her in a long embrace. Overwhelmed, Katie couldn't understand what had gotten into David. He pressed his expert lips on hers, kissing her longingly. Locked in his embrace, Katie went along with the flow kissing him passionately.

"Great to see you again," he whispered, releasing her from his strong, firm grip.

"Ditto. And congratulations on signing the contract."

"Thanks. Now the real work begins. How's business? Have you had a good week?" said David.

Katie nodded affirmatively. "It's been smashing. I'm organizing a couple of forthcoming film premier events and that's really been the highlight of my week. I'm keeping my fingers crossed that it'll all run smoothly without any hitches," she said returning to the roses, cutting the stems. "Why don't you open a bottle?" Katie indicated, pointing the scissors at the wine rack.

"Don't mind if I do," said David, sauntering over. "Now let's see," he said, reading the labels. He pulled out a bottle of Californian Chardonnay and waved it in the air, waiting for Katie's approval. "Would this do the trick?"

"Anyone'll do really but, yep, I'll go along with that," said Katie, crossing the kitchen floor to the lounge, carrying the roses neatly arranged in a white porcelain vase. David poured the wine into the waiting glasses Katie had left on the breakfast bar earlier and brought them into the lounge.

"They're beautiful," said Katie, placing the vase on the window ledge, standing back, admiring the display, before nestling comfortably next to David on the couch. David handed her a glass of wine. Taking a sip of wine, Katie picked up the remote, aimed it at the DVD player and pressed play. She tossed David a sultry glance and provocatively pointed a warning finger at him. "And now for the movie which, this time, we'll watch from beginning to end," said Katie.

"You look so refreshingly beautiful and cuddly this morning," he said, slowly running his forefinger up and down her arm.

Weak, Katie put her glass on the side table and threw her arms around David's neck. They locked in a passionate embrace, kissed, stroked and undressed one another. David unbuttoned the dress revealing Katie's nudity. He exhaled in delight and need of her. Positioning herself, Katie lay back on the couch. With David on top of her and Katie wrapped her legs tightly round his waist. David penetrated her hungrily. Gripping his shoulders tightly, Katie vaguely heard the theme music of The Instigation movie playing loudly in the background. Half an hour later, smothered in David's embrace, Katie awoke from her recovery period to the pleasing sight of his cute, boyish profile and his ruffled blond hair. Stirring contentedly, she smiled smugly at him.

David responded without taking his eyes off the screen. "Sssh. I'm determined to watch this to the end. I've missed a few minutes but I've got the gist of the storyline now," he said, taking a sip of wine.

Feeling self-consciously exposed, Katie got up and slipped on her dress she'd noticed David had neatly folded and draped on the back of the couch. Thirsty, she poured herself a full glass of wine, returned to the couch and snuggled up to David. "What do you think of the movie so far?" Katie whispered, nibbling his left earlobe, ready for more lovemaking.

David gently pressed one finger on her lips. "Hush. Quiet," he whispered, watching the movie to the end in complete silence.

"Sheer brilliance," said David, jubilantly.

"Your mission to watch it from beginning to end has now been accomplished. Well done," said Katie, raising her glass at him.

"Careful, this movie watching caper may develop into a regular habit."

Katie welcomed David's flippant remark without any opposition. "That can be arranged," she said.

"I need to freshen up. Can I use your shower?"

"Feel free," said Katie, pleased he'd asked her first rather than take over her apartment like other men she'd known. David pecked Katie on the cheek then made his way to the bathroom. At ten-fifty-even, it was still early morning and so much had already taken place that Katie prepared to take another short nap on the couch hoping that, after David had taken his shower, he'd come in, arouse her and make love to her again. The telephone started ringing and Katie answered it blissfully. "Hieee."

"Hello. David White, please?" said a woman.

Bemused, Katie wondered why anyone would call her private home number asking to speak to David.

Scratching her head in disbelief, Katie was lost for words. Why would David have anyone call him on her private number and not on his cell-phone? Katie eased herself upright on the couch. "I think you may have the wrong number," said Katie, knowing full well that it was too much of a coincidence. Despite Katie's surmise, the woman continued determinedly.

"Go tell David that his wife is on the telephone," said the woman, dictatorially.

Absolutely fuming, slumped in the couch, Katie looked towards the lounge door, happy that David wasn't in earshot. Noises emanating from the bathroom confirmed he was still taking a shower. Somehow, she had to get the woman, who was claiming to be his wife, off the telephone. "I'm sorry, but I do believe that you've dialed the wrong number," said Katie tersely.

"Don't be a fool. I know he's there. He was careless enough to leave your number lying around."

Mixed feelings of weakness, anger and rage, her heartbeat violently pounded from the shock of it all.

None of this is making any sense, Katie thought, reluctant to hand the woman over to the David. "You've dialed the wrong number," said Katie, hanging up. After a few seconds the telephone inevitably started ringing again. Katie aggressively snatched the receiver from its cage.

"I suppose he's told you he'd been in Dubai all of last week. Has he?" the woman shouted before Katie had a chance to speak.

"That was smashing," said David, boisterously entering the room, appearing before Katie's eyes, resembling a spruced up Greek God with nothing but her thick, white, Ralph Lauren bath towel wrapped round his waist, a little water slowly trickling down the few faint, soft hairs of his chest. It was too late to cover the mouth-piece as the woman had undoubtedly heard David's voice in the background.

"PUT HIM ON THE 'PHONE. NOW," the woman demanded, yelling at the top of her voice.

David sensed there was something wrong from Katie's demeanor, her stiffened shoulders and her not so friendly facial expression, fully focused and directed at him. "Who is it?" mimed David, a look of concern written on his face. Speechless, Katie got off the couch, walked over to David and thrust the telephone at him. Retreating one step back, David refused to take the telephone. He shook his head from side to side, crossed and waved his hands in the air. "You want me to take care of this?" he mimed.

"Yes," Katie hissed loudly, her anger surging through.

David whispered, "Who is it?"

"The call's for you."

"Me?" said David out loud.

"Yes. You. Just take the call and be done with it," said Katie, slamming the telephone on his chest.

David fumbled awkwardly with the telephone and brought it to his ear.

"Hello," he said in a pathetic and sheepishly low voice.

"You bastard!" screamed the woman.

Katie stood facing David, her arms folded matronly in front of her, raising her eyebrows at him as his wife hurled abuse at him.

David swiftly turned his back to Katie. "Who do you think you are? And how did you get this number?" he shouted.

"That's a stupid question. How could you? Where are you? Who is she?" Hurt, enraged, overhearing the ferocious barrage of questions, Katie wanted to join in. "You slime ball. You've only just crawled out of our marital bed at seven o'clock this morning. I really hope you haven't …"

"OK, OK, OK," David loudly interjected, "you'll see me in an hour. And don't call back otherwise you'll run the risk of not seeing me at all today, if you piss me off any further." He slammed the telephone down.

Katie immediately wrenched the telephone cord out of its socket. David turned around and faced Katie. Clearly embarrassed, David gazed at Katie apologetically. They were both caught in an acrimoniously silent moment for a few agonizing seconds, agonizing seconds torturous to Katie. Saddened, David looked at Katie remorsefully.

Katie finally broke the silence, "I dare you to look me in the eye and tell me this is all a bad dream. Is it? … Yes?" she yelled, on the verge of succumbing to David's pitiful expression. "Don't you dare look at me in that way, it's not going to work," she blurted angrily. But, it was working. David was an amazing sight. Silently facing her, motionless and beautiful. Shower fresh, her Ralph Lauren bath towel hitched on his waist. Gorgeous chest. Rippled stomach. She yearned to hold him, to feel the warmth of his skin, the pressure of his body against hers that Katie had to muster every bit of strength in every bone, every muscle, every nerve, every cell, in her body and her entire will, to stop herself from walking over to him and tenderly taking him in her arms.

"Katie, please, I can explain," pleaded David, in a low, pitiful and feeble voice.

Katie swung her head back and laughed, mockingly at him. "Three little words. *I can explain?*"

David interjected. "Look, I've taken a massive risk coming here. I'd planned to discuss my present situation with you in greater detail in a few days or so, not right now but, now this has happened …" His eyes fell to the floor.

Katie reluctantly gave David the forum to offer his rendition. "I'm listening?" she said, making her way to the kitchen, opening another bottle of wine.

David followed Katie into the kitchen saying, "Zowie likes to keep tabs on me. She snoops around my stuff, looking for evidence of an affair. I've never cheated on her and … I've warned you about this, about getting involved. I visited the children recently and she must have gone into my cell-phone and made a note of a few telephone numbers. Goodness knows who else she's called today before finally tracking me down. I dread to think … oh! … thank you, ... Katie," he said guiltily, visibly shocked that Katie had poured him a glass of a full bodied, red wine.

"And Dubai?" said Katie, imperceptibly fighting back her tears. She drank her wine and refilled her glass.

"Dubai?" said David.

"Yes. Dubai. She ... Zowie I mean ... said something about you not having gone there at all."

David sighed long, hard and deep. Beads of sweat formed on his forehead. "Can I sit down?"

"Go ahead. Be my guest." Katie remained standing in the middle of the kitchen with one hand on her hip and a glass of wine in the other.

David wandered over to the breakfast bar and sat down, assuming the stance of a broken man. "We'd discussed making a go of things ... a reconciliation ... for the sake of the children and I'd informed everyone, family, friends, business associates, everyone that I'd be away in ... that I'd be in Dubai for a week on business so that Zowie and I could make a go of things, at home in Richmond, for a week with the children, get to know each other again," he said, coughing nervously, sitting on the edge of the chair. He brought his wine glass to his lips and gulped the wine down in one.

"So, you'd intentionally lied to me?"

"Yes," David snapped, ashamedly bowing his head, avoiding eye contact. "Look, Katie, I'm sorry."

Jolting her head backwards, Katie laughed out loud. "You're really with it today. Another lot of three little words. *I am sorry*," she said, sardonically.

David was greatly relieved by Katie's laughter but also confused, ignorant of the real reason behind her laughter. Steering away from the possibility of a backlash of incriminations, David opted to play it safe by keeping a straight face. "I was hoping you'd understand once I'd explained it all to you. Er ... if it's any consolation, there will be a signing agreement scheduled to take place in Dubai in a few weeks, I'm just waiting for firm dates."

"You're clutching at a poor and ghastly attempt to justify yourself. .It's pathetic, giving me all this bullshit now and, you know it. It's too late. All that stuff about signing a deal and contracts and lawyers and blaming visiting the kids as the reason for her getting hold of my number. It's all lies. You disgust me. And sleeping with me assists you in making a go of things with your wife for the sake of the kids, I suppose?" Katie poured her third glass of wine.

"No. You'll probably find this hard to believe but, I contacted you today because I couldn't get you out of my mind all week—ever since our first ...

well, you know what I mean. I don't need to go into it all. It was such an unforgettable moment. Zowie doesn't turn me on the way you do. She doesn't take care of herself like you do. You're refreshing and Zowie's not. You've certainly made an impact on me. And I've not slept with any other woman other than Zowie during our marriage. You're the only one Katie, the only one. I'm actually smitten by you, can't you see that?" he blabbered, desperately.

"Huh?" retorted Katie bluntly, gulping her third glass of wine in one swoop, topping up David's wine glass and pouring her fourth. Yearning for him, her eyes danced at his semi-nudity, damp ruffled blond hair, cute, boyish features, dazzling blue eyes, full pleasure waiting to serve her, there and then. Defeated, Katie felt herself about to break down under the stress and strain of the whole situation. She seethed with anger at the acute sense of betrayal, convinced herself that she'd get over it in no time and continue to live up to her reputation as good old Katie, the tough cookie. A cold shower to wake her up, to rid her of the stupor of her emotions, to knock some sense back into her head was in order. "I'm going to take a shower," she said.

"OK. Enjoy," said David, breathing a great sigh of relief. He ran his fingers through his hair, confident that all was not lost with Katie. Before Katie had left the kitchen, David got up, walked over to her and stopped her in her tracks. Facing her he said, "Let me hold you?"

Advancing towards him, Katie smiled sweetly, screening him adoringly, their eyes locked, unblinking. Then Katie spoke slowly, accentuating, "*Get dressed and get the fuck out of my face.* I don't ever want to see you again." Stepping aside, Katie marched out of the kitchen with the bottle of wine in one hand and a glass in the other, slamming the door violently behind her.

CHAPTER 10

Saturday, at six in the morning, Amy waited around Heathrow airport in the vicinity of the airline check-in desk where she'd arranged to meet Mike. She paced back and forth, looked left and right, keeping a watchful eye. Her cell-phone rang. She glanced at the screen and reluctantly accepted the call.

"Have a great girlie weekend won't you honey and send my regards to Rochelle," said Jenson.

That was it with Jenson. He was so easy, Amy thought. She'd told him how she'd come to be in possession of the free trip and that she'd be traveling with a colleague. She hadn't specifically stated that it would be Rochelle. Not very astute at the best of times, Jenson had jumped to that conclusion himself. He trusted her, rarely questioned her and took her word for granted on virtually everything. He'd seldom go over anything she said. Lately, he'd told her that he'd considered himself lucky to be dating the likes of her, a city corporate executive. He'd said she was refinement, finesse, different, discreet, in a class of her own, nothing like the other women who were constantly throwing themselves at him, lustfully in want of his body and a piece of his semi-celebrity status as DJ and national radio show host. "Thank you, Jenson."

"Amsterdam's also a place for lovers. Maybe we can plan a weekend trip of our own when you get back?" said Jenson, amorously.

"Sure," said Amy. Mike was running late. Amy had checked in over half an hour ago. According to her estimation, check-in would be shutting down in fifteen to twenty minutes. Amy wandered into the main concourse area and checked the screens. The flight to Amsterdam would be boarding in twenty minutes and the gate was due to close in forty minutes. "Jenson, I'm about to board," she told him, anxiously desperate to end the call.

"Yes, I know. I can hear the usual airport pandemonium in the background taking place. Have a safe trip, honey."

"Thanks," she said, clicking off and hurrying over to the airline attendants standing at the enquiry desk. "Excuse me. Would it be possible to find out whether a colleague of mine, his name is Mike Brandleton, has checked-in or not?"

"Certainly." The airline attendant keyed in the details taken from the itinerary Amy had handed to her. "No. He's not checked in I'm afraid. Sorry."

"Are you sure?"

"Yes I am. Now, would you excuse me, I've other things to do," said the airline attendant curtly.

"Could you delay closing the gate for at least another five to ten minutes?" Amy demanded.

"You say this is a colleague of yours?"

"Yes. And why do you ask?"

"You seem to be quite concerned," said the airline attendant.

"And, what are you implying?"

"I'm not implying anything. You just seem to be overly concerned."

Fuming, Amy stamped her foot, took a deep breath and told herself to stay calm. Snatching the itinerary out of the airline attendant's hand, Amy marched off to call Mike on his cell-phone. She listened to his voicemail prompts in annoyance. Resignedly, Amy entertained the thought of possibly flying to Amsterdam alone should Mike prove to be a no show when, by chance, she spotted him racing through the automatic doors towards the check-in desk, looking superb, wearing a pair of smart casual blue slacks, matching blue shirt and a white PGA golf cap. With overwhelming relief and joy, Amy ran over to meet him. "Mike, you've made it, at last," she said, breathlessly placing the itinerary and travel documents on the check-in counter.

The airline attendant rushed over to the check-in desk. "Is he the colleague you've been waiting for?" asked the airline attendant, hastily checking them in, radioing their luggage onto the flight.

"Yes," said Amy proudly. Amy caught the airline attendant admirably eyeing Mike. Her eyes slowly wandered all over his body from head to toe.

"You're in luck. You've ample time to get to the gate. You'd better run on ahead. I'll notify the team at the other end that you're on your way. Quick, you'll need to clear security."

Amy turned and smiled apologetically at the airline attendant saying, "Thanks for rushing us through."

"My pleasure. Mr. Brandleton would not have been able to check-in without the eticket—that you had in your possession." said the airline attendant, smiling in armistice.

Amy said nothing as she rushed through the airport with Mike, successfully clearing security.

"I'm sorry. I had an unavoidable delay," said Mike.

"Don't worry about it. Let's just board the flight."

"Yes, you're right," said Mike, sprinting on ahead of Amy to the departure lounge.

"Welcome to the Woedenberg Hotel Mr. and Mrs. Scott. Your passports please?" said the reservations clerk. The Woedenberg Hotel (Veedenberg) was conveniently located in a peaceful area in Leidseplein, a few minutes outside the city centre of Amsterdam.

"Actually, it's Miss Scott and Mr. Brandleton?" Amy pointed out.

The reservations clerk bade them a smile, the type of smile normally reserved for customers, pulled out a sheet and ran her finger down a list. "Yes, I see it here. The booking is in the lead name of Scott. Ah, yes, I see the discrepancy now. I'll have to make a few minor adjustments. May I ask you to complete these forms, please? It's mandatory that visitors complete the forms, a requirement of the Dutch government." said the reservations clerk, handing them each a small sheet of paper. Mike and Amy quickly filled in their details. "Your room is on the third floor. Enjoy your stay," said the reservations clerk, handing the passports to Amy, hotel paraphernalia and two swipe cards for room entry. The bellboy took their luggage and directed them to the elevator.

"I need to get out of these clothes," said Amy, catching a glimpse of her reflection in the mirrored elevator.

"We can go out on a leisurely stroll once you've changed. Do some browsing around," said Mike.

"Yes. And a lot more. We've got plenty of time to really pack the day. It's approaching ten," said Amy, checking her watch as she stepped out of the elevator. They were met by the obsequious bellboy and quietly followed him along the hushed passageway covered in deep pink, plush carpeting and dark wood paneled walls to their room. The bellboy swiped the door which opened to a fairly luxurious, deluxe room housing a King-sized bed.

"The room is of a pleasingly acceptable standard," Mike commented, nodding in approval. He walked around and inspected the en-suite shower and bathroom, closets, furniture, windows and balcony. Visibly comfortable, he

golf hat on the bed, found the remote control and switched on the
r tipping the bellboy hovering in the doorway, Amy unpacked and
took a quick shower. She heard the roar of cheering cricket fans blasting from
the TV and Mike cheering along with them. His team is obviously at an advantage, Amy thought. She emerged from the shower, pulled on a pair of Versace
jeans and a crispy white t-shirt and spent ten minutes lingering around the
hotel room bored, waiting for the cricket match to end. "Ready?" she asked.

"Yes," said Mike, fixated to the TV.

"You're quite at liberty to remain here," Amy joked.

Mike grabbed the remote control and switched off the TV. "No, I'd rather
we hit the streets."

Amy paraded on the steps of the Woedenberg Hotel and basked in the warm,
bright sunshine. "Left, right or right on ahead?" she said, slipping on a pair of
Chanel sunglasses.

"Shall we cross the street and head for the park?" asked Mike.

"Right, into the park it is," answered Amy, jumping playfully off the steps. A
green metal signpost read Vondelpark in gold lettering at the park's entrance.
Mike and Amy entered and strolled along the footpath teeming with tourists
and the Dutch alike. They found amusement in a bunch of young lads who'd
speedily raced along on roller skates, crisscrossing, performing athletically
impressive stunts. Cyclists rode along the allotted bike paths on tandems, tricy-
cles, bikes with baby-seats and shopping basket attachments. Children played,
lovers kissed and frolicked and picnics were had on the grass.

Mike alerted Amy's attention to a woman pushing an unusual perambula-
tor stacked with three screaming babies. "Look at that. What on earth's that
thing she's pushing?" he asked, laughingly.

Amy giggled.

"More like shoving, you mean! Looks like a puppet theatre on wheels. We
are cruel," said Amy.

"No harm done. She didn't hear us. Look! There's some activity down there.
It's some kind of cafeteria. I could do with a drink," said Mike, quickening his
pace, advancing to the open air café, filled with tables and chairs scattered
around. None were vacant. People formed an assortment of disorderly queues
for ice cream, snacks, hot and cold beverages, the bar and the women's rest
rooms. A queue for the men's rest rooms was virtually non-existent. Whatever
the establishment and whatever the country, Amy wondered why men's rest

rooms seldom suffered the agony of long queues. The subject took her a few seconds to figure out the obvious.

"I could murder a sparkling water," she said, joining the queue at the bar.

"Where shall we sit? It's far too noisy around here. On the grass?"

"Yes. I much prefer that idea," said Amy. The queue moved steadily. Amy purchased two bottles of sparkling spring water and followed Mike. He weaved through the crowded tables out of the packed open air cafe and onto the expanse of grass. Mike nestled in the shade under one of the Elm trees dotted along the tree lined park.

"Ah—this is nice," said Mike.

Making the most of the space, Amy sprawled out freely, legs fully stretched out in front of her. She leaned back propped up on her elbows. The Elm leaves warmed in the late morning sunlight and gently flittered in the subtle breeze. It had finally hit home to Amy that she had Mike to herself, completely, utterly, totally and unequivocally. Tossing her head backwards, Amy tingled at the thought of romancing Mike. Wonderful, she thought.

"I'd like to do some shopping later. I've seen something on the website that I'd like you to wear for me over the weekend. Would you mind?" Mike peered straight ahead of him.

"Not at all," said Amy, accommodatingly. Stunned at the idea, Amy was also honored. Speculating, she hoped that it would be a garment made from PVC or leather. No bondage or sadomasochistic gear. There was one subject she had to get to the bottom of. "You believe that I'm the best person for this?" she said, eyeing the distant expression on Mike's face, which she couldn't quite read or place.

"Yes, you most certainly are."

"I had it in mind to buy something memorable for you. Something you could take home with you, to put on display."

"Thank you," said Mike, smiling warmly.

"And what would you tell your other half when she sees my gift?"

Mike paused. Amy waited.

"What else would I say other than the fact that it is a gift from a friend?" said Mike staunchly.

"Let's cut the crap," said Amy, lying on her back, running her fingers along the shaded blades of grass.

Visibly stunned, Mike managed a contorted smile. "I don't quite copy. Crap? What are you inferring?"

Gazing up at the small clouds floating across the romantic blue sky, Amy nibbled the tip of a long reed. "I want real conversation from now on, Mike. Agreed?"

Mike shifted awkwardly. "Then, talk to me," he said, smiling faintly.

"When exactly are you getting married?" asked Amy, pangs of jealousy surging through her.

"That bothers you, does it? I'd rather not discuss it but, as you've mentioned it." Mike's faint smile contorted and metamorphosed into an ugly grimace, delaying his response. Amy gave him all the time he needed. "Erica's a friend of the family. We grew up together. She's the daughter of my father's best friend. Our fathers went to Eton together."

"I see," said Amy, painfully braving the news, feeling an inferiority complex. A glutton for punishment and unprepared for the news, Amy's feelings of jealousy, inferiority and insecurity intensified. But she wanted to know everything, regardless. "You're childhood sweethearts?"

"No. That, we are most certainly not," Mike refuted.

Amy sat up alertly. "No? I don't understand."

"I've got to marry her, set a date for the engagement whether I like it or not. I'm being pressured into this marriage, some life long promise or pact made between our fathers—it goes way back, the pact is years old."

"I see," said Amy again, although she didn't. It wasn't clear. It was all too mysterious, as mysterious as Mike.

"I need to stretch my legs," said Mike, leaping onto his feet.

Amy leapt up and flicked grass off her jeans and t-shirt. The subject on hold, Amy turned her mind to things of a more pleasant nature. It was a beautiful morning and she didn't want to be the one to ruin the moment and, despite the shroud of mystery surrounding Mike's engagement, Amy was determined to have enormous fun. "Where to now?" she said with a ring of excitement in her voice.

"Shopping. We can take the tram to the centre," said Mike.

Mike and Amy hopped off the tram in the centre of Amsterdam. Like excited school children, they roamed in and out of an endless emporium of shops. On sale was every conceivable and inconceivable adult only gadgetries, toys, sex aids and lingerie.

"Mike, take a look at this!" Amy held up a life-size, blown-up male doll, complete with pubic hair.

Mike howled with laughter. "Over here," he said. Mike took Amy by the hand and marched her over to his exciting discovery, luring customers.

"Wow. Now, that smells like the real thing. Read the packaging, it states, deliciously fruit flavored condoms," said Amy. "Oh, my gosh. Look at this, pink champagne and chocolate flavors!"

"Try one. Go on. I dare you. Taste one of the testers … here," said Mike, coaxing Amy.

"No thanks. I'm not hungry. You try one?" she said giggling, backing away from him. She caught Mike attempting to place a chocolate flavored tester under her nose. Her attentions distracted by another display a few feet away, Amy turned her head in a double-take. "They're not!" she exclaimed in disbelief, nudging Mike.

"Oh yes they are." he said in pantomime style, laughingly.

Amy advanced closer to the display. "I've got to get a closer look at this," she said. The shelves were stocked with candles in a variety of sizes and colors ranging from pink, blue, brown, red, multi-colored and glittered. Amy gawked at the lit candles. The flames flickered and the wax flowed.

"Would you like one?" said Mike.

Laughing, Amy shot Mike a quirky glance. "Twelve inch penis candles are not my forte," she said

"Excuse me, sir," Mike called out to one of the sales staff.

"Don't you dare," Amy scowled under her breath.

"I'd like to …"

Amy raced out of the store and blindly darted into the store next door. A strange smell emanated from the packed café situated at the back of the store, an unfamiliar smell that reeked of burning grass. Scrutinizing one of the varied artifacts on display, Amy couldn't decide the nature of the store she'd darted into and was freely wandering around in, whether it was a museum, café and art gallery all rolled into one.

"There you are. I thought I'd lost you," said Mike, clearly relieved and out of breath.

Deliberately ignoring Mike's concerns, Amy deflected his attentions to the various artifacts she'd observed. A sail cloth attached to the remains of a purportedly ancient sail boat, in particular. "I'd no idea Hemp was also used in this manner in historical times. I'm intrigued. Read this," said Amy, pointing to the descriptive and historical information printed on a placard that hung on the wall alongside the sail cloth.

"Um … Yes." Nondescript, Mike skimmed through the information. "When you're quite finished," he said. Amy sensed his disinterest. "I'd spotted a wine store a couple of shops away after you'd scampered," Mike continued.

"I didn't want to be seen with you buying those, those … candles," Amy joked.

"What? The cock candles? You weren't embarrassed were you? Surely not!"

"Oh Mike, dick candles, penis candles, willy candles, ding-a-ling candles whatever, let's go." Amy shivered, flash backs of her escapade on Mike's lap in Candies infused her mind.

"No harm in having a bit of fun," Mike teased, "We're going to have more fun, savoring a good bottle of wine tonight."

"Good, why not," said Amy. She kept in close step with Mike walking briskly out of the shop and into the wine store. A novelty shop in close proximity caught Amy's eye.

"Take your time. I'll be browsing around over there whilst you make your wine selection," said Amy.

"I'm not in the habit of tendering wine in haste. I'll browse at my leisure." said Mike profoundly, strolling slowly around the wine store, reading the labels on the wine bottles as though they were fine pieces of literary. Amy wandered into the novelty store for the discerning tourist. She flicked through a selection of postcards and felt it was hardly worth mailing to anyone, as she'd have returned to the UK days before delivery of the cards to the recipients. Pairs of handmade ornamental wooden clogs colorfully painted with intricate floral and windmill designs, hung on a stand-alone display. Tempted to purchase a couple, Amy decided against taking gifts back to the UK. Her weekend in Amsterdam wasn't common knowledge, save for Richard and Jenson, and she hadn't informed Katie. Retracting, Amy selected two pairs of ornamental clogs, a pair for Katie and herself. "These, please?" she muttered to the counter staff. Amy left the store pleased with her gift wrapped purchases and wandered back into the wine store.

Mike hoisted a bottle of red wine at her. "Chateau Larrivet Haut-Brion. Not had one of these lately," he said decisively, wandering over to the cashier. Amy strolled out of the store and waited for Mike outside. Mike emerged reading a piece of unfolded paper he'd fished out of his back pants pocket.

"What are you reading?" enquired Amy.

"A map. I'm trying to pinpoint the location of a particular shop." Mike moved off briskly to the right. "Ah, we should be walking in this direction, if my navigational skills serve me well."

"You've come prepared. What shop are you hoping to find?"

"Ah hah," Mike joked, leaving Amy to wonder.

Amy shrugged her shoulders. "OK. I'll gladly traipse and trundle along."

A Dutch windmill crystal paperweight on display in a shop window caught Mike's eye. He pressed his nose against the shop's window. "That's unusual," he said.

"Yes, it is" said Amy, peering through the shop window. "It's pretty and quite ingeniously crafted. Shall we pop inside?"

"And why not. After you," said Mike, holding the door open.

Inside, the store was quieter than most. Mozart's exquisite symphony number 40 in G minor played in the background. Mike and Amy were met by a plump, white haired, red faced elderly man slouched behind the counter.

"Can I help you?"

"Yes please. We'd like to look at the windmill crystal paperweight in the window," said Amy indicatively, carefully quiet and polite. The elderly man slowly got out of the seat, shuffled over to the window and unlocked the door of the window display. His hands trembled as he placed the paperweight on the counter, reflecting a prismatic spectrum of rainbow-like colors around the store. "Beautiful," said Amy, admiringly.

"Very nice," said Mike, casually nodding.

"I'll take it," said Amy, rummaging threw her handbag. Mike casually wandered around the store prospectively browsing the vast array of silver engraved snuff boxes, enamel pill boxes, pipes and pipe holders.

"Thank you for your custom," said the elderly man, his hands trembling as he handed the small bag to Amy.

"Are we ready?" said Mike, standing at the shop door patiently waiting.

"Yes," Amy answered brightly. "By the way, this is for you," she said, as they left the store.

Mike stopped walking. His eyes fell on Amy in disbelief. "Thank you," he murmured, taking the bag. They walked for what seemed to be an endless fifteen minutes, the time it took to locate the store Mike had been searching for, stopping a pedestrian only once to ask for directions in the warm and sticky heat of a progressively glorious sunny day. The air conditioning cooled Amy as she followed Mike into a lingerie boutique. A sales assistant eagerly approached them.

"Can I help you?" asked the sales assistant.

"No. We're just looking, thank you," said Mike, waving the sales assistant out of his midst.

"We have a His and Hers collection if you'd care to come this way," suggested the sales assistant unabatedly, keen to secure a sale.

"No, thank you. I'm quite capable of finding my way around," said Mike adamantly. He picked up a white leather teddy thong complete with gold chains. "What's your size? Would these fit?" Mike asked Amy.

Bracing herself, Amy raised her eyebrows and took a deep breath. "A size twelve should do it," she said.

Mike fiddled inside the garment in search of the label depicting the size. "This is your size."

"Good," said Amy, taking the teddy to the dressing room.

"This way, madam," said the sales assistant, closely following Amy. "Should you need me, I'll be right outside."

Staring at herself in the full length mirror, harnessed in a private moment, Amy slowly revisited the transformation an item of clothing can make. She looked and felt absolutely fantastic and sexy in the tiny teddy that fitted her like a glove, enhancing her curves, tightening her waist, bolstering her bust, the distinctive designer high cut lengthening her legs. She tiptoed out of the dressing room.

"You look a picture," said Mike, standing back. "Turn around let me see you at every angle."

Amy strut an elegant pose. Sales staff and a few patrons gawked at her. Not accustomed to the attention that she was now drumming up, Amy began to feel uncomfortable and embarrassed.

"A pair of white, fish net, hold-up stockings will go quite nicely," said Mike.

"Please, I'd like to take it off now," Amy whispered to Mike.

"Of course, go ahead." Amy hurriedly scuttled back to the dressing room.

"A fresh teddy from stock, please? And a pair of white, fish net hold-up stockings? A medium size would be about right." Amy overhead Mike place the order and preparing to purchase the items. Her pulses raced as she wondered what adventures were in store over the weekend. She'd never had such an experience with any other man. Her world would constantly shift, change and evolve as long as Mike remained in her life. She slipped out of the dressing room.

"One more shop and I'm done with shopping for the day," said Mike.

"Another shop?" asked Amy, exasperated.

"This won't take long," said Mike reassuringly, consulting his map again. "In fact, it's close by, and besides, I could do with another long, cool drink," he said, swinging the shopping bags as he departed the store. He entered a pub,

went straight over to the bar, ordered a pint of Danish lager, a gla—
water with a slice of lemon and headed out to the beer garden. "This is a —
spot," he said, settling on a wooden bench. Amy sat, facing Mike, on the bench
opposite. Mike sipped his Danish lager. "What's on the agenda tonight?" Mike
quizzed.

"You tell me! I hadn't planned anything, I must confess. Spontaneity is the
name of the game on this trip, I'm afraid," said Amy, tossing her head back and
slipping off her Chanel sunglasses.

"Good. That's what I like to hear," said Mike, relaxing in silence, spending
the next half hour people watching as he basked in the glorious sun.

I'm becoming a dab hand at this game now, Amy thought, twirling around the
shop floor, modeling a floor length, figure hugging black leather dress.

"A divine fit," said Mike, throwing on a black leather jacket.

"Now, that fits you superbly," said Amy.

Mike strode over to Amy across the leather boutique's highly varnished
Mahogany floor and pressed against her whispering, "Remember, I love the
feel of leather rubbing."

"How can I forget?" Hot from rubbing leather, Amy retreated to the dressing room. Eavesdropping, Amy felt guilty overhearing the cashier loudly stating that the cost of Mike's transaction, a black leather suit and her dress, had
totaled over two thousand euros. Mike wouldn't have spent hoards of cash had
it not been for her invitation, she thought. "I'll take one of those bags," Amy
offered, emerging from the dressing room, swiftly grabbing a bag before Mike
had time to decline her offer.

"If you insist." said Mike, obligingly, strolling out of the store, triumphantly.
With a complete outfit and underwear to boot, Amy found it hard to imagine
what Mike had in store for her over the weekend.

"We'll take the shopping back to the hotel, change, go out to dinner and
maybe visit a nightclub or two. How does that sound for spontaneity?" said
Mike.

"Great," responded Amy, vacantly.

"Or, would you have any other ideas in mind?"

"Oh no, Mike, you go right on ahead, you're giving me less to think about,
honestly," she said, knowing that Mike preferred to take charge.

"Good."

Back at the hotel, Amy massaged her aching feet. "We did some serious walking today. How many hours were we on our feet out there? Five hours or so?"

"Yes, about that," said Mike, arranging the dress, teddy and fish net hold up stockings neatly on the bed. He hung his black leather suit on the closet door and took a shower. Amy showered quickly after Mike and slipped on the new garments.

Fully dressed, suavely adorning the leather suit Mike said, "You are breathtakingly beautiful," He filled a glass of Chateau Larrivet Haut-Brion wine and handed it to Amy.

Amy sipped daintily. "Delicious," she said, giving Mike the thumbs up. She indulged in savoring the taste, although her knowledge of wine bordered on the very miniscule. She glanced at Mike. He didn't appear to be in any hurry. In fact, he appeared to have slowed down the pace now that they were dressed for the evening.

"Take another sip," he said.

Amy duly complied. The more she drank, the more delicious the wine. "This is magnificent wine, Mike."

"Yes, it is special," he said, topping up her glass. He moved closer and pecked her on the cheek. "Drink more," he coaxed.

"Hey, you too," Amy laughed.

Mike sipped his wine then, gently took the wine glass out of Amy's hand and placed both glasses on the side table. Leaning and rubbing against Amy, Mike pecked her forehead, eye-lids, cheeks, and nibbled at her ear lobes. Her body heat rose sharply to the sensuousness of Mike's kisses and the rubbing of leather. He pulled Amy's zipper down and pressed his fingers on the small of her back. He assisted Amy in pulling the dress down to her ankles. Then, Mike stood back. "Step out of the dress for me and, slowly," Mike calmly instructed. Amy stepped out of the dress crumpled in a heap around her ankles. I need more wine, she thought, feeling vulnerably self-conscious standing before Mike in the teddy and stockings. "You're a picture," said Mike breathlessly. He held her in his arms and lifted her onto the bed. He removed his jacket with a helping hand from Amy. They rolled around the bed kissing, groaning and moaning in pleasure. Mike broke the links, ripped the chains from the teddy, stroked her, and entered her, surprisingly. Amy gasped and gushed in ecstasy, arching her spine, wrapping her legs round Mike's waist, tightly gripping his body. Mike winced and groaned. He gripped the tops of her stockings, slowly pulled them down to her thighs. Amy compatibly grappled with the strenuous movements of Mike's passion-filled body. Opening his shirt, he pressed his torso against her in growing and heightened passion. His hot flesh and soft skin took Amy to the edge of mindless pleasure. Feelings of love and lust for Mike trickled through her whole being. Thrusting, she hoped he felt the same way about her too. They were compatible. She gave him her all, making sure he'd never forget this moment. Never. Ever.

Mike slept whilst Amy remained awake holding him tenderly in her arms, running her fingers through his sleek black hair, listening to his breathing, feeling the rhythmic pulsations of his heartbeat. Amsterdam was known to come alive at night and, Amy wanted to experience the night life, although she was having the time of her life, laying there with Mike asleep in her arms. Another ten minutes had gone by when Mike eventually stirred. He awoke, pecked Amy on her cheek, got up and moved around the hotel room, selecting a smart and casual outfit from the closet before taking a shower. Amy steadily raised her body off the bed. Her muscles ached. She felt like she'd endured a twenty-four hour workout. Mentally perking herself up and putting on a brave face, Amy forcibly moved around the room with agility, selecting a smart green, tight pants suit for the evening then slipped into the shower when Mike had done. Mike, dressed and ready, sat back in the armchair and leisurely drank the remainder of wine he'd left in his glass. Reclining the armchair, Mike silently waited for Amy to complete her finishing touches. "Now, where were we before we got so rudely sidetracked?"

"Nightlife?" said Amy.

The woman in the large picture window stared back glaringly at Amy with eyes that read, *"Who do you think you are? You're no better than me. I hate doing this shit. I need the money."*

Amy felt compassion for the woman in the notorious red light district, her body, well groomed, poised alluringly in a yellow and elegantly revealing mini negligee, delicately accentuated with soft ruffled feathering around the neck and cuffs. All the women Amy viewed along the alleys appeared to have enjoyed their expediencies. Amy opined that the woman in the yellow negligee, the most beautiful by far, clearly hadn't. Tall, owning exotic features, caramel colored skin, Amy had difficulty in pinpointing her origin. Men ogled at her, fantasizing. The woman stepped down from her high chair prop, stepped towards the window and fixated her eyes on Amy. *"Who, the fuck, are you looking at? You're no better than I."*

Determined, Amy locked her eyes on the woman's gaze in the hope that she'd detect that Amy was merely viewing her in admiration of her beauty, not in revulsion, mockery, judgment or disdain. *You won't be doing this for much longer. It'll be over soon. It won't be long before it's all in the past,* Amy's eyes vowed. Amy bowed her head slightly and felt a wrench in her gut as the woman abruptly and swiftly closed the curtains, blocking Amy out. Stunned, Amy lowered her eyes and looked down at her feet.

"What are you waiting for? She won't be back for at least twenty minutes," said Mike.

"How would you know that?" enquired Amy, suspicious of Mike's knowledge.

Mike continued on further up the bustling alley. "Closed curtains signify that she's got a punter and the curtains will reopen once she's taken care of business."

"Oh," exclaimed Amy ominously, stomach grumbling from the effects of eating a large portion of chips and mayonnaise walking along the bustling streets thronging with tourists mingling with Amsterdammers. She regretted agreeing to the daring decision to waiver the civility of fine wine and dining that evening in favor of chips and mayonnaise.

Sex sells, thought Amy observing the amount of sex aid merchandise being sold at the variety of shops and assorted establishments packed with people purchasing the products, furtive favors and services.

"This looks interesting," said Mike. He stopped suddenly in his tracks and peered through the square glass window of a bar. "Shall we give this place a try?" It was the only bar that had umpapa, umpapa sing-a-long music bursting out of the steamy windows.

"Yeah. Great," said Amy inquisitively, taking position behind Mike, arms wrapped round his waist, shuffling into the crammed bar to a confined space. It was hot, dark, steamy and loud inside. The crowd sang loudly in Dutch to the umpapa, umpapa beat which made a welcoming change to the mainstream sound of techno, house, garage, reggae, R&B, rock and pop that was streaming out of most of the establishments. Amy amusingly picked up the beats and hummed and swayed along with the crowd to the simple melodies. Each song sounded exactly the same as the previous one. Umpapa. Umpapa. Mike followed suit waving his pewter tankard in the air along with the crowd, mimicking them, splashing and spilling his Dutch brewed ale in the process, which he miraculously managed to purchase amid the furor. Punters, who had no way of getting to the bar, gave their orders to waiters, paying them in advance in return for a metal disc with large white numbers painted in white which the punters held in the air until they'd received their corresponding drinks order. Amy watched in awe the mechanics of barmen mounted on raised platforms behind the bar, ingeniously distributing filled pewter tankards overhead ~~that were~~ slotted in a ring at the end of long poles to the thirsty punters whose disc numbers matched the numbers on the pewter tankards. The noise levels were at a high pitch, drawing in people to an already overcrowded bar. No words were needed between Mike and Amy, their eyes and radiant expressions of enjoyment sufficed. Amy felt giddy from the wonderment of it all. Half an hour, four songs and Mike's empty pewter tankard later, Amy's ears throbbed and hissed to the crowds' endlessly loud cheers and singing to the high volume of music. Having had her enjoyment for the day, Amy wanted to head back to the hotel, but was conscious about not ruining Mike's night. They'd been on the move non-stop since their arrival. Testing, Amy made an eye gesture towards the exit and Mike acquiesced. Amy tightly held Mike's arm. He tugged and pushed through the crush of people as he headed to the exit. Outside, Amy deeply inhaled the night air. A welcoming and cooling breeze swept across her face.

"Fancy dancing tonight?" said Mike.

Amy's heart sank for a second on the looming prospect of having to find energy to go dancing and cope with another deafeningly loud and noisy venue. "Yes, why not," she said, wondering what had gotten into Mike as he performed a jig along the street ahead of her singing, "umpapa, umpapa. Only joking," he said, laughingly. "Oh, Mike," Amy stared at Mike adoringly, "you are funny. I'm having an immensely enjoyable time with you," she said, grabbing Mike playfully by the arm.

"Hotel?" said Mike.

"Yes please," said Amy relieved.

Mike wrapped a protective arm around her shoulders and, pushing any unwanted thoughts of home at the back of their minds, for the time being, at least, they set off on the long walk back to the hotel singing umpapa, umpapa to the tops of their voices, laughingly sharing their elevated happiness that cities like Amsterdam made possible, enabling them to limitlessly enjoy and indulge, openly and freely, without any restrictions, judgments or constraints, whatsoever.

"It's nothing serious … it's a casual affair." Amy felt a little uncomfortable being in the hot seat at eight o'clock on a Sunday morning in June, in bed, in a hotel room in Amsterdam with a man she hardly knew, convinced she was slowly but surely, falling in love with. It was her turn. Fair's fair, she'd put Mike through a similar question and answer session the day before and had every intention of revisiting the subject at a later stage.

"How long have you known him?"

"Not very long. A year, I think. Not really given the length of time much thought, really." Amy was doing her utmost best to convince Mike that Jenson was not an important factor in her life.

"Do you return to him when you get back today?"

"No. It is not that type of a relationship. I probably won't see him for a couple of days," said Amy, knowing full well that Jenson would be at her apartment, waiting for her with open arms. "My head's killing me," said Amy agonizingly, perching on the edge of the bed.

Mike sprang to his feet. "Relax. Lie back. Here, let me help you." He rummaged through his travel bag, pulled out a packet of pain killers, poured Amy a small glass of bottled mineral water and placed two capsules in the palm of her hand. "These should do the trick," Mike reassured her.

Amy accepted the pain killers. Mike's caring quality had an impressionable impact on her, intensifying her need to keep hold of him, not let him easily slip through her fingers. He's worth pitching for, she thought, swallowing the pain killers, lying back and resting her head on the pillows.

"Get some rest. I'm going to breakfast."

"OK, Mike. I'm sorry I couldn't join you for breakfast right now."

"No need to apologize. Get some rest," he said, shutting the door quietly as he left the room.

The painkillers took ten minutes to ease the throbbing head pains. Almost refreshed, Amy got out of bed, had a shower and hurried to the breakfast room in the hope that she'd have at least five to ten minutes of cherished moments with Mike during breakfast. She'd pack later. Sat hunched-back at the table in the corner of the breakfast room, staring gloomily and blankly ahead, Mike was a sorry sight, Amy observed. He hadn't noticed that Amy had been watching him for five minutes from a safe distance prior to joining him. He remained motionless staring into space, slouched like a man with problems of the entire world on his head and shoulders. It was hard to imagine what thoughts were burdening his soul. Amy crept over to the breakfast table. "Hi," Amy whispered sheepishly, sitting opposite him.

"You've made it," said Mike, dazzled by her surprised appearance.

"Yes, I'm feeling much better now, thanks to you," she said, pausing for a moment. "Is there anything wrong? Only you appear to look a little withdrawn?"

"Just putting a few matters into perspective, really. I've got a lot to do when I get back to the UK."

As far as Amy was concerned, Mike was in denial and not very good at hiding the guilt riddled look of having cheated on his fiancé written all over his face. The table settings remained clean and untouched. Mike hadn't had any breakfast since he'd left their hotel room.

"I've worked up quite an appetite. I'm famished. Can I get you a coffee?" Amy urged tactfully.

"No. The waiter will be coming round with fresh coffee soon. I've turned him down twice already."

"Order a fresh orange juice for me would you please, Mike, once the waiter re-emerges? Thanks." Amy left the breakfast table, served herself an ample bowl of tropical fresh fruit salad from the buffet, returned to the table and ate in reflective silence, waiting for the day to move on to a happier note. "What shall we do today? We've a few hours before we leave for the airport?" Amy sipped a tall glass of freshly squeezed orange juice the waiter had poured.

"We could head for the park again. I could do with some relaxation, I hardly slept a wink last night," Mike revealed. Unbeknownst to Amy, Mike had spent most of the night awake. He'd watched her sleep, immersed in the joy and the lasting effects of having made passionate and exciting love to her in the shower, massaging her, smearing her with a range of Egyptian oils he'd conveniently brought along with him, delighting her. The appreciative sounds of her sweet groans rippled through him and would remain with him forever. Her beautiful baby pink, silk panties, trimmed with silk satin ribbons she'd worn to bed had aroused him. Ravishing her, he'd gotten carried away and had ripped the panties when he'd applied a little too much force removing them. He'd promised her that, as a compensatory measure, he'd purchase her the most luxurious panties from Victoria's Secret and have them delivered to her apartment.

"Sure," said Amy, in response to Mike's suggestion that they vacate their room after breakfast. Any had hoped there would be enough time to mark the end of their weekend by way of a short, romantic pleasure trip, sailing along the River Amstel. After breakfast, they returned to the room and packed their bags. Amy was beginning to feel slightly nervous and edgy as Mike remained in the quiet state, a state she hoped wouldn't go on for the entire day. She thought he'd

enjoyed himself the night before, that she'd given him yet another unforgettable session of love making that a man would've willingly died for. So, what was
his bloody problem? Their flight was due to depart at seven that evening and
she didn't want to endure this spell of silence all day. Amy banked on Mike
perking up once they'd checked out of the hotel. Inhaling the fresh air, taking
in the park's beauty and feeling its ambience, Amy believed would culminate in
altering his mood, if not she'd have to come up with something. Amy had
noticed that Mike hadn't packed the white leather teddy and black leather dress
in his baggage and smiled as she tossed them in her weekend case.

"I'll call room service to inform them that our bags are ready for collection,"
said Mike, locking his weekend carry case.

Amy thanked Mike and dropped her bags on the floor alongside his as she
left the room. Mike remained silent at the check out desk. Checking out of the
hotel was simple enough, lasting all of five minutes. The reservations clerk was
satisfied that there were no additional expenses incurred and confirmed that
the cost of the room would be borne by the promotions company sponsoring
the trip.

"A courtesy car has been arranged to take you to the airport at four o'clock,"
the reservations clerk informed Amy.

"Please, may we have our bags stored in a room for safe keeping for the
day?"

"Certainly," said the reservations clerk.

Amy thanked the reservations clerk and tucked a copy of the hotel receipt in
her Versace hold-all.

"You'd caught me off track. Erica had called several times, pestering me and I'd
thought you were her, calling me again," responded Mike, sipping a tall glass of
orange juice with crushed ice. There were a lot of things that needed clarifying
and Amy attempted to clarify them all. They were sitting in the sun around a
wrought iron, green table they'd luckily found outside one of Vondelpark's
packed bars. Mike had bought Amy a sparkling water with a slice of fresh
lemon. Emerging from his spell of silence, Mike explained the reason behind
his cold reception the day Amy had called him at the office inviting him to
Amsterdam. "Erica had things to discuss. Neither was it the right time nor the
place. I was extremely busy. And when you'd called, I wanted you to be brief
with whatever it was you had to say and, thankfully you were," said Mike,
vaguely answering Amy's question.

"Discuss things? What things?"

"We're not getting on very well and … I'd rather not go into that right now," said Mike, clearly agitated adding, "Erica's great as a family friend and, I wholeheartedly believe that we weren't meant to be partners. She adores me … quite obsessively really, it's worrying."

Amy drifted. She needed a little time to come to terms with the information. Somehow, she had to let Mike know that she adored him too. But how? It was worth a try. The prospect of Erica becoming his wife due to the pact made between their fathers made her skin crawl that she began to mentally prepare for the grief and loss she'd undoubtedly experience on inevitably having to let go of Mike indefinitely. "How much do you know about the pact? What does it actually mean?" asked Amy, earnestly.

"Quiet frankly, our fathers built their empires from scratch. My father's an hotelier and Erica's, a financier. They'd helped one another, scratched each others backs, if you like, laying foundations, putting all the components, fundamentals and mechanisms in place long before they'd finished Eton. They'd collated the required information, researched their businesses and sealed many influential contacts that the foundations for success were in place, set in stone, ready to make their mark on the business forum well before they'd left Eton for further study. They'd promised that they'd make it an absolute certainty that their children would be bred and groomed for the sole purpose of inheriting their businesses and wealth, bringing the families together as one through marriage. It's ludicrous if you ask me. The idea is that, the children and their off-spring would pass this nonsensical pact of theirs down the line. Here is the most ridiculous part," said Mike tersely. "This pact forms as one of the bases of their wills and testaments, carrying a clause stating that, anyone who broke the pact would forfeit their inheritance and face being ostracized. And whatever it takes, the joint names at the top of the wealth of the financier and the wealth of the hotelier should infinitely be a Brandleton and a Cunningham.

Astonished, Amy raised her eyebrows. "What if Erica was a boy? What then?" argued Amy.

"Adoption of the most carefully handpicked child," said Mike dryly. "Erica's father would have had to adopt if he couldn't bear children and vice versa."

It was valuable insight of Mike's world. The world of the rich and wealthy, creating blood lines and blood ties and family heirlooms and heritages, passed down from generation to generation, she had no idea that these lifestyles were still in existence and being fully practiced. It had clearly struck home. She didn't stand a chance in having anything realistically concrete with Mike in the love department. It was all falling into place. Mike became distant and withdrawn whenever he'd spent time with her. Having learnt more about his background and hardships surrounding Erica and the family ties, Amy refrained from asking him to explain the reason behind his disappearing act on the Sunday morning after Candies. As time went on, she'd have to figure that one out herself. Was he getting attached? Was he fighting his feelings? Was he trying to protect her? Clutching at straws, Amy premised over the idea of becoming Mike's mistress, the only option she'd envisioned a woman of her, not so quite up to standard caliber, status and life position could afford. From an ordinary working class background, she was hardly the type he could take home to meet his mother. He would obscurely drift out of her life as obscurely as he'd drifted in and Amy would shoulder all the pain as she'd done all the pursuing. None of this was Mike's fault. She imaged Erica endued with more than her fair share of beauty, leading a debutante lifestyle, spoilt and rich, never having done an honest day's work in her life, living a life of inherited wealth. A waitress noisily cleared the tables, clattering glasses, shaking Amy out of her miserable thoughts.

"Another orange juice and water, please?" Mike called out to the waitress scuttling off with a tray full of empty glasses and bottles, frantically nodding her head in acknowledgement.

"What about the PVC gear you like to wear that no-one knows about? Does Erica know?" Saying her name felt unpleasant on her tongue.

"I introduced the idea to her once which resulted in her unreasonably going into ballistics, citing that it appealed to perverts and sick minded people, adding that it would be her uncompromising duty to the family to inform them if she'd discovered that I'd spent my own personal leisure time indulging in such exploits."

"Oh, I'm sorry to hear that," said Amy.

Mike shuffled uncomfortably in his seat. "Out of all the people you could have invited to Amsterdam, you'd chosen me. I want you to know that I appreciate the invite," said Mike, spreading his arms out wide, embracing the expanse of the park. He tilted his head backwards. The sun shone directly on his face.

"Don't mention it. It's been a pleasure."

"Literally," said Mike in a sexy voice arousing Amy as she baked in the heat of the sun. Her mind conjured images of making love on the grass in the nude, just the two of them, alone in the park. Humored by his response, Amy was astoundingly happy that Mike had perked up again.

"You looked smashing that night at Candies. I hadn't known that having someone share my interests would have been so dammed enjoyable. You had no qualms about me introducing you to any of it. Had you? You enjoyed it all, did you not?"

"Yes, it was all fun," said Amy. A lump formed in her throat, stunting her from elaborating on the memorable events at Candies.

"Thank you for modeling the teddy. You looked amazing in that too. It's yours to keep, including the dress."

"Thanks. I've packed them both," said Amy quietly.

"I'd noticed … And thank you again for the paperweight which will have pride of place on my desk at the office."

The waitress left their drinks on the table. Mike sipped his orange juice. "Well, time's pressing on. Once we've finished our drinks, I suppose we'd better be heading back to the hotel, collect our bags and head for the airport when our car arrives," said Mike resultantly.

"Yes. We don't want to miss our flight now, do we?" responded Amy in finality. It was all too final. Amy was going to miss Mike, terribly. She had to shut down, not lose control. Composure. Maintain composure, she thought repeatedly, coldly shivering in the sun, picturing the unwanted aspect of falling into Jenson's open arms back in London.

CHAPTER 11

Amy ploughed herself into her work. The Del Mar casino project served as a useful obstacle and occupational measure, safeguarding her from driving herself crazy, pinning and yearning for Mike. Three weeks had elapsed since Amy's return from Amsterdam and she'd not touched based with hardly anyone in that time, but determinedly kept Jenson at bay, preferring to spend her weekends at home in solitude. Jenson had taken up being grouchy of late, accusing Amy of avoiding him since her return from Amsterdam. He'd moaned that she'd not had much to report about her weekend in Amsterdam, that she'd withheld the identity of the colleague who'd accompanied her, when he'd learned that it wasn't Rochelle, heightening his suspicions, leading him to question why she'd chosen to adopt such a notion. "I've only seen you once since you've been back, Amy." Jenson pleaded over the telephone, at eight o'clock, Saturday morning when he'd asked to come over. "Honey, you've not been the same. You've changed. What the hell happened out there? Who is this pal of yours you're not naming? If it wasn't Rochelle, then who was it? You could've told me from the beginning," he'd pressed on dejectedly.

"What are you talking about? I've not changed. I'm still the same person. You're just imaging things. I'd merely stated that I was going away with a friend. You chose to assume that it was Rochelle. Come on, Jenson, do you really and honestly expect me to mention every single Tom, Dick and Harry that passes through my life? Give me a break, honey. Pleeeese, relax. Quit belly-aching. I think you're the one who's changed not me!" said Amy, passing the buck, "Anyway, I'm working from home this weekend."

"Alright. What about next weekend?"

"That's out too."

"Why?"

"I've got to go in next weekend to assist with the set up of a data room. That's why," she said, pertinaciously. "We are completing a deal, and dedicating all the hours that God sends, and that includes weekends otherwise, non-delivery on the project will cost us millions in revenues and ..."

"OK. You win. Name the day."

Amy couldn't name a day. She was resolutely working Jenson out of her system. He'd lost his appeal and his persuasion skills had died a death. Influentially charming Amy into changing her mind from a no to a yes was progressively proving to be a lost cause. She was aware that she was becoming hard work now, work Jenson wasn't accustomed to. She knew he was accustomed to women saying yes, always, immediately or eventually to him. But Amy was an exception and she sensed Jenson's frustrations but, felt he had to learn to practice a little patience and understanding and yes, he was right, she wasn't the same, thanks to Mike

"I'll call you in a couple of days, Jenson."

"OK. I'll wait. I've no other choice, have I?" he said, hanging up. Jenson had many choices and was free to exercise them. He scoured through a contingency list on his Palm Pilot. "Cassandra, no ... Anita, maybe ... Sandra, so, so ... Bianca, all-nighter ... Jacqueline, nice. Bianca, the all-nighter. She'll do," he said out loud, calling her on his cell-phone. "Hey B, it's been a long time."

"Oh, my word! J? Is that you?" Bianca purred.

Amy was hardly able to contain her excitement.

"Very, very busy these few weeks. I'm sorry I'd not contacted you before now," said Mike.

Three weeks had gone by, three weeks exactly to the day, Amy thought. Three weeks of working long hours to distract her from agonizing over him since he'd dashed off at the UK airport when they'd returned from Amsterdam. He'd given her a quick peck on the cheek with no promises to contact her that she'd believed it was the end of her, that Mike had hurried off to assume a life of compliance with his family, conforming to marry Erica.

"In fact, I need to talk to you," said Mike, his voice trailing off solemnly.

Perking up, Amy was all ears. "Is everything OK, Mike?"

"She's trashed our apartment."

"Are you serious? You do mean, Erica? Right? Erica's trashed the apartment?" Amy was shocked and bemused as she'd no idea that Mike and Erica had been cohabitating.

"Yes. Erica. She'd called the office to discuss our relationship problems. I'd refused, which resulted in an inevitable disagreement. I got back last night, to discover that she'd trashed the place. Cups ... glasses.... plates.... All the porcelain's been smashed and strewn all over the kitchen floor ... papers ... pages ripped out of books, torn to shreds ..." Mike sighed. "There is clutter and damage everywhere. The apartment's in a complete mess. Well, there's no point going on."

"Gosh, Mike! Are you sure it was her, not a break-in, vandals, hooliganism?"

"Yes. I am certain. To top it all, she had the audacity to call me last night at a time when she knew I'd be back from the office. She started blaming me for what she'd done. She said it was my fault for calling off the engagement."

"You've definitely called off the engagement?" asked Amy, affirmatively. Her heart sang and her ears danced to the most endearing news.

"Yes, last week Saturday night, after we'd returned from a boring and ghastly dinner party my mother had laid on for the family and a few of her boring old codgers."

Amy noted his impressive calm, his exquisite handling of the stressful situation. "What are you going to do?" Amy enquired, consciously controlling her tone, mirroring Mike's.

"I'd managed to sort through some of the stuff and salvaged a few personal items. I'd stacked them in the car, drove to my parents' house in Bath last night where I've stored the items for safekeeping. On my arrival, I'd discovered that Erica had already broken the news to them. My father was extremely angry, insistent upon me rethinking my decision."

"You're in the apartment now?"

"Yes. I'd checked out of the hotel in Cumberland Place, Marble Arch this morning and returned here to continue the job of sifting through, attempting the painstaking task of putting everything back together again, somehow."

"I can't believe that you'd driven all the way to Bath and back last night."

"Yes. I did. It was worth it. And I'd booked myself into the hotel in order to detach myself from the onslaught of Erica and my parents, who were all causing so much of a fuss. I had a good night's sleep, soundly and peacefully under the auspices of my comfortable hotel room," he said. "She's got such a temper. There's so much damage here that I'm almost tempted to take out a legal writ." The sound of broken items crunching under Mike's feet, traipsing through the debris emanated down the telephone.

"Would you really go down that route?"

"No. It's no use nor is it an option. I'm more or less shot of her now and I'd like to keep it that way."

Amy had Jenson to contend with. Although her time with Jenson was going through a cooling off period, he wasn't completely out of the picture and, without doubt, Jenson was becoming an increasing worry. He had a key to her apartment. It was time to get it back and get shot of Jenson too. "What are your plans for tonight?"

"I'll remain here for the night, clear up, have it out with her when she resurfaces at some stage, let her know that I'm moving out and I'll sleep on the couch until I do."

Amy beamed widely, from ear to ear. "If you're in need of any help Mike, please call me. And if it's any consolation, you're free to use my spare bedroom until you've sorted things out."

"Thanks. That's kind, but I couldn't … You know, since our chat in Amsterdam, I knew I could count on you. And by the way, my decision is final. Calling off the engagement is definite. It's over. There'll be no going back," he said, staunchly. "I'd better be getting on, register with a few real estate agents, get some properties lined up for viewing next week. I'll call you during the week. Maybe we could do dinner?"

"Yes, I'd like that very much but, don't worry about me, take your time, we can do dinner when this has all sorted itself out."

"Shouldn't be a problem, I'm not very busy most evenings over the coming weeks. And I don't suppose viewing properties will take up an enormous amount of time."

"Whatever you say, Mike."

"Good," said Mike.

Amy continued her day reveling in the bitter sweet, replaying Mike's words over and over again in her mind. Inextricably overjoyed that the engagement was off, Amy basked in the fact that Mike had also found solace in her. His utterances revealed how much he had begun to count on her. And inviting her to dinner amid his domestic problems lifted her spirits. Amy calmed herself down, sat at the kitchen table, switched on her laptop and commenced producing a first draft document that had to be duly completed and emailed to Vincent no later than noon the following day. Dressed snugly in a long, baby-pink, silk satin kimono covered with intricate embroidery of Japanese blossoms, and baby-pink silk satin slippers, in true Planet Management style, Amy placed her elegant fingers on her keyboard and began thrashing out her contribution.

"... London, Paris and New York offices shall adopt a governance model to monitor and co-ordinate the implementation of the Pre-Closing Separation Projects, and the provision of transitional services to each other (Services). The model shall provide for regular meetings, reports and information sharing. Each party's Project Coordinator shall assume responsibility for overall co-ordination for the Pre-Closing Separation Projects ..."

Amy worked solidly throughout the day, halting briefly at five-thirty to eat a small portion of green salad, washed down with a tall glass of vegetable juice. Two minutes to midnight approached to the sound of the intercom interrupting the completion of her final edit. Frowning cursedly, Amy saved the document and wandered reluctantly over to the intercom system to give Jenson a piece of her mind. But, Amy stumbled, shell-shocked at the image that appeared on her security camera. She repeatedly pressed the entry button calling frantically through the intercom, "Mike? Mike?"

"Yes, yes it's me, no need to panic. Just let me in, would you?"

"Come in, come in, it's open," she said in urgency, dashing down the hallway to meet him. Mike leaned in the doorway of the main entrance firmly pressing a white bloodstained handkerchief on his lips. A little blood trickled down his chin. Beads of blood oozed out of long scratches on his cheeks. His slicked black hair was ruffled and unkempt. "Oh, my God. What on earth's happened?" Amy blasted, extending a helpful hand, leading him into the kitchen.

"Clean this up, would you? Damned if I'm going to sit in A&E all night. I hate hospitals."

"Oh, Mike. I'm so sorry. Please, sit down." Amy dashed to the bathroom and whipped her mini first aid kit out of the bathroom cabinet.

"It's hot in here." Grimacing, Mike removed his jacket to reveal a ripped blue and white gingham shirt. The bottom half was held together by two buttons. There were four holes at the top half where four buttons had once been, but were evidently ripped forcibly from the shirt. A long deep scratch on his chest and bruising to his stomach were exposed through the opening of his shirt. Amy acted as calmly as she possibly could. She took deep breaths at the kitchen sink, washed her hands thoroughly in warm, soapy water and instinctively prepared the medical kit. Mike sat at the kitchen table in an awkward crouching position. He dabbed his swollen, bleeding lips and wearily observed Amy systematically laying out the contents of the first aid kit on the kitchen worktop. "I'm sorry, you were in the middle of something?" he said, glancing at the coral reef screensaver on Amy's lap top.

"No, no, no, I'm drawing to a close on a document. I can finish it in the morning. Anyway, let's clean up this mess. This may sting a little," she said, warningly. Amy gently dabbed a moistened medicated swab on Mike's left cheek.

"She—she's attacked me ... I've been attacked by that bitch, Erica."

Astonished at Mike's aggressiveness, Amy's mouth dropped wide open, momentarily hampering her gentle dabbing. "Erica?" she said.

"Appeasement," began Mike, "she said she wanted to put forward some form of an appeasement."

"I don't understand! Appeasement?" Amy placed her forefinger under Mike's chin and tilted his head upward in order to gain a closer inspection of his wounded lips. "Ooh, that's a nasty gash," she whispered, bathing and coating his lips with soothing antiseptic healing cream.

"No idea what she'd meant. It made no sense to me. She pleaded for another chance and due to my outright refusal she suddenly erupted into a violently crazed woman."

"It must have been quite difficult to restrain her from the looks of things," said Amy, taking a closer look at the injuries sustained to his chest and stomach.

"Very difficult, I regret to admit. There is only so much physical force a man can use against a woman. We shouldn't wrestle with them but I had to put her in an arm lock. She was screaming and struggling, kicking and spitting trying to wriggle free. And once I was suitably convinced of her total exhaustion, I then released my grip. She fell out of my arms and collapsed in a heap on the floor like a limped and washed out rag-doll. Ouch! Amy! Steady on." Mike flinched as Amy applied a little extra pressure to remove dried blood that had caked on his left cheek.

"Sorry. Hold still. I'm trying. I'm doing my best," she said, nervously finishing off, moving over to his right cheek.

"We talked about making plans to move out, terminate the rental agreement, permanently give up the apartment, but she wouldn't hear of it. She just wouldn't accept it. She's in complete denial ... Erica's a spoilt, rotten, neurotic cow, accustomed to getting her own way, if not," Mike leaned back in the chair and pointed at his face saying, "this is the result, ashamedly. A prime example of what she's capable of doing."

"You mean, there've been other incidents?"

"She's had outbursts, but nothing to this extreme," he said.

The job of nursing Mike's wounds completed, Amy made a final check of his face. Satisfied, she washed her hands and packed the medical kit away. "You'll be pleased to know that you won't be bearing any physical scars. You'll heal soon enough," she said optimistically, inspecting the deep scratches that were now appearing a lot less severe than she'd originally feared.

"I do appreciate this, Amy."

Amy noted his weariness and reddened eyes, filled with disillusionment, pain and confusion, tired with the game of life. "Your shirt," Amy pointed out.

"What about it?" Mike gingerly laid his hand on his groin. "Sorry, this doesn't look very nice, but she'd kicked me there. I'd jumped out of the way in time to miss the full impact of her heel, thankfully."

"Yes, thankfully," said Amy, openly relieved, rolling her eyes exaggeratingly towards the ceiling. "Shall I check down there for any damage?" she said smirking, attempting to invite humor to the unpleasantly heavy atmosphere.

"No, I'll be fine," said Mike, grimacing, breaking into a bruised and hurting smile. "Don't worry about the shirt. Before the attack had taken place, I'd decided that checking into the hotel again for at least a week would serve as a better option than sleeping on the couch. So, this afternoon, I'd packed a few items and dropped them off at the hotel. I envisage moving into an apartment within a few days or so, two weeks at the most. The real estate agents are lining up a few properties for viewing around the Baker Street, Bloomsbury, St John's Wood, Holborn areas."

"I don't suppose you could manage a drink?" said Amy, switching on the espresso maker, in need of a caffeine fix in order to stay awake.

"A cool beer … with a straw might work."

"You're in luck. I have them both." Amy took a beer, normally reserved for Jenson, out of the refrigerator. She popped a straw into a tall glass and poured.

"Just what the doctor ordered, thanks," said Mike, cautiously sucking at the straw.

Amy's thoughts trailed on the day's events, her heart secretly filled with compassion, reaching out to Mike. She poured herself a cup of espresso. "So," she said, taking a deep breath as she sat down at the kitchen table, graciously crossing her slender legs, revealing her smooth, recently waxed shins, "calling off the engagement has caused quite a stir. Had you a date set?"

"No. I deliberately held off firming up on a date, left it to drag on really … I don't wish to talk about it any further tonight. It's off. Over. Finished."

Amy shut down her PC.

"My apologies for disrupting your evening."

"No. No. Please don't mention it again. The work's almost completed."

"What exactly are you working on?"

Shop, thought Amy, wishing she could change the subject. "I'm producing a draft TSA … a transitional services agreement, that is" she explained.

"Yes, I'm familiar with the term."

"The project involves the lucrative acquisition of a casino in del Mar, California on behalf of clients who also happen to be personal friends of Vincent, making things even more critical. And as it's quite a sensitively in-depth project, Vincent has selected a dedicated team to work on the deal. He requires the TSA by noon tomorrow so, I'll continue with it in the morning."

"Sunday? I'm impressed. I take my hat off to you. Sounds like I ought to be networking with a company such as Planet Management. Have you networked with anyone from the workshop by any chance?"

"No. Not really. Well, there's Katie, whom I've communicated with from time to time, purely on a social level and, I've taken part in a market research survey for Antenna Associates at Petra's request. And, you, of course." Amy poured herself another espresso. "More lager?"

"Sure. Thanks." Mike glanced around the kitchen. "The truth is, I don't love her." he said, re-opening the subject.

"That's fair enough." Amy eased herself back into the subject.

"And the not so simple truths are that Erica doesn't love me either. What she loves or, more appropriately, wants, is status. She's faired implicitly well to date, courting a Brandleton, masquerading in various hotels and stores, charging our accounts, brandishing the name in almost every establishment she walks into, a nonsensical and foolish privilege afforded her by my stupid father," said Mike. "Marrying me would put her in good stead and set her up for life. Our offspring would be the rightful heirs to the Cortland Group for the enablement of the legacy."

Nice catch, Amy thought. She was reservedly shocked, learning the true realization of Mike's social standing and apparent wealth. It was obvious, Mike was rich and wealthy, but she was ignorant of the extent of his wealth. She'd heard of the Cortland Group, seen the name on the London Stock Exchange FTSE 100, Bloomberg, in the odd business periodical and, not having had the need to conduct any research on the group, she'd never really taken very much notice of them.

Mike glanced around the kitchen again, his mind adrift.

Amy searched his expressionless face, wishing she could take an exploratory journey, delving into the length, breadth, depths and recesses of his mind. In her heart of hearts, without a doubt, Amy wanted Mike.

"Shattered dreams," Mike began, shaking his head from side to side in a regrettable manner. "Do you know, I'm being held responsible for the shattered dreams of both our families, my father let it be known today? And, thrown in, for good measure, he's threatened me with disinheritance, promising to have me written out of the family's fortune and, he was kind enough to grant me an ultimatum of one month to rethink my decision. Should I not have a change of heart, then ..." Mike made a slash of the throat gesture across his neck from right to left.

"Oh, my goodness, surely that's rather a drastic step. Your father is simply angered, he'll back down."

Mike rose from the chair. "You don't know my father, the all powerful, all important, indispensable, infinitely formidable, Carlson Henry Brandleton," he announced, in the style and pose of a master of ceremonies. Mike looked at his watch. "Look, I'd better be heading off. I've kept you up long enough, it's nearly three o'clock in the morning, it won't be long before the birds start tweeting," he joked, showing strains of fatigue.

The espresso hadn't done its job of keeping her awake, Amy got up, shattered and barely able to keep her eyes open, desperate to get a good few hours sleep before contemplating the TSA in the morning. "I welcome you to stay," Amy offered again, hoping to change Mike's mind.

"No. I'll head on back to the hotel. There shouldn't be any problems now that I look more presentable, thanks to you. I couldn't have walked into the hotel foyer looking disheveled."

"Just do your jacket up and you'll be fine. I'll escort you to the door," said Amy, fiercely holding back a yawn.

Mike looked at Amy with longing in his hurting eyes as he ran his fingers up and down her spine. "No need. I'll see myself out. You've done enough already," he said affectionately.

Amy wrapped her arms round Mike's waist and squeezed him gently, reassuringly and affectionately. Their faces drew closer and the tips of their noses touched. She gazed into his eyes—wanting to say "*I adore you*,"—but dismissed the urge hoping that he'd intuitively connect with her feelings.

Mike inhaled Amy's rose scented perfume. "My lips are in a sorry state, I'm unable to kiss you, damn it," he remarked cursedly, slowly unraveling himself out of Amy's arms. He proceeded along the hallway to the apartment door.

"Goodnight, Mike," Amy whispered wearily, leaning in the kitchen doorway, watching him as he disappeared from view. Yawning massively, Amy made her way sleepily to her bedroom and crawled into her cold and empty bed. Her head sunk on her pillow, cushioning the intensity of her swirling heady thoughts. She couldn't foresee any problems in meeting the Sunday afternoon TSA deadline, no problems at all. It was her deep concern for Mike's welfare that was now weighing heavily on her mind. Mike left, quietly, closing the main door behind him. Exhausted, Amy closed her eyes and went to sleep.

CHAPTER 12

Late Saturday evening, Katie returned home exhausted from an arduously long shopping spree in Knightsbridge. She hauled her expensive purchases into the lounge and peeked at the telephone. Six voicemail messages were waiting to be heard. Both hands heavily weighed down, Katie dropped the designer bags on the floor, kicked her shoes off and, sluggishly with her feet, shoved the bags into the corner of the room. She then waltzed into the kitchen and poured herself an unconventionally tall glass of red wine. After a few large gulps, holding her near empty glass in one hand, Katie shoved the bottle under her arm, grabbed the note pad and pen off the breakfast bar and waltzed back into the lounge. Placing the bottle of wine and glass on the side table, Katie activated the answering machine. Ungraciously flopping on the couch, with the notepad and pen on her lap, Katie commenced listening to the messages.

"Hi Katie, It's me, David. We need to talk. Please call me." *"Message received at two twenty-six pm, beeeep."*

"Yuck," Katie cried out loud, rolling her eyes around contemptuously.

"Hello, It's me again, David, waiting for your call." *"Message received at three forty-three pm, beeeep."* "Katie. I hope you've got my previous messages. Call me. David." *"Message received at five fifty-three pm, beeeep."* "I need to talk to you for five minutes. I miss you. I sincerely mean that. Call me. Please. All I want are five minutes." *"Message received at six forty-seven pm, beeeep."*

Frustration and anger festering, Katie dragged herself exhaustively off the couch and walked over to the answering machine. She was about to erase all the messages, including the ones she had not yet heard, when the message that followed wasn't another from David.

"Hi, Katie. Amy calling. How are you? Hope all's well with you. We must have a chat. I'll try again tomorrow. Bye for now." *"Message received at seven twelve pm, beeeep."* Arms folded and toes tapping, Katie patiently listened to the final message.

"Hello, Sweetie. Mum and Dad here. We've landed safely. Benidorn's lovely. A bit too hot, mind. We'll ring back soon, Sweetie. Big kisses. Cheerio." *"Message received seven forty-six pm, beeeep. End of messages."* Katie erased all the messages, returned to the couch and began scrawling on her notepad. Mum and dad calling back. Call Amy. Call 'phone co. Change 'phone number. She got up, slammed the notepad and pen on the side table, poured another full glass of wine, switched on the TV and stared blankly at the screen. Slightly tilting her head backwards, Katie brought the glass to her lips and knocked back her wine. She unsteadily refilled the glass to the rim, spilling wine on the cream colored carpet. She cursed under her breath and left it, outraged at the prospect of having to personally wipe the carpet clean. Nestling restlessly on the couch, Katie placed the glass and bottle of wine on the floor directly under her nose and remained there until the following morning.

Katie awoke to the telephone ringing. She clumsily rolled off the couch and grabbed the receiver, accidentally banging her head on the wall in the process. She cursed and swore under her breath. Hauling herself upright, Katie leaned against the wall. "Hello," she answered croakily, breathing heavily, head spinning and thumping in agonizing pain.

"Hi, Katie"

"Hello?"

"Katie? It's me, Amy."

"Hello? Who?"

Amy double-checked the time on her watch. It was eleven-thirty. She considered eleven-thirty on a Sunday morning a reasonable enough time to call and hoped that she wasn't wrecking Katie's morning.

"Who?"

"Katie, it's me, Amy. Are you alright?"

Katie had enormous difficulty stringing two words together. Her tongue felt dry, gritty and swollen. She was thirsty and in need of a drink. She focused her eyes on the quarter bottle of wine left on the floor overnight.

"Katie. Can you hear me? It's Amy."

Dropping the telephone, Katie got on her knees, crawled on the floor, brought the bottle to her mouth and drank the remainder of wine. She crawled

...hone and picked it up. "Hi … of course I can hear you. Keep ...top the bloody shouting!" A nauseating feeling overwhelmed ...he'd just swallowed started traveling upwards.

"I'm sorry if you believe that I'm raising my voice. If you don't mind me saying, you don't sound yourself this morning. Have I called at a bad time? I can always …"

"I think I'm going to be sick," Katie butted in, regurgitating and vomiting on the floor.

Amy overheard Katie's wrenching, coughing, heaving, vomiting and her pitiful sobs. "Katie? Katie? Are you, OK? Do you need any help? I can come over if you like."

"Come," said Katie, sobbing loudly.

"I'll be over in a shot."

Amy jumped out of the taxi, paid and tipped the driver modestly for taking the back streets to Bayswater, rushing her to her destination. She thought how lucky she was to be able to recall Katie's address from memory having shared taxis with her on only two occasions. Using the tip of her American manicured finger nail, Amy pressed the number eight button on the aluminum exterior wall panel keypad and waited a few long and lingering minutes. There was no sound of Katie. Amy began to worry. "Come on. Come on. Open the door," she said, under her breath. Tapping her feet, Amy meandered at the main door, anxiously waiting for Katie to activate the entry system. Eventually, Amy heard a crackling sound and a buzzing noise emitted from the highly polished, chrome grilled fitment on the exterior wall.

"Hi," said Katie. The sound of her voice crackled out of the grilled fitment.

"I'm here."

"To your left are the lifts. I'm on the second floor. It's the Mahogany door, third on the right."

"Thanks." There was a clicking sound and Amy gently pushed the door. It automatically swung open. Amy stepped in and the door closed automatically behind her. The smart lobby area had brass light fittings, oil paintings and wood veneered paneled walls. Amy athletically trotted up the four flights of stairs to the second floor. The thick velvet deep maroon colored carpet sound-proofed the staircase. Ajar, Katie's door was easily spotted. Amy approached cautiously and tapped lightly on the door as she entered. "Hi? … Katie?" she called cagily, turning her head from left to right. She closed the door quietly behind her. The hallway to Katie's apartment was also smart, but dark, hot and stuffy.

"I'm in here."

Amy walked along the hallway towards Katie's voice, locating her in the lounge. Katie sat on the couch in the darkened room. Holding her breath, Amy idled in the doorway for as long as she could. She rubbed her nose with her right hand as she inhaled the offensive blend of body odor, rank and stench of vomit, vehemently reluctant to enter the torturously stuffy room that was desperately crying out for light and fumigation. "Ah, here you are," said Amy, bravely smiling at the scene of Katie, slouched slovenly on the couch. Her immaculate French plait had fallen out of place. Scruffy, Katie wore a pair of creased, black slacks and a plain white crumpled blouse. Amy suspected that Katie had slept in her clothes all night. She was an awfully depressing sight, disheveled, haggard and bleary eyed, aiming the remote control at the TV, mindlessly flicking channels. Amy observed the total mess of the room. An untidy pile of shopping bags lay on the floor in the corner. A pair of black court shoes was slung at the end of the room. A scattering of vividly red unsightly stains were on the carpet. The pinewood slats of the Venetian blinds were shut. Amy felt a certain sadness witnessing Katie's dismal conditions, finding her first visit to the apartment unsettling, wishing she'd gone there on more pleasant terms, a Sunday lunch or a dinner party.

"There's never anything good to watch on a Sunday afternoon, lately. It's all bullshit, politics. As if we don't get enough of it during the week. Give it a rest! Sundays are meant to be the day of rest, anyway."

"I've brought something for you," said Amy, entering the room, placing the gift she'd purchased in Amsterdam on Katie's lap.

Katie continued staring, unfocussed, at the TV. "Thanks. I'll look at it later," she said, leaving it on the arm of the couch.

"Take your time," said Amy, sinking in the armchair near the window. The atmosphere was tense, gloomy and depressing. Amy wanted to launch straight into learning about Katie's problem, the reason behind her sobbing down the telephone. But, judging from the scenes and not wanting to rush Katie, Amy disguisedly shocked at what she'd seen so far, decided that it would be best to wait a while. There was no need to hurry and, she was free all afternoon. Perplexed, Amy looked at Katie questioningly. Where is that fun loving person? What's happened to her? The lounge was proving to become unbearably stuffy, nauseating. "Can I get you anything? Tea? Coffee?" Amy asked as an excuse to get out for a breather.

"No. I'm OK. But you can help yourself. It's not a big apartment, so you'll easily find the kitchen out there."

"I could do with some company. Come with me. You're going to have to show me where everything's kept, anyway," said Amy, attempting to get Katie up and moving around, her blood circulating and air in her lungs."

Katie switched the TV off and tossed the remote on the other end of the couch. "There's never anything good to watch on a Sunday," she groaned, lifting herself off the couch. Amy glanced suspiciously at the empty wine bottle on the floor at Katie's feet and refrained from making a comment. "Oh. My head spins," said Katie, swaying as she got on her feet.

"I'm not surprised. It's stuffy in here. Here, let me open the window for you. You're in need of fresh air." Amy quickly located the cord, pulled the blinds up, opened the window, poked her head out and inhaled deeply. Katie placed both hands on her flushed cheeks and staggered out of the lounge into the kitchen. Amy quickly followed. The kitchen was in total disarray. Dirty cups, plates and cutlery littered the worktops. Biscuit crumbs on the floor felt like grit under the soles of Amy's shoes. Turning a blind eye, Amy lifted two clean mugs from the mug tree. "Tea?"

"Please. And no milk for me," said Katie, pointing at the cupboard where the tea bags were kept as she hoisted herself wearily onto one of the four high-chairs at the breakfast bar.

"Rubber gloves?"

"What?"

"Gloves. I'm going to have to do some clearing up before making tea."

"They're under the sink. But don't, Peggy will be here in the morning," said Katie, frustratingly.

Amy remained silent. Brown rings on the worktop blazoned.

"Who's Peggy?"

"My cleaner."

"It's OK. I won't do everything, just the bare essentials. I'll clear the worktop, stack the dishwasher and leave the rest for Peggy to do." Where do I start? Amy thought. She poured mineral water into the kettle. "So, what's going on, Katie?"

"How much time do you have?"

Amy switched the kettle on and popped herbal tea-bags in the mugs. "Loads. I'll be here for as long as you need me."

"Thanks ... It's David,"

"David?"

"Yes. David. I got a little bit too involved and—Zowie 'phoned.'

"Zowie? Who's Zowie?" Amy located a bottle of disinfectant, a cloth and a pair of bright yellow rubber gloves in the cupboard under the sink.

"Mrs. White. His wife."

"His wife?" said Amy, opening the bottle, sprinkling disinfectant generously on the worktop and wiping the surface clean.

"Yep."

"I see. So, Zowie 'phoned who?" The water had boiled. Amy removed the rubber gloves, dropped them in the sink and poured steaming hot water from the kettle into the mugs.

"Me. David … Well, like I said, I got a bit too involved and everything's a complete mess … a bloody nightmare. Lies. Lies about going to Dubai."

"Lies?"

"Oh. Sorry, David. I'm not making very much sense, am I?"

Amy brought the mugs of tea over to the breakfast bar, handed Katie a mug and perched herself on a high-chair opposite Katie. Amy cupped her mug in her hands and sighed. "Take your time. Start from the beginning."

"So much has gone on, Amy, OK? David and I, were an item … at least I thought we were. But, I was wrong to believe that."

Amy realized Katie's matchmaking skills hadn't worked out in her favor; quite like a doctor who could administer care of his patients but, couldn't take care of himself. "When did this happen?"

Katie shrugged. "A few weeks ago, now. I don't know exactly how many,"

"I recall you had a date in the park."

"Yes. That's when it all started and gradually progressed to this." Katie let out a nervous giggle. "He's fantastic on the sex front."

Amy's body heat rose. She removed her jacket and hung it on the back of the high-chair. She started to relax, feeling happier now that Katie was giggling, appearing to be in better spirits. "Well, we don't need to go too deep into that subject. But if you really want to talk about it, then fine, if it helps."

"We had a good thing going until his wife called—this might sound crazy but, I owe her one. If it wasn't for her, I'd still be with David, being lied to." Katie ran her fingers nervously through her tangled hair.

Amy was having a hard time trying to form a picture of Katie's illustrations. "Sounds like a messy jigsaw puzzle to me."

"It is … How's Mike? Seen him lately?"

Startled, Amy didn't quite know what to come back with. She wanted to avoid speaking about Mike, how blissful and confident she'd been feeling about him lately. "Yes. I have."

"Any news on the fiancé?" Katie climbed off the high-chair and shuffled over to the wine rack.

Amy took a deep breath, dreading the thought of Katie opening another bottle. "Not very much really. But … I'm concerned about you. I really want to talk about you, David and Zowie. What's going on?"

"He's lied to me. His wife found my telephone number. She caught him here … with me," said Katie. Deliberating on whether to open a bottle of wine, Katie refilled the kettle, to Amy's relief.

"Right," said Amy. She had a mental aberration, scaring herself, wondering whether Mike was trustworthy.

"He's been separated six months," said Katie.

"Separated? I don't believe it. Separated! I'm sorry, Katie."

"I want him to stay away from me. I didn't mean to get carried away like this. This wasn't meant to happen. I'm not meant to be feeling like this."

Amy felt compassion for Katie but she couldn't stop the niggling voice in her head blaming herself for Katie's plight; perhaps she could have done more to steer Katie away from David.

"He's called me a few times. I've not spoken to him. He wants to talk … I can't make up my mind …" Katie started crying.

Amy got up quickly, ripped off a few sheets of kitchen tissue and handed them to Katie. Katie snatched the sheets out of Amy's hand, slumped on the kitchen floor and cried, convulsively.

Devastated, Amy took a few steps back. Stinging tears began to well in her eyes. Lost, not knowing what to do, Amy watched Katie. Stunned, willing herself to remain calm and strong for Katie's sake, Amy took over from where Katie had left off making more teas, placing the mugs on the breakfast bar. Then Amy calmly bent down and began stroking Katie's back. She moved Katie's wet fringe from her eyes. Katie's sobbing began to subside. She made a movement, an attempt to stand up. Amy assisted her to her feet. "More tea?" whispered Amy.

"I just want to get back on the couch."

"OK. You go ahead and I'll fetch the teas in." Amy quickly popped tea bags into the mugs and poured hot water in them. Katie blew her nose in the kitchen tissue and made her way, shoulders hunched, out of the kitchen and into the lounge. Amy followed, carrying the mugs of tea, smiling as she entered the room in sheer relief now that the lounge was brighter and the stench, stuff-iness and odors were thinner, practically unnoticeable. "What does David want to talk about?"

Katie sniffled. "What is there to talk about?" She lay flat on her back on the couch. "More lies I expect."

"What did his wife talk about?"

"I didn't conduct a conversation with her as such. But David hadn't gone to Dubai."

"He may stop telling lies now. Maybe it's worth speaking to him. Hear him out. Let him know how you feel. How much he's hurt you. Then, say your final goodbyes," said Amy, easing in the armchair.

"I'm unhappy, alright. There's nothing he can say or do to change the way I feel."

"You'll get through this, Katie. I know you will. You'll bounce back."

"Bounce!" Katie laughed.

Amy laughed nervously. The designer shopping bags, stacked in an untidy pile on the floor caught Amy's attention. "Harrods? Louis Vuitton? What have you been buying?"

"Oh. Impulse shopping."

"Dangerous," said Amy, shaking her head.

"I know. I know. I bought a load of stuff and, here's another crazy thing, I don't want any of it. Buying them felt great for the moment, stepping out of the stores, swaying the bags along Knightsbridge, but the feeling doesn't last, it soon wears off."

"Then I suggest you return them all."

"Maybe." Katie sat up, took a sip of tea and peered thoughtfully at Amy. "You're right. I think I'll talk to him."

"Good. Think things through. Give it some clear thought. Clear your head. Don't rush into it. To start with, freshen up a bit, take a shower, you'll feel much better for it."

Katie continued peering at Amy. Her haggard face had a grateful expression. "Thanks for coming over, Amy. I appreciate it. I'm feeling a lot more positive now, thanks to you. You're a good person."

"Don't mention it, it's not a problem," said Amy embarrassingly, blood rushing to her cheeks.

Katie took a deep breath, put her mug on the floor and, with a new lease of energy, got up and rushed towards the door. "I'm off to take that shower. I won't be long."

time. I'll be here," said Amy. Looking around, Amy wondered ...... she should start cleaning up first.

Amy had just finished vacuuming the stained lounge carpet when Katie came storming in, smelling of perfumery, looking refreshed, wearing a large, white toweling bath-robe. "You really shouldn't have done all this, you crafty thing," said Katie, arms flailing. "You'd waited until I'd disappeared into the shower then you started doing all this. I faintly heard the racket of the vacuum cleaner and wanted to come out to stop you but, I was stark naked and dripping wet. I've already told you that Peggy will be here in the morning."

"Honestly, it's no trouble. I don't mind. I just wanted something to do." Amy wheeled the vacuum cleaner back to the storage cupboard in the hallway.

"OK. I'll let you off," said Katie, guiltily.

Amy returned to the lounge. "When are you going to make that call?"

"I don't know. I need some wine."

"Please. No. Give it a break," pleaded Amy.

Katie paced around the lounge, sat on the couch and abruptly got up again. "I'm worried. I've got to call David. God knows I've got something very important to tell him."

"And what would that be?"

"I ... I ..." Emotionally distraught, Katie had difficulty in getting her words out.

Amy placed her reassuring hands on Katie's shoulders, fearing she was about to burst into tears again, "Relax, Katie. Calm down. We'll sort this thing out together. OK?"

"I'm pregnant," blurted Katie.

Amy freed Katie's shoulders and covered her mouth with her hands instead. Her eyes bulging at Katie's stomach, Amy took her hands away from her mouth saying, "Fuck. Shit. That's a bummer."

"Precisely," said Katie.

CHAPTER 13

Wednesday night at eleven fifteen, Amy was Mike's last port of call from the office before wrapping up for the night. "Dinner. Friday night. How are you fixed?"

He sounds fine. Weary, but fine, Amy thought. "Friday? At what time?"

"We could sit down at eight?"

Amy checked the calendar on her laptop. "Yes, that would work. Where ~~should~~ shall we meet?"

"Beaujolais. I quite liked it there. Would you mind booking the table again, please?" said Mike, locking his desk.

"Not at all," Amy enthused, pleased at Mike's favorable regard for Beaujolais, since she'd introduced him to the venue.

"Good."

"How are you?"

"I'm well. Very busy. And you? Busy? Oh, by the way," said Mike, "I've moved into temporary accommodation."

"That's good news. When did this take place?"

"Last week. I'll invite you over."

"Thanks," said Amy, pacing her kitchen floor, swooning. "Local?"

"Yes. Quite. Bishops Avenue, Hampstead Gardens."

Amy raised her eyebrows. "Nice," she said, calmly suppressing her thrill.

"I'm scooting off now. It's been a long day." Mike sighed adding, "So, it's Beaujolais on Friday at eight?"

"That's a definite yes. I'm confident we'll get a table. I'll make the reservation. See you then," said Amy, sad that the conversation had to be brief, so brief that she didn't get the opportunity to broach the subject of Erica to remain ɔreast of things. Nevertheless, chuffed, Amy grinned and clamped her long arms round her small waist.

"Reservations?"

"*Oui, madam.*"

"I'd like a table for two, at eight, this Friday night in the name of Amy Scott, please?"

"Ah, Madam Scott. For you, a table for two has been reserved, right away."

It had been two and half weeks since Amy had patched-up Mike's wounds, but she'd willingly withstood the time it took to hear from him. The picture of things was becoming clearer, now that Mike had called off the engagement. She'd had a lot to think about in the meantime, what with Vincent keeping her on her toes, working long hours on his latest Latin American project and Katie's lamentations on whether or not to terminate the pregnancy playing havoc on the forefront of her mind, in fact, the thought of Katie terminating the pregnancy mortified Amy.

At ten forty-five, Mike and Amy were boarding their waiting taxi conveniently parked outside the Beaujolais restaurant.

"Food and service were superb," said Mike, duly fortified, sliding into his seat.

"I agree. They've not disappointed me to date, always coming up trumps, fiercely living up to their reputation."

"Quite." Mike nodding in agreement turned and smiled widely at Amy. Her body tingled in anticipation.

They sat in silence whilst the taxi driver sped off to Mike's recently acquired accommodation, hurtling them rapidly over speed ramps, causing an uncomfortable and incessant churning in Amy's stomach. She'd over indulged again on food, champagne, wine and liquor. Amy closed her eyes in an attempt to ignore the discomfort, imagining affectionately clasping Mike's hand for the entire journey.

"Voila, we're here," Mike announced effervescently, hopping out of the taxi, extending his right hand to Amy.

Gasping, Amy held Mike's hand and stepped out of the taxi onto the gravel driveway. "Mike!" she exclaimed.

"Wonderful, is it not? Wait until you see the interior." Mike released Amy's hand and reached for his wallet. He paid the taxi driver, tipping him generously. Amy didn't think the driver deserved such a generous tip, of twenty pounds, hurtling them, quite inconsiderately, over speed ramps, stomach. Luckily, her stomach had calmed down a bit and she was feeling slightly better now, but her head was spinning. The taxi driver thanked Mike appreciatively and sped off. Amy took a couple of deep breaths to clear her head as she admired the floodlit grounds. It wasn't what she'd imagined. Mike used a remote control, to open the ornate wooden double doors to the huge mansion styled property. The entrance was supremely opulent. Spectacular. Mike took Amy on a grand tour of the house of many rooms, comprised of a ballroom, cinema, seven bedrooms, six bathrooms, catering kitchen and a triple garage, all marble throughout.

"Why all this?" said Amy, in sheer astonishment.

"It was a toss up between a Penthouse in Belgravia or this place. The greenery of the Heath and its wonderfully elevated heath-land were the deciding factors. The property's owned by a wealthy businessman who's happy to accept a nominal sum for the right occupant. He's a personal friend of Roderick, the proprietor of the real estate company."

"A form of house sitting service, if you like," said Amy, her eyes darting here, there and everywhere in utter amazement.

"In a nutshell. Yes. Theoretically speaking, he's not rented the property but, having someone here periodically ensures the property maintains a lived in feel to it. For instance, during the winter months, regular use of the hot water prevents the pipes from freezing or bursting, that sort of thing. He resides here for a maximum of three months in a given year."

"Who is he?"

"No idea to be honest but, according to Roderick, he's in the oil business." Mike sighed. "In view of all the shit that has been going on in my life, I've made a conscious decision to enjoy making my life long decisions in opulence, luxury, style and comfort. Fitting, I'd say." Mike leaned luxuriously against the balustrade of the gallery on the upper floor. He turned Amy round to face him and, with a glint in his eye, planted an unexpected kiss on the tip of her nose. "Come this way. This is where I've been sleeping." The master bedroom had an ornate white marble fireplace and an Emperor size, ostentatiously decorated, white four poster water bed as the focal point. Mink rugs were scattered on the black marble floor. A black leather couch and a black, glass coffee table were situated a few feet away from the fireplace. Black framed mirrors lined the white walls and ceiling.

Amy couldn't hold back any longer from demonstrating an ostensibly calm reaction. "Incredible. Absolutely fantastic," she shrilled excitedly, wide-eyed and breathless, clasping her hands.

"I thought you'd approve," said Mike, smugly.

"How long do you intend to remain here?"

"Six months with the option to extend." Mike walked Amy over to the black leather couch. "Make yourself comfortable. I'll be two minutes." On his way out of the master bedroom, Mike flicked a brass switch on the wall above the white marble mantel, igniting a fire. Flames instantly flickered, a warm, burnt orange glow behind black tinted glass, giving the room a romantic incandescence, hypnotizing Amy's already aroused senses to the extent that she was almost tempted to slip off her clothes and lay in the nude on the Mink rugs arranged directly in front of the fire. But, she opted to remain seated, orderly and demurely on the couch, sitting with her back straight, not too complacently or overly relaxed with her eyes following Mike strolling out of the room. He's so full of life, she thought. Reviewing the evening, Amy thought he'd been amusedly funny and witty over dinner, happy, transformed to a degree. He looked very well, handsomely fit and adorably healthy, sporting a subtle tan. He'd probably been to France and back, again, Amy thought. His cheeks, lips, including his spirits had all healed, showing no scars or any other tell—tell signs that he'd recently been caught up in a violent fracas with Erica. The clinking of glasses interrupted Amy's thoughts. She glared dreamily at the tranquilly dancing flames. Mike entered the room with a pair of champagne flutes and a bottle of Bollinger Grande Annee 1997 vintage in a champagne bucket packed with ice. On that premise, Amy began to wish. Her eyes flittered discreetly towards the water bed. "More champers. Great," she managed to say.

Mike poured the champagne and handed a glass to Amy.

"I've a cause for celebration. Salute," he announced.

Amy gracefully rose to her feet and tapped Mike's flute. "Salute," she said, savoring the champagne. "What's the occasion?"

"Divorce."

Dismayed, Amy returned to the couch. "Divorce?"

Mike smiled and sighed. "Indeed. My father made an important decision. With effect from today, I'm an outcast, no family fortune, my inheritance forfeited. I'm no longer a member of the Cortland Group."

Horrified, Amy's heartbeat quickened. She was also enamored by Mike's ability to maintain full control of his feelings. She took two large sips of champagne and thrust the glass at Mike. "Pour me another, please?" Doubting whether she could be of any real concrete use to the likes of Mike Brandleton, a big cheese, not sharing the same wealth and powerful connections in her life he was generally accustomed to, Amy desperately hoped she could prove to be of valid use to him, in her own little way. Shocked, Amy suspected a long night ahead and prepared herself to listen, attentively, to Mike's problems. Mike topped up Amy's glass with champagne. She took a sip. A concerned expression was etched on her face. "Thanks. I'm sorry about the state of affairs concerning your father. Wasn't there anything either of you could have done to prevent such a drastic outcome?"

"Yes, me literally agreeing to marry Erica, which would be an outrageous act on my part." Mike sighed.

"What are you going to do?"

"New roads, new beginnings and new risks are the spices to a new life ahead. I've some ideas I'm itching to explore." Mike sat on the couch.

Amy eased her feet out of her shoes. "Are you willing to share any of these explorative ideas?" she asked, keenly.

Mike smirked, stared at the flames, momentarily transfixed. "Nannies," he said, brusquely. "Nannies tended to my every need during my childhood. My mother is a kept woman. Socializing has always been her life. She was always far too busy to cater for the needs of her son. Tea parties here, garden parties there, dinner parties, cocktail parties, the bridge club, the ladies club, etcetera, etcetera, etcetera. That's all I've ever known. Nannies took care of me during my times of sickness. I remember being covered in ghastly spots and scabs caused by chicken pox, my parents weren't there for me but my nanny smeared the sickly, putrid lotion on my skin and comforted me. When I'd contracted measles, my mother never came to bid me comfort. Each night, I'd cry myself to sleep. Erica, she only cares about herself. My mother enjoys being the wife of a Brandleton and Erica had hoped to follow in her footsteps."

Filled with overwhelming compassion and empathy, Amy was thankful for the eye-opener into Mike's inner thoughts and painful memories of his childhood. Placing her glass on the coffee-table and cupping Mike's face in her hands, Amy stared caringly into his eyes. "How on earth have you managed to get through all this? What on earth have you been doing to avail yourself of such misery?"

Mike stared back at Amy, an *"are you ready for this?"* type of stare.

Amy placed her hands on her lap.

Mike turned and focused his eyes on a small black wooden box in the centre of the coffee table. He leaned forward and opened it. The interior was com-

Inside the box

partmentalized. There were three, very small, inconspicuously concealed pack-ages. Mike placed each package, side by side on the coffee table.

Clueless, Amy glanced at the packages and smiled curiously. "What the hell are they?" Mike sniffed.

"Go on! What are they?" Amy demanded, nudging Mike.

Mike pointed at each item, naming them, saying, "Lebanese hash, mari-juana and cocaine—grade A, of course."

"Oh, my God, Mike … I don't … you're not …"

"*No*. I'm no junkie." Mike looked at Amy searchingly. "You've not tried any of these—not once in your life?"

Amy looked at Mike, ashamedly. "Well, yes … I'd dabbled once or twice with marijuana in the girls' toilets at school … but cocaine and hash, no."

"OK," said Mike, smiling, "Shall we snort cocaine, tonight?"

Amy shook her head adamantly saying, "No thanks. The cocaine is a defi-nite no, no. N. O."

"OK." Mike sighed, reopened the box and returned the items to their respective compartments.

Shell-shocked, Amy wondered how many more surprises Mike might have had hidden up his sleeves and the incongruous ways he'd planned to spring them on her. She hoped that he'd have the consideration to spare her a bomb-shell of a shock surprise. He could be an imposter, a rapist, a serial killer, a murderer. Who knows? Amy thought speculatively, scaring herself, almost giv-ing herself the creeps. Hiccupping, Amy quickly retrieved her glass. "Excuse me. Too much champagne," she said, embarrassingly, gently tapping her chest.

"Can I fetch you anything?"

"No thanks. I'm perfectly fine. Really, thanks" said Amy, her hand waving him off. "Let's celebrate the new beginnings you'd mentioned earlier. Life goes on, as they say."

"You are a woman after my heart, Amy."

Blushing, Amy was deeply moved. She managed to maintain her compo-sure, stopped hiccupping, keeping herself in check. "That's lovely Mike. Thanks."

"No. I meant that most sincerely, so much so that I've told my parents about you."

"Me! There is nothing about me that they would remotely be interested to note," said Amy in a high pitched voice, her body heat rising from the lus-ciously flickering flames or was it the champagne or both? Amy couldn't differ-entiate.

"Let me be the judge of that," said Mike, topping up their glasses.

It's the room. The room's getting hot. Amy thought. She removed her jacket and slung it on the arm of the couch. Her head swimming, Amy yearned for a conversation to keep her mind alert. Tonight was magical even with its intricate twists and turns, throwing Amy's already swimming thoughts into a chaotic whirlwind. She closed her eyes, took a deep breath, exhaled and commenced a mental count from one to ten.... *four, five, six.*

"We're compatible, you and I. And this aspect has made me very happy. It's not something I can truly and honestly say I've experienced with any other woman."

Speechless, not fully apprehending Mike, Amy burrowed her toes into the Mink and scanned her clouded mind for a fitting response. "I'm nipping to the en-suite;" she said, putting her glass on the table. Clutching her handbag, Amy got off the couch and walked shoeless across the master bedroom, trying not to stagger on each cautiously planted step. "It's this door here, right?" she guessed, pointing at one of many doors in the master bedroom.

"Be my guest," said Mike jovially, removing his jacket.

Critically scrutinizing her reflection in the full-length mirrors of the beautiful white and gold Roman themed bathroom, Amy thought she was looking better than what she was actually feeling—hot, flustered and nervous. She spotted half liter bottles of sparkling mineral water and a range of fruit and vegetable juices through the mist-proof glass door of the wall inset refrigerator, adjacent to the steam room, opposite the most luxurious marble hydro-massage spa bath she'd ever seen. Dehydrated, Amy helped herself to a bottle of water and drank the entire contents. Refreshed, she discarded the bottle down the disposal shoot, raked her fingers through her hair, applied more lip gloss and exited the bathroom. She feasted her eyes on Mike, his eyes closed, laid comfortably on his back on the couch. Her initial thoughts on seeing him were to kiss him all over and devour him lavishly but, Amy tiptoed across the room, sat at the end of the couch and stared at the black silk socks on his gentlemanly feet.

Sensing Amy's return, Mike opened his eyes, immediately sat up and yawned. "Pardon me. How rude. It's been a long day. I'd dozed off."

"Please, don't let me disturb you," Amy whispered.

Mike stretched and yawned.

Amy saw the fatigue in his eyes. It was evident to her that Mike was forcing himself to stay awake, just for her sake. "Well, I'd better be heading off home."

Before Amy had a chance to get up, Mike moved swiftly across the couch and grabbed her arms.

"No. Please. Could you spare a few more minutes?"

Amy, acknowledging the pleading in Mike's tired eyes said, "Yes, of course."

"Where were we? Ah, yes." Mike pressed a couple of buttons on a large remote control that rested on the coffee table. The sound of soothing, Peruvian piped music filled the room. Looking round about her, Amy had a hard time locating the speakers.

"More risks are to be taken. Like, tonight for instance."

"Tonight?" Amy exclaimed, hydrated, accepting another full glass of champagne Mike had just poured.

"I've made it emphatically clear to my parents, and Erica, that there is a formidable woman in my life. She's beautiful, intelligent, unique, easy going and doesn't cause a fuss about anything at all, whatsoever."

A tinge of envy surged through Amy. "I'm pleased for you," she said ostensibly, wanting to leave.

"Thank you." Mike's smile was full of contentedness and Amy's envy lingered.

"Obviously, they were all very alarmed by this fact. They'd no idea that I'd someone in my life. You see, it'd been over between Erica and me for a long period of time. I dilly dallied in doing something about it. To be perfectly honest with you, our relationship hadn't taken off, really. We're just not right for each other. I've not felt anything for her. My father had stated that whoever she is, the woman of my choice would never be accepted. Do you know, I'd informed my father that I'd never loved Erica and, do you know what he'd said?"

Amy raised her eyebrows and shook her head. "I've no idea."

"It went something like this, "You don't have to love Erica. Cultivate her into becoming a good wife and the bearer of your offspring, but find a mistress and love her, that's what'll keep your marriage going. Look at your mother and me". Well, words to that effect."

Amy found the whole matter painfully sad, and yet she was intrigued that Mike had been ostracized. "My take on this is that there's a possibility your father had a mistress or mistresses throughout his entire marriage and expects you to follow in his footsteps, fall into line," Amy analogized.

"Absolutely. We could theorize on that. This explains why I've not had meaningful relationships. I'd received no love from either of my parents simply because they hadn't the foggiest idea how to truly love as they'd been too busy taking care of their own agendas." Mike shrugged. "I don't remember ever playing rugby in the park with my father or the joys of my mother cuddling me during my childhood."

Amy was shocked at Mike's ability to emotively express himself. She respected him for the risk he'd taken, bravely bearing his soul to her. "Please put it all behind you, Mike. Look ahead. You've so much to look forward to now. The world's your oyster."

"Yes, you're quite right. It'll take some getting use to but, I'll battle on, as per usual," said Mike retrospectively. "Only time will tell. I've a few tangible assets, private investments held over the years which I could use to offset my own businesses."

"What businesses are you going into?" Amy asked shortly.

"I'll remain in the hotel industry but outside of Europe, purchase an ongoing concern, in the Caribbean perhaps."

"That's wonderful. But would your father object? It is a competitive aim."

"Mark my words, he'll not only object, he'll do whatever it takes to block my path and sabotage my aims, but I'll do everything in my power to make this thing happen. I'll fight his every intransigence. By the way, Planet Management could come in very handy here."

"Meaning?"

"Transitioning is one of their many specialties, is it not?

"Yes?"

"I've given this idea some careful thought in that, I could use their services to locate an island, hotel, legal provisioning, accountants, everything. What I'm saying is that, I'd like to go on the books. Would there be any possibilities?"

As the night progressed, Amy became increasingly impressed and at awe with Mike's tenacity and unpredictability. Although, surprised at the concept of Mike Brandleton, the man whom she was intimately acquainted with, his company becoming a portfolio of Planet Management, Amy also envisioned herself doing her utmost to ensure that Mike, would not only benefit from her providing him with her full support, but she'd ensure that he'd also be continuously furnished with an exceptionally valuable service under the condition, that he would be in agreement to keeping their intimacy a closely guarded secret. She'd personally see to that, if need be. Business is business. "I can certainly make arrangements," she said in an efficiently official tone. "You'll need to provide a blueprint in a set format. We'll put a dedicated team together to consistently work quite closely and expertly with you every step of the way and beyond if you wish."

"I'm duly impressed that I can hardly wait to get things moving." Mike leaned back in the couch, clapped and rubbed his hands together victoriously.

Amy noted, from the self-assured look on his face, that Mike was a man with a vision and a plan, curiously wondered what slot she'd effectively fallen into and hoped she wasn't being used, caught in a trap for his own personal gain. Taking a risk, she had to be more scrupulous on this, not let her heart rule her head. "With a positively conscientious plan, the sky's the limit," she said.

Mike advanced closer to Amy. "I've a proposition to make," he said, nibbling her earlobe.

"Yes?" she said, pecking his cheek, rubbing his shoulder with her free hand, balancing her glass in the other, hellishly curious about the proposition, furiously getting hot and sexually aroused.

Mike sat upright, looked into Amy's eyes and gripped her shoulders with both hands. "Be my business partner. Join me in my venture."

Amy quivered at the noble thought of the proposition. It was all too much. She was out of her league. She didn't have the funds, and yet, this was the realization that her dreams were finally coming true. The success, recognition, credibility and respectability she'd hankered and worked so hard to achieve. She'd grafted to, one day, realize her own personal fortune. Totally unprepared, Amy couldn't turn Mike down, let herself down or allow an opportunity of a lifetime slip through her fingers. This was the break she'd been waiting for, playing a key and major role, owning a stake in a high level concern. She'd dreamt of this and worked so hard to achieve it.

"Take your time. I'll grant you one week," said Mike, freeing her shoulders.

"No … yes … my decision is, yes … I don't need a week … Yes. It's now," babbled Amy, trying desperately to stay in control.

Mike roared with laughter. "You're so enchantingly pretty when you're flustered."

Amy was relieved that Mike saw the funny side, that she'd fallen apart like butter in his hands, but she was also a little angry with herself on her delivery she believed lacked the strength and confidence that Vincent had worked so hard cloning her.

"Great. We're a team and we'll start immediately. It's all in your hands. I'll leave you to make the necessary arrangements concerning your end."

"Thanks. I'll get the ball rolling, first thing, Monday morning," responded Amy more confidently, not knowing what the hell was going on, how the hell she was going to pull this thing off, raise the money, an amount her bank manager would be prepared to loan to her. She'd seek Vincent's advice first thing on Monday morning. She could kick herself for leading Mike along, she thought. He'd acquiesced to the worldly image she'd falsely portrayed of herself. The conversation over, Amy had an inkling of the next inevitable event to follow. Mike stood up, held his hands out to Amy and beckoned her to come forward. Amy daintily held the long stem of her glass, relished the last few sips of champagne. She rose demurely out of the couch, left the empty glass on the coffee table and slowly walked the few paces towards Mike. They faced each other. Peruvian piped music played softly in the background. The fire glowed flames of a rich romantic blend of colors, red, yellow and orange. "I think I'm experiencing love for the first time in my life," Mike whispered solemnly. He lifted Amy's slender body into his arms and carried her to the bed. Ecstatically silent, speechless that Mike had literally uttered sentiments of love to her, helplessly believing him, Amy wrapped her arms round his neck. Her eyes filled with tears on the realization that the formidable woman in his life he'd spoken so highly of was, in fact, her. Her heart lurched. Things were moving too fast. Without any resistance, Amy allowed a blissful tear to fall freely. The solitary tear moistened Mike's lips. He laid Amy gently on the bed, her body bobbed up and down to the ebbing movements. Mike lifted her white silk camisole and fondled her breasts. Amy raised her arms and Mike pulled the silk camisole over her head, undressing her. She lay topless, her nipples protruded, Mike took a deep breath and marveled at her breasts. "Wait there," he whispered huskily, climbing off the bed. Amy closed her eyes, patiently waiting for Mike to return—she heard him opening another bottle of champagne. Surprised, Amy yelped softly and oozed in excruciating pleasure as Mike trickled droplets of ice, cold champagne on her nipples, sucking and nibbling them gently, circling champagne around her breasts with his finger tips. Amy squirmed. "Wait," Mike said abruptly.

Amy grabbed his arm and pulled him towards her. "No," she said.

He tugged at her skirt, placed his hand under her arched back, located her zipper and wrenched at it. He unzipped his pants.

Amy tugged at his waistband, pulled his pants down. He removed his shirt and groaned as he lay on her naked body. Amy heard keys jingling.

Mike had whipped out a pair of handcuffs from under the pillows and was dangling them at her.

Amy smiled. She had no time for games tonight. She wanted pure sex. She grabbed his head and pulled his hair.

Mike winced and groaned pleasurably.

She held his erect penis in her hand and squeezed. "I want you now," she said groaningly.

"Wait," he said, panting and groaning in painfully agonizing desire. He grabbed her left ankle with one hand, swiftly yanked her across the bed and handcuffed her ankle to the post.

"This had better be good," said Amy, surrendering herself to him, pulling him towards her.

"Get ready," he said.

Amy raised her right leg. Mike mounted her. He groaned loudly, plunged himself forcefully and deeply inside her. Amy tightened her lips and sucked in the air as she hissed from the sweet pain. She gritted her teeth, took a sharp intake of breath, and watched in the mirrored ceiling as she embedded her long manicured nails into Mike's spine.

They kissed, licked, scratched, clawed, nipped, slapped, grappled, swore, cried, frolicked, talked dirty and obscenely and changed positions. They'd released their tension, anger and frustration, satisfied their animalistic urges and finally climaxed simultaneously. Amy knew Mike was a happy and contented man evidenced by his deep, loud groans. The beauty of Mike's masterfully sculpted back muscles reflected in the mirror as his body contracted in a surging force of inexplicable pleasure. Their legs intertwined, Amy held Mike tightly and coped with the force and strength of his body, his heartbeat pumped rapidly as he gushed inside her. They continued, insatiably into the early hours of the morning.

Amy lifted her head off the warm pillows and smiled contentedly. Licking her parched lips, she purred as she extended both arms to feel, embrace, frolic, and liberally smother Mike with adorning kisses but felt nothing, only the cold patch where he'd slept. She turned round and, as suspected, Mike was absent. Wonderful, she thought. Her body ached all over and her ankle tingled. Twiddling her toes helped to diminish the tingling sensations. Funny, she thought, mind boggled, she'd no recollection that Mike had unlocked the handcuffs. Looking around the luxurious master bedroom, Amy half expected an English butler or a French maid to come walking in to pamper her and make a fuss. The room was cheerfully bright in the daylight and the welcoming fresh air gently blew in through the opened windows. Life couldn't get any better, Amy mused, ducking her head under the sleek satin covers for an extra five minutes snooze, dreaming of eating toast on the top deck aboard a luxury cruise liner sailing along the Mediterranean, listening to the mesmerizing sound of Mike's beautiful voice whispering her name against the sea breeze.

"Amy? Amy? Wake up. Amy?" said Mike, softly blowing in her ear, "Amy?"

"Uh, Mike," Amy stirred, sleepily.

"Ah, at last, you're awake."

Squinting and incoherent for a few seconds, Amy slowly gathered her senses. She was completely astonished and taken aback to find that the smell of toast wasn't part of her dream after all, but the real thing. Mike stood at the bed, enrobed in an elegant black and gold, silk gown. He held an exquisite bamboo and rattan tray to serve breakfast in bed for two of fresh orange juice, organic muesli, delicately chopped fresh fruit salad and lashings of home baked granary toast with wild organic honey. A single red rose resting on a crispy, white cotton pleated napkin and the Saturday newspaper bulging with supplements completed the tray arrangement.

"Come on, sit up, lazy bones!" ordered Mike.

Reveling in Mike's attention and taking her own sweet time, Amy made herself comfortable, propping herself up against a stack of pillows.

Mike sat on the bed and put the tray between them.

"My gosh … this is wonderful and so generous, kind and thoughtful of you. You shouldn't have, Mike." Famished, hunger pangs noisily played an away game in her stomach. Eyes on the toasted granary bread, Amy wanted to spend the rest of her life with Mike. Forever.

"Enjoy. Ladies first," said Mike.

Amy bit daintily into a slice of toast.

CHAPTER 14

Amy stepped into the marble hydro-massage spa bath with Mike. Water cascaded along a wall softly beaming rainbow colored lighting. They sat closely together, indulgently allowing the thrashings of jet powered water massage their bodies. Amy sank deeper into the spa. Her mind engulfed on the rapid change of her life, unbelievably transforming before her eyes. Elated, Amy turned her back to Mike and he gently massaged her shoulders.

"Ah. Yes, that feels so good," Amy cooed contentedly.

"Cascading … Cascades Hotel … Suite Cascades … Suite Cascades … Cascadia. Sounds like a good name for our hotel," said Mike. "Just think, we'll be running our own unique, one of a kind suites hotel. Each suite will have its own rainbow illuminated waterfall cascading into a spa overlooking ocean views."

Amy blinked splatters of water from her eyes, turned to Mike and, barely able to fully harness his dreamy concept, lapped up in the privileges of the luxurious surroundings and settings said, "Cascadia. Yes, I too like the name."

"That's settled. Cascadia it is."

"I'll certainly go along with that."

"I hope we can agree on most things as simply as this," said Mike laughingly, sprawling his arms out wide.

Amy laughed. "Should we choose to discuss business matters incongruously, hot, wet and naked in influentially compromising positions, I'll be inclined to guarantee that we'll undoubtedly reach an agreement on most things ninety-nine, point nine percent of the time," said Amy, raising her eyebrows and blowing Mike a kiss.

Mike threw his head back and laughed out loud. "I cannot begin the number of strangest and most bizarre circumstances, innovative and inge-nious business ideas and decisions being made right now, as we speak," said Mike. ∧that are ̶S̶T̶E̶T̶

"Nothing wrong with being imaginative, I suppose. One should be able to launch ideas, make creatively constructive decisions from wherever they are."

Mike closed his eyes and smiled. "Agreed. Agreed. Whilst we're on the sub-ject of launching, I'm aiming, ultimately for the triple A, four diamond rating."

"Superb," said Amy excitedly, still feeling a little out of her depth.

"One needs to follow their hunches. Plainly speaking, I'm confident that I've made the right decision here in choosing you as my business partner. I've observed your numerous qualities, your unobtrusive style and commanding strength and, I particularly admire that you tenaciously give your all to Planet Management. There's so much more to you than meets the eye. Arduously demonstrating a great deal of dictative flair, you deserve to reap the rewards and benefits from your own exclusive incentives that it makes sense you've joined me."

Amy suspected that Mike had put her through many a test and monitored her reactions. She'd not nagged him or panicked when he'd failed to call her as promise. Daringly putting her on the spot at Candies, Amy had complied, adapted and enjoyed where other women would've crumbled. "Thank you, Mike. You're flattering me far too excessively," she said coyly. Feeling vulnera-ble, not certain what to make of it all, she was coming to realize the over-whelming affects she was having on Mike. She adored him more and more at every passing moment, but knew she had to get a grip, tread carefully, one step at a time, one day at a time.

"I, by no means, intend to cause you any discomfort," said Mike contrarily

"I know," said Amy lethargically, lost in the moment, the combination of heat, steam, effects of inhaling the potent scent of Ylang Ylang aromatherapy oil, excessive thrashings of water massaging her, sending her into a deeper state of relaxation, depleting her energies. "I'm hopping out. Goodness knows, we've been in here for ages. My skin's beginning to wrinkle."

"You go on ahead. I'll be out in five minutes." Equally depleted of energy, Mike chose to immerse himself deeper.

Amy stepped out of the spa bath and wrapped herself in one of the guests' bath sheets. She drank a bottle of sparkling mineral water and headed back to the master bedroom to recuperate. The aftermath of breakfast lay scattered on the bed. Having no intentions of clearing up, Amy moved across the room to the couch. Lying on her back, Amy smiled thankfully, enjoyably reflecting dinner at the Beaujolais, their rampant lovemaking, breakfast in bed, the remarkable things Mike had said to her and, the business proposition. Her watch lay on the mink rug, Amy picked it up and looked at the time. It was approaching four o'clock. She slung her watch on her wrist, rose sharply, let the bath sheet fall to the floor and began putting her clothes on. She had a lot of thinking, planning and researching to do on her new business and she had to consult Vincent's invaluable advice. Amy was slipping on her shoes when Mike strolled in, wrapped in a guest bath sheet.

"Leaving?" he asked, strolling over to the couch, lackadaisically.

"I'd love to stay but, I'm afraid I have to leave now. I've so much to …"

"There's no need to explain. You run along. I'll be in touch," said Mike sullenly, sitting on the couch, not doing a very good job of concealing his disappointment, sulking openly.

Feeling guilty about leaving Mike, Amy was hoping that she wasn't ruining any further surprises that he may possibly have had in store. She sat on the couch and smiled into his eyes. "Thank you very much indeed for an absolutely splendid weekend. I truly appreciate everything."

"Oh, don't mention it. Come back tomorrow for lunch. I'll call a taxi."

Mike and Amy stood holding each other in a loving embrace behind the ornate wooden double doors. Their taxi driver waited in the driveway with the engine running.

Amy beamed into Mike's eyes. "I'll work on scheduling our initial meeting to take place within a week," she said.

"Sure," said Mike nodding, pressing his lips gently on her forehead.

Amy reluctantly pulled herself away, walked out to the driveway and climbed into the taxi. She waved at Mike as the taxi driver pulled away. Admiring the rows of palatial residential properties along the Heath Street, Amy grew apprehensive about Mike's proposition and hoped that she'd made the right decision. "Stop doubting. Get your fucking act together," said Amy.

"Sorry luv. I didn't hear that," said the taxi driver.

"Excuse me? Oh, I'm sorry," said Amy surprisingly, shaking her head. She'd spotted that the passengers' microphone had picked up her voice. "I was thinking aloud."

The taxi driver chuckled saying, "You know what they say about people who talk to themselves."

Amy said nothing. She'd dialed Vincent's cell-phone number, it was ringing and she was waiting for him to answer.

The taxi driver pulled up outside Amy's apartment. Amy thanked, paid, tipped him modestly and fished her apartment keys out of her handbag. Her cell-phone rang. Jenson's number flashed up on her screen. Frustrated, Amy rolled her eyes. "Yes, Jenson," she barked.

"That's hardly a nice way to answer the 'phone. And, a good afternoon to you, too!"

"Jenson, I've had a hectic weekend."

"I'd noticed. I'd popped round twice today. You haven't been home since last night, have you?" he returned, cynically.

Amy let herself into her apartment, slammed the door and stood rigidly in the hallway. "What has that got to do with you?" she said, wary that Jenson may have been keeping tabs on her.

"What's up with you lately? How long has it been since we've made …"

"I'd rather not talk about that."

"I think you've got something to say to me and, I'd rather you say it than keep me hanging on like this. How long do you think a man can wait?"

Amy was in no mood to argue. "Alright, alright," she said. "I don't want …"

"To see me anymore? I know that's what you're about to say."

Amy took a deep breath. Jenson wasn't making things any easier for her. "It's over. Us. We're through. I've moved on, Jenson. Sorry?" she spurted remorsefully. Jenson hasn't done anything to deserve this, she thought.

"Just like that? Over the 'phone. As simple as that, is it? Just as I was getting sucked into you … Talk to me, woman."

Amy cringed. The pained tone of Jenson's voice cut through her. "No, I won't, to be honest. It just won't help matters. We've been going along casually and uncommitted to each other, Jenson." she said, coldly, not doing her best to placate him.

"What about my stuff that I've left in your apartment?"

"I'll send them to you by courier. And by the way, I'd appreciate you dropping my keys in the mailbox, please." Amy continued along the hallway, unlocked her door, entered her apartment and slammed the door.

"Don't I get a chance to see you, one last time?" Jenson pleaded.

Guilt riddled, Amy's stomach jerked, churned, twisted and turned at Jenson's desperate pleas. "No. Jenson. Please don't make this any harder for us."

"Why?"

"Get a grip, Jenson. These things happen," she said sternly, slumping on the couch.

There was a brief pause. "I'd like to ask you a question before I go?"

"What is it?" Amy wasn't prepared to discuss Mike and hoped that Jenson hadn't found out about him.

"Can I call you, in say, a month's time to see how you're getting on, compare notes, touch base with you, we could lunch …"

Amy sighed. "You just don't get it, do you? Familiarity breeds contempt and all that jazz. It's over. I've got to go now, Jenson. Hope all works out for you. I'm sorry, Jenson." There were tears in her eyes.

"You condescending little bitch …"

"I'm hanging up," Amy shouted shakily, switching off the cell-phone. In a fit of exerted anger, guilt and frustration, Amy threw her cell-phone on the floor, marched into the kitchen, slung open the refrigerator and pulled out a Bud. She sat down, slammed the Bud on the kitchen table, held her head in her hands and cried. Twenty minutes later, her telephone rang. Amy had stopped sobbing five minutes beforehand, finished the Bud and moved on. She grabbed a tissue, blew her nose, got up quickly and answered the telephone.

"I've picked up your message, called your cell-phone, but got the voicemail. What can I do for you, Amy?" said Vincent hurriedly.

"Thank you so much for returning my call, Vincent." Amy, pulled herself together quickly in order to expedite the matter as Vincent wasn't one for small talk and his time was very limited. "Could I arrange an early morning meeting with you on Monday to discuss a new business venture? An hotelier associate of mine proposes going onto our books."

"Could you not pass this one over to the guys in the new business section?"

"Well, I would also like to seek your personal advice on this, if I may. I've some personal involvement in this particular venture and …"

"Amy, let me stop you there to inform you that I don't have any free time on Monday morning. I'm back to back in meetings."

Amy's heart sank.

Vincent continued, "You're seeking my advice therefore, this must be important to you," he said, sighing.

"It is important."

"I can fit you in at six AM."

"That'll be great."

"Monday morning, in my office, at six."

"Thank you, Vincent."

"Would there be anything further?"

"No, that was it."

"Very good," said Vincent hanging up.

Amy took a thankfully deep sigh and stared up at her kitchen ceiling. She switched on her lap top and began her research on every conceivable aspect to do with the hotel industry. She emailed Richard a list of instructions, alerting him on the anticipated work and long hours planned ahead, returned to conducting her research and concluded at four ~~am~~ in the morning.

Amy awoke Sunday morning feeling different—on top of the world. She lay in bed deliberating her life, her now, her present and her future, optimistic, her future was looking promisingly bright due to the potentiality of becoming a wealthy woman, going into partnership with a wealthy man whom she adored and admired. It was ten minutes past eleven. Amy smiled and wondered how Mike was feeling and what he'd planned to do for lunch. Her concerns grew for Katie and the abortion. Only a week to go, Amy thought. She reached for the telephone and dialed Katie's number. Katie's telephone tripped over to the voicemail. "Hi Katie, Amy called. Please call me. Bye for now." On that note, Amy decided to get out of bed. She showered, ate a light breakfast, and when she'd settled down on her lap top to continue her research on the hotel industry, Katie returned her call.

"Hi. How are you feeling today?" Amy asked Katie.

"Do you really want to know?"

"Try me."

"I'm ravaged, owed to morning sickness all weekend."

"Oh! How awful."

"But, I've great news for you. How much time do you have to spare?" asked Katie.

"Fire away," said Amy, sitting comfortably, bracing herself eagerly awaiting the news.

"I've changed my mind. I won't be going ahead with the abortion next week and, I've just got off the 'phone to the clinic. I've cancelled it. They tried to talk me out of it. Can you believe that?"

"That's great news, Katie. I'm so pleased for you and the baby. Now I can look forward to making his or her acquaintance." Amy had offered Katie her unequivocal support and promised to remain with her, on the fateful day. The news of Katie's decision freed Amy from the daunting prospect of having to live with the heavy burden of guilt resting on her shoulders as an accessory to the act of, murder, in effect.

"And ... there's, David," Katie added with an air of confidence.

"Oh yes. What's the latest?"

"He regrets the way things have turned out between us. He's very sorry," said Katie, saddening her tone.

Amy, opposed to David's re-emergence, sternly asked, "Have you told him that you're pregnant"

"Of course I have, Amy. A few days ago, once I'd decided to keep it. How could I not let him know?"

"Where do you both go from here?"

"David's visited me and wants to be a part of the baby's life. He intends to be there for us and he's offered to kit the baby out with everything it needs. So, I'll be turning the spare bedroom into a nursery and...." Katie went on and on about David this, David that, that Amy was finding it all so appallingly boring, her mind was shutting down as a result. "... boarding school. That way I can return to work ..."

"Katie? Slow down, will you?"

"Yes, you're right. I know. I'm getting over excited. I know."

Irritated, Amy couldn't help but feel pity for Katie. He has her wrapped around his tricky little, nasty fingers, she thought. "What about his wife and kids?"

"I was just coming to that bit. He's left her."

"Left her? Are you sure? How do you know it's the truth?"

"You've got it wrong. He's provided me with proof," said Katie, proudly.

"Proof?! What proof?"

"Don't get annoyed, Amy, it's not been easy for me. Please try to understand."

"Understand? I'm under-the-standing that you could get hurt again, Katie? Why are you doing this?" Amy poured herself a glass of water and sat down at the kitchen table. Her positive state slowly ebbed away to one of sullenly that Amy willed positivity to come flowing back.

"Because I want to make things work ..."

"Katie, let me be frank with you. Don't kid yourself into believing or dreaming that you will be playing happy families, living happily ever after with David. Be careful. He's lied to you before and he will lie to you again."

"No, he won't. How can you be so sure? Look, he's going ahead with the divorce and he's shown me a copy of a letter from his lawyer and photocopies of other legal documents. He's fully going ahead with it."

Amy had heard enough. "As long as you're happy," were her final words on the subject.

"Thanks, Amy. I knew you'd understand. Come shopping with me next week, I've seen lots of cute baby gear in the stores."

"It's a bit early to be shopping don't you think? You're not that far gone."

"I know, but, I just want to be prepared for when the baby comes."

"It's an excuse to go shopping," Amy joked.

Katie laughed. "You hit the nail on the head."

Amy sighed. "Sure, I'll be happy to come along. Where shall we meet?"

"We could kick off with coffee, here, at my place next week Saturday morning for say, come round at ten. I'll prepare you a figure conscious, low calorie breakfast of melon and blueberries that you can burn off walking around the shops."

"Sounds like a smashing plan."

"Good stuff. I'm looking forward to it. And, Amy?"

Amy held her breath.

"Thanks."

"Don't thank me," said Amy awkwardly, "See you next week." Amy was slowly coming to terms with the ironical fact that Katie was pregnant with David's child.

CHAPTER 15

Amy sank her tall and slender body in the black leather, executive couch, conveniently situated outside Vincent's office. Yawning, Amy nervously tapped her feet and scanned her notes repeatedly in the hope that the outcome of the meeting would be a successful one and, that Vincent would agree to Planet Management adding the business venture to their portfolio. Amy whipped out her cell-phone vibrating in her handbag and inserted her ear-piece. Vincent's cell-phone number appeared on her screen alongside the time of ten minutes to six. "I'm on my way in, approaching Cino's. Would you care for a coffee?" Vincent's firm and sturdy footsteps stumping along the pavement reverberated through Amy's ear-piece.

"Yes, please. A small latte with skimmed milk. No sugar. Thanks."

"Good, right you are."

Amy's heartbeat quickened in apprehension. She returned to her notes, re-read them and stopped at six o'clock when Vincent stumped out of the elevator. He swung an old, tanned leather briefcase that had seen better days in one hand and a small white paper bag with Cino's emblazoned in large italic black print in the other. "Ah, Amy. Come in. Come in," Vincent beckoned, stumping over to his office. He dropped his briefcase at his feet, pressed his right thumb firmly on the thumbprint reader which automatically unlocked his office door. Amy rose quickly to her feet and followed Vincent into his office. Vincent perched himself on the edge of the black leather, high-backed reclining chair behind his desk, carefully took the Styrofoam cups of basking hot coffees out of the Cino's bag and handed Amy a cup of latte. "Right," he said, grabbing a note pad, jotting Amy's name, date, time and prospecting as the heading at the top centre of the page. Sitting opposite, Amy was able to decipher Vincent's notes, reading upside down as she leaned forward putting her cup of latte on Vincent's desk. Her throat was parched. She felt slightly nervy. Amy coughed then took a careful sip of latte.

"Thank you for agreeing to see me, Vincent."

"Now, fire away, Amy."

Amy sat up powerfully in her seat. "I'll be as quick as I can. An associate of mine proposes to purchase a hotel. He has invited me to become a partner and, I wondered whether I could ask you for guidance and advice in this area. Not having ventured into anything of this sort or magnitude, I must confess that I've very little working knowledge on the subject."

Vincent looked inquisitively at Amy. "I don't need to tell you that you need to know exactly what it is that is being proposed and required of you. I'm assuming this associate of yours has the necessary knowledge, skills and expertise in this field and easily accessible capital?"

"Yes, indeed, most certainly, Vincent, in fact, his family own hotels in Europe but, he has planned autonomy, to run his own hotel, that is." Amy avoided going into the underlying deliberations of Mike's disinheritance and family problems.

"Good," said Vincent, pausing briefly, "That'll make things a lot easier to progress, less work and more cost effective where time's concerned. What is the name of your ... your associate? I may know of him."

Amy froze in her seat and hoped that Vincent hadn't had any encounters, professionally or otherwise, with Carlson Brandleton or anyone related to the Brandleton clan. Amy coughed again to rid the discomforting parched feeling that still nagged at her throat that the latte failed to quell. "Mike Brandleton," she said calmly.

Vincent jotted down the name, held his pen between his teeth, swiveled around in his recliner and gazed out of the window in contemplative silence.

Amy silently panted in her seat, anxiously waiting for Vincent's response.

After a few moments, Vincent swiveled around and faced Amy, saying, "No. Nothing. The name doesn't come to mind."

Relieved, Amy crossed her legs and leaned back in her seat in regained comfort.

"Would he, by any chance, be prospecting a small group of investors to purchase an immediately self-sufficient hotel or an empty hotel requiring refurbishments and, in what locations?"

"I would say something immediately self-sufficient. The location is yet to be decided upon but, it would be overseas, that I'm most certain about. The Caribbean looks favorable. He hadn't mentioned getting any other investors involved although, I don't think he'd rule out that option. It depends on how much autonomy he'd be aiming to achieve. I believe, at present, this venture would be between us both." Amy uncrossed and stretched her numbed, long legs and allowed the blood to flow and circulate freely.

Vincent sighed. "You do intend to remain with us long term? It would be a shame to lose you, Amy."

"Of course, I do, Vincent. In fact, the next question would be that we'd like our venture to be considered by Planet Management and wondered whether we could go on the books." Positioning her note pad on her lap, Amy prepared to jot down a valuable list of bullet notes.

Vincent raised his eyebrow. "Forgive me, Amy, but there isn't sufficient time to go into the pedantries in this hour. We'll most certainly run out of time. I have another appointment, due to arrive at seven. We'll have to wrap this up, unfortunately. Make an appointment for you and Mike Brandleton to come along and see me in the next couple of weeks. Prepare a draft list of team members to work on the prospect of a new project and have the list brought to that meeting together with a blueprint. That way, we can immediately start the ball rolling. Subject to you both meeting the book criteria and, once we've completed the necessary searches, we'll decide on a definitive team to work on the geographical dynamics, supply and demand, markets, political and economical climates. Should you not have a specific hotel in mind, the team'll research hotels that are not purely esthetically appealing but, more critically, delve into how well they're run, look into some of the terms of the original purchases and related loans and whether the owners or owner is current on any loans, bills, real estate taxes. Plans of remodeling the hotel could influence the asking price and offset financial factors in that, one would have to look at negotiating a reduction of the purchase price. This way, you could free-up some equity. Failing that, you'd have to finance the remodeling and this may result in secondary financing. The hotel's cash flow would have to be carefully examined and may help to pay for any refurbishments. There is the whole package on offer that needs to be seriously taken into consideration to ascertain whether the hotel would meet your basic criteria and indeed, those of Planet Management. The physical facilities, surrounding areas, competition and market demands are to be researched. How do you intend to raise your side of the capital?"

"I had thought of asking my bank manager for a business loan. And I've a little bit of savings and investments put aside," said Amy, speed writing, exasperated by Vincent's rapid flow of information, her thoughts heavily preoccupied on creating ideas on how to come up with the funds, hoping that any financial sacrifices she'd have to make wouldn't prove to be too adverse.

"The overall sum could be quite sizeable. How much capital are we talking about here?"

"We are looking in the region of, circa three million, to start with, at least."

"Three million's a good start for a small concern. Should you envisage any problems in raising the finance your end, please come back to me. I can work out a number of ways where Planet Management would be able to assist you personally. Let me know how you get on there. I could also recommend the locations of St. Barts or the Turks and Caicos as highly prospective locations in the Caribbean. Not only do I personally own investment property in Provo particularly, I do have excellent connections and contacts at both locations."

Astonishingly impressed with Vincent's offers, Amy struggled to contain her excitement. "This is more than I'd expected that I'm truly taken aback by your generosity, Vincent. Thank you very much."

"Not at all," said Vincent, raising his left arm, glancing at his yellow gold Rolex watch. "It's been my pleasure discussing the preliminaries with you this morning. You possess astute business acumen and I have full confidence in you, Amy, that this venture will be a great success for you. Draft that team together in order that we can start rolling straight away." he said, rising sprightly out of his seat.

Amy stood and Vincent walked towards her. "Should anything further cross your mind prior to our next meeting, please give me a call and I'll assure you of my best endeavors to clarify any queries in a timely manner," he said, walking Amy out of his office.

Amy paused at the door and turned to Vincent saying, "Once again, I thank you so much for your kind support."

Vincent made no further comment, but nodded and smiled stiffly. As he swung the door open, the retired barrister, Bernard Wilson, an elderly, white haired, distinguished looking gentleman and an old friend of Vincent, paced back and forth in the spaciously expansive reception area outside Vincent's office. "Bernard it's great to see you, old boy, do come in, come in," said Vincent, ushering Bernard into his office. Bernard winked at Amy as he entered the office.

Stunned, Amy stood motionless and mischievously wondered whether Bernard could be a clandestine member of a Fetish club. Taking a deep breath, Amy looked around the open planned office and relished the welcomed silence. She looked at the state-of-the-art, hi-tech Platinum clock hanging from the ceiling above the reception desk. It was approaching six-fifty. Telephones hadn't started ringing and staff hadn't started arriving. Amy strode slowly over to her desk and immediately started transposing her meeting notes onto her PC. She emailed Richard a brief overview of her prospective project. With a list of suggested names to serve as members of the draft project team, Amy instructed Richard to set up a new project meeting. By seven-twenty, Amy concluded the transposition of her notes and instructions to Richard and, thirsted for another cup of latte. The staff restaurant was due to open at eight o'clock, Amy couldn't wait and she'd never cared to drink coffee from the vending machines. She downloaded her notes from her PC to her lap top and, armed with her notes and her cell-phone, Amy headed to Cino's. Floating along the street, she felt like she was the luckiest woman on the planet to have such a great boss in Vincent. She desperately wanted to call Mike to relay the good news. It was seven-thirty. Cino's were relatively empty, peaceful and quiet. Amy viewed that Cino's would be the perfect spot and ideal place to call Mike from her cell-phone. She wandered over to the counter, purchased a cup of latte, sat down at her favorite table, sipped her latte, read through her notes and called Mike at seven fifty-five. Amy lightly tapped her French manicured nails on the table. "No definitive date has been set for the meeting with Vincent. We're to come up with the blueprint within the next two weeks or so to present to Vincent. I'm in the process of getting a select team together to work on the project from its inception and on an ongoing basis."

"Thanks for getting it all organized. I trust that you'd have matters in hand and all under control," said Mike, commendably.

"How flexible is your diary?"

"Quite flexible. I've a few meetings in place with my lawyer and accountant, nothing my secretary couldn't reschedule. I'll work around you. We need to get this thing off the ground."

"Expect an imminent call from Richard, my managing assistant, in connection with setting up a date"

"I'll inform my secretary to expect a call from Planet Management regarding our meeting and that she treats it as priority."

"Great," said Amy, sipping the last mouthful of latte. Amy needed something to work with, something to focus on, something to visualize, when she returned to her desk. "Are you any closer on what it is you'd like to invest in?" she enquired, proactively.

"It would be an ongoing business and my plans are to renovate the top floor during the out of season period into the most luxurious Penthouse suites ever, once I've found the appropriate hotel that feels right," Mike responded. "All in good time."

"I know. I know exactly what you mean." Amy's thoughts traveled back to when she'd viewed her apartment. She knew it was the one for her the moment she'd stepped into the entrance hall, she'd felt it and had purchased it. "Moving on to the location, if I may?" she said.

"Sure."

"Vincent had suggested the Turks and Caicos, and St. Barts as possible locations. He has influential contacts at both. Bear that in mind, would you? There is the possibility that he might be able to swing a few ropes for us," she said, hoping she wasn't being too pushy.

"Interesting." There was a silence. Amy waited. "I'll certainly bear that in mind. Barbados appeals to me. Hotels are thriving out there."

Amy didn't fully share Mike's choice of location. She preferred the more affluent locations of St. Barts and the Turks and Caicos, locations that appealed to her yearnings of the prestige she desired and aspired to, fully conscious of the fact that, owing to her present status, she had no other choice and would have to humbly settle for Barbados if need be. A progressive number of patrons flowing into Cino's purchasing coffees to take-away, caused the noise levels to rise steadily. Amy had to head back to the office to commence work on the project, the most important project she'd work on to date. She strolled out of Cino's and joined the army of office workers, all doing the habitual morning melancholy march, the majority going in the same direction. "Let me know whether you'd be requiring any input from my side with regard to the blue-print," said Amy.

"I'll have you cast your eye over it once it's done."

"I'm certain that you'll complete an impressive job. By the way," said Amy, replaying the arousing images of Mike sensually licking-off fresh cream he'd smeared over her hardened nipples. "Thanks for Sunday lunch, especially dessert."

"My treat," said Mike, chuckling sexily. "We must do it again, and soon."

"Yes, we must." Excited, Amy rushed back to the office as horny as hell.

Richard was reading through Amy's emailed instructions as she walked into the office. "Red eye hours are in order by the looks of things. Let me congratulate you on your personal involvement on this project," said Richard, confidently boisterous and enthusiastic in his ambitious aim to place himself on a par with Amy.

"This is a special project shrouded in confidentiality. Prior to the commencement of works, signatures of all involved would be required on a confidentiality agreement which I'm presently in the process of drawing up," said Amy.

Richard wasn't certain what Amy was getting at. All projects came with signed confidentiality agreements, it was standard procedure. He listened half-heartedly whilst Amy scanned through her emails. Impressed with her stake in the new business, Richard was also a little envious. "I'd welcome more of an involved role on this venture. Perhaps, when you're fully up and running your own lucrative hotel business, I could become an employee of yours. I hope you'll bear these thoughts in mind?"

Irked on the one hand at Richard's casually pledged interest, on the other hand, Amy admired his audacious spirit. She wandered over to Richard's desk, placed both hands firmly on her hips and looked at the back of his thin frame sitting in the chair.

Richard swiveled around in his chair and looked bravely into Amy's eyes, something he very rarely did.

Amy glared coldly into Richard's eyes.

"I'll do a damned good job for you, Amy. If only you'd consider," he pleaded, fuelling Amy's annoyance.

"Let me be honest and frank with you, Richard. Your offer would not be considered as an option and, knowing this, should you prefer to be taken off the project, please let me know, as soon as possible, so that I can call someone else in."

"I'll be more than happy to remain on the project," returned Richard, stoically enthused, his feelings hurt and ego bruised. Richard knew within himself, and by the look in Amy's eyes, that he'd made a precocious fool of himself. Frustrated, he turned round and gazed blankly at his computer screen.

"How soon do you think you can arrange the first meeting to be attended by Mike Brandleton, Vincent and I?"

"I'm in the process of firming up a date."

"And, how soon do you think you'll have the list of names of the team members confirmed and drafted up for me to take another look at?" Amy was fully aware of her bullish and demanding attitude but, she wasn't in the mood to mollycoddle Richard. Nervous about the whole concept of going into the venture, she was intentionally using Richard as her punching bag. Even with Vincent's backing and support and the information she'd gathered from a variety of sources, Amy was beginning to entertain doubts as to whether she'd be able to work wonders on the venture. She allowed her insec᠁ imagination to run wild, conjuring nightmarish images of ᠁ thoughts about her should she fall short of coming up trumps, not m᠁ high expectations. She was totally convinced that things were going to be tough for her walking on new and alien grounds that she didn't want anything to go amiss.

"I'm working on the list of names as we speak. Give me at least a couple of days," said Richard, slightly harassed.

"Forward what you have now would you, please?"

"Sure." His lips tightened in annoyance, consciously concealed from Amy, Richard forwarded the list to Amy and immediately pressed on with arranging the meeting.

Amy scanned through the names, made a few adjustments and returned the updated list to Richard. "I've added a couple of people to the list. Go ahead with arranging informal one-to-one discussions with them. There'll be some inevitable shuffling around of duties, moving people from one project to another but, that can easily be remedied," Amy commented. "Go through all their projects and arrange informal one-to-ones with them all, would you?"

"Right away," said Richard. Increasingly getting more aggravated by Amy's shortness in manner and tone, Richard urgently needed five minutes away from her. "I'm popping out for five minutes," he announced abruptly, almost tempted to tag on "any objections?" but thought wisely against doing so.

Amy peered across her desk at Richard. "Fine," she said. "See you in five minutes, or so."

Seething, Richard slipped his cigarettes and lighter in his shirt pocket, threw on his black and white, dog-toothed check tailored jacket and dashed to the elevator.

Conscious of Richard's mood and feeling reproachful about her attitude, Amy closed her eyes as Richard stepped into the elevator. Regretful, Amy promised herself that she'd go easy on Richard when he returned from having smoked his much needed cigarette.

Amy had a quick bite of green salad for lunch in the staff restaurant, returned to her desk, and flashed Richard a side-eyed glance. He munched on a chicken salad sandwich with mayo on brown bread and refused to acknowledge that Amy had returned. Amy checked her inbox and sighed at the numerous emails that had arrived during her short lunch break and noted that Richard had finalized on the meeting arrangements to be held between Vincent, Mike and

Amy. He'd proactively added his name to the new team. Pleased, Amy wanted to thank Richard for his expediency. She glanced sneakily at him, sensed his irritability, felt the cold enmity between them and, opting to make amends, she thought she'd thank him later—after she'd called Mike. Amy got up abruptly and made her way to one of the vacant meeting rooms. She hoped that no-one would require use of it whilst she was engaged on a private call, she'd pull rank, if need be. "We've email confirmation. The meeting is scheduled to take place in a week's time, next Monday at three to be exact, that's sooner rather than later. How are you getting on with the blueprint? Will it be ready on time? Is there anything you'd like me to...."

"Amy, slow down, slow down. Everything's in order. I've set the specifications in motion with my business lawyer and accountant. I'm ready," said Mike.

"Great. I didn't want to come across as being pushy or over keen or anything, it's just that I want this as much as you do and ..."

"There's no need to explain. I perfectly understand your concerns," Mike interjected.

Amy strolled over to the other end of the meeting room and leaned on the window. "I'd like to come to an agreement with you on a delicate matter," she said, staring out of the window, admiring the view of the city, the clear blue sky and the sun's vying to burst its rays through the tinted smoky-grey sun screened window.

"I'm all ears," said Mike, curiously.

Amy coughed nervously, moved away from the window and paced up and down the expansive, twenty foot meeting room. "Our intimacy ... our relationship. It would be best if we could refrain from allowing our intimacy known to Vincent or anyone else during our business transactions."

Mike laughed heartily. "Agreed. It's unprofessional. I'm more than happy to go along with you on that."

"Perfect," said Amy, relieved at Mike's jovial response.

"On the subject of business, with the blueprint ready, you could browse through it at my place over lunch on Saturday if you like," Mike suggested casually and invitingly.

Amy pictured Katie getting all upset and furious with her for canceling the breakfast morning and shopping excursion. "Sunday would be better," she said, crossing her fingers, hoping he'd say yes.

"That'll be fine. Shall we say between twelve forty-five and one? I'll pick you up and we can continue from where we'd left off," Mike said teasingly.

Amy giggled, slightly. "Yes. That'll be fine. I'm looking forw
tinuation," she said, acquiescently, making a mental note of the ⌐ ,
lay in wait ahead. The closure and debrief of the Del Mar casino project, the
inception of the new Latin American project, work on her new project, ending
with her entire weekend being taken up by Katie and Mike.

"Smashing, darling," said Mike.

"Darling? Did you say darling?"

"Yes. I won't do so again should you have any objections to me using …"

"No, Mike, please, quite the opposite. I welcome the term of endearment,"
she informed him pleasingly.

"Fine … darling. I'd better be pushing off now. I'll catch-up with you before
the end of the week."

"Fine," said Amy, blowing Mike a kiss. She returned to the window, looked
out and admired the view of the city again. Happy, she later strolled out of the
meeting room, relieved there were no interruptions during her unofficial
occupation of it. Re-energized, Amy returned to her desk to find Richard
working mirthlessly at his computer. "Thank you, Richard for getting the
meeting arranged so quickly. Please, if I'd appeared to be short with you, don't
take it personally. You are fully aware that I'm working on a number of projects
and the demands set on me," she said, reconcilably.

Richard swapped his concentrated gaze at the screen for one of an apologetic beam at Amy as he tossed sheets of paper into the recycling bin conveniently situated close to his desk.

"Not at all. I understand. We're both busy. Don't worry I'll assist you as best
I can," said Richard

"Thank you, Richard. Your assistance is highly valued and appreciated."

Richard blushed slightly, turned to his computer and resumed typing.
"Thanks," he whispered, embarrassingly.

"'Right. Now that's settled, I'd better crack on with producing the confidentiality agreement," said Amy, pleased she'd succeeded in clearing the brief
enmity that had lurked between them.

CHAPTER 16

Amy heaved her body out of bed and slumped lazily on the edge. She shielded her eyes from the dazzling sun blazing through the slits of her venetian blinds. "This is sacrilegious," Amy moaned, burying her head in her hands. At seven-thirty on a Saturday morning, her stomach buckled at the thought of eating a large portion of breakfast. Food was the last thing on her mind. She'd give anything to pass on breakfast, much preferring to settle for the shopping trip. Given the choice, spending virtually the whole day wrapped in Mike's arms was what she'd sooner opt for. Dragging her fingers through her hair, Amy drudgingly slid off the edge of her bed. Stretching, she looked back and stared yearningly at the brilliant white ruffled goose down pillows, crumpled duvet and fine Egyptian cotton sheets. Desperate for an additional ten minutes of beckoningly blissful sleep, Amy weighed up that, crawling back into bed could possibly prove to be a fatal move, vowing that Katie would never forgive her for missing their appointment due to oversleeping. Amy yawned. There's only one thing for it, she thought. Tossing her white silk kimono over her shoulders, Amy slipped her feet into a pair of white, silk slippers and, inhaling a few deep breaths, she shuffled hesitatingly slow to the bathroom to negotiate a cold shower.

"AMSTERDAM!" Katie admired the keepsake clogs that hung ornately on the kitchen wall, gracing its pride of place. "You dark horse," Katie teased, a shocked expression written all over her face, nudging Amy, accusatively. "I thought you'd bought them here, in London."

"Sorry, but with all that's been going on lately, I hadn't had an opportune moment to update you on Mike and me."

"I guess you're right. It has been a bit of a trying time for both of us," said Katie, agreeably. "Well, well, well. Amsterdam. How was it then?" she continued, shoving a large spoonful of cereal in her mouth, a large chunk of full cream, milk chocolate closely following.

Amy smiled reminiscently. "Delightful. We had a brilliant time."

"Have you fallen in love with him, then? Only, you look at bit blurry eyed, caught in a daze."

Amy sighed contentedly. "You could say so," she said coyly, sipping a cold glass of home made Elderberry Flower juice.

Katie shook her head and looked at Amy. "That's unbelievable."

Drenched in private wonderment, Amy gazed into her half-filled glass and shook her head from side to side. "Tell me about it, I don't believe it myself at times. So much has happened. So much," she said, moving finely chopped lettuce around her plate with her fork.

Katie got up abruptly, gathered her breakfast dishes and dashed over to the dishwasher. "Time's moving on," she said in urgency, stacking the dishwasher, clatteringly loud. "We'd better be moving on or I won't get any shopping done."

"Of course!" Amy looked at Katie, admiring the intricacies of her pregnancy, her radiance, her bloom and her blatant weight gain.

"Right, let's shop." Katie slammed the dishwasher door, switched it on, grabbed her keys and rushed out of the kitchen.

Disheartened at Katie calling an abrupt end to breakfast, Amy dropped her fork in her plate, grabbed her black leather, petite handbag and dashed closely behind Katie, leaving her unfinished homemade Elderberry Flower juice, salad and untouched melon and blueberries on the breakfast bar.

Katie bombarded Amy with non-stop news about David and the baby for the entire forty-five minute drive to the North London indoor shopping mall in Golders Green. Offering no comment and, listening in sheer and utter boredom, notwithstanding the fact that Katie hadn't allowed space for any commentaries, Amy gazed at the traffic ahead. Talking incessantly, Katie parked on the seventh floor of the multi-storey car park in an ideal spot within close proximity to the entrance of the shopping mall. She clambered out of the car, slammed the door and walked briskly to the entrance. Katie repeatedly looked back at Amy who lagged a few short paces behind her. "Come on, Amy," demanded Katie, aiming the fob at the car, automatically locking the doors and immobilizing the engine.

Amy was amazed at the amount of energy Katie had expended as she eventually caught up with her in the store. "I'm blown away at the vast array of items on sale here. Every conceivable idea that could possibly be produced is manufactured and put on sale," said Amy, entering the baby department, appraising the merchandise in sheer astonishment.

Katie glared at Amy in disbelief. "Come on now! Surely this isn't your first ever visit to a baby store, surely not?" she said laughingly, hoisting a handmade Moses basket in the air. "Cute, don't you think?" she said, her eyes darting everywhere.

Amy was contemplating an answer to Katie's previous question. "Yes. It's very pretty."

Katie exhibited a pair of satin and silk, pale blue booties from the footwear range. "Oh, I do love these."

"They're blue. Are you having a boy?" Amy asked, imprudently.

"Haven't got a clue. I'd rather wait the full term, see what pops out. These days, the color's not important." Katie paused. "I thought I'd let you in on that one," she said, winking knowledgably.

"Thanks for the update," said Amy, her patience waning.

"I think I'll buy a pair of these booties and a matching outfit," said Katie, swiftly crossing the shop floor to another section. Amy walked along wondering how much longer the shopping expedition would last "I'll take a few feeding bottles, cups and plates in advance, for when the baby gets older," said Katie, awkwardly clutching the Moses basket, booties and two layettes, she'd picked up indiscriminately.

Amy rushed forward. "Your hands are full. Let me help you or at least get you some assistance or something."

"Don't you start! I can manage, you know. They're not heavy. Gosh, you and David are so alike. He won't let me do anything either. Alright, I'll leave them on the reserved goods counter."

Amy held her hands above her head, signifying a truce. "Good idea. You've everything all worked out," she said, taking a step back, amused at the sight of Katie hobbling over to the reserved goods counter in a proud figure of motherhood, balancing her goods like a circus juggler.

"Where next?" said Katie returning breathlessly, scrunching the goods collection ticket in her purse.

"My, you've been hyperactive all morning. You ought to calm down on the rushing around front."

"I know. You're right. I get puffed out quite quickly nowadays. I need to s̶
for a bit." Katie turned abruptly, wandered out of the store and made a quick
bee-line to the self-service coffee shop directly opposite.

"This place looks relaxing. Take a seat. I'll get the refreshments."

"I'm so thirsty. I could murder a bottle of water," said Katie, gaspingly.

"I second that. I could easily demolish two bottles," said Amy happily,
relieved to be out of the baby department.

Leaning back exhaustively in her seat, envious, Katie watched Amy's tall,
slender body and gracious gait to the self service counter. It was evident that
Amy had increased vivacity. Feeling onerously fat and trapped, Katie bowed
her head and glared at her growing bump. "You little brat," she scowled, patting her stomach.

Amy returned with four bottles of mineral water and two glasses. She
opened two bottles and poured the contents in each glass.

"Thanks," said Katie, gulping her glass of water.

Amy sipped graciously and stared ahead into space.

Katie slammed her glass on the table. "So, what else has been going on
between you and Mike? You know virtually everything there is to know about
David and me. Surprise me more. Amsterdam! Well, I never."

Amy wondered how much she should wisely reveal as her relationship with
Mike wasn't completely certain, concrete or set in stone, not yet, although she
curiously wanted to learn Katie's views and opinions. Riskily, Amy spurted
whatever came out of her mouth. Hesitating, she coughed gently before pro-
ceeding. "Mike has asked me to go into business with him … the hotel industry," she said, bracing herself for Katie's response.

There was a long and painful silence.

Katie raised her eyebrows and frowned slightly. "You're not kidding? You've
shocked me now. Doing what?"

"I'd effectively become his partner in the ownership and management of a
hotel," Amy proudly announced.

"You're going to need to raise shit loads of money. Who does he think he is
asking you to come in? You haven't got that kind of money or even know anything about running a hotel," returned Katie, acrimoniously. Katie's open
brashness stopped Amy in her tracks that she held back on relishing in her
delivery of the remainder of her newly prized and treasured proposition.

"How would you know what I know from what I don't know? As the saying
goes, where there's a will there's a way. And besides, I can always learn the
ropes, hands on, as I go along. And who but Mike could I have as a better men-

tly, allowing herself the right to show her annoyance of

shoulders, snatched a bottle of water, opened it and
another glass. "Well, OK, you've made your point. I suppose it'll
work with Mike doubling up as your mentor. I'd better look out, if you carry
on at this rate, I'll be out of your league," she joked, enviously.

Amy sadly detected Katie's resentment and susceptibility to jealousy. "We're
only at the preliminary stages. Nothing's actually materialized yet but, if all
goes well, I've no doubt that our business partnership will flourish."

Katie patted her stomach. "My plan to run my own business will have to go
on the back burner for now or at least until this little brat gets older."

"Well, you've motherhood to look forward to. And you can't beat that. It's
much more of a precious, meaningful and rewarding role in life."

Katie gulped more water. "I'm not sure that I want to go ahead with having
this baby after all."

"WHAT? Why the sudden change of heart?" Amy sat up sharply. Shocked
and mortified, she slammed the palms of her hands on the table.

"Hey, calm down, Amy. What's with the shouting?" Katie whispered loudly,
her eyes flitting around the coffee shop. A number of onlookers were already
intruding on their conversation. "Now you've drawn attention to us."

Her eyes fixated on Katie, Amy ignored the onlookers. "Answer me. You
seemed so happy." Amy lowered her voice, a fraction.

"I'm just pissed off with the whole thing … David and his divorce proceed-
ings … everything. I feel I'm going to regret having this baby … after David's
been very supportive."

Speechless, Amy took a deep breath and slouched back in her seat; she fidgeted, having great difficulty in finding a relaxed position. Katie's words hung
densely in the air between them. They're eyes met for a few fiery seconds. Amy
turned away. She grabbed her glass and swallowed a large gulp of water to sub-
due an encroaching lump in her throat. Amy broke the edgy silence that hung
between them. "So, do you have plans to reschedule the …" Amy paused,
unable to say the word outright.

Katie came to Amy's rescue. "Termination? … I don't know. I just don't
know," she said, sighing, clutching her half-filled glass of water with both
hands. "A look at more baby gear might change my mind."

Amy rose swiftly from her seat. "Let's go for it," she said, tentatively waiting
at the table to whisk Katie back into the baby store, hoping the merchandise
will influence her to alter her decision.

Katie looked at Amy strangely and confusedly for a few short seconds and lethargically heaved herself out of the chair. "I need to look at cots and toys and things for the nursery," she said tiresomely, strolling out of the coffee shop.

Relieved, Amy smiled warmly. "That's more like it," she said, strolling closely beside her.

"I adore all the gadgets on this one, but there's just something about it that I'm not sure about," said Katie indecisively, critically scrutinizing all angles of the state-of-the-art playpen.

Amy exercised her trying patience whilst Katie mused over the playpen for nearly half an hour. "I'll purchase it for you. When you've decided, let me know."

"Thanks for the generous offer. David mentioned he'd commissioned the nursery to be custom built by some Swiss organization. I'm wondering whether there would be any scope to build a replica of this playpen into the plans."

"You'll have to ask David that one. Let me know once you've decided. I could always make an alternative purchase of clothing or …"

"Oops, I need to find a loo," Katie interjected. "I'm bursting. It's ridiculous. I go about ten to twenty times a day," she exaggerated. Grimacing, Katie placed her hand gently on her bump and dashed to the rest rooms.

"I'm not surprised, you'd downed two bottles of water rather quickly," commented Amy, waving Katie to go along ahead of her.

"It doesn't make any difference," argued Katie, hurriedly entering the rest rooms, diving into the cubicle. "With this lump pressing against my bladder, I tend to go a million times a day, regardless of the amount of liquid I consume," she shouted from the cubicle.

"Oh well, it's all part of the process I'd say." Amy smiled, looked at her reflection in the mirror and tousled and brushed her hair. She frowned vainly at her lips requiring a touch of lip gloss. She rummaged through her hand bag, fished out her lip gloss then, leaning forward, she applied it to her lips. Amy smiled at her reflection in the mirror and popped her lip gloss in her handbag. A sudden piercing, gut wrenching scream from Katie's cubicle jolted Amy.

"Oh, my God. Help me, Amy," Katie screamed.

Without thinking, Amy dropped her handbag in the sink and dashed to Katie's cubicle. The door was locked. Clenching her fists, Amy repeatedly thumped at the door. "I can't get in there. It's locked. Unlock the door. Open the door, Katie," she shouted, in restrained panic.

"I can't," said Katie, sobbing uncontrollably.

"I'll get help," a woman said.

"Please, and hurry," said Amy, without looking at the woman, kicking the door, leaving a few ominous smudges on the white paintwork. Amy was about to launch into another kick when Katie unexpectedly opened the door. Amy entered the cubicle. Katie leaned against the cubicle wall. Blood clots were splattered on the white tiled floor around her feet. Amy took one apprehensive step out of the cubicle. Her eyes welled. Unable to hold back the raging feelings of horror and helplessness, Amy broke down and cried. She wrestled with the thought that she was letting Katie down by falling apart. Behind the tears, Amy told herself that she had to be strong for Katie, convinced herself that they'd get through the trauma together. Katie cried convulsively. Amy wiped her tears away from her cheeks with the back of her hands, stepped two paces back into the cubicle, maneuvered herself in the confined space, closed the door and facing Katie, she placed her arms on her shoulders, caressing Katie.

"Call, David," Katie spluttered, her tears dampening the left shoulder of Amy's sports jacket.

"What?"

"'Call, David!.'"

"But, you need an ambulance," said Amy, sniffling. "I'll call an ambulance then I'll call, David."

"No. Call, David before an ambulance. I want him here with me," pleaded Katie, hysterically. There were sounds of footsteps, a few muttered voices, followed by a gentle tap on the cubicle door.

"An ambulance is already on its way," said the woman, Amy had heard earlier as the one who'd gone to fetch help. Amy opened the door slightly and poked her head out.

"Thank you, so much," said Amy, to a petite, middle aged woman with a gentle manner and a pleasant disposition, dressed in an elegant pastel lemon suit, her rose blond hair softly swept back and neatly tucked under a pastel lemon summer hat.

"Do you think you'll be requiring any further assistance?"

"No. Thank you. You've been a great help," said Amy, gratefully.

"Very well," said the woman.

Amy noticed that her handbag was still in the sink. "I'll give David a call now. I need to get my cell-phone. It's in my handbag. I've left it outside. Wait here."

"No. Use my cell-phone," Katie insisted, nodding at her handba
floor, propped up against the cubicle wall, inches away from the blood clots.

Amy closed the door, reeled out a large wad of toilet tissue, picked up Katie's handbag, wiped it clean, retrieved Katie's cell-phone and scrolled to David's cell-phone number.

Katie winced and groaned.

What do I say to him? Amy thought, pressing the call button.

"Hello, my love."

There was a hard knock on the door. "No! It's Amy. Give me a second would you, David?"

"Hello, Amy?"

"Members of the ambulance crew are in the building. They're on their way up to you now via the goods elevator. Are any of you able to come out?" a man said.

"Hello, hello, Amy? What's going on, Amy?"

"Hold on, David."

"Please clear the ladies room. They are now out of bounds until further notice," the man announced.

Amy popped her head out. A tall, slim man waved Amy's handbag at her.

"Is this your handbag?"

"Yes, it is," Amy responded quickly.

"You ought not to have left it out here, madam. This could've been stolen."

"I know. I do have an emergency situation on my hands. I'll be with you in a moment, I just need to finish this call," she said.

A female security guard worked tirelessly at the main door of the rest rooms ushering women out, blocking women hovering outside trying to gain entrance, purely to speculate.

Closing the door, Amy brought the cell-phone to her ear "David, I'm with Katie. She's had an incident. I think there's a threat to her losing the baby."

"Oh no! An accident? Are you certain of this? That's devastating news. Can I speak with her?"

"An … an incident, David. Yes … speak with her. Here you are." Amy handed the cell-phone to Katie.

Grief stricken, unable to speak, Katie shook her head and refused to take the call.

"Now's not a good time, David. I'll call you back as soon as I can."

"Where are you? What's going on? Where's Katie?"

"Everything's going to be OK, David. We're at the Golders Green shopping mall. I'll call you," said Amy reassuringly.

"Don't leave it too long in getting back to me, will you?" David stressed anxiously. "I can hear ... Is that Katie crying?"

"Don't worry, David, she's in safe hands," said Amy, abruptly ending the call, switching off the cell-phone.

The ambulance crew rushed into the restrooms. A medic banged on the door. "Can you make it out of there?"

"Yes. I could give it a go. I'm feeling a bit weak and in excruciating pain," said Katie, breathing heavily, crouching against the wall.

"Then wait. Don't move," ordered Amy. She stepped outside to allow the medics room to enter the cubicle. A crew member swiftly assembled a wheelchair.

"Excuse me, young lady," said the man, approaching Amy amid the pandemonium of two medics rushing into the cubicle, systematically administering medical assistance to Katie, incessantly sobbing, leaving most of the medics' vitally important medical questions unanswered. "My name is George Mason and I manage the shopping mall. What exactly happened here?"

"I suspect she's losing ... having ... or ... has had a miscarriage," said Amy.

The name, George Mason was calligraphically engraved in black and gold on a white identity badge pinned to the left lapel of the man's smartly tailored navy blue suit "Oh, that's quite serious. I'm sorry to hear that. That explains the blood on the floor," he said frowningly, looking sheepishly at the floor.

"Quite." Amy diverted her attentions to the medics, intently listening to their conversation.

"She's showing all the signs of having had a spontaneous miscarriage."

"We'll have to get her down to the treatment centre to identify whether it's incomplete or not and have her uterus checked."

"Right."

Two paramedics lifted Katie and eased her into the assembled wheelchair.

"Is it safe to have the cubicle cleaned now?" George asked the medics as they were wheeling Katie out.

"Yes, it's all yours now."

Two middle-aged female, Hispanic cleaners clutching their buckets and mops hovered around mutely. George instructed them in Spanish to sanitize the entire ladies rest rooms from top to bottom. "Security guards are on standby and will escort you to the goods elevator." George informed the medics.

Katie looked at Amy forlornly. "Coming with me?" she whispered.

"Of course," said Amy, entering the goods elevator. "Where are you taking her?" Amy asked one of the medics.

"The Women's Hospital along the Marylebone Road," said the medic.

"Great." Amy glanced at Katie caringly and reassuringly. "I'll give David another call once we get out of the elevator."

As Katie was being lifted into the ambulance, Amy switched on the cell-phone and called David. He answered on the first ring, minus any greetings.

"I'm worried. What news do you have on Katie?"

Amy climbed into the ambulance. "We're getting into the ambulance now. They're taking her to the Women's Hospital on the Marylebone Road. We're making our way there now."

"How is she bearing up?"

Amy heard the agonizing quiver in David's voice. "She's doing fine."

"I'll meet you at the hospital. Tell Katie that I'm on my way."

"Will do." Amy switched off the cell-phone and sat on the bench opposite Katie. "David's making his way to the hospital now."

"Thanks," said Katie, sniffling and crying. The medics rushed to her aid, monitoring and preparing her for the treatment centre. Amy shifted out of their way as best she could in the cramped space. The ambulance moved off. Adjusting her senses, coming to terms with the unfamiliar devices and medical equipment surrounding her, Amy was desperately wishing that she was having a bad dream. It was her first experience, traveling in an ambulance, witnessing a miscarriage, Amy solemnly prayed that it would also be her last.

In the hospital waiting room, Amy paced the floor, back and forth, wringing her hands nervously.

David arrived five minutes after Katie had been rushed into the treatment room. "I got here as soon as I could. How is she? Is she going to be alright?" he asked, flustered and out of breath. Visibly shaken, he looked a sorry sight.

Amy felt no sympathy for him. She cursed under her breath and blamed David for getting Katie into this mess. "She's in the treatment room."

"Oh, my God," said David, slapping his forehead with his right hand. "How serious is she?"

"The doctors are carrying out a routine procedure," she told him icily. Amy refused to look at him. She disliked David, tremendously. And David detected it.

"I feel just as bad you do about all this—Katie's loss. It's my loss too, you know," he said remorsefully.

Amy avoided going into an in-depth conversation. "I need some time alone. I was about to step outside for some fresh air," she said, pretentiously.

David sighed. "I understand."

Amy turned to leave the waiting room. "Amy?" said the doctor. "Yes, Doctor?" Amy eyed David awkwardly. "Doctor? Let me introduce you to, David … the father of … Katie's partner."

David shook hands with the doctor.

"Hello, David. I'm Dr Amir. The bleeding's subsided," the doctor informed them.

"Thank goodness," said David, breathing a huge sigh of relief.

"We're conducting an ultrasound to detect whether any of the pregnancy has remained inside the uterus and, if Katie hasn't fully miscarried, where some of the placenta was unable to be naturally expelled, we'll have to perform a D and C. It's routine. Nothing major."

"Thank you, Dr Amir. She'll recover quite quickly, I hope?" David had a worried look on his face.

"I see no reason why she shouldn't. Katie's a young, fit and healthy woman. There's no reason why she shouldn't." said the doctor, tactfully.

David smiled worriedly. "When can I see her?"

The doctor pulled out a silver watch-face from the top left pocket of his white coat. "In approximately an hour," he said, retreating swiftly to the treatment room.

"Thanks again, Doctor," said David, gratefully.

"If you'll now excuse me, I'll pop outside for a while," said Amy.

"Sure, Amy," said David.

Amy strolled around the hospital grounds in a dazed and depressed mood. I've got to be dreaming, she thought. "God, tell me this is all a bad dream," she said out loud, tilting her head back, looking searchingly up at the sky. She glanced from left to right, relieved that passers-by hadn't seen her talking to herself. Progressively feeling the strain of Katie's plight, filled with remorse, emotionally and physically weak and exhausted, Amy sat on a vacant bench. Pigeons scrambled aimlessly at her feet then took sudden flight. The bench was cold, hard and uncomfortable. Her thoughts drifted to David, his ghastly attempts to flirt with her in the champagne bar, his deceptiveness, lies and the messy conditions Katie would have had to endure embroiled in his divorce. Timing of the miscarriage concerned Amy as an ironical coincidence happening too soon after Katie had intimated her thoughts of rescheduling the termination, provoking Amy to momentarily wander into disturbingly suspecting Katie of maybe secretly damaging herself. Who knows? Amy thought, visualizing Katie locked in the cubicle, where no-one could see her or would ever know what had actually taken place in there but, Katie. Amy sighed dismissively, denouncing her thoughts as cold, cruel, extremely evil, irrational and far-fetched. She consoled herself saying, "Every disappointment is a blessing in disguise," and fervently hoped that Katie would view the miscarriage as an omen to end her affair with David, once and for all. Tears flowing, Amy clutched at Katie's handbag. She shuddered at the thought of Katie in the treatment room, her body being subjected to injections and prodding by the medical team. Amy opened Katie's bag and helped herself to a few sheets of Katie's tissues. Baffled, she couldn't possibly imagine what having a miscarriage felt like, mentally and physically and hoped that, once the event was all over, Katie would return to her cheerful self in a very short space of time. Amy cupped her face in her hands and sobbed loudly and openly.

"Are you alright?" said a young man.

Annoyed, upset and curious to see who was at the end of the sound of the young male voice, Amy sheepishly looked up and locked her reddened eyes on the young man standing in front of her; attractive, an Adonis, Mediterranean or something, young, of medium build and height, in his mid to late twenties, smiling handsomely, standing attentively in front of her, ready to bounce into worthy, caring and assertive action. Too teary-eyed and distraught, Amy looked away. "No, I'm not alright. My friend has just suffered a miscarriage. What the hell do you really want?" Noting Amy's expression of annoyance, the young male wasted no time in briskly continuing on his way. Men! They're all the bloody same. There's no let up, Amy thought. Against her will, but for Katie's sake, Amy decided to keep up appearances by conversing civilly with David when she returned to the waiting room. Consoling and forcing herself to take control, prevent another breakdown, after blowing her nose, wiping her face and refreshing her make-up, Amy followed the guided footpath to the waiting room.

"How are you bearing up?"

"I'm OK," said Amy icily. Remembering the pact she'd made with herself on the bench, Amy coughed and altered her stance. "And you? How are you bearing up?" she asked, attempting a naturally caring tone of voice.

"I'm desperate to see her. I just want to know that she's going to be alright."

"Call me over-confident, if you like, but I believe Katie will be as right as rain and bounce back to her usual form in no time."

"Ah, David," said the doctor, suddenly emerging, removing his white coat. "You can go ahead and see Katie now. She's in a private room on the fourth floor. I'm keeping her in overnight for observation and once I'm fully confident of her condition, I'll discharge her in the morning."

"Why keep her in overnight? Is there something wrong?" David questioned frowningly.

"Not at all. It's just a precautionary measure. I'd like Katie to rest. She's lost quite a lot of blood." The doctor, worked at putting David at ease.

"Thank you, Dr Amir," said David.

"The lifts are at the end of the corridor, second turning on your right."

"Thank you, again, Dr Amir." Exiting the waiting room, David broke into a jog along the corridor.

"David, stop running," Amy called, rushing behind him.

Panting, David glanced back at Amy. "I really need to see her."

"I know. I understand."

"Bloody hell," David moaned. "Come on. Come on," he went on impatiently, waiting for the elevator to arrive.

Amy turned to David and laid a reassuring hand on his shoulder. "Calm down, David," she said comfortingly, surprising herself.

Looking into Amy's eyes, David welcomed her touch. "These past few months have really been tough for me that I …" The elevator's arrival stopped David in midstream. Insensitive, Amy wasn't the slightest bit interested in what David had to say. They stepped into the crowded elevator which stopped on every floor to the fourth. Restless, David frowned, sighed and cursed. "Maybe I should've bought some flowers," he said.

"Take her some in the morning."

"That's a good idea."

The fourth floor was exceptionally quiet, almost too eerily quiet, Amy thought. David went on ahead to the reception desk and asked the nurses for directions to Katie's room. A nurse escorted Amy and David to Katie's private room, paid for by Katie's private health care plan, one of a number of perks afforded her by her employers. David entered the private room, ergonomically furnished and tranquilly illuminated. A nurse sat in a chair close to Katie's bed. Katie appeared to be asleep. David launched forward and pressed his lips softly on Katie's forehead. Amy stood at the foot of the bed scanning the room, admiring its spatiality. Katie slowly opened her eyes.

"Hi guys. It's all over," she whispered groggily, managing a weak smile, secretly happy that she was no longer pregnant.

David took her hand.

"Hey, Katie," said Amy, welcoming Katie's smile.

Katie closed her eyes, appeared to drift back to sleep. "Afresh. I'm going to have to start afresh," she said, deliriously.

David glanced worryingly at the nurse

"She needs to rest. She has lost a lot of blood," said the nurse.

"Yes. I am aware of that," said David, crouching. He whispered into Katie's ear. "If there is anything I can do, please ask me, Katie. I'll take care of everything for you."

"Please, take her handbag, David. Her car keys and fob are in there. She's left the car in the shopping mall car park. The car parking ticket is also in there." Amy placed the handbag at the foot of the bed.

"I'll take care of everything. Katie won't have to worry about a thing," said David, responsibly.

Amy had to leave, she hated hospitals. Feeling ghastly, emotionally wrecked, relieved that Katie was making a recovery and slowly warming to David, Amy handed him one of her business cards. "I'm about to leave now. Please, call me tomorrow. Keep me informed, would you?"

"Thank you. I will," said David, keeping a watchful eye on Katie.

Admirable, Amy thought as she slipped quietly out of the private room.

Amy boarded one of the taxis parked at the hospital's taxi rank. Deeply saddened by Katie's plight, Amy gazed sightlessly out of the window at the slow moving traffic. David's apparent care and concern for Katie impressed Amy, forcing her to alter her unfavorable opinions of him and assisting in lessening her paramount concerns for Katie's welfare. The taxi approached Amy's apartment. She was desperate to take a shower. Dreaming about the pleasant times she'd share with Mike, ambitiously playing with avant-garde ideas on their new business, lifted her spirits. Yearning Mike's touch, Amy fantasized about giving her all to him before, during and after their forthcoming Sunday lunch.

CHAPTER 17

Mike scratched the stubble on his chin, yawned and threw on a deep blue, Chenille bathrobe. He made his way down the grand, winding staircase to the kitchen and fixed himself a cup of black coffee. His lips barely touching the rim of his coffee cup, Mike blew the fiery hot steam away, took a couple of sips and sighed appreciatively. He strolled over to the breakfast bar and sat comfortably in the chair. The doorbell chimed. Mike sighed and looked at his watch. Eleven thirty. He was about to take another sip of coffee when the doorbell chimed again. Eleven thirty on a Sunday morning is far too early a time to be making such a racket, Mike thought, slamming his cup on the breakfast bar, spilling coffee on the white, ceramic tiled surface in the process. He rose out of the chair, tightened the belt round his waist and marched out of the kitchen to ward off the unwanted visitor. The doorbell chimed again, continuously this time, like it had been jammed. "What the blazes?" Mike cursed aloud. Yawning, he approached the door and glanced through the peep-hole. He scratched the back of his head in bemusement. Amy? She's early! Mike thought, swinging the door open. Amy lunged forward and wrapped her arms tightly about his waist in a desperate embrace. Mike stumbled and clasped his arms unnervingly around her. The door swung shut. Amy's heartbeat pounding against his solar plexus aroused him. "Hey," he whispered gruffly, directly into her ear.

"Please. Don't let go," pleaded Amy, gripping him tighter.

"Let's go inside. Has something dreadful or wonderful happened?" asked Mike, freeing himself, taking Amy by the hand and leading her into the lounge.

Amy slumped in the couch and tremblingly allowed herself the moment to relish being back with Mike, adorningly robed in her presence.

"I was just having a coffee." Mike scratched his chin and strolled casually out of the lounge. "What can I get you? Tea? Coffee? Something strong or light?" he called from the hallway.

"Champers," Amy called back, pulling her cell-phone out of her handbag, distractively glaring at the screen, anticipating a call from David.

"Champers it is," Mike called back from the kitchen agreeably, and without question, as he reached for two champagne flutes, in silence and suspense, stealing time to ponder.

The rest room scenes, the sound of Katie's cries roved around disturbingly, in Amy's mind. She swallowed saliva to moisten her parched throat. Her eyes glistening, Amy desperately blinked to prevent a threatening flow of tears.

Mike returned with filled champagne flutes and caught Amy's dismal facial expression before she'd time to alter it. "You can trust me with whatever it is that's upsetting or bothering you," said Mike sympathetically, handing her a flute.

Amy took a few dignified sips. The liquid bubbled lusciously on her tongue, drenched her parched throat, doing the trick it lived up to, altering her mood. After a few more sips, Amy felt stronger and regained visible control and emotional composure. "It's an acquaintance ... a friend of mine ... she's ... she'd suffered a miscarriage yesterday."

"I'm sorry," said Mike, sitting on the couch, inching closer to Amy.

"It's quite devastating, really."

"Is there anything I can do? I mean, you're free to talk about this for as long as you'd deem necessary," returned Mike, consolably.

Amy thought it was remarkable that Mike's present encompassing ability to administer tender care and attention to her, made her all the more susceptible to losing her self control, almost tempting to cry her heart out in his arms but, Amy decided that talking about it would serve as the better option, more notably, serve in her better interests and favor in Mike's books.

Mike listened, uninterruptedly, to every detail as Amy delivered a full account of the events. Amy hoped that, in time, she'd quickly recover from the experience. The distraction was untimely, Amy could make mistakes, overlook important aspects, put the venture in jeopardy and she was sure that Mike wasn't prepared to lose his project, his baby, due to someone's miscarriage. Amy finished giving her account of the ordeal and a long, dense silence presided over them.

Mike shook his head from side to side in a demonstrative show of sympathy. "Take as much time as you'd deem necessary to get through this dilemma. Naturally, you'd want to give valuable and timely support to your friend in her time of need," he said attentively. "You needn't worry about our business venture. Take a break. Take all the time you need. And I want you to know that I'm also here for you and, if there is anything I can do to help you ..." Mike stopped.

Amy had put her flute on the floor at her feet and had cupped his face in her hands.

Mike put his flute on the floor at his feet and started stroking Amy's thighs.

Amy shuddered, held her breath a few seconds and exhaled whispering, "On the contrary, that would be defeating the object. I need to be kept busy. This new business venture will keep my mind off the miscarriage. Besides, her partner is doing a grand job of taking care of her needs and he's the only person, I'd expect, she'd want rallying around her."

"I'm totally prepared to go along to the meeting to take care of matters on-spec until you are ready to jump back onboard."

"I'm staying put, remaining onboard. The venture will not be compromised and that's final," said Amy adamantly.

Elatedly relieved, Mike arched an eyebrow.

"In fact, we can get down to a bit of business now if you like," suggested Amy, pecking Mike's cheeks.

"Oh, you mean this business," said Mike, gliding his tongue slowly along her lips.

"Yes," said Amy.

Amy awoke exceedingly happy. She welcomed the images reflected on the mir-rored ceiling, laid dead-beat, closely snuggled, arms clamped awkwardly around Mike, their bodies intertwined on crumpled cotton sheets. She smiled sleepily, gladly remembering their pleasurable and strenuously long love mak-ing sessions on the couch that she'd built up a fierce appetite, hunger pangs rumbled in her stomach, she squirmed quietly.

"Huh, yes, what do you want? Huh?" said Mike, nonsensically and half asleep.

Amy snuggled up closer to Mike. "I could murder a coffee," she intimated.

"And I could murder a piping hot and steaming shower," said Mike, yawn-ing loudly, unraveling their interlocked arms and legs and slipping out of bed.

Amy tugged at the sheets and pulled them over her head.

Mike checked his watch. It was three-thirty-five in the afternoon. "Great Scott!" he exclaimed loudly. "Do you have any idea of the time?"

"Yes. My body feels like the day's almost disappeared," said Amy croakily under the sheets.

Mike dashed into the en-suite bathroom and clambered into the shower. The strong force of hot water lashed fiercely on his back. Mike got out of the shower, left the water gushing, wrapped a bath sheet round his waist and wandered back into the master bedroom. "Darling," he said, "Fancy joining me in the shower?"

Feeling needed, Amy smiled satisfactorily under the sheets. "Of course," she said.

"We're all agreed on the high level milestones set," Amy confirmed, updating her notes and disguising an overwhelming sense of anxiety.

Vincent had spent hours in meticulous scrutiny, previewing, reviewing and digestively scanning the blueprint, project inception documentation and contract schedules Amy had furnished him with a few days prior to the meeting. He'd finalized matters by procedurally complying with the company policy of securing the legal department's endorsement.

"Splendid," said Mike.

"Take your time on deciding where you'd eventually like to travel," Vincent advised Mike.

Observing their interactions, Amy was aesthetically pleased that Mike and Vincent had evidently gotten along smoothly and were genuinely relaxed with each other.

"The decision is quite a simple one to arrive at, really. We've covered the ground on Barbados and St. Bart's and, with the information on the Turks and Caicos, I'll opt to go there as soon as arrangements can be made. My decision's based on a number of optimal factors, one of which is tourism. A key mechanism serving the strength of the economy alongside offshore financial services tallying UK onshore finances and, more importantly, the islands are a British territory with the inclusion of a legal system fashioned on the laws of England and Wales. These are a few factors that have made a tremendous impact on influencing my decision."

"Good choice," said Vincent, nodding affirmatively.

"Planet Management will organize all your travel arrangements customized to your personal requirements," Amy informed Mike, scouring through pages of the draft contract schedules. "You'll be accompanied by our team member, Stefan Regis," Amy continued.

Stefan Regis, the project team leader, waved his hand indicatively at Mike.

Mike bowed at Stefan in acknowledgement.

"Rory Gibson, will meet you at the airport. He's one of our team members permanently based in the Caribbean. He'll expertly advise you on all aspects relating to the business climate of hotels in the region and, on your behalf, organize a schedule of inspection visits and meetings with key officials. I also hold the view that for the sake of true cost effectiveness, I'll opt to travel to the Caribbean during the completion process of the deal, remaining in the UK, holding the fort, as it were, during the initiation process of the project," Amy concluded.

"I agree with your feasible approach," Mike responded, addressing Amy in a formal business tone, his face expressionlessly bland, eyes piercingly blank.

Amy detested Mike's too formal attitude towards her and, although she found it quite tediously off-putting, she couldn't afford to have Mike conduct himself in any other way. Mike was merely giving her what she'd asked for. Professionalism. Their intimacy kept as a closely guarded secret. Anyone observing the level of communication they'd conducted between them throughout the meeting would never suspect their intimacy, Amy figured. Her thoughts irrelevantly returned to the workshop's boardroom role-play where Mike had done a great job in conducting a non-reactionary and expressionless approach to Belinda's antics and innuendos. Amy had difficulty speculating the ruminations of Mike's inner thoughts back then, but felt confident in her present position that her perceptions of Mike were now bordering on the fairly accurate.

"We could aim to be there in say, seven to ten days. This would give Rory time to take care of the necessary arrangements, Mr. Brandleton," said Stefan, filling the silence.

"Let's get out there in seven days shall we? We'll need roughly ten days there at the very least."

"Of course, Mr. Brandleton," Stefan dutifully replied.

Amy regrettably danced with the damned prospect of not having Mike around for an unbearable week to ten days that her concentration levels began to wane.

"With no adversity, legal implications or disputes noticeably evident or highlighted, confirming the successful engagement of Project Cascadia, I can safely wrap up our session. I'm fully satisfied that we've thoroughly covered all the relevant aspects foreseeing the way forward. Please add Project Cascadia onto our portfolio, would you, Richard? Going forward, we'll meet on a monthly basis."

Fantastic. A done deal. Sealed. Amy thought, burning in the combinational sensations of excitement and fear with the added entertainment of lustful thoughts of Mike, throwing in the reminiscence of where it all began from snatching at the opportunity of daring to leave Wellings, attending the workshop, to the present day. The grass was definitely looking greener over here, Amy thought. Sipping mineral water, her eyes snatching the time from the chrome, digital wall clock, Amy noted that duration of the meeting calculated to an hour and twenty minutes with a capacity of time remaining to speed through any other business prior to wrapping up. Richard had generously allowed two hours in case of any technicalities, issues or disputes which were known to crop up occasionally with Vincent being such a perfectionist. Meeting concluded. So far, so good, we're on our way, Amy thought, thankful Vincent hadn't caused any waves on this one, delaying the process, sending them all back to the drawing board. She'd done her homework, made certain no loopholes appeared in the documentation prior to handing them over to Vincent by appointing the legal department's shit, hot services of Shelley Craig, legal assistant to the legal counselor, Kevin Doherty, who'd also attended the blueprint meeting, asking her to run her intelligent eyes over the documentation. Shelley was enthusiastic, quick witted and sharp eyed. She'd developed an admirable and growing reputation within the company on her accuracy in pinpointing every important detail realistic to the success or detriment on any given project. Richard proudly walked around the enormous oblong shaped, maple walnut table, distributing the confidentiality agreement to each individual, pleased to be part of it all, but equally desperate for more of a juicier piece of the action, he envied Amy her stake.

"Once you've all read and understood the contents of the confidentiality agreement, I'd most appreciate your expediency in signing and returning the agreement to Richard within twenty four hours. Please may I also remind you all of the fact that, no work on the project is to commence prior to signing the agreement and no discussions are to be entered into on Project Cascadia during and after its life as stated in the agreement bearing in mind the potential negative impact this could place on the project and Planet Management. A material breach of this confidentiality agreement could lead to serious consequences," said Amy, rising from her seat. "Now, if you'd all excuse me, I have a conference call commencing in five minutes." Gathering her paperwork, lap top and handbag, Amy quickly left the meeting room with no looking back. Watching Amy exit the room, Mike yearned for her.

Amy raced back to her desk and made a mental note to call Mike that night, at home. Her ploy to ravish him that evening in celebration to mark the success of getting on the books of Planet Management was not going amiss. Unbeknownst to Amy, Mike was entertaining the exact thought.

Amy let herself into the apartment at eight-thirty in the evening. She kicked her shoes off in the hall-way, whipped her cell-phone out of her bag and called Mike. "Are you free tonight? Only, I thought I'd pop over to finalize on a few items relating to our meeting today."

"Sure, come over," said Mike. "It's rather late in the evening for a discussion?"

"You'd better get accustomed to it, Mike. This is how things are going to be from now on," said Amy, firmly.

"Then, make your way over."

"Thanks. I'll be there within the hour."

Amy hopped out of the taxi a little after nine forty and hadn't gotten to the door when Mike swung it open. Amy screeched, as Mike had caught her by surprise, swept her into his arms and athletically tossed her over his shoulder. Kicking the door shut and, ignoring Amy's pleas to put her down, Mike climbed the stairs, two at a time, brought her into the master bedroom and laid her gently on the inviting rugs. Astonished, Amy laid, wide-eyed and speechless calmly awaiting Mike's next unsuspecting move. He undressed her, kissed her, teased and played with her, made love to her tenderly, slowly and pleasurably in a special way she'd not experienced, taking her to un-chartered heights that Amy cried tears of indescribable ecstasy.

Amy reached for Mike. The bed felt cold and empty without him. She yearned for the feel of his delectable body under the goose down duvet. The delicious aroma of coffee intruded Amy's thoughts, serving as a welcomed distraction. Amy lifted her investigative head off the pillow, sniffed at the coffee filled air and peered at Mike as he crept quietly into the dimly lit room, tall, robed, freshly shaved and alert. He sipped coffee from a huge mug in one hand and held a replica mug with piping hot coffee in the other. "Pleased to see you're awake. You've saved me the job of waking you up for coffee," said Mike, brightly.

"Thanks," Amy croaked, wrapping her slender fingers around the mug, the comforting heat warming her fingers and palms.

Mike sat on the ottoman at the foot of the bed, leaned forward and commenced flicking through the pages of one of several documents strewn on the floor at his feet.

"I'd better be heading off home once I've finished my coffee," Amy sheepishly announced, aware of Mike's engrossment in the paperwork.

"Very impressive," said Mike. "You're infallible. It's great that you'd mentioned during our meeting and are actively mindful of the importance of cost efficiencies from the onset. I couldn't have opted for a more suitable business partner," he continued, complimentarily.

Flattered, Amy could hardly believe her ears. Not completely awake, her mind wishy washy, Amy wanted to lazily relish in the joy of light conversation, sip coffee, exclusively prepared by the hands of Mike. A business discussion was the last thing Amy wanted to venture into. But, in her desire to remain infallible to Mike, Amy desperately foraged to come up with some form of a fitting response. Clutching the mug of coffee in one hand, Amy clambered out of bed and arduously wrapped the large bed sheet about her. The sheet swished about Amy's ankles and swept along the floor in a long trail like an extravagant wedding gown as she wandered wearily over to Mike. She glanced at his watch. Is he crazy? Is he going out of his mind? Amy thought. "It's four in the morning, Mike!" she moaned.

"You'd better get accustomed to it, Amy. This is how things are going to be from now on," Mike responded, shooting Amy a mischievous smirk.

Touché, Amy thought, recalling her words that now came back to repay her. "Maximize revenues, minimize expenses," was her best shot.

"Agreed," said Mike, breaking into laughter.

Convinced that she'd made a fool of herself, Amy shrugged her shoulders and laughed wearily with Mike. Busily wrapping the sheet around her more securely and perching on the edge of the ottoman, Amy took a few more sips of coffee before carefully placing the mug at her feet. Loathed to interrupt Mike's thoughts, Amy decided to take a shower and head off home.

"Just think, I'll have a grand opening to commemorate Hotel Cascadia," said Mike out of the blue, dreamy eyed. "A ribbon cutting ceremony will go down a treat."

Amy's mind now verging on the fully awake state, she saw the need to join Mike in living the dream but, more importantly, she was conscious of the fact that, in recognizing the need to keep abreast of things, she was also aware that she had to work at keeping Mike's feet firmly on the ground. "Have you given any further thought to the superior experiences you plan to offer our Penthouse guests?" asked Amy in an air of soberness, gently coaxing Mike away from intoxicating himself any further.

"Oh yes, there are many. Each Penthouse will be equipped with indoor and outdoor rejuvenation spas. Glass bottomed swimming pools, on the roof of each Penthouse where underwater swimmers look directly into the interior of the Penthouse and the indoor rejuvenation spa beneath them. One of an array of distinctive features would be that residents will have the option to close off the pool by either the press of a button on the control panel affixed to the wall or by remote control that'll operate the movement of ceiling panels. Shall I go on?"

Visualizing, Amy found herself drifting into the dream. "Sounds absolutely perfect. With maximization of revenues and determination, we'll get there."

"And further. Don't forget my aim to achieve the ultimate diamond class rating."

"I haven't forgotten. That comes with secret inspections. I hope you're aware of that."

"I'm completely aware. We'll be inspected all the way from inception and on, and on, and on," said Mike, resignedly.

"We'll need to work on the artwork of the company logo," said Amy.

"I'll leave that with you, if I may. Go with whatever looks and feels right."

"Sure. You can count on me and Planet Management to provide virtually every conceivable service with departments equipped to provide most business requirements. Everyone's on the payroll, and wherever possible, Planet Management strictly refrains from using middle men or private contractors."

"It makes a lot of business sense."

"Yes. There is one exception," Amy warmed, unraveling the sheet.

Mike raised his eyebrows. "And that is?"

"Legal counsel. It's stipulated in one of the contract clauses somewhere and worded along the lines of, in the avoidance of doubt, lawsuits and conflicts of interests, Planet Management, meticulously scrupulous in its approach in conducting all business activities, will not provide legal services nor recommend or quote names of legal representatives or institutions to quote the client unquote. Well, in similar wording."

"Ah, yes, I do remember reading something of that nature. I've no intention of relinquishing the services of my personal lawyer whom I've known for many years now. I'd be very reluctant to do so. He knows and understands me and my business affairs entirely."

"Good. Going back to what you'd mentioned earlier regarding the ribbon cutting ceremony, that can easily be arranged, in fact, the public relations professionals are a mint at putting together ads on the radio, in newspapers, hotel and leisure industry periodicals and magazines that matter, but they all come at a price," said Amy, desperate to get into the shower. Dawn would soon be breaking. She had to return home to prepare for an early morning meeting with Vincent, both the subject matter and start time escaped her for the present.

"We'll decide on the most relevant and cost effective forms of publicity and exposure at a later stage," said Mike, flicking through paperwork.

"Yes, and Rory, our guy in the Caribbean, will show you what works. Back here in the UK, Planet Management will work on the most imperative considerations and generate forecasts of revenue and expenditure that would enable justifications on a case by case basis, check viabilities and possibly offer advice, where necessary, on making adjustments to plans which would enable more profitability." Amy went on tirelessly.

"With all this support and backing, we're deemed to succeed. How could we possibly fail?" said Mike.

Cutting the discussion short, Amy got up and headed for the en-suite bathroom. The sheet swished about her ankles and swept along the floor in a long trail. "It's time I was heading home, Mike," she said, apologetically, hovering in the doorway of the en-suite bathroom.

"Yes, it's getting lighter. I'll call a taxi."

"Thanks, to arrive, say in forty-five minutes, one hour max," Amy called out, closing the door. Taking a deep breath, Amy stepped out of the sheet and into the shower, flipped the switch, and selected number four, power jets and maximum as her options on the selection dial. "Why hasn't David called me?" she muttered, switching the power on, standing in the centre of the shower room, amid the power jet sprays shooting water from the top four corners of the spacious shower room at maximum force and speed, battering and washing her frustrations, worries and fears away. Groaning, Amy closed her eyes, shut off her mind and surrendered to the cleansing and therapeutic powers of the gushing water.

CHAPTER 18

Amy hadn't taken in a word at the cost review meeting. It had been scheduled to take place at seven thirty in the morning. Disorientated, she'd made an unprecedented entry, arriving five minutes late. "Apologies," she whispered sheepishly, cracking an embarrassingly lethargic smile. With concealed embarrassment, Amy walked commandingly over to the blatantly vacant chair at the table in Vincent's large and spatial office. Seated around the table with Vincent were an accountant, a statistician, a senior cost analyst, an actuary and Richard actively taking the minutes. Amy's entire muscles ached as she slid into the chair. Her concentration levels on matters relating to cost reviews at an all time low, Amy amiably reflected on Mike serving her coffee at four in the morning. She then consciously shifted her thoughts to the acquirement of funds towards the venture, doubting whether she'd the ability to raise a worthwhile sum. She'd scheduled a lunchtime appointment with her bank manager that afternoon and had provided him with the business loan application form beforehand. She'd taken a photocopy of the form and repeatedly mulled over it, hoped that she hadn't, inadvertently omitted important factors that would weaken her borrowing power. She'd failed to spot any tell tale signs that could cause a delay in the process or cause the bank manager to draw any doubts about her application. Amy couldn't avoid feeling self-admittedly impressed with how strong her credibility appeared on paper, she was more than hopeful that she'd met the bank's stringent credit scoring criteria. She'd applied for just a little over two hundred and fifty thousand pounds, had found the amount hugely worrying and wondered whether she'd borrowed out of her depths, foolishly cajoling herself into believing that she could keep up with the likes of the Brandletons of this world.

"Thank you. And that wraps up this morning's session," announced Vincent, the first to vacate the table.

Fully aware of Vincent's impatience and abhorrence to unpunctuality of any sort, Amy searched his facial expressions and physical composure for clues in reaction to the impertinency of her late arrival. Vincent hadn't displayed any obvious signs of annoyance, although Amy was fully conscious of the fact that she hadn't gotten away with it Scott free. Vincent would have it out with her at a later stage, Amy intuitively guessed, at the arena of their impending one-to-one where she'd planned to simply and confidently win him over. Her thoughts then diverted to working on winning the confidence of the bank manager in agreeing to grant her the desired funds. The meeting delegates gathered their documents amid mutterings. Not having fully participated in the cost review meeting and, with Richard attending, Amy decided that an in-depth, one-to-one briefing session with Richard during the latter part of the afternoon, following her meeting with the bank manager would suffice. Amy gathered her unread meeting documents and followed Richard out of Vincent's office. "Are you free this afternoon from four o'clock onwards?" she enquired, walking alongside him back to their desks.

"Hypothetically speaking yes, without checking my calendar."

"I'd like to go over the entire cost review with you. Can we arrange a time?"

"Sure, although I'll be completing the minutes and distributing them within a day."

"I know. Ignore the minutes for the moment. It's a more in-depth perspective on the cost review I'm more concerned about," she said, withholding the fact that she'd not fully grasped the crux of the meeting and that she vitally needed Richard to bring her up to speed.

"Right you are," said Richard, self importantly.

"Book a small meeting room, would you? We should get this thing done and dusted in under an hour," said Amy, sitting at her desk, leaning back in her seat, delicately nibbling the edge of her silver, slim-lined, Mont Blanc pen.

Richard stooped over his desk, and started typing swiftly on his laptop. "Yep, will do," he said.

Amy jotted down a reminder on her notepad to call David and spent another twenty minutes meticulously going over the photocopy of her business loan application form.

"Management of your accounts has been most impressive, Miss Scott. You've kept to a definite and consistent pattern, evidenced by the solid growth on your savings and current accounts. Have you given any further considerations to crossing monies over to one of our high yielding savings accounts? You're receiving the mail-shots on-line, am I right?" queried the bank manager, in his effort to maintain a permanent hold of Amy's accounts.

"Yes, I'm receiving them all and I'm yet to make a decision on the account that'll be of most benefit to me in the long term," said Amy agitatedly, fully aware of the bank manager's subtle use of soft-sell tactics.

"Is there one in particular you'd like to go over now? I'd be more than happy to run through the ramifications with you," offered the bank manager, handing Amy a couple of glossy informational booklets on high yielding savings accounts, persistent in his aim to achieve on-target earnings for his branch and region.

"Not particularly. I'm suitably happy at present," said Amy in finality, smiling stiffly.

"Borrowing towards this business venture of yours, although quite an ambitious feat and brave on your part, releasing equity from your property can be an enormous risk to you and, you're quite right and sensible in putting your bonds and shares safely aside to serve as a buffer should adverse conditions arise. However, having said that, I'm confident, according to the excellent business plan and forecasts you've presented here and, dare I say, the powerful partnership you're entering into, with the support and backing of a strong company, a major key player in the field of global corporate consultancy, in the short term, you could envisage enjoying a personal high net worth."

"You've given me so much sound advice throughout my application, backed up with literature, I can hardly thank you enough," said Amy, feeling overwhelmingly light-headed, elated and fearful of the size of the business loan standing at two hundred thousand pounds, eighty thousand pounds release of equity on her apartment and a five thousand pound increase on her overdraft to cover expenses and incidentals, all on competitive interest rates. She'd not factored in her personal cash savings of twenty-seven thousand pounds, an amount she'd managed to save over the years and, on numerous occasions, she'd agonizingly fought off temptations to dip into it during hard times. Stretching herself to realize the sum of thirty-thousand pounds, Amy treated her savings as something to imperatively fall back on, savings for a rainy day. Neither was it raining nor was she imperatively falling back, well, not yet, she thought. Astonished at the amounts borrowed, thrown at her at ease, by her bank manager, it was all proving to be too much to take in, although she'd viewed the amounts as laughably miniscule in comparison to whatever Mike would be contributing. "I'm absolutely pushed for time. I've got to be heading back," she said, desperately in want of solitude in order to wrap her head around ideas and meditate on the progressively rapid whirlwind changes her life was potentially undergoing.

"I shan't delay you any longer," said the bank manager, urgently springing from his seat in conscious avoidance of taking up any more of Amy's time. "Please contact me once you've made your final decision and I'll allocate one of our experienced personal bankers to you, who'll take you through the process," he went on.

"Thank you. I'll get back to you before the seven day ruling with regard to signing the loan and re-mortgage agreements." Amy neatly tucked the small pile of business literature in her brief case.

"I'm most looking forward to hearing from you." The bank manager vigorously shook her hand and escorted her out of his office.

Cautiously elated, struggling to hold back on getting excessively egotistical about the stark potentiality of becoming rich and wealthy, Amy slowly wandered back to her office in a fixed daze.

Perched at the opened window, elbows rested on the window ledge of her private room, Katie waited patiently for David to arrive. She inhaled the scented air of the freshly mowed lawns, marveled at the colorful assortment of flowerbeds bordering the hospital grounds and the spread of Oak trees dotted along the concrete pathways whilst deeply re-evaluating her life and future. Battling with the torment of her recent loss, Katie wondered about the sex of the baby and swore she'd never fall pregnant again.

"I won't be a second," said the nurse, hastily leaving the room, returning precisely in one second, as promised.

Katie held a booklet in her hand on counseling Dr Amir had asked her to take home and read. She flicked through the pages and screwed the booklet into a ball. The nurse watched and said nothing. Finding the garden scenery more refreshing and uplifting, Katie resumed her marveling of the Oak trees, metaphorically comparing herself to a tree that changes with each season, shedding the old and sprouting anew, vowing to make positive changes in her life from that point forward. Change scenery, change everything or go mad, Katie thought. A large guilt filled lump forged in her throat as she thought about David's show of genuine compassion and tireless support, forever present, at her beck and call, providing her every need, unaware that she'd decided his days with her were numbered.

"Are we ready?"

Katie shuddered at David's sudden entrance, automatically recalling their first date, when they'd met in the park and he'd crept up on her and startled her then. Katie remained perched at the window.

David crossed the room and hugged her gently.

Katie turned to David and looked into his eyes, weak and undeniably fond of him, battling with the need to shake off the emotional feelings, for her own sake.

David returned her gaze. "I'm so sorry, so truly sorry. We can always try again," he said earnestly.

Katie held back her horror saying, "Yes."

David thanked the nurse and assisted Katie to Dr Amir's office for the final meeting and official discharging process. After the meeting, David whisked Katie home in his newly acquired Silver Land Rover, breaking speed limits and jumping a couple of red lights.

Unimpressed, Katie gripped her seat and threw David a disapprovingly side-eyed glance which he hadn't noticed. Katie stared ahead thankful of the idea that fate decided that she was not chosen to be the mother of David's child after all, that Zowie had been chosen to be David's wife, albeit allegedly divorcing, and mother of his children. The daunting prospect of having Zowie in the midst of their lives should she choose to remain with David, was not something Katie would ever wish for or entertain, nor did she want to play Stepmother to his children, aspects she was finding immeasurably unappealing. Laying her head back on the leather head rest during the fast speed, non-conversational journey home, Katie wondered what the hell she ever saw in David, summing up that, without paying attention, she'd just simply got caught up in one of the numerous games of life, an obscure game that went terribly wrong, beyond what she'd ever had imagined but, she was glad to be getting shot of him, sooner rather than later.

David pulled up outside Katie's apartment, halting sharply on the brakes. He jumped out of the vehicle, grabbed Katie's overnight case, ran round to the passenger side of the vehicle, opened the door and assisted her climb out of the vehicle. He helped her into her lounge and assisted her on the couch. He got on his knees and removed her shoes, brought a blanket out of her bedroom storage cupboard and covered her with it, wrapping her up snugly. The anesthetic and pain killers began to wear off, leaving Katie with the feelings of stress and discomfort. She moaned, twisted and turned contortedly, aiming to find a comfortable sleeping position.

"Can I fetch you a bite to eat?" David asked.

"No thanks. Food's … I think I'm going to be sick."

"Oh, heck," said David, making a panicked dash to the kitchen. Looking left and right, David grabbed the fruit bowl off the centre of the breakfast bar and tossed the fruits on the kitchen floor. Making a mad dash back to the lounge, David placed the fruit bowl under Katie's chin and stared at the ceiling.

The post cost review meeting between Richard and Amy was held at five-thirty and concluded by six fifteen. Suitably up to speed and fully conversant with the figure-work on the summation of Richard's impressively accurate and informative delivery, shattered and hungry, Amy strolled slowly back to her desk. She drummed her French manicured nails lightly on her desk as Richard logged out of his computer preparing for his departure home. After bidding Richard a quick farewell, Amy called Katie. David answered. "Oh! Hi, David. How's Katie coming along?"

"Somewhat depressed, but that's to be expected. All in all she's coming along."

"I've been waiting for your call. I would have called earlier on today but I've been quite busy. I'd love to speak with her."

"Not a fat chance of that, I'm afraid. Katie's asleep right now."

"Oh dear, I've missed her," Amy sighed. "How long have you been back from the hospital?"

"Since this afternoon, only her doctor had held her back, doing his best to convince her to attend a … well … he'd asked me to come along too … to some support group meeting amongst a host of other things he went over with Katie before giving her the all clear."

"Theoretically speaking, her doctor suggested you both attended post miscarriage consultative group therapy sessions together?"

"You've got it in one."

"There are a number of positive benefits that could be derived from attending such sessions. I think it's a super idea."

"No. Katie ferociously refused to take part."

"I know, I know. Well, that's Katie for you," said Amy profoundly.

"You've developed quite an acquaintanceship. Katie speaks quite highly of you."

"Oh. Really? Does she? Such as?" said Amy, taken aback.

"Nice things, generally. She admires you, your personality," said David. Amy listened on intently, cringing, shutting her eyes tightly, mentally urging

David to get on with it, spare her the flattery. "It's quite something, I'd no idea you and Mike were partnering in more ways than one. It's great," he went on, sniggering.

Deeply regretting having divulged her intimate thoughts and business relations to Katie, Amy pondered on the threat of her treasured secret being revealed before she'd time to make discretionary announcements to her parents, selected family members, friends and associates. The idea of David candidly spilling the news to Mike, possibly subjecting him to the third degree was unbearable to think about. It's such a small world, Amy thought, fearing the worst, imagining the nightmare of it all should critical business information get into the wrong hands. Her heart quickening, imagining Vincent stumbling across the leak and subsequently treating it as a material breach, Amy saw fit to delve deeper. Investigative of the details, stifling her anger, she asked, "From what Katie's discussed with you, what specifically stood out the most regarding Mike and me?"

David sniggered pathetically remarking, "Well, that was strangely put, but I'll answer it anyway. Going away together to … you know where. I suspect that was a bundle of fun. And the whole idea of a joint business enterprise, that's smashing news. What a lucky man. I'm in awe and envy of him."

Amy had heard enough. She now viewed Katie as a potential threat and instantly arrived at the conclusion that it would serve in her best interests to put Katie on hold for a while. Empathetic, Amy understood the inevitability of the emotional and physical aspects Katie had endured and suffered, but she also wanted Katie to make a speedy recovery, get back to her senses before divulging any further information that could detrimentally affect her relationship with Mike. Muddled with mixed feelings and brain weary, Amy tirelessly convinced herself that she was perhaps being presumptuously over-sensitive and overly speculative in her reaction to the news and that she could be far wrong in her wild assumptions about Katie. "How much longer do you intend to stick around with Katie?"

"However long it takes. However long she needs me to be around. Why do you ask?"

"Expect flowers to be delivered to Katie's place in a day or two."

"That's so sweet of you. I can relate to every word she's said about you."

"I'm off," Amy pitched in abruptly.

"I quite understand you having to dash off and all that. You must be quite busy, juggling several things all at once."

"Yes, David, you're absolutely right. Good night." Amy hung up before David had a chance to say another word. Amy's eyes flittered around the silent, empty office. Speechlessly in dread, nagging feelings of anger slowly emerging, envisioning Katie tearfully getting emotionally lost and carried away, spurting to David a full barrage of information on both her prospective business interests and intimacy with Mike, left her feeling hurt, confused, betrayed and decisively alone. She leaned back in the chair, raised her legs, laid them outstretched on her desk and breathed deeply, in and out. Ten minutes had flown by and, with no secretaries on hand, Amy was left to carry-out the final task of ordering the flowers herself prior to heading off home. She swung her legs off the desk and, satisfied that she'd left non-confidential paperwork on her desk, neatly arranged in preparation for the following morning, Amy logged out of her computer, retrieved her handbag, briefcase and cell-phone and, wandered to the secretaries' area. She tossed her briefcase on the floor at her feet and intrusively, fumbled around at one of the secretary's cluttered desks until she came to a small, dark grey plastic box, inconveniently tucked away behind the secretary's telephone. Perching her left buttock on the edge of the desk, Amy plucked out the small grey plastic box and flipped up its cover. It was filled with business cards filed in alphabetical order. Selecting *F*, Amy walked her finger tips through the cards and fished out the printed card, *Flowers Unlimited 247*, depicting a twenty-four hour telephone order line. Amy pulled her purse out of her handbag, slipped out her credit card, displayed Katie's home address on her cell-phone, picked up the secretary's telephone and dialed the twenty-four hour number. Obediently following the prompts, Amy painstakingly placed an order of Dendrobium Orchids for next day, early morning delivery. The instructions of a woman with an annoyingly mechanical voice spieled, "Please state, slowly and clearly, spelling any unusual names, your message, not exceeding ten words, you require to be printed on the presentation card," triggered Amy to keep things plain, short and simple. Robotically drawling her message, Amy said, "To Katie. Best wishes. Love, Amy."

Amy stepped out of the elevator at eight o'clock on a fresh and sunny Tuesday morning. Her cell-phone vibrated in the top, right-hand pocket of her navy blue, tailored blazer, stopping her in her tracks. She determinately answered according to whose number flashed on her screen. On recognition that it was one of Vincent's company cell-phones, Amy coughed the frog out of her throat and aptly took the call. "Good morning, Vincent."

"A good morning to you, too, Amy. Please, pop by my office this morning, would you? Anytime'll do, say, between now and eleven," Vincent politely commanded.

"Right you are, Vincent. I'll pop by in ten minutes, if you like."

"Fine," said Vincent disconnecting the call.

Amy quickly swept across the office floor to her desk. The path of her sweet, floral scented perfume intoxicatingly danced in the air. "Morning, Richard," she greeted hurriedly, throwing her bag on her desk. Hot, she removed her blazer and slung it over the back of her chair.

Richard swiveled round in his chair and faced Amy. "Morning. Vincent's been enquiring your whereabouts," he informed her warningly.

"I know. He's just called me. Thanks for letting me know. Any mention of what he wanted to see me about?" Amy switched on her computer, logged on and scanned her incoming emails in search of clues.

"Nope. Sorry," said Richard.

"I'm just checking my emails. There's nothing here, only the usual, routine stuff." Amy fished her Mont Blanc pen out of the top, right-hand pocket of her blazer, flipped to a clean page on her notepad and, warily unprepared, wandered over to Vincent's office. On entering, Vincent's eyes remained fixated on his computer screen. He appeared to ignore Amy by not acknowledging her presence, increasing her wariness. Amy gently closed the door and crept across the room to the mineral water dispenser. Tucking her note pad under her arm, she filled two plastic cups with chilled water and quietly wandered over to Vincent's desk. On edge, secretly fearing bad news, Amy sat in the chair and placed both cups on Vincent's desk. "Would you care for some water?" she offered anxiously.

"Thank you," murmured Vincent. He immediately reached for a cup, brought it to his lips and gulped the entire contents. He put the cup on his desk, faced Amy and deliberately locked his eyes with hers in warrant of her full attention.

"I've given Stefan the responsibility of discretionary portfolio management to transact on our behalf."

"Yes. Great. A good decision." responded Amy.

Vincent turned to his computer screen. "Mike Brandleton intends to inject five million pounds, I note here from Stefan's email that has only just arrived. What would be your proposed injection?"

Amy shifted nervously in her seat. "In the region of a little over a quarter of a million pounds," she announced shakily, the termed amount rang better than two hundred and eighty five thousand pounds, she thought.

Vincent turned back to Amy. "You've comfortably come up with that amount, have you?"

"Yes, broken down, it's comprised of a bank loan, an increased overdraft amount and a re-mortgage."

Vincent bowed his head in wisdom. "You believe in this. It shows. Good. And are you happy with the bank's terms and conditions against the amounts borrowed?"

"Although preferential, the interest rates could be a little lower, I must confess. However, all in all, I'm confident that I would be capable of comfortably meeting the loan repayments."

"My recent offer to assist you financially still stands. Planet Management is willing to offer you a similar amount, in fact, more on a lower interest rate than what I imagine is being proposed by your bank, with attractively manageable payment terms where you could commence a repayment scheme in six months, one year from now or whenever suits you best."

Fully aware that everything came at a price, Amy found Vincent's munificent offer appealing and tempting but tenaciously wanted to safeguard her autonomy. "That's a very flexible and extremely generous concept, Vincent. How would this affect my combined position within the business and Planet Management?"

"You'll not lose or be restricted any of your employment rights, nor would there be any re-writes to the contract that would effect change. The only definitional difference is that your injected amount would be marginally higher and recorded as such. Finally, you'll not have to release equity on your property should you opt to accept my consideration, as I won't be asking for any collateral." said Vincent. "Where Planet Management is concerned, you are at liberty to delegate more of your work on existing projects to other team members who are not too overly busy. Take it that I've granted you authority to do so with immediate effect. We could look at promoting Richard, providing him with an assistant. Under your jurisdiction, he's been productively impressive of late, he deserves it."

Almost short of breath, Amy's eyes began to sting. With such irresistible offers, only a blithering idiot would turn them down, Amy thought. Although Amy trusted Vincent implicitly, she was sneakily suspicious of his offers and questioned his motivational factors, if any, that lay behind his excessive generosity, and wondered whether it was his way of keeping her tied-in with Planet Management until full payment of the loan, at the very least. It took only a few seconds to figure that she was on a winning edge and forcibly displaying emotional balance and, in true Planet Management style, Amy accepted the offer graciously. "I've considered the feasibilities and long term fiscal sense of your gestures, Vincent that, with no alternative or more favorable options, I provisionally accept accordingly." she responded, tugging at a dainty Victorian laced-edged, white cotton handkerchief, tucked up the left cuff of her white, made to measure shirt.

"Splendid," said Vincent, appearing not to have noticed Amy fighting back her tears.

Dabbing her eyes, Amy said, "Excuse me, but, I've something in my eye." Vincent made no comment and looked away. "What sum are we talking about?" asked Amy composedly.

"I'll have the loan agreement drawn up ready for signing in twenty-four hours in the sum of one point five million pounds or whatever's in the asking."

Amy almost choked. "One point five million pounds is an acceptable offer. One has to speculate to accumulate, as the old adage goes," she said spontaneously, nervously repeating the figure several times over in her head.

"That's the spirit. I agree to the old adage. You're under no obligation I hasten to add. Take your time in your decision making. And should you wish to change your mind in any way, you're at full liberty to exercise that right," Vincent cautiously advised Amy adding, "On further review of the potential business and with Stefan's trusted management of the portfolio, I thought I'd bring to your attention that I propose to inject two million pounds of my personal funds into Project Cascadia, as a silent investor, of course, written into the project as Planet Management's stake towards the business. Between you and me, call the move integration methodology if you like. The stake will have to be unanimously accepted and agreed, and the contract updated to reflect this."

Astounded, Amy nodded definitively. "I perfectly understand, Vincent. I'll run it by, Mike, my business associate. I'm sure he'd be more than happy to accept Planet Management's injection."

"Jolly good, then," said Vincent sighing. "Before you go, your late arrival to the cost review meeting hadn't gone unnoticed. Are there any special reasons?"

"I apologize. Time had overrun. I'd, I'd gotten carried away researching Project Cascadia. It was only five minutes, which is no excuse, I know, and … and … and I can only reiterate my apologies," responded Amy, speaking rapidly, coming up with her best response, shooting from the hip, reminiscing on

her time spent discussing the project with Mike, at four in
wrapped in a cotton bed sheet, hating herself for arriving late, with the re̶s̶̶
ant potentiality of letting Vincent and the side down.

"Make full use of the expertise and resources you have at your entire disposal here at Planet Management. There is no need to spend excessive time on
projects unnecessarily. Work smart. We have great teams working on all
aspects. You simply overseer," said Vincent, glancing at the telephone as
though he was expecting it to ring at any moment.

"I'll bear that in mind."

"You've a number of projects you're doing great work with and heading up
remarkably well. With my silent vested interest in Project Cascadia, I'll be
keeping a close eye on it, as I do on all projects across the board. Therefore,
please do not worry. That'll be all, Amy," Vincent concluded, dismissively.

Amy gracefully rose to her feet. "I'll make myself readily available to sign the
loan agreement and, either myself or Mike, Mike Brandleton will get back to
you on your … on Planet Management's invitation," she said, turning on her
heels, quickly exiting the room.

"Right you are, Amy."

Consumed with heightened feelings of indescribable awe, Amy strutted
over to her desk. Her meeting with Vincent and the whole idea of the venture
was proving to be too much for her to wrap her head around and take in all at
once.

"All's well?" Richard remarked inquisitively, pouncing on receiving Amy's
attention before losing her to commencement of work now that she'd returned
to her desk. "I've read the email update," he continued enthusiastically.

"Yes. All is well, Richard," Amy responded pleasingly. Stefan had copied
Amy and all project team members in on the email he'd sent to Vincent and
had attached emails sent by Mike's business lawyer and accountant confirming
the five million pound-inception. With Project Cascadia enjoying the initiate
sum of eight point five million pounds, Amy fiercely struggled to come to
terms with the concept of being personally involved in a small project with the
potential to mushroom, limitlessly. With the huge sums of money involved,
the whole idea of Mike as her lover and business partner and, Vincent coming
in silently, flabbergasted her. Stiflingly hot and in need of fresh air, Amy felt
impelled to physically jump for joy, shout and scream out loud to release her
stifled excitement. "Richard, please take all my calls. I'm popping out for a
quick coffee. I'm reachable on my cell-phone if anyone needs me," she said.

"Sure, Amy," said Richard.

Amy made a vivaciously energetic dash towards the approaching elevator and dived into it just in the nick of time.

Franco served Amy a cup of latte in his usual suave, Latin manner. Amy thanked Franco sweetly. Sitting comfortably in her favorite spot, enjoying the familiar sounds of Cino's, Amy stared out of the window in absolute bliss. Slowly feeling at ease with accepting Vincent's offer, Amy decided that she'd do everything in her power to make the necessary changes, compromises and sacrifices, alter her spending habits, tone down her lifestyle, in order to meet the company loan repayments. She'd give both her venture and Planet Management her all. Work hard on maximizing revenues to achieve huge returns that would assist in her capability in making the repayments and re-investment in the venture. The bank loan had to be cancelled and Amy wasn't so readily at ease having to call the bank manager to decline his offer. Shrugging her shoulders in a true "what the hell" style, and to avoid having to go through the ordeal of walking the bank manager through a soft explanation behind her deciding factors for no longer going ahead with the loans, Amy dialed the customer services number from her cell-phone. After clearing a routine security check, a cheerful call centre operator cancelled the loans with no questions asked, informing Amy that a covering letter confirming the cancellations would follow in seven days. Satisfied, Amy switched off her cell-phone and gazed through the window at the steady flow of people moving through the morning rush hour. *"You cannot serve two masters,"* Amy murmured the old biblical saying knowing that eventually she'd inevitably have to serve one master. Embellishing ideas of becoming a woman to be reckoned with, her latte untouched, Amy vacated her table and winked at Franco saying, "And may the best man win," as she switched on her cell-phone and walked swiftly out of Cino's to embark on giving her best shot to both masters, wondering whom she would ultimately serve.

Katie awoke on her couch. She raised her right hand and shielded her eyes from the sun bursting its rays into her lounge. She squinted around the room. A blanket lay tossed over the armchair where she assumed David had slept, bringing with it the unwanted reminder of the day before. She looked the other way surprised at the Orchids adorning her Mahogany mantel fireplace, softening her mood.

David entered the room wrapped in one of Katie's bathrobes. He walked over to the Orchids, picked up a small, sealed white envelope and handed it to Katie.

"Thanks. They're gorgeous," Katie croaked.

"Open it. They're not from me."

"Oh?" Bewildered, yawning, Katie opened the envelope, pulled out the card and read the brief printed message. Katie's face lit up. "They're from, Amy?" she gasped.

"Yes. They were delivered this morning." David smiled warmly.

"But I didn't hear the intercom. I'd slept through it?"

"Yes." David coughed nervously and cleared his throat. "Amy telephoned last night. You were asleep. She'd mentioned that she'd send flowers so, to avoid disturbing you, I adjusted the intercom to the lowest volume in case the flowers arrived early in the morning. And they did, at seven forty-five, to be precise."

"Amy, called last night? But I didn't hear the telephone ring. You hadn't lowered the telephone's volume too?"

"Yes, because I didn't want you disturbed. You've been through a very traumatic ordeal and …"

"Please, stop. I don't need you telling me what I've been through, thank you," Katie howled. "You could've woken me up. I would've gladly spoken to Amy."

David stood in silence.

"Did she say anything else, or leave a message or anything?"

"No," said David, bluntly and quietly, head bowed.

"Then, I'll return her call. I must call to thank her." Tossing back the blanket, Katie dragged herself slowly and wretchedly off the couch. She shuffled unsteadily over to the Orchids and admired them closely. Yawning, Katie turned to David and glared at him. David glared back at Katie looking very unattractive. Awful. As ugly as her mood. "After our cheerful chat about Amy and stuff, you then went on to kill the moment, moaning and groaning, going on about Zowie and the kids. I'd fallen asleep, bored with it all."

Stunned and visibly hurt, David arched an eyebrow and looked away in contemptibility at Katie's statement. "You could have simply asked me to talk about something other than my family. I had no idea you were bored."

"It's all an absolute bore and I hope she won't be calling here again." Katie pushed David out of her way and headed to the kitchen.

Casting a look of disdain at Katie, David decisively and convincingly put her disparaging comments down to the trauma she'd suffered over the weekend. "I don't understand! What's gotten into you, Katie?" he pleaded, teetering behind her.

"It's not working for me. You've been a great sport. I couldn't have gotten through this without you, David. Now, it's time to move on. I'm handing in my resignation and I'm going away for a few months. I need to spend time with my family. I may spend some time with my parents, in their villa in Spain. I'll probably let this apartment for six months or more. Then, I'll review my situation."

"Run home to mother! Where's the good in that gesture?" bellowed David. "You've no idea what you're talking about. It's the trauma you've suffered. Why won't you re-think this thing through?"

Katie noisily prepared herself a cup of coffee, banging and slamming everything down heavily on the work tops. "I've done my thinking and there's nothing you can say to change my mind."

"We ought to attend one or two of the meetings your doctor had quite rightly suggested. I think they'll do us both the world of good," David desperately reasoned.

Katie turned her back at the agonizing sight of David remorsefully appearing closely on the verge of coming to tears. Katie was sick of tears. She'd spent the entire weekend crying for England. "Please leave me now. It's all over," she demanded tersely.

"You're such an ungrateful woman. After everything I've done for you. I was prepared to change my life for you. Women, you're all bloody alike," David sneered dejectedly, exiting the kitchen in a huff.

Feeling faint, Katie slouched over the breakfast bar, listening out for David, praying that he'd leave her apartment. He got dressed, gathered his items and marched out, slamming the door behind him without saying good-bye.

"Yes," Katie bellowed triumphantly. Smirking, she reached for the telephone and called Amy at the office.

"Any messages?"

"Yes. Only one. Someone by the name of Katie? She didn't leave a number. Said it was a personal call," said Richard.

"Thanks," said Amy.

"Anyone to do with Project Cascadia, perhaps?" asked Richard, fishing.

"No," said Amy, bluntly. "Whilst we're on the subject of Project Cascadia, going forward, please arrange daily briefing sessions to take effect round about five-thirty, the first of which is to commence today, would you?" Settling at her desk, Amy began the long, testing and grueling tasking exercise of accelerating the remainder of projects under her jurisdiction, kicking ass if need be, she thought.

"Certainly. Anyone in particular you'd like to participate?"

"No. Just you and I for the present. I want nothing going wrong with this project."

"To date, nothing drastic has gone wrong on projects that we couldn't fix."

"Rightly stated, Richard. However, there's always an exception."

Refusing to return fire, Richard threw his arms in the air in an un-opposed I give up fashion saying, "I'll get on to it right away, Amy," bouncing into efficiency.

Amy wandered into a vacant meeting room, closed the door behind her, picked up the telephone and dialed Katie's number. "Hey, Katie. Got your message. I'm about to get a bite for lunch but thought about returning your call before I do. How are you?"

"Bearing up, bearing up, slowly but surely, considering, thanks to you. And thanks so, so much for your support and the beautiful Orchids, they'd arrived this morning. Sorry, I haven't sent you a thank you card or anything for all the support you've shown," said Katie, babbling gratefully.

"I'd ordered them last night."

"They're gorgeous, thanks. I don't need to tell you that you can pop round any evening convenient to you. I'm taking lots of time off work."

"How about tonight?"

"Tonight's fine."

"Will David be there?"

"No. I won't be seeing him for a while."

"Oh. Why's that?"

"I'll explain it all to you later."

"I'll be there at eight sharp."

CHAPTER 19

Amy stepped into the hallway of Katie's apartment.

"Spot on. It's exactly eight and not a second later," said Katie, energetically planting Amy a continental kiss.

"I wouldn't possibly dream of keeping you waiting," said Amy, amusedly moved by Katie's come-back, her vibrant spirit and fresh appearance, flatteringly dressed in a warm, peach and white jogging suit, her hair neatly styled in her signature French bun. Exhausted, hungry and lacking sleep, Amy was desperate for a long earned rest. Primarily focused on getting home at a reasonable hour, Amy consciously aimed at keeping the duration of her visit to one hour. "So, what's the story?" Amy followed Katie into the kitchen.

"Have you eaten? I've freshly prepared salad in the refrigerator or I could rustle up a hot snack?" Katie offered, pouring two cups of freshly made Colombian black coffee.

"I'm famished. The salad will be just fine," said Amy gratefully, sitting comfortably at the breakfast bar, placing her handbag on the floor at her feet.

"There'll be no turning back. I've had it with David. It's all over," Katie suddenly blurted.

Here we go, Amy thought.

"What I saw in him, I'll never know. I mean, he's hardly my type now, is he?" Katie busily served up a plate of salad, a condiments tray, a glass of chilled filtered water, the cups of Colombian black coffee with a jug of skimmed milk and a bowl of assorted sweeteners.

Amy selected two sachets of low calorie sweetener, sprinkled the contents into her coffee and stirred. "Thanks," she said. She brought her cup to her lips and sipped the coffee. "Coffee's delicious. Aren't you eating?"

"No. I've already eaten."

Keeping a mental track of the time, Amy commenced eating her salad, a succulent array of Chinese leaf lettuce, cherry tomatoes, aubergine, green beans, thickly chopped red, yellow and green peppers, served with a sprinkling of mixed herbs soaked in French wine vinegar. "What's the deciding factor behind your conclusion only, under the circumstances, you both appeared to be doing fine when I'd last seen you together? And what about the plans you'd so endearingly talked about? Have they now been blown out of the window?" Amy probed, deliberately asking a multitude of questions, between mouthfuls of food, implicating Katie to engage in most of the talking, which freed her to eat, drink and listen, half-heartedly.

Katie pulled up a chair and sat at the opposite end of the breakfast bar facing Amy. "David has been very supportive, admittedly," she said, waiting patiently for Amy to source her with some form of invaluable endorsement. Chewing graciously, Amy glanced at Katie, smiled warmly and nodded in acknowledgement. She reached for the jar of olive oil on the condiments tray and poured a modest serving over the Chinese leaf lettuce. "Well, now that I'm not having his child, I don't see the need to remain with him. Anyway, life with David would have been quite boring. Then, there's the question of his wife. I'd envisioned her deliberately coming between us, repeatedly putting a spanner in the works," Katie went on. "I couldn't live with David having his wife constantly in our lives once the divorce had gone through. There is the problem of taking on his kids, playing second mother. No thanks. Call me selfish, if you will but, I don't want to take all that on."

"No. I'd not call you selfish. Sounds like you've thought things through." Amy washed her salad down with a few generous gulps of water.

"Oh yes, I've thought things through, alright. And there's more," said Katie, pausing, deliberately conjuring an atmosphere of suspense.

Amy chased cherry tomatoes around her plate. She pronged at them with her fork and missed each time. They would have been better cut in half, Amy thought. Giving up the chase, Amy dropped her fork in her plate, picked up a cherry tomato with her fingers and popped it in her mouth. "I'd love to hear it!" she said, prompting Katie.

"I'm resigning. Taking time out. Going to Spain for a while."

Amy swallowed. "Resigning? Moving to Spain?"

"No. I'm not moving, not indefinitely anyway, just spending some time with Mum. God knows, she's been on my case, begging me to join her on one of her frequent stays in the villa she'd purchased in Benidorn two years ago."

Katie breathed deeply. "I can't wait. I'll be out there as soon as I've cleared things up this end."

"I'd no idea. Well, putting your directorship and your life here on hold, no doubt, your mother will be pleased to have you all to herself," said Amy, struggling to find the right words.

"She knows nothing about David and me, or the pregnancy," revealed Katie.

"Why ever not? Why would you not inform your mother of such an important occurrence in your life?"

"You don't know my mum. Drama. Always drama. She over-reacts, over-dramatizes, causes scenes and she'd probably go as far as naming the child, mention it during conversations as though it was once here. She wants grandchildren and moans at me for not getting married and having children. And as for the company, I can easily re-introduce myself into the working world again having built up dossiers of influential contacts. I really need the time off, a good, fresh, clean break, in the sun."

Amy raised an eyebrow, "I see," she said politely, her thoughts trailing back to the hospital, particularly reminiscent of David's demonstration of his caring side. "Would you not consider giving David another chance?" said Amy, hardly able to believe herself that she'd actually posed the question. She scraped her leftovers into a tidy heap at the top right hand corner of the plate and left the cutlery neatly in the centre.

"Amy!" cried Katie, "you're beginning to sound just like him. He had the cheek to believe that we could try for another baby!"

Amy sipped her coffee that had now gone unpalatably warm and tasted bitter. "So, the decision to end isn't an equally shared view?" returned Amy, calmly and controllably.

"No. I'd effectively ended it all. Sent him packing. Anyway, he was getting on my nerves."

"Well, it's great to see that you've made a remarkable recovery, returned to the Katie I know, full of fighting spirit." Amy put her cup aside.

"More coffee? Any water?" asked Katie.

"I wouldn't say no to more water."

"Sure." Katie rose nimbly to her feet, busily cleared the breakfast bar and stacked the dishwasher.

Amy vacated her seat and paced around the kitchen, stretching her long legs. "Any firm ideas on the length of time you plan to be away in Spain?"

"Two months. Three. Six at the most should do it."

Amy walked over to the kitchen window and peered out admiring the stylish wooden vertical blinds, hanging smartly in the kitchen window of the apartment opposite. "You do intend to remain in touch whilst you're out in Spain living a life of leisure in the sun," said Amy, teasingly.

"Of course I do. You never know, I may invite you over."

Amy wandered back to the breakfast bar and sat down. "Thanks, I may take you up on the offer, but I wouldn't want to get in the way, impose on the valuable time you'd otherwise spend with your mother."

"Take it from me, I'll be finding things to do and ways to escape my mother's smothering and suffocation. And that's after I've finished stuffing my face with her scrumptious roast dinners and steamed puddings," said Katie laughingly, pouring Amy another glass of chilled filtered water and handing it to her.

Amy smiled, delightedly pleased at having the real Katie back in full swing, bravely moving on with her life with no obvious signs of wallowing in misery. Yet, in another vain, Amy wondered how much emotional pain Katie might actually be furtively struggling through, articulately suppressing her pain, keeping it well concealed.

"What do you plan to do out there, exactly?"

"For starters, I could earn money letting this apartment. And I may look at a possible career change, dabbling here and there. Don't know what doing specifically, but who knows what'll happen. The truth is, I need to get away, get David out of my mind and think about where I'm going with my life."

"I see," said Amy, hiding her puzzlement.

"What about you?" Katie poured herself a glass of chilled filtered water and sat down at the breakfast bar. "What's the latest on the Mike front? Seen him lately? How's the fiancé thing?"

Amy recalled snippets of her telephone conversation with David. "Things have been very quiet on that front. We've both been extremely busy that we've hardly laid eyes on each other." The dishwasher hummed quietly in the background.

"How's the hotel business going between you and Mike?"

"No change. Stagnant. It'll be a good few months before anything really concrete kicks off," said Amy, resignedly dull, persuasively lacking luster in her deliberate refusal to reveal latent facts about the venture.

"The concept sounds great and I hope you'll both be able to pull it off successfully."

"Thanks. We'll see," said Amy.

"What's that supposed to mean? You're either going ahead with it or you're not, and what about you as a couple, any plans or developments there?"

"There is nothing new to report. We've not made any significant progress on the venture. And as for us, we're developing, but very slowly. There's nothing much to report, really."

"Oh?" said Katie, clearly unconvinced, throwing her arms up in the air.

Amy hunched her shoulders. "OK. OK. Don't get me wrong. As time progresses, there's no denying, my feelings for Mike grow. Naturally, I'd like nothing more than a fully fledged relationship with him but, like I've said, we're coming on very slowly, who knows what'll happen between us." Amy kept Erica out of the equation.

"You're right. Who knows? Who in damned hell knows about anything?"

Amy drank all her water, put her glass down, leaned sideways and picked up her handbag. She rose out of the chair and stood on her feet. "It's time I was heading off. We can talk about this another time," she said hastily, avoiding further debate on the sensitive subject dominant in her life.

"I'll certainly hold you to that. You know me. I want to know everything."

"That's my girl," replied Amy smiling, "And thanks for the salad, coffee and everything."

"That was nothing. Thanks for coming over, I know you're pushed. I'll see you out." Amy glanced at her watch and lifted her cell-phone out of her handbag. "It's eight-fifty. We've got a few minutes yet. I'll call a taxi."

"We must meet again before I depart for Spain."

"Yes, we must. By the way, when are you likely to be heading out there?" said Amy, calling the taxi company on her cell-phone.

"As soon as things are physically and viably possible. Give me a couple of weeks to a month max."

"I see." Amy nodded at Katie signaling that she was about to speak on her cell-phone. "Ah. Hello there. It's Amy Scott. I'd like a taxi. Pick me up right away would you please? From ..."

Katie got up and busied herself around the kitchen.

Amy looked forward to the prospect of finally heading home. She waved at Katie as she boarded the taxi. Slamming the door and positioning herself comfortably, Amy gazed out of the window as the taxi pulled away. She reflected on the tactful hour spent with Katie, mulling over the news of the break-up with David, the temporary move to Spain, skirting around the miscarriage without mention to silently chuckling at not having laid eyes on the Orchids she'd sent.

taxi

The cab pulled up outside Amy's apartment at approximately nine thirty. Exhausted at the end of a highly taxing day in the office, Amy took a long, hot and relaxing shower and crawled blissfully into bed. Her hi-tech digital clock radio beamingly displaying the time of ten twenty-two was set to alarm at five thirty in the morning. Amy switched off her bedside lamp and snugly settled down to sleep. The telephone rang. Her eyes closed, Amy reached clumsily for the telephone and narrowly missed knocking the digital clock radio on the floor. She grunted, squinted and switched the lamp back on.

"Have I caught you at a bad time? I love the sound of your voice when you're semi awake."

"Yes, Mike. In fact, you're right, I'd fallen sleep, only just. You've caught me in time. It's been a long day. What can I do for you?" Amy turned on her side and propped herself upright on her elbow.

"Are there any items you'd like to go over regarding the venture?"

Amy glanced at the digital clock radio beaming the time of ten forty-three. She'd actually had a few minutes sleep although she didn't feel she'd slept at all. "Not exactly," she said, covering the mouthpiece, letting out a fiercely, eye watering yawn, wanting and adoring Mike, wishing he'd pass on the preamble and get on with whatever it was he'd called to discuss.

"Any plans for the weekend?" Mike asked.

"Work on Latin American projects."

"Fancy a night out at the theatre, Sadler's Wells to see Swan Lake this coming Saturday?"

"That would be very pleasing," Fatigued, Amy responded, enchantingly. She pulled back the covers and slithered out of bed. *insert ellipse* X

"Great. It's my final weekend in the UK. Ideally, my thoughts were that we'd spend the entirety of it together, theoretically speaking, if you're free, of course. How does that sound?"

"Wonderful," said Amy ponderingly, pacing up and down her bedroom floor. Richard had confirmed during their first update briefing session that Mike and Stefan were due to fly out to the Turks the following week and Amy effectively began missing Mike from that point. "Yes. So, you're off to the Turks next week, Wednesday to be exact," she went on confirmedly, fighting back an emerging yawn.

"Right. Stefan and I have conducted short impromptu discussions on the proposed schedule of meetings and travel itinerary, yet to be finalized."

With the cordless telephone pressed against her ear, Amy made her way through the darkened apartment to the kitchen. She poured herself a glass of chilled Chablis, wandered back to her bedroom, sat carefully on the edge of her bed and savored a couple of sips. "Planet Management injected two million pounds into our venture today," she announced, consciously heeding in keeping Vincent's name out of the conversation.

"Noted. We couldn't have wished for a more valuable interest. I'm astoundingly pleased by that aspect. Not only are we on the books, but we're enjoying the added bonus of the company's vested interest, leveraging us very nicely within the leisure industry. This act demonstrates the good faith shown in the project, that we're bound to go from strength to strength," said Mike.

Amy's head weighed a heavy ton on her shoulders, induced by the quick, large gulps of Chablis, triggering the swift return of sleep and lethargy to her entire body that Amy battled with paying cautious attention to Mike's every word. Draining the glass, Amy placed it on the mirrored bedside table and lying back, she gently nestled her head on her pillow. Satisfied that Mike had no qualms, questions or stipulations surrounding the injection and, to avoid making any incriminating statements caused by the lack of concentration and the desperate need to go back to sleep, Amy sought to bring the conversation to a close. "I agree with your sentiments entirely, Mike," she said, struggling to sound sharp and alert.

Mike paused. "Well, if you're certain you've nothing further to discuss, I'll contact you soon with news of the ballet."

"I'm so looking forward to our weekend, how exciting, thank you," Amy enthused.

"It will be, mark my words. It'll be one to enjoy and remember. Sleep tight." he said, hanging up.

Amy switched off the telephone, tossed the goose down duvet over her head and slipped blissfully back to sleep wearing a smile.

Amy worked ambitiously through the remainder of an exciting week, chiefly highlighted by Friday afternoon's signing of the company loan of one point five million pounds in the presence of Vincent and the legal counselor, Kevin Doherty. Both officials serving as witnesses to the contracted loan agreement was icing on the cake for Amy, marking a significant end to her week. Amy confirmed to Vincent the joint acceptance of both herself and Mike of Planet Management's injection. Finalizing on Richard's promotional matters with Vincent and Human Resource representatives, escalating projects to meet a number of milestones set on service level agreements and, with Mike's imminent business trip on the horizon, Amy bravely prepared herself with the daunting prospect of conducting a long distant relationship with Mike. "Richard, please make certain that I'm provided with final copies of the travel itineraries and meeting schedules in duplicate."

"I'll get on to that right away. The meeting schedules will be confirmed by Tuesday afternoon, I believe."

"The timing's rather tight! That's one day before they're due to depart," Amy expressed alarmingly.

"I know. We're still awaiting confirmation on a couple of key meeting arrangements, Rory promised to us no later than Tuesday."

"Fine."

"If it's any consolation to you, what I can tell you now is that they're booked first class on the overnight direct flight to Providenciales."

"That's fine, Richard," said Amy, appreciative of Richard's efforts to constantly please her, keep her up to date with as much detail as possible.

Richard handed Amy an A4 brown envelope marked in black ink and bold lettering, *Strictly Private and Confidential. To Be Opened by the Addressee Only*, delivered by the messenger on his final mail run for the day.

Amy slashed it open with an elegant Turtle Shell letter opener, peered inside and read the top line of the document. "Book a meeting room scheduling a meeting between you and I today, would you?"

Richard looked at his watch depicting the time of four twenty-five. "The subject matter being?"

"H.R. See whether you can get something in, say, half an hour."

"Right away." Richard peered at his computer screen, exercising his privileged rights to access sensitive information on Project Cascadia. He eagerly entered the password allowing him entry to the restricted server, opened files enabling him to read through Amy's signed loan agreement in pdf format, loaded on the server by the legal department.

Amy made her way to the staff coffee lounge to sufficiently familiarize herself of the envelope's contents. She noted Richard's impressive credentials, length of service, career path to date, offer of an attractive middle management position, negotiable remuneration package and sign-off of Vincent authorizing his approval of the appointment. Amy returned to her desk with a view to making the meeting with Richard a quick and easy one.

"If you're agreeable, we can commence our HR meeting at five-fifteen," Richard informed Amy.

Amy smiled warmly at Richard. "That would be fine," she said.

Richard entered the small meeting room with Amy. "Amy, I hope you do not object to what I'm about to state. It's just that I couldn't face another human resource maneuvering task, painstakingly reshuffling staff. I've just completed the onerous task of reappointing staff to other projects you'd instructed, most willingly accepted their moves, whilst a couple attempted to give me a hard time. I'd resolved matters swiftly and amicably, aware of the importance of maintaining good relations with my peers as much as possible, including those I totally loathe, a fact I'm sorry to state."

Amy skirted around Richard's statement. "I've called this sudden meeting in order to present an offer to you on behalf of the company, Planet Management." Adorning the wall, above Richard's head, was Johannes Vermeer's aesthetic portrait, The Girl With A Pearl Earring, momentarily stealing Amy's attention. Owing to Vincent's passion for the arts, masterpieces by Rembrandt, Picasso, Monet, Vermeer and more, ubiquitously graced the walls of Planet Management's buildings, worldwide.

Stunned, Richard remained speechless, intrinsically using the gap to mentally register Amy's statement.

"A management appointment is in order, the title being Senior Project Manager. What this entails is that you'll continue working for me, managing my projects on a more involved scale. This would release certain aspects of the management side of things from me onto you, freeing me up to work on overseeing projects more in-depth. You'd be reporting to Vincent on a regular basis and get involved in the decision making side of things. All that's left is your acceptance or decline. The decision is entirely yours."

Richard blinked. "I'm absolutely flabbergasted. I'd no idea that this was in the pipeline."

"I'm pleased for you, Richard. I sincerely mean that," said Amy, encouragingly.

"I'm absolutely stunned," said Richard. He held out his hand across the small meeting room table. Amy took it and engaged in a vigorous handshake. In an unprecedented move, Richard brought Amy's hand to his lips, grazed the back of her hand and remained in that position longer than warranted. The bristles of his soft moustache making contact with her skin and the pressing warmth of his firm lips caused the trickle of desperately unwanted sensations. Hating herself, regretting the handshake, Amy tugged her hand free.

"Thank you very much, indeed," Richard continued, bowing his head at Amy in eminence.

Amy slid the envelope across the small round table towards Richard saying, "I've been asked to bring the remuneration package and benefits to your attention. It's all in there. I suggest that you thoroughly read through everything, carefully. It's all self-explanatory and, should you wish to discuss anything further, please let me know and I'll ask one of the secretaries to arrange an appointment with a human resource representative who'll be assigned to you, taking you through the mentoring, career package and your overall development once you've formally accepted the appointment and signed the relevant documents." Richard whipped the offer documents out of the envelope and immediately started reading.

"One final thing. You've seven days to sign the acceptance. Failing that, the offer will be automatically withdrawn," Amy heeded.

"I accept now, verbally, in principle, subject to the contractual terms on offer, of course." Preoccupied, Richard flicked through the pages.

"Great. You won't be disappointed. There's also the proviso to furnish you with an assistant, something I know you'd welcome highly," said Amy.

Richard glared at Amy in amazement. "Terrific. Would there be any scope to participate in the selection and interview process of the candidates. I would be the better judge as to the one who'd best fit the role?"

Amy smiled. "I'm sure that can be arranged. I'll run that by the human resource representative. Are there any additional items you'd like to discuss before we move on to Project Cascadia?"

"No. I'll look at this over the weekend and get back to you by Monday. Amy, I'm pleased with the fact that I'll be working with you on a continual basis on all projects."

"Likewise. You're being granted more responsibilities. Use of your recognized skills, hard work and expertise are not only highly valued but are also valuably required, hence the appointment."

"I'm aware of that and will not let you down."

Amy smiled tightly. "Thank you, Richard and, well done." At the close of their brief Project Cascadia daily meeting, Richard proudly clutched the envelope under his arm and walked swiftly out of the small meeting room back to his desk.

"I'm leaving shortly as I've a hectic weekend ahead," said Amy.

"I'd be inclined to follow suit. Doing anything interesting?"

"Theatre. Tomorrow night."

"That's grand. Is it a play?" asked Richard, casually.

f mine is busily making all the arrangements. Therefore, I'll
details tomorrow," said Amy, rushing to the elevator, deter-
to maintain her stance of exercising discretion of her private life and as
little familiarity as possible with Richard. Appointment or not, she hadn't
planned to relax formalities.

"Good night, Amy. Have a wonderful, wonderful weekend," called Richard
exaggeratedly.

"Thanks. And you too." Amy eased herself into the packed elevator.

Richard reached for the telephone and called Nick, an assistant manager,
based in the Alternative Assets department. "Hey, Nick, I've been promoted to
senior project manager to Amy Scott and, hear this, I get my very own assistant," Richard bragged in full knowledge of Nick's recent dilemma, failing to
reach his targets, deferring his career plan.

"Good for you, Rich. Well done," said Nick pretentiously, seething with
envy.

Amy stepped out of the packed elevator, raced through the glass revolving
doors and hailed a taxi. The Friday evening traffic moving slowly, Amy decided
to make positive use of the time spent sitting in the taxi. She opened her briefcase, pulled out the company loan documents and attempted to understand
the agreement clauses, contractual notes and glossary of terms. Incomprehen-
sibly lost by certain aspects of the stated terminology, Amy self-professed that
she couldn't grasp the full meaning or the true implications of what she'd
effectively agreed and signed to, thus influencing her decision to appoint her
own personal business lawyer. Everyone else has got one, so why should I not?
she thought.

CHAPTER 20

"Amy! You lucky bastard!" David ranted, standing propped up against the bar of The Precedence, a drinking haunt in the city they'd arranged to meet for a general catch-up during David's brain-picking midweek telephone call to Mike.

"Fortunate, my man. Fortunate," said Mike. "But, Katie? The one who'd attended the workshop? I'd no idea you were in contact with her," returned Mike, clearly astounded.

"Yes, I've certainly been in contact with her for my sins. Yes. Katie, indeed," said David sorrowfully, drumming his fingers on the bar. "Katie's also told me you're embarking on some sort of business scheme with Amy?"

Mike lifted an eyebrow. "Really?"

"Amy!" David signed. "How did that all happen?"

"Happen?" said Mike, perplexingly. He'd asked himself that question a million times, each night before settling off to sleep, wide awake, in his master bedroom, laying in the nude, flat on his back on the Emperor sized, four poster waterbed, needing Amy, imagining her snuggled close to him, her long, strong, smooth and slender legs intertwined with his, her soft, long capable fingers expertly and sensuously stroking his entire body, soothing him to sleep after satisfying her, climatically. "To further elaborate on my answer to your question, I'd made use of one of the numerous benefits associated with networking. For some time now, I've toyed with the idea of hiring the services of an apt management consultancy to establish a business concept of mine I've long been itching to get off the ground and, Amy's expertise fitted the bill perfectly. Grasping the opportunity, I took the liberty of propositioning her and, it appears to be paying off rather handsomely in more ways than one," said Mike, nonchalantly.

"I'm pleased to hear it. What business are you embarking on?" said David, brandishing his glass of vintage Albert de Prumeac Tres Vielle Reserve Grande champagne cognac towards the light.

Mike shrugged his shoulders. "I'm expanding, growing, running more hotels. It's early days yet, as we're only at the implementation stage," said Mike in general, protective of his plans.

"Excellent! You're taking on the expertise of Amy's employers with Amy being the prime link and target should I say. You crafty bugger!" cried David.

Mike sucked a pre Cuban embargo, expensively rare Hoyo de Monterrey panetela. "Well, not quite along those lines. Although Amy's a bit of a leggy stunner and a worthy catch, she's also packed with potential. I have the utmost respect for her and esteem her highly." he said, chuckling proudly, silently in trouble. Women! Mike thought. Where should I go with this one? They always start off like this. They know what to do. They tantalize you. Reveal a little cleavage here. Wiggle their asses a little there. Pout their lips at you in their own special way when they speak. They know how to make you go weak in the groin and suffer under the captivating tones of their soft, sweet and sexy voices. They know exactly where to apply their perfumery in just the right places and in the right measures to steal your mind and send your thought processes into mindless shock waves. They know how to make love to you in such a way you'd never thought possible, that your eyes roll to the back of your skull while they send you straight to heaven, beyond and back.

David sighed. "Things haven't worked out as successfully for Katie and me, I'm sorry to say."

"No? Why ever not?"

"We started off having a fun fling but, she'd fallen pregnant and I'd made the mistake of getting far too intimate with her. We lost the baby last weekend."

Mike blinked. "I'm sorry," he said grimly, awkwardly looking away from David, his thoughts racing back to Amy falling distraughtly into his arms, sharing the tragic news of the miscarriage. Casting his memory back to that memorable Sunday, Mike hadn't recalled Amy mentioning that it was Katie who'd, in fact, lost the baby. Markedly obvious, putting two and two together, Mike summed up that it was Katie whom Amy had been distraught about. He admired Amy's discretion and loyalty. Stunned, Mike stared gloomily ahead at the lively Hoorah Henry types propped up against the long saloon styled bar.

"I've had it with women," said David, sourly, "It's time I took a break from them. My marriage is a joke and practically over. Women! They're a bloody pain in the neck!" David tossed his head backwards and gulped the remainder of his cognac in one swig. Exhaling loudly, he let out a beastly roar. Swiftly bringing his head forward, David landed his chin on his chest and slammed his glass down on the bar.

Mike fidgeted uncomfortably. He had no intention of playing consoler to David for the night. "My man, take heed in what you care to utter about women, from your personal distraught. Women? I'd be very reluctant to dismiss them all. There's always an alternative to an alternative," Mike grinned inwardly, determined to finish the night on a happy note.

Confused, David looked quizzically at Mike. "What are you getting at?"

"I've an idea. You need a change of mood and scenery. I know of an excellent, private establishment in Pont Street, Mayfair where you can cast your eyes on the most exquisite of women, women whose sole purposes are aimed at making a man very happy. Very happy indeed. No questions. No strings. No ties. No clinging."

David's face lit up. "What a bloody good idea. What are you waiting for? Let's go," he said.

"Great. I'll settle the bill, leave you in the capable hands of the exquisite beauties and head off home," said Mike.

"Won't you be joining me?" David looked at Mike through glazed eyes.

"Certainly not!"

"Ah! Amy's well and truly got you hooked, eh?"

"Something like that," said Mike.

CHAPTER 21

The cell-phone text message alert awoke Amy. Groaning, Amy stumbled out of bed and crept precariously across her bedroom floor over to the white, Wicker armchair where she'd tossed her gold studded, black leather Dolce & Gabbana handbag the night before. She opened her bag, retrieved her bleating cell-phone and squinted at the brightly lit screen. Slumping in the armchair, scrolling, Amy forcibly strained her eyes to get a clearer vision of the blurred words. *"Swan Lane. Sadler's Wells. Meet me @ 7PM for pre show drinks. Show starts at 7.30. Mike."* It was two minutes past three in the morning. Amy noted that Mike had sent his text message two minutes earlier, at three, precisely. Gladdened, Amy re-read the message in consolatory relief, thankful that the message wasn't an emergency. She smiled warmly and almost laughed out loud. He's crazy. He could've sent this much later on, she thought, yawning. *"Thanks. See you there. Amy,"* she responded fumblingly. Slumbering heavy eyed in the chair, Amy mentally ran through her wardrobe not knowing what to wear to the ballet and composed a text message to Robbie Black. *"Home appt today at 3PM? Hair, Nails & full make-up from the Elite range. Thanks. Amy. xx."* Tackling a slight tinge of guilt, Amy pressed the send button. She hoped that Robbie wouldn't be too disturbingly awakened by his cell-phone alert, a few minutes outside of three in the morning. Her cell-phone bleeped. Amy checked the screen. The battery had run low. She switched it off, heaved herself out of the armchair and crept unsteadily through the darkened apartment to the lounge. Feeling her way around, Amy located the battery charger, connected it to her cell-phone and set it down on the desk to complete a full recharge. She crept back to her bedroom, crawled lethargically into bed and nestled down to sleep, undecided on what dress to wear to the ballet.

Disorientated, Amy picked up the telephone at eight thirty in the morning, frustrated that, yet again, her sleep had been disturbed. "Hello," Amy rasped. "That's twice in one morning," she hissed silently.

"Amy, love. How are you? You certainly sound rough this morning."

Irritated, Amy wanted to hang up, but sensibly chose otherwise. Gathering her thoughts, she climbed out of bed, threw a silk kimono over her shoulders, walked unsteadily over to the white Wicker armchair and slumped in it again. "Oh. Robbie. Hi. Thanks for getting back to me. Don't worry about me. I'm great. I hope you can make today's appointment?" she croaked anxiously.

"But, of course I can. That's the whole purpose of my call. I'd received the text message you'd sent at such an ungodly hour. My answer is a firm, yes. I can make the appointment, but it'll cost you," Robbie warned Amy cheerfully.

"I know, I know, I know. I'm sorry. Had I disturbed you at all?"

"No. I only do specially commissioned work during the early hours of the morning, booked in advance. Luckily, my mobi was switched off. Three AM's a strange time to arrange an appointment let alone by text messaging. It's so unlike you, Amy!" exclaimed Robbie, "Were you out partying or something?"

"No. It's a long story," Amy sighed apprehensively.

"Ah! One of those is it? I can't wait to hear all about it."

Amy rolled her eyes, glad Robbie wasn't there to witness it.

"Tell me, what look are you hoping to achieve from the Elite range? Where are you off to?"

They discussed, in detail, the overall image Amy aimed to achieve, hair style, colors and shades of make-up, a French manicure and Mike's text invitation. Robbie couldn't resist tagging on a bit of catty gossip regarding certain members of his clientele and Amy couldn't escape it that easily.

"You'll look like a princess when we're done. I'll see you at approximately two forty-five. My assistant and I'll need the extra time to set up all the equipment."

"Thanks a lot, Robbie. That's fine by me. I'll have your favorite bottle of Californian Chardonnay on the chill, ready and waiting for you."

Robbie let out a high pitched, effeminate shriek of delight. Shuddering, Amy held the telephone a good distance away from her ear. "You've always been one of my best clients, if not theeee best," sang Robbie.

"You're too kind," said Amy ending the call. She set the alarm clock to go off at twelve noon, disconnected the telephone and climbed back into bed.

Robbie, wide-eyed and open-mouthed, both his palms pressed firmly on his cheeks, his lips perfectly formed in the shape of an O said, "You look like a fucking dream, honey."

"I wouldn't have put it quite so bluntly, Robbie. But, thanks anyway," said Amy, laughingly, equally astounded by the outcome of Robbie's creation. According to her estimations, she looked great. She'd never conceivably or conceitedly imagined she could ever, remotely look that great, great, but not that great. But, she'd opted for the Elite range, normally enjoyed by a handful of Robbie's VIP clients, those who could afford or were prepared to pay the associative high costs in order to gain that special look, for that special occasion, be it a wedding, ball, gala, royal function, occasions among occasions.

Robbie's eighteen year old Japanese female apprentice, Sukyi stood and faced Amy. Like a Siamese cat, Sukyi gracefully raised her petite leg in the air, took one step back and, in close inspection of Robbie's work, ran her penetratingly studious eyes over Amy's face. Suitably satisfied, she quietly muttered something illegible and turned her fastidious attention to packing the used equipment in a recycling container.

"You're simply gorgeous. All eyes are on you tonight. Swan Lake! What a magical time you're going to have. You look absolutely wonderful," Robbie went on.

"You're too kind, Robbie. Thank you. This is all owed to your artistic work."

"Don't mention it, honey. Having an already beautiful face to work on darling, made the look easier and such fun to accomplish which is more than I can say about some of the transformational work I have to regularly perform on some of the ugly girls finding their way into my salon, sacrilegiously sitting their fat butts in front of my mirrors," he sighed, hot and bothered, patting his brow with a multi-colored cotton handkerchief, highly perfumed with a sickly, sweet scent.

What a bitch of a man, Amy thought, refusing to comment on Robbie's latter remark, twirling around in front of her full length mirror, scrutinizing herself at every angle. Robbie had put together a superb job on Amy's hair and make-up that Amy hardly recognized herself. She thought she looked like a fantasy that she was almost afraid to leave her apartment. She could easily pass herself off as a glamorous top model or a movie star with ease, she thought, exaggeratedly. Robbie had swept her hair into an elegantly swirled bun, bedecked with pearl beading and Austrian crystals artistically woven in. Sukyi had done an excellent job of the French manicure. Robbie had spent hours applying Amy's make-up, gluing each long strand of top quality human hair evenly to her eye lashes, creating a full bodied natural look, sculpting her eyebrows to an enviable arch, delicately stroking soft and subtle colors and tones on her eyelids, sweeping blusher, accentuating and contouring her high cheekbones, finishing with perfectly outlining her lips gleaming a subtle satin glow and boasting a natural shimmer. Her face was a masterpiece. Amy settled for a figure hugging, ankle length oyster colored dress she'd worn to a family wedding the previous year. Low cut from the shoulders, Amy recalled turning a few heads and had heard a few gasps and whispers then as she walked down the aisle at the church a few paces behind the bride. Oyster colored beading and crystals tastefully adorned the bodice. Her elegantly plain hand made shoes of woven silk added the finishing touches to the fish tail design of her dress that swished about her fine ankles as she walked.

"I'll submit an invoice to you in about two weeks so, don't worry about settling the bill now," said Robbie.

"Whatever suits you best, Robbie," said Amy, fully suspecting the bill had, no doubt, run into hundreds of pounds, the majority of it being the hourly labor rate charged on the three hours Robbie had spent working on making her look exceptionally beautiful, with a couple of breaks in between, constantly gossiping, telling the odd joke over sips of Californian Chardonnay. Amy mused on Robbie's plusses outnumbering his minuses as he'd never let her down, was consistently accommodating and expert at his craft that she willingly tolerated his idiosyncrasies and would hire another beautician most reluctantly if he ever became unavailable. As long as Robbie was around, Amy would quite happily use his services, willingly meeting whatever price he'd demand.

"Enjoy. And I'm waiting to hear all about it," Robbie yelled on his way out of the apartment.

It was approaching six fifteen. Amy called a taxi. She had under an hour to get to the theatre. She hoped that traffic would be light.

Amy gently nudged her way through the crowd to the bar at the Sadler's Wells. She heard the familiar gasps of gawking onlookers. Her head perked upwards, Amy stared straight ahead in search of Mike and spotting him almost immediately, she strode gracefully towards him. His eyes sparkling, Mike greeted Amy with a broad and approving smile. He leaned forward, placed his hands gently on her waist and pecked her on her cheeks. Cupping his elbows, Amy moved closer towards him. There was no denying, she was falling hopelessly in love with him. Amy let her silk shawl fall to her waist and gracefully wrapped the shawl's tails loosely around her slender arms.

"Champagne?" said Mike, motioning to the bar staff.

"Why not?" said Amy, looking left and right, meeting a few glances of a number of curious onlookers.

Mike handed Amy a full glass of champagne. "To us. May we fully prosper," he said, gazing meaningfully into her eyes.

Dumbfounded, Amy was almost speechless. It all felt like a fairy tale fantasy. Unaccustomed to classical music, Amy instantly developed an appreciation to Tchaikovsky's, Allegro Molto Vivace playing in the background. "To us. May we go from strength to strength," she saluted, tapping her glass on Mike's.

Mike leaned forward, pressed his cheek against hers and whispered huskily in her ear saying, "You look divine. I want you now."

Smiling blissfully, Amy breathed softly in his ear. "I adore your attire and you smell exceptionally good, I wouldn't hesitate in taking you now," she teased whisperingly.

"You like my scent? It's a pure Clive Christian. Number one, I think. Or is it 1872? Last year's Christmas present from Mother. She'd bought near on the whole range, four bottles of a variety of fragrances." Amy said nothing. Mike moved closer and brushed his closely shaved cheek against hers. Amy inhaled deeply, her senses captivated by the sensuous potency of Mike's unusual fragrance. "We must exercise a degree of decorum here. I'm getting far too excited," said Mike.

"It's your doing," said Amy, her cheeks flushed.

Mike chuckled. "Blame me! Thank you!" He turned and faced the bar. Amy fitted herself into a small gap between Mike and a distinguished looking elderly gentleman who'd shuffled around, courteously making room for her. Mike turned and faced Amy. His solitaire diamond pin in the centre of his deep blue cravat sparkled at her. His tailor made Savile Row, blue-grey suit fitted him perfectly, like a glove.

"Congratulations. Well done. You've exercised your investment opportunity. Now, that's more money than I'd expected you to come up with. I'm duly proud of you, Amy." Mike spoke appreciatively, intuitively sensitive to her means, he was clearly surprised at Amy's ability to raise such an amount.

"It's the best sum I could raise. May I also thank you for the ambitious investment opportunity and invitation to become a partner in your business. It's great to be part of it all. That makes a total injection of eight point five million so far," Amy accentuated casually in strength and confidence, cautiously peering over her shoulders, wary of candidly discussing their private busines. affairs in a public area. Amy continued. "Do you intend to invite further investors?"

"No. Not at this stage. I prefer that things remain as they are for the present. Close knit. This venture is very special to me, being appropriately ensconced, subsequent to my indignant release from the reigns of my father, as it were. We'll see how matters progress once I've returned from the Caribbean prospective. I look forward to strategizing with you then."

Shying away from entering into a conversation regarding the delicate subject of Mike's family feud, Amy took a large sip of champagne and held out her glass towards the barman for a top-up. The barman poured her another glass. "I too look forward to strategizing."

"Thank you, Amy. To further our celebrations, I've presumptuously scheduled lunch tomorrow. One o'clock at Beaujolais. Are you free to join me?"

Testing the water, bravely assured of her readiness and ability to openly express her emotions in a way she'd not demonstrated said, "But of course, Mike. There's no one else I'd rather be in the company of," melting away, looking round about her, asking the Gods what she'd done to deserve all this.

Mike blinked, nodded and smiled faintly. "I'm flattered by your kind remark. Dress casually, wear comfortable footwear. I thought we'd finish the day by rambling on the Heath after lunch."

"Great thought. I love the outdoors."

"Nowadays, I ramble around the Heath as often as I can. It's a glorious expanse of greenery," said Mike introspectively.

Obsessed in wanting to look her best in maintaining a trim figure, Amy was willingly paying the all too subsequent price eating an insubstantially light salad for lunch before Robbie's arrival and nothing since. Although Amy proudly and flatteringly modeled a flat, tight stomach in her dress, the champagne played havoc on her relatively empty stomach. A glutton for punishment, Amy continuously sipped at her champagne.

"Shall we watch the show?"

"Yes, of course" said Amy, sipping the last drop of champagne.

Mike cupped Amy's elbow and led the way into the semi-lit auditorium where staff waited to usher them to their premium seats situated in the first circle.

Amy hadn't revealed to Mike that she'd never been to the ballet. She'd not seen the need to inform him of such. Sitting quietly, waiting for the show to begin,

229

…he pages of the Swan Lake program and read the story of …uish and humor with great interest. Mike was right, Amy …ging by the way things had progressed the weekend had all the …ments of becoming one to remember. All in all, having Mike in her life was proving to be an unforgettable experience in itself, Amy mused. The theatre lights dimmed, the stage lit up and the show commenced. Enveloped in the unfamiliarly pleasurable melodies of Tchaikovsky's classical melodies, Amy found the spectacularity of the show, special effects and the power of the choreographic skills, speed, energy and graceful athleticism performed by the dancers captivating, breathtakingly beautiful, unforgettably impressive and very entertaining, that she came to realize why the award winning production enjoyed raving reviews. She was awestruck by the muscularity of the male dancers, the beauty and the excessively thin bodies of the ballerinas. Her eyes followed their tiny, petite and fragile frames flitting around the stage in fabulous tutus and costumes, possessing inexhaustible strength and energy than she'd ever thought possible or could muster herself. Mike remained silent throughout the entire show but shot Amy the odd quick intermittent glance, returning his attention to the stage immediately after. At times, Amy was almost tempted to take Mike's hand in hers and give it a gentle squeeze but declined the notion. She thought that it probably wouldn't be quite the etiquette during a ballet. She kept her hands gracefully on her lap, discreetly slipped off her shoes and enjoyed the show. "Bravo. Bravo. Encore. Encore," the crowds erupted amid rapturous applause. Amy clapped loudly, slipped her shoes on and stood to face the entire cast bowing to the audience in the grand finale. Noise gradually lulling and the lights brightening, Amy turned to Mike.

"That was magnificent. Sheer magnificence," she murmured thankfully.

Mike smiled and raised his eyebrows. "Yes, it certainly was. Would you care for more champagne?"

"Yes, please. Happy to," said Amy.

Ten tea-light candles romantically illuminated Amy's bedroom. She'd scattered the white musk scented candles around the room, strategically. Enraptured, Amy engaged in a long embrace with Mike. Shadowy reflections of their silhouettes danced on the walls to the movement of the delicate tea-light flames. Amy closed her eyes, inhaled the aroma of white musk that wafted around the room. She turned her back to Mike. "Undo my zipper, would you?" she whispered.

Mike pecked the nape of her neck. "No. I'll take you just as you are." Her body tingled intensely. Mike trailed his fingers slowly upwards, along her stomach to her breasts. Amy shrunk at his touch. Desperate to get out of her dress, Amy hoped Mike would relent on his decision to undo her zipper. His fingers crept along the beading of her bodice. He fondled her breasts. Amy wriggled and turned to face him.

"Mike, I need to get out of this dress," she whispered, pleadingly.

"No," Mike breathed, releasing his cravat, pecking the tip of her nose. He took her by the hand and led her to the bed.

Amy lay on her back in anticipation, desperate to get out of her bra. Her breasts swelled, her nipples hardened, she ached for Mike to kiss, suck, nibble and play with them with the tip of his tongue in his usual way. She wanted Mike in every way. He knelt down in front of her and pulled Amy's dress up from her ankles to her waist. Amy arched her back and Mike neatly tucked the dress under her, gently parted her legs, flipped her silk thongs to the left and tucked it under her buttock. "Mike," Amy whimpered weakly, grabbing his head, pressing him firmly against her, tonguing her exquisitely, licking her expertly. She was oozing wet, contracting, pulsating and groaning loudly. Mike pulled off his jacket and shirt and tossed them on the floor, stood up, unbuckled his leather belt and stepped out of his pants. He stroked and massaged Amy's thighs. Amy writhed breathlessly saying, "Mike, I want you now." Mike groaned, reached under Amy's spine and dragged her towards him until her buttocks rested on the edge of the mattress. Amy raised her head and her eyes fell on Mike. Heavenly, Amy thought as Mike entered her, groaning ecstatically from the back of his throat.

Amy and Mike arrived at the Beaujolais at one o'clock sharp. It was busy and a lot noisier than usual. Mike took Amy by the hand as Giselle, the waitress, led them through the crowded restaurant to their table. She allowed them a few minutes to browse through the luncheon menu, returned and flirtatiously took the order from Mike, conversing purely in French. Observing Mike cautiously and feeling totally at ease and unthreatened, Amy found the whole scenario both pathetic and hilariously amusing. Mike hadn't appeared to have taken a blind bit of notice of Giselle's suggestively subtle and wanton antics. "Would there be anything else, Monsieur?" Giselle enquired sweetly, hovering unwarrantedly and unnecessarily around the table after Mike had fully completed the order.

Mike smiled courteously. "No. Thank you, Giselle. That'll be all for the present, unless?" still smiling, Mike looked questioningly at Amy.

"Not for me, thanks," said Amy, looking directly at Mike then turning, shooting Giselle an expressional, *"I know exactly how you feel,"* look in her eye together with a, *"he has the same affect on me too, darling!"* twist in her smile. Smart enough to have comprehended Amy's facial expression and, embarrassed at having been caught out, Giselle speedily scuttled off to the kitchen, whilst Amy watched her young and pretty frame disappear.

"Is there something wrong?" Mike enquired.

Amy fidgeted in her seat and bravely met Mike's eyes, hesitantly saying, "I'll … I'll surely miss your presence once you've flown out to the Turks on Wednesday." Amy took a gambled risk of allowing the emotionality of her inner thoughts and feelings known to Mike.

Mike frowned. "Join me? Reconsider, although, I do see the sense in your initial concept to remain here in London."

Amy was almost tempted to arrange a last minute booking, but knew she had to remain in London to ensure the smooth running of the venture. Loyal to Planet Management and fully committed to overseeing the projects under her jurisdiction through to fruition, Amy judged that now wasn't the right time to consider relieving herself of her duties on a temporal basis. An inkling of strain being torn between Mike and the company was beginning to get the better of Amy that she feared her allegiance to Planet Management waning fractionally. "I'd love to reconsider. However, it wouldn't serve as a practical move at this stage."

"We'll both be so busy that you'll hardly notice my absence," said Mike.

"I'll notice not having you around and in my arms and …"

"Just as I'd inclined to believe that your statement regarding my absence was shot from a business angle as opposed to an intimate level?" Mike interjected.

"Well, you could say my statement was shot from both angles really, but admittedly leaned more on the intimate level," she said quietly. The activities of the entire weekend, the ballet, the lovemaking the night before and the sporadic lovemaking back at Mike's place when they'd stopped off, en-route to Beaujolais, so that Mike could change into something casual, were vividly at the forefront of her mind.

"We must keep everything under due perspective. We cannot afford to lose our heads, as it were?"

"Absolutely, Mike. I can assure you that I'm not out of sorts going out of my mind."

"Of course, I'm confident you'll not indulge in anything of the sort."

Growing nervous, unable to place Mike's tone, Amy coughed and cleared her dry throat. "I'm in the throws of researching a personal business lawyer." Amy informed Mike. She shrugged her shoulders, forcing herself to refrain from taking the risky gamble of making any further emotional statements for the remainder of the day.

"Well done, Amy! That's splendid news. You'll need to perhaps get a personal accountant or financial advisor. With an initial eight million pounds plus at stake, we'll both need to keep our heads, working on not allowing anything to falter."

"Agreed," said Amy, feeling tactfully slapped down and silenced by Mike. Giselle approached their table with a bottle of Beaujolais' house white wine Mike had ordered.

"Let's drink to that," said Mike. Giselle busily uncorked the bottle, poured a little in a glass and waited, professionally attentive, for Mike to conduct the wine tasting. Mike held the glass a few inches away from his nose, sniffed, swirled and tasted.

"*C'est bon, Monsieur?*"

"*Oui. C'est bon.*" Mike handed the wine glass back to Giselle saying, "That'll go down nicely with the fresh water trout." Blushing, Giselle poured two glasses and promptly left the table. Mike raised his glass. "Cheers," he said, jubilantly.

"Salute," Amy returned, taking a couple of delicate sips. "You've made a good choice of wine, as always. No doubt its taste will go down nicely with my smoked salmon."

Mike lifted the bottle of wine out of the ice bucket and scanned the front and back labels. "Made from fermented young grapes, you'll find that this particular wine will be quite light on one's head and stomach it'll not affect our stroll on the Heath later on."

"I'm so looking forward to that," said Amy sipping generously, battling to keep her emotions at bay, Mike consistently blowing her mind.

Giselle returned, accompanied by a waiter assisting her in serving up their main course dishes of fresh water trout, smoked salmon, a selection of side dishes of steamed vegetables, leafy salad and a couple of crystal jugs of mineral water.

"That was quick. I'm impressed with the service, yet again," said Amy, chirpily.

Mike glanced around the busy restaurant and did a quick headcount of the clientele. "I take my hat off to the management in their preparatory measures enabling them to consistently deliver a wide range of dishes in a timely manner during their busier periods. One has to constantly think ahead. Make good and profitable judgments. Be constantly aware of consumers' imminent desires, almost become a constant mind-reader, if you like, in order to stay one step ahead to maintain a first class service as enjoyed by Beaujolais' regular client base," said Mike, tucking in heartily, evidently enjoying the succulence of his fresh water trout.

Amy popped a wafer thin slice of smoked salmon on her tongue. Savoring it, she found the taste and texture exceptionally delectable. "Although I've not had Sunday lunch here until today, I'm certain, in your capacity as a connoisseur of food and wine that you're absolutely right in your observations and judgments on such matters and, as time goes by, in the interests of our hotel, I intend to learn, hands on, the ramifications of the restaurateur's business," said Amy.

Mike smiled broadly. "As this is your first lunch here, maybe we could do Sunday lunch here more often."

Nodding affirmatively, Amy ate the remainder of her meal in silence, with her mind heavily occupied on the subject of routine. Thriving on the unpredictability of Mike's personality traits, she loathed routines at the best of times, preferring variety and surprises from a man and hoped that Mike would continue to excite and surprise her, rather than see the unpredictability of their courtship fall into one of mundane routines. Amy had eaten enough and patted her lips with the red linen napkin.

"Coffee? Desserts?" Giselle enquired, clearing the table.

"Not for me, thank you," said Amy, waving her hand at Giselle, gesturing her to pour her a glass of mineral water from the crystal jugs on the table. Giselle, a little flushed, smiled and poured obligingly.

"L'addition, s'il vous plait et pouvez-vous m'appeler un taxi?"

"Oui, Monsieur."

"Translation, please?"

"I've requested the bill and ordered a taxi," Mike answered. Giselle disappeared into the kitchen, carrying their used dishes stacked neatly on a silver tray.

Amy set her napkin down on the table, stood up and clutched her handbag under her arm. "Excuse me. I'll be five minutes," she said moving away.

"Take all the time you need," said Mike.

Giselle returned to the table. She handed a red leather wallet to enclosing the bill. Bad timing, Amy thought as she continued through the restaurant to the ladies room, leaving Giselle at the table alone with Mike.

"Stop here. Smashing. This'll do." The taxi driver pulled up on the West Heath Road opposite the Whitestone Pond. Mike stepped out of the taxi, paid the driver, included the usual generous tip and strolled wordlessly along the Heath's concrete path and then onto the grass. ~~Exasperated, Amy was taken in by~~ the picturesque scenery of the Heath's emerald green grass, tended shrubs, fine old trees and the sky boasting its perfect azure. Suddenly, ~~Mike~~ broke free and leapt into a spontaneously carefree jog.

"Hey! Where are you going?" yelled Amy in puzzlement, watching Mike's athletic build bobbing up and down, diminishing before her. Agile, Amy caught up with Mike and remained in pace, jogging alongside him, grateful that the light lunch and light wine, washed down with plenty of mineral water hadn't adversely affected her performance. Powering her pace, Amy kept her breathing steady.

"We'll jog to that tree over there by the bench then take a break," said Mike, barely out of breath, pointing directly ahead of them.

Amy focused on the tree in question. It was way off in the distance. It would take at least five minutes to get there, she thought, calculatingly. "Sure, Mike," she said, saving her breath for the home run.

Mike leaned against the tree and waited for Amy. A park bench in focus, Amy looked forward to collapsing on it in a heap to indulge in an energy recouping exercise.

"No. It's better to remain standing," said Mike, breathing heavily, his arms outstretched, beckoning Amy to join him. Reluctantly relinquishing the park bench idea, sweating and panting, Amy collapsed contentedly into Mike's outstretched arms. Mike quickly lifted her and laid her on her back on the grass. Like nature's carpet, the cooling texture and lusciousness of the shaded emerald grass cushioned her body. Mike kissed her longingly. It happened so quickly that Amy had no time to protest. Hot, panting and out of breath she returned a passionate kiss. Mike propped himself up on one elbow. He stroked her cheeks with the backs of his fingers. His fingers traveled to her breasts. He squeezed them gently. He tugged at her sweater and attempted to undress her.

Amy firmly gripped his hand, stopping him. "Mike. No. Stop it. We mustn't. Not here, out in the open!" gasped Amy weakly.

"And why the hell not?" whispered Mike huskily, blowing his warm breath down her chest.

Amy groaned and loosened her grip. "We'll get caught ... arrested and charged ... with ..." kissing her lips, Mike smothered her words, "indecent behavior or ..." Mike kissed her lips again, "exposure ... or some sort of ... Mike!" Amy yelped.

CHAPTER 22

Amy took the thirty page report on the Caribbean Economic Analysis to bed with her and read it through to its entirety. Wide awake, she'd spent the majority of the night tossing and turning and hadn't slept a wink since climbing into bed at eleven forty-seven. She caught sight of the time. It was three in the morning. The alarm was set to go off at five. She had to get into the office early. It was Mike's last day in the UK. Tonight, he'll by flying to the Turks, she thought. The itinerary and meetings schedule hadn't been finalized and, Richard had informed her that, at the last minute, Mike had requested that Stefan alter the trip to an open return. Amy was furious that Mike hadn't informed her personally, although she'd also picked up the information from an email she'd been copied in on. Amy drifted into reminiscence of her recent encounter with Mike where he'd cut short their romantic stroll along the Hampstead village on that memorable Sunday afternoon. He'd suddenly hailed a taxi, put Amy in it, paid the driver a huge advance and sent her home. The memory annoyed her. Grunting, Amy pulled the sheets over her head and forced herself to sleep.

All was peaceful and calm at the office when Amy arrived at seven AM. Duplicate sets of the final itinerary and meetings schedule were on her desk. Yawning wearily, Amy perused them thoroughly. The meetings schedule had an impressive line-up and all appeared to be in order. Amy sighed, neatly folded a set in half, tucked it in her briefcase and attached the other set to the action notice board, strategically situated directly opposite her desk. I could scream for not having wangled myself on the trip, she thought.

"My God, Amy, you look rather fatigued today!" announced Richard concernedly, storming in overzealously at seven twenty-two.

"Morning, Richard."

"Is there anything in particular you'd like to go over on Project Cascadia? I'd left the preliminary budgets, itinerary and meetings schedule on your desk last night, along with an executive summary on Latin America," said Richard informatively.

"I've looked at them all thank you. And with regard to Project Cascadia, we're as up to date as we can be for the present. It's all down to Mike … Mike Brandleton and what transpires from his fact finding mission. Let's hold off on any further processes for now, apart from the obvious business as usual." Closing her eyes, with her elbows on the desk, Amy placed her head in her hands.

"You ought to leave early today. You've worked flat out over the last couple of days, pushing the teams along that we're fairly up to speed on all projects, thanks to your expert delegation. Vincent's impressed by the way."

Amy opened her eyes and peered drearily at Richard.

"Is he?"

"Yes. He'd stated something along those lines, last night."

"That's good to know," said Amy, breathing deeply, feeling slightly feverish. "I'm popping out," she said.

"The fresh air'll do you the world of good. Take all the time you need. I'll take care of things here."

"Thanks," said Amy yawningly, hoisting her handbag over her left shoulder and clutching the executive summary under her right arm. "On second thoughts, I'm taking the rest of the day off. Call me if you need me, Richard."

"But it's only quarter to eight and the final day of Project Cascadia before the overseas trip. What I really want to point out is that, should anything … anything could crop up at any given moment …"

"Then take care of things, will you?" Amy cut in dryly, making her way to the elevator.

Encouraged, Richard turned his back to Amy, stood rigidly at his desk and realized that, he'd be in charge, in complete power and control, and that managing the department for the day wasn't going to be such a bad idea after-all.

Amy slept uninterruptedly until six in the evening. She checked her emails and voicemails. No news from Mike. To refresh, Amy drank two cups of organic green tea, showered, logged on her laptop and worked solidly until nine o'clock, then fixed herself a warm bowl of organic Muesli. Amy dropped the spoon in her bowl of Muesli when the telephone rang.

"Hallo. Amy Scott speaking."

"Hi. I called you this afternoon at the office. Richard informed me that he was holding the fort, effectively in charge for the day, that you were otherwise engaged but, reachable if it were absolutely necessary. All is well I hope?" said Mike hurriedly.

"Of course, Mike. I'd taken the decision to catch-up on some well earned rest and worked from home today. Sorry, but Richard should have called me or patched you through to me," Amy explained apologetically, angry on account of Richard's faltering.

"As Richard hadn't reported any issues or matters outstanding or arising on the venture, it wasn't absolutely necessary that I spoke to you then."

Amy strolled into the lounge. "All appeared to be up to date on my final check. And I've not received any last minute emails or calls," she said.

"Jolly good. Stefan and I are all set now. We're in the executive lounge waiting to depart."

"What time is your flight due for take off?" Amy ran her index finger along the itinerary pinned to the notice board, in case she'd overlooked any minor details.

"In approximately forty-five minutes. There've been no changes. The flight's on schedule."

"Great. Hopefully, you won't be suffering any undue delays. I note that your first meeting will be taking place on Friday. This should give you time to recuperate from any jet lag as it were," said Amy, running her index finger along the first page of the meetings schedule.

"Yes. You're quite right there."

"You've extended the trip I've noticed. To what length of time may I ask, Mike?"

"I thought I'd make use of the maximum thirty day stay with the option to extend as I've a gut feeling that I'll be making an initial expression of interest during this visit, which would warrant extra time putting all the legalities in place."

"Good idea, only I hadn't received due notification of your plan to extend the trip," Amy put it to Mike.

"I knew the information would've filtered itself through to you in due course," Mike explained. "Amy? Am I right in assuming that you might be entertaining reservations on my business decision to extend?"

Amy nervously clutched at the telephone in fear of causing a rift between them. "No, Mike. In fact, I'm all for it. It's a good decision. To be honest, I would have ideally preferred to have learned about it sooner and by you directly, perhaps?"

"Next time, I will endeavor to keep you more aptly informed," said Mike dryly.

Finding the conversation utterly straining, Amy steered on regardless. "You'd said you'd call me when I saw you last and, I'd hoped to have had a call from you before now," she said, having difficulty in disguising her annoyance of Mike's timing, calling her a forty-five minutes before his flight was due to take off.

"My apologies. There were unavoidable delays. And a number of tasks all required my immediate attention."

"I perfectly understand."

"I knew you would."

Amy walked into the kitchen and leaned on the worktop, lost. "Stefan. Is he within earshot?"

"No. He's wandered over to the bar. He'll be back in a tick. Would you like to go over any items with him?"

"No. I just wanted to say, I'll miss you and, have a safe and pleasant journey. Call me when you get an appropriate moment and best of luck on finding a concern that'll lead to our success," Amy spewed nervously.

"You're too kind. I'll call you as soon as I get a chance."

"Well, do you have anything further to say?"

"No. I believe we've covered everything, really."

"Yes, I believe we have," said Amy, peeved that Mike hadn't returned any words of endearment, words to sleep on, words to hold on to, words to reminisce on, words to get her through his absence … words …

"Stefan's making his way back. I'd better be setting off now."

Amy strolled into the lounge. A lump wedged in her throat. "Right you are, Mike," she said hanging up. She picked up the executive summary on Latin America, slumped in the couch and commenced reading it.

Words monotonously scrolled down the computer screen. Words debating the concept of whether there'll be a positively marked change in the economic performance currently enjoyed by most of the countries of Latin America. Amy had difficulty in mustering up passion for the subject. She simply wasn't in the mood. The telephone rang at seven forty-five AM. Her throat went dry. It wouldn't be Mike, his flight hasn't yet landed, she thought. She'd opened the small bottle of fresh orange juice she'd purchased on her way into the office, took a large gulp, wetting her throat. "Good morning, Amy Scott speaking."

"Amy!"

"Katie! What a surprise calling me at this hour!" she said startlingly pleased.

"I had a sneaky feeling I'd catch you in the office."

"What owes me the pleasure of your call?"

"Come on, Amy. No need to address me in that fashion."

Amy giggled. It's far too early in the morning for this, she thought. "I'm in office mode, me dear."

"So, be it," scoffed Katie, in a poor impersonation of Amy. "I've booked a flight to Spain."

"Well done. You've finally done it!"

"Yep. I'll be leaving this Saturday morning."

"That's rather sudden."

"I don't see the need to stick around for much longer, what with all that's …"

"I know. I know. You don't need to explain."

"Can you do coffee at all this week?"

With Mike away, apart from plans to visit her local health club to work on maintaining her tone and, more importantly, thrash out her frustrations, Amy had nothing planned otherwise. "Yes. I'm available this week."

"Smashing. Then, how about tonight?"

"Tonight would be fine."

"Good. I'll travel into town. We can pop into Cino's or some place else. How does that sound?"

"Sounds great! We can meet initially at Cino's and move on from there, if you like. What time did you have in mind?"

"Let's see. Would seven suit you?"

"Yes, that'll work," said Amy.

"See you in there," said Katie. "Bye for now."

Another one bites the dust, Amy thought, hanging up. Richard arrived. She met his gaze.

"Good morning, Amy."

"Good morning, Richard." Amy switched her gaze from Richard and darted her eyes at the computer screen. "How did you get on yesterday? Any items worthy of report?" Amy clicked her mouse.

ℕᴏ. Not to my knowledge. Nothing to report. It was business as usual. Quite a wheel churning day, really," replied Richard abstractly, sliding his sports rucksack off his shoulder, shoving it under his desk as he sat down in his chair. ~~deleted~~ on

Amy sighed. "I understand Mike Brandleton called. Were there any other callers?"

"None actually. Mike Brandleton hadn't left a message. I'd offered to take one. However, he'd stated there was no need and that he'd call you later," said Richard defensively, switching on his computer.

"Thank you for that, Richard. May I kindly ask that, in my capacity as a partner on the venture, it's absolutely imperative I'm duly informed whenever Mike Brandleton calls, regardless of whether he leaves a message or not. Is that clear?" she said, disguisedly impressed with Richard's overall success in running the department single handedly and problem free.

"Certainly. I'll not forget in future," said Richard, nervously running his fingers through his hair. With nothing further to state, Amy ploughed solidly through her work, speaking to Richard as and when necessary.

Two rounds of espresso amid lively conversation and rapturous laughter was had at Cino's. With Katie back on form, as a farewell treat, Amy decided to frivolously commemorate her leave for Spain by going to one of Vincent's favorite jaunts, the Fabrizio Italian restaurant, and summonsed Franco to order a prestige car to take them there. Not having had the pleasure of dining at Fabrizio, Amy had earmarked the pricey establishment for a suitably fitting occasion. She also requested Franco reserve a table for two in the name of Vincent Laidlaw. The clout of Vincent's name pulling rank on Fabrizio's long waiting list, secured the table at short notice.

"Are you sure your boss won't have any qualms about you using his name?"

"Of course not. Our relationship is infallibly professional. There's nothing to worry about. I'll say we're guests of his, if anyone asks. There won't be any problems. I'm pretty certain of that," Amy assured Katie.

"I've heard of the place. I believe it's quite expensive there?"

Amy arched her eyebrows. "Gosh, Katie. Quit worrying. Besides, we deserve it."

"You're right."

"Your car is waiting, Miss Scott," Franco announced.

"Thank you, Franco. Put the car and coffees on my account, would you?"

"Of course, Miss Scott."

Franco raced on ahead and waited outside the gleaming black Mercedes people carrier. The engine ran whisperingly. Franco opened the passenger door. Amy and Katie climbed in and strapped themselves in their seats. Franco closed the doors and tapped the bonnet signaling to the driver to move off.

"Wow, that Franco, he's such a hunk," Katie remarked lustfully.

"And young too," said Amy. She turned and watched Franco through the rear window, perched on the edge of the curb, waving at them until they were out of his sight.

"Age is nothing but a number," Katie quipped.

Sitting back, Amy smiled warmly and closed her eyes saying, "No comment." They arrived at Fabrizio ten minutes later and were seated at their table with no questions asked. Awestruck, Katie gawked at the lavish décor. The gilt and bronze Florentine crystal chandeliers caught her eye.

"They're gorgeous. I wouldn't like to guess its worth," she said. The waiter overhead Katie and approached their table.

"They date back to the 1920's," he said.

"I see. Yes, they're elaborate. Priceless, no doubt?" said Amy, equally impressed.

"Of reasonable worth, they could each fetch anything from a thousand pounds upwards," said the waiter, handing them a menu each.

"Thank you for the information."

"I'd caught snippets of your conversation and knew you'd be interested in learning more. Customers often enquire about them and, one or two have made offers. They're not for sale."

"I'm not surprised. They're gorgeous," said Amy, wishing the waiter would leave, give her some space, stop crowding her. She kicked Katie under the table. Katie jolted and instantly cottoned-on to Amy's cue.

"Come on. You've gotta be moving up in the world to be eating in a place like this!" said Katie loudly, flitting through the menu.

"Credit card, darling," Amy returned casually. The waiter mumbled something illegible under his breath and walked away.

"OK, but what's the occasion?"

"To celebrate your temporary move to Spain and our friendship, you know, eat and drink, to everything!" said Amy, shrugging her shoulders.

"That's great. Thanks a lot for this, Amy. And now, your business. What's the latest?"

"Mike's in the Caribbean prospecting hotels."

"Nice. Where exactly?"

"The Turks."

"Very nice. Tell me more. You're keeping me in suspense. Why aren't you with him? Shouldn't you've gone too?"

Amy browsed through the menu strategizing how best to tackle Katie's relentless barrage of questions.

"On a serious note, please don't utter a word of this to anyone," said Amy, warningly.

Katie shot Amy a look of concern. "Is everything kosher?"

Amy smiled relaxingly. "We're progressing slowly but surely now. Mike's prospecting hotels out in the Turks and he hopes to make a decision on this trip. I had to remain here to keep an eye on things."

"That's fantastic, Amy. Shouldn't you've been there to share in the decision making process?"

"At this stage, it wasn't imperative that we both attended. Mike would be the better judge in the area of selecting the hotel that has the right fit and, call me crazy, but I am inclined to trust in his decision making." said Amy, throwing her hands in the air.

"I'm sure you've done your homework and that, in time, you'll learn the trade and grasp it well," Katie philosophized.

"Thank you for that, Katie. I need all the positive support and encouragement I can get right now, treading on new ground as it were."

"You'll be fine. I know you will," said Katie confidently.

Amy, reluctant to reveal all the intricacies of the venture, took careful note of Katie's positive attitude and seemingly genuine support.

"Let's order," Amy suggested, putting the subject on hold. They spent a few minutes browsing the menu in silence.

"I'll need a couple of weeks, a month max, in order to get organized in Spain then, I'd like to invite you over for a long weekend break."

"That's most kind of you. I accept and look forward to, not only spending some time with her, but also meeting your mother."

"I couldn't possibly put you through such an ordeal of spending too much time with her. Adorable, at times my mother can be overly accommodating. She'll smother and suffocate you to death."

"I do not view that as a problem at all," said Amy politely.

"I've a better idea. A weekend break in Barcelona is what I'd had in mind." Katie winked at Amy craftily.

"You're on," said Amy, winking at Katie.

Amy signed the credit card receipt, averting her eyes from the bill's three figure sum. "I've eaten too much that I can hardly move," she said, patting her stomach.

"Ditto. The food was fantastic. Thanks a lot for that, Amy," said Katie, her speech slightly slurred.

Amy checked the time on her watch. Eleven ten. "Don't mention it. Time's pushing on. I'd better be making tracks." Amy asked the waiter to arrange a taxi.

"I can have a taxi arrive in twenty minutes. Would you like to order a drink whilst you're waiting?" asked the waiter.

"No thanks. I'm stuffed," said Katie, hiccupping.

"Nothing for me, thanks." Amy leaned back in her chair and mulled over Katie not having mentioned a word about David during the entire evening. "Any news on David?" Amy felt pangs of guilt emerging, intrusively prying unceremoniously into the painful side of Katie's personal life.

Katie flashed a pained look at Amy. "That name makes my skin crawl," she said in a shaky voice.

Amy shook her head and held her hands up. "Sorry. Forgive me, I shouldn't have asked," she said, feeling like such an insensitive idiot.

"I've changed my mind about not having something to drink. I'll have a neat brandy," said Katie.

"I'll join you." Amy waved her hand beckoning the waiter over. Why am I doing this? Amy asked herself. "Two glasses of brandy, please? Any brand will do." Amy delved into her handbag and fished her credit card out of her purse.

"Put that away, I'll foot the bill for this lot," Katie demanded.

"OK. Thanks." Amy slid her credit card back into her purse.

"This is a good quality brandy. Fogolar. Italian, of course," said the waiter, approaching their table with two glasses of neat brandy on a tray. Katie lifted a glass from the tray, brought it to her lips, took a large gulp and in an uncouthly manner, made a strange guttural sound.

Quite un-lady like, Amy thought, looking round about her.

The waiter placed Amy's glass on the table and walked away. Amy picked up her brandy glass, sipped graciously and coughed suddenly.

"Are you alright?" asked Katie, her slurring speech progressively worsening.

"I'm fine. I need water to wash this down," said Amy, spluttering and eyes welling.

"Waiter. Fetch a glass of water for my friend, here." bellowed Katie.

"My gosh. It's so devilishly potent," remarked Amy.

"You're a true lightweight. There is an art to drinking brandy," said Katie wryly.

"I really don't wish to learn, thank you," said Amy

The waiter returned carrying two glasses of water on a tray. Amy drank her water thirstily.

Katie leaned forward *and* snatched Amy's glass of brandy. "I'll finish this. It'll be a shame to waste it or have it poured back into the brandy bottle," she said, taking one gulp of the contents then slamming the brandy glass on the table.

Embarrassed, cheeks flushed, Amy looked around, pleased to discover that their table hadn't caught the attention of the few diners that were left. Mentally willing the immediate arrival of the taxi, Amy checked her watch. "The taxi shouldn't be much longer now," she said, desperate to leave the exquisite surroundings of Fabrizio, before Katie performed any further embarrassing exploits

"The taxi's here," said the waiter, rushing over to their table.

Relieved, Amy breathed deeply. My wish has been granted, she thought, heralding the taxi's perfectly timed arrival.

Katie pushed her chair back, folded her arms on the table, and nestled her head on her arms. "I'm dead-beat," she groaned.

Amy sighed, pushed her chair back, stood up behind the table and viewed Katie contemplatively. "Let's get you in the taxi," she said slowly, hoping to accomplish the task with minimum difficulty. She tapped Katie's shoulder. Katie stirred, raised her head and looked at Amy groggily.

The waiter, observing the scene, shook his head sympathetically at Katie and then glanced at Amy. "I'll assist you in getting her into the taxi," he said, advancing towards Katie.

"Thank you," said Amy irritably.

The waiter took Katie's hand and helped her out of the chair. Disorientated, Katie shoved her handbag under her arm, maneuvered herself unsteadily on her feet and allowed the waiter to put his arm round her waist. He lifted her with ease. Moaning, Katie clasped her arms instinctively tight round the waiter's neck as he carried her out of the restaurant to the waiting taxi.

"This is all I need. What a way to end an evening," Amy whispered under her breath. She left fifty pounds on the table to cover the cost of the brandy, water and any change to be served as a tip and followed the waiter out to the taxi. The taxi driver leapt out of his cabin and assisted the waiter in getting Katie into the taxi. Amy thanked them and climbed in. Katie had fallen asleep with her head precariously propped up against the passenger window. To awaken her, Amy gently nudged Katie's arm. Katie jerked, shifted and groaned. "Katie, you must stay awake. You'll be home soon," whispered Amy. Katie raised her head, squinted at Amy, rubbed her eyes and peered out of the window.

"Where are we?"

"You're nearly home."

"How much do I owe you?"

"Nothing. Just get your keys out of your handbag."

Katie's handbag was sandwiched between them on the seat. Katie placed her handbag on her lap, fumbled around inside and pulled out her purse. "I'm paying the fare. I won't settle for you paying for everything," she said.

"If you insist," said Amy.

Katie leaned back, closed her eyes and continued the remainder of the journey in silence. The taxi pulled up outside Katie's apartment fifteen minutes later.

"I'll be one minute," Amy told the driver as she clambered out of the taxi to give Katie a helping hand.

"That's alright, me love," said the taxi driver.

Amy gripped Katie's arm and staggered a little as she walked with her to her main door. After a few unsuccessful tries, Katie eventually inserted the key in the lock. "Coming in for one last drink?"

"That's really kind of you, Katie, but I'd better be heading home. It's late."

"OK. Thank you for everything."

"Thank you too, Katie."

Katie staggered into the hallway and turned to Amy saying, "*Adios, Amiga.*"

Amy smiled and waved. "*Adios,*" she said. The main door closed automatically. Amy returned to the taxi and climbed in. It reeked of alcohol, so she opened the windows either side of her. As the driver sped off, Amy sat back and dwelled on the latter part of the evening. Feeling a surge of compelling concern for Katie, Amy pulled out her cell-phone and dialed Katie's cell-phone number. Katie answered sleepily.

"Hel, hello?"

"Hi. Just checking that you're safely in your apartment and there are no hitches?"

"I'm in, safe and sound. Sleep tight, Amy" said Katie, clicking off.

Smiling amusedly, Amy whipped out her purse and, whilst preparing to pay the cost of both journeys Amy switched her thoughts over to Mike.

Early in the morning, Amy jogged sluggishly to the gym to the sound of birds chorusing harmoniously. Dragging her weight, she felt heavier than normal owed to excessively eating at Fabrizio the previous night. Focusing on maintaining a beautifully toned body, Amy determinedly burnt off the excess calories gained with a strenuously ferocious cardio vascular work-out, ending her fitness session with ten lengths of breast stroke. Vincent had recently appointed Amy to spearhead an asset management bid worth three hundred million pounds. The bid involving a high profile, Swiss bank, was her largest and most challenging piece of business undertaking since joining Planet Management. The early morning exercise boosted her endorphin levels that Amy successfully drove her resolutions forward during the tough off-site negotiations held at eight o'clock. The morning had quickly disappeared with the meeting closing at eleven forty-five. At ten minutes past twelve, Amy was back at her desk drafting an incentivisation agreement. Counting the days, hours, minutes and seconds, Amy eagerly awaited news from Mike. She worked exceptionally hard on suppressing her emotional yearnings engaging everything in her mental power to snap out of her stupor. Amy called her health club and booked a sauna followed by a head to toe massage. That'll knock me out. A good night's sleep is guaranteed, she thought.

CHAPTER 23

Not having much of an appetite, at two thirty, Amy sat down to a late lunch in the modern surroundings of the staff snack bar. The smoked salmon and cucumber on Swiss rye lacked flavor. Nibbling disinterestedly, Amy washed it down with a few sips of sparkling water. Her cell-phone vibrated and rumbled on the round glass table. Amy jerked her head down, read the number and answered her cell-phone. "Yes, Richard," she said, dabbing her lips with a paper napkin.

"My apologies for interrupting your break but, I've Mike Brandleton on the line for you. Should I take a message?"

Amy's pulses raced uncontrollably. "No, that won't be necessary, Richard. I'll take the call now, thanks. Please, put him through," she said eagerly. A concoction of anxiety, relief and exhilaration permeating her being, Amy inserted her earpiece and wandered out of the staff snack bar to the expansive corridor. There was a clicking sound.

"Hello? Can you hear me?"

"Yes, Mike. I can hear you clearly. How are you? I'm so pleased to hear from you."

"Marvelous. I won't keep you. No doubt you're busy. Hope I haven't called at an inappropriate time?"

"No. No. I'd taken a break. Had a bite to eat, only just. I've oodles of time before I head back to a meeting."

"Good. Stefan and I spent the best part of yesterday getting our bearings and are ready to kick-off the first of our schedule of meetings."

"Yes, the first of which commences in just under an hour, at ten thirty, a preliminary prospect introductory meeting with the head of the hotelier real estate broker prior to viewings, right?" Amy had intensively memorized the entire meetings schedule.

"Precisely," said Mike.

"Are you comfortable? How is your accommodation? And, our Caribbean representative, Rory … Rory Gibson, that's it. How is he? Has all gone to plan? Are you happy with arrangements so far?" Amy rambled on brightly, pacing the corridor back and forth.

Mike laughed. "My answer is an emphatic yes to all of your questions. Rory's great. All's gone well. No hiccups. We're comfortably accommodated in executive apartments. The luscious surroundings are quite lavish."

"Good."

"Social activities have been organized throughout the weekend and, by the way, tonight's dinner, venue to be confirmed should now read, the Grace Bay, Blue Ocean Club. The three of us, Rory, Stefan and I, will be dining in the club's oceanfront restaurant at eight after our quick informal hand shaking session with a couple of the islands' dignitaries. They're in the area this evening for the primary purpose of attending some private event of sorts. Acquaintances of Vincent's, I've gathered from Rory."

"Good public relations tactic of Vincent's I suspect, preparing the dignitaries for our possible investment on the island. Thank you for the information, Mike. I'll take care of the prompt update and re-circulation of the meetings schedule on formal appointments only, disregarding all informal events, of course," said Amy joking lightheartedly, enviousness consuming her.

"Fine. Rory kindly gave us a tour of Provo and had pointed out the dinner venue whilst cruising past it. Interestingly enough, Rory had also highlighted the fact that the chef's French," Mike paused for a moment. "I've been thinking, as Nassau is only a hop away, I'm seriously considering a trip there too, at some stage." Amy, perplexed by the concept, walked aimlessly to the elevator.

"To prospect?"

"No. To play," said Mike teasingly.

In no immediate mood for mind games, Amy checked the time on her watch. It was approaching three ten. She had a few minutes to spare before commencement of the asset management meeting scheduled at three thirty with Vincent as chairperson. She'd spent the entire morning keeping up to speed, studying the documentation Vincent had sent to her the previous day. "To play? What exactly do you mean, to play?" she enquired naively.

"The tables?"

"Gambling! I'd no idea."

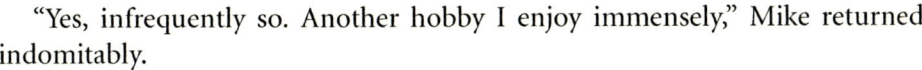

"Yes, infrequently so. Another hobby I enjoy immensely," Mike returned indomitably.

"I see."

"I've other ideas beaming on the horizon," Mike volunteered.

"Such as?"

"Well, for one, I wouldn't rule out relocating here."

Amy made a detour from the elevator to a quite and conveniently private corner of the corridor. "Relocate?" she said in a voice both loud and astonished.

"Why ever not? One of us would have to remain here for a while to keep an eye on the business, I'd expect. Besides, I like the feel and the smell of the place. The moment I'd arrived, set foot on the soil, I'd decided that in a short space of time I'd be making an offer and staying awhile."

"But, not having inspected any hotels, how can you be so adamantly certain about arriving at such decisions?"

"I instinctively trust in my hunches and gut feelings." Mike breathed heavily.

Frowning, Amy longed to join Mike. She inhaled deeply, closed her eyes and leaned her back against the wall.

"When you eventually get out here, you'll judge, on your own merits, precisely what I'm talking about and, I know, you won't be displeased. All one could wish for is here. Sun, scenery, golf, diving, sailing, the pace of life …"

"Enough, Mike. You're torturing me, let the truth be known. I can hardly wait to get out there," said Amy, breathlessly surrendering to the idea.

"That's the spirit. Grant me no more than two weeks and I should've made a firm offer. In the meantime, I'll keep you posted on developments and I'm open to whatever views you may undoubtedly have."

"Before you come go … I … I just wanted to say one final thing to you and, that is, I sorely miss having you around, Mike."

"Then fly out here! Join me!"

Stiffening, Amy found the conjuring images of Vincent's objections to her untimely request to travel without the offer of due rationale, unnerving. "Mike, things are not that simple. I've landed an important contract that's near on impossible to wangle out of or even handover without a measure of unnecessary duress that would most certainly be experienced by a number of officials here. To be the cause of such an unfair upheaval, I'm just loathed to consider," she said, moving away from the wall.

"You're the best judge of that. Think it through. If the situation's right and you've scope to travel, call me," Mike duly concluded.

Amy advanced towards the oncoming elevator. It had stopped momentarily on the second floor. The clock on the wall above the elevator door was displaying the time of three twenty two. Amy impatiently tapped her feet in fear of arriving late for yet another meeting caused, yet again, by the fact that she'd had great difficulty tearing herself away from Mike. The fact that the meeting was being held in Vincent's office, a short elevator ride away, served as a positively hope-filled consolation. "I'll consider it, Mike. Good luck," she said softly. The sound of the bell signaled the elevator's arrival. The steel doors hissed open. Amy stepped aside allowing room for the people to spill out.

"Thank you, Amy. I too bid you good fortune," Mike reciprocated.

Amy beamed with joy. "That's sweet. Thank you, Mike. Well, good-bye for now," she said, reluctantly disconnecting the cell-phone. She stepped into the empty elevator. It ascended non-stop to the eighteenth floor. Amy scooted out, dashed to her desk, grabbed the meeting documents and bolted to Vincent's office. She arrived in the nick of time with one minute to spare.

Duration of the asset management meeting lasted two hours. Amy emerged from Vincent's office with the action point to produce a sizeable initial due diligence request list document in fourteen days resting heavily on her shoulders. The effects of the measure of time and intense energy spent on discussing, in varying degrees, from rudimentary to critical fiduciary aspects of specialized financial mechanisms, left Amy mentally exhausted. It was five thirty in the UK and lunch time in the Turks. Amy wondered how Mike had faired with the head of the hotelier real estate broker, how well the tour of hotels had gone and what fine culinary delights he'd be savoring for lunch. Taking a deep breath, Amy sighed and slipped into a daydream wondering how sweet life could be, living prestigiously with Mike in the Turks. Amy shuddered. "Unimaginable," she whispered. She sat at her desk, leaned back in her seat and presided how best to divide the task of producing the sizeable action-pointed document.

"I'd welcome five minutes of your time, if I may please?"

Vincent paused. "I'm about to leave the office. I've a dinner engagement with Lord and Lady Riley. Do send me an email, would you, Amy?"

"I'd rather address the items very, very briefly with you, face to face, at this point, please?" said Amy preemptively.

"I'll spare you a couple of minutes. Please, come to my office now, Amy," said Vincent agitatedly.

"Thank you." Amy hung up, raced to Vincent's office, tapped lightly on the door and entered the room.

Vincent busily shuffled his papers on his desk and threw documents into his briefcase.

"Thank you for sparing the time. I'll be as brief as possible," said Amy, closing the door quietly.

"Please, take a seat," said Vincent, slamming shut his briefcase.

"Mike Brandleton called. He hopes to make an offer in no longer than fourteen days. I understand that he plans to remain in the Turks to ensure the smooth transition of the purchase."

Vincent paced back and forth behind his desk. "A feasible concept, I'm sure," he said.

"I'd like to fly out there to assist in the purchase and transitioning process."

Stony faced, like a man on the verge of losing something precious, Vincent abruptly turned his back to Amy and gazed out of the window. "When?" he asked gruffly.

Amy attempted to present a believably fair option. "As soon as the asset management contract has been completely signed-off by all the parties, I would then like to handover the ongoing management of the contract to a suitable successor for a temporary period."

"What period of time do you have in mind to be away in the Caribbean?"

"A couple of months—three at the most, with a view to returning as soon as the hotel is up and running to a fiscally satisfactory standard in its first few weeks."

Vincent threw his jacket on, picked up his briefcase and began walking out of the office. Amy leaped out of her seat and closely followed Vincent.

"I agree to your terms on the proviso that you'll leave on full completion of the signed contract. Thereafter, whilst in the Caribbean, you'll maintain continuous contact with your temporary successor to ensure the smooth running of the contract. I have total faith in Mike Brandleton's handling of the business affairs. Additionally, Stefan's quite adequately skilled. Project Cascadia is in safe hands enjoying the advantages under the auspices of Planet Management, one of the most significant management consultants in Europe," Vincent paused contemplatively, "in the world I should correctly state. I admire your robustness and fastidiousness brought with you to my company. You're good at what you do, Amy that I'd much prefer that you consider the option to remain on the asset management contract during its entire phase. I'm truly reluctant to see you go, temporarily or otherwise." Vincent stopped rigidly at the door and turned authoritative eyes on Amy.

Guilt riddled, Amy detected a note of concern in Vincent's voice that was impossible to ignore. She felt the urgent need to provide him with some form of reassurance. "I'll see the contract through to its signing and remain abreast of its developments. I'll ensure ease and accessibility and fully guide and advise the temporary successor. I have no immediate intentions to leave the company, therefore, please dispel any possible notions of concern. I'll return to resume my full duties and responsibilities as I'd already stated. You have my word on that, Vincent."

"Thank you, Amy." Vincent gave her his most formal smile. "Now, I must be off. My car is waiting. I shan't delay any longer." He swung the door open and lead Amy out of his office.

Stunned, Amy stood motionless outside Vincent's office. He entered the elevator and turned around. Their eyes met. Amy smiled warmly. Vincent smiled formally. The elevator doors hissed closed and Amy wandered slowly back to her desk.

"Shelley has agreed to write the legal section, subject to receipt of all relevant information, instructions and briefing documentation," Richard hastily informed Amy.

"Terrific," said Amy, rummaging around her desk.

Richard stroked his chin, "And the auditors will inform me of a nominee, no later than ten on Monday morning."

"Fantastic, Richard." Amy busily scribbled a list of names of potential temporary successors on a sheet of paper. In need of five minutes on her own to contend with the fact of the possibility of flying to the Turks, sooner than she'd originally expected, Amy stepped away from her desk. "I'll be no more than fifteen minutes," she said.

Nodding, Richard glanced quizzically at Amy as she strolled to the elevator.

Pacing outside the office block building, feeling torn between Mike and Vincent, the old biblical adage, *"you cannot serve two masters,"* echoed repeatedly in Amy's mind. "Something has got to give. I cannot continue like this for much longer," Amy whispered, walking around the block, deep in thought, searching for a fair and beneficial solution.

Amy met her deadline. Exactly fourteen days of strenuous hard work amalgamating four segments of the initial due diligence request list document into one final document. Vincent highly commended Amy along with the contributed efforts of Richard, Shelley and the nominated auditor. "Outstanding." Vincent had commented. Amy agreed it was a sexy document. Feeling sluggish, she hadn't made it to the gym in those two weeks nor had she called or heard word from Mike. She called her health club and booked a ninety minute, Saturday morning circuit training session and Astanga Dynamic yoga for the following Sunday morning.

Sunday night, overstretched by work and exercise, Amy retired to bed early, at nine. She awoke to the telephone ringing and glanced at the clock. It was two minutes past four in the morning.

"Hello?" she croaked drowsily.

"Amy," Mike whispered.

"Ha … Hallo, Mike." Amy stirred in desire.

"Forgive me, I wanted you to be the first to know."

Flattered but half asleep, Amy dragged herself up. Her muscles ached. "Let me guess, you've found the hotel," she said, yawningly.

"You're perfectly right. The Crystal Waters Hotel."

"Congratulations, Mike. Well done. The name has a nice ring to it. What were the unique selling points behind your decision making?" continued Amy, gradually becoming more alert, doing her yoga breathing exercise.

"Quite a few, actually. It's a small, humble and fully operating establishment, secluded, tucked away in its own impressive position. Enjoying a good clientele, the hotel is frequented by a mixture of business people, locals on weekend breaks, vacationers with the majority coming in from Miami. It's well appointed on the waterfront. Therefore, the hotel has the potential to become a real money spinner that, not much time was spent pondering on this one. I plan to make an initial expression of interest tomorrow morning."

Overwhelmed, Amy was also irked at not having been there to take part in the viewing process and negotiations. She agonized at not being there with Mike, period. "What is the asking price?"

"Six point five million pounds."

"Good heavens! That's around twelve million dollars! That's way within our budget," cried Amy optimistically.

"The real estate broker stated that, for a quick sale, the proprietor would be open to offers. He's getting old, has had enough of the game and wants out."

"Sounds like a solid opportunity. This is good news."

"Put the London team on stand-by, would you? Vincent Laidlaw in particular," Mike ordered.

"I'll get onto Vincent although, the team's on stand-by, ready to spin into action on the acceptance of your offer to purchase."

"Rory and Stefan are aware of my interest. However, I'll inform them both in the morning of my final decision. No doubt, Stefan will inform London once the initial offer has been accepted, expediently setting all the legalities in place"

"I'll re-alert the marketing department to prepare the write up for the Caribbean press releases and major hotel and industry trade publications and travel magazines which will firmly establish our public relations strategy. There are so many options open to us, I could go on and on here," said Amy.

"The Crystal Waters would require some renovations such as repairs, remodeling and refurbishments. I'll suitably raise its current three-star rating and quality of service to the desired five-star rating," Mike enthused.

"Well," said Amy jubilantly, "we're certainly on our way. I distinctly remember you'd mentioned your ambitious aim to acquire the triple A, four or five diamond rating," Amy reminded Mike.

"That dream will soon become a reality where I envision our clientele will verify the superiority and outstanding quality of service as an unforgettable experience, nine stars Michelin chefs sensationalizing their palates. The list goes on. One hurdle at a time, Amy. One day at a time." Amy immersing herself in the ambitious concept of Mike's words floating in the air delayed her response. "Hello?"

"Sorry, Mike, I'm still with you. Yes, you're right, one hurdle at a time. When do you propose to arrange a full inspection?"

"As soon as. Prior to a written offer, I'll arrange a reasonable inspection of the property. And, once we have a tentative agreement in place, I'll ascertain the proprietor's willingness to allow the company lawyers the right to examine the records held on financial statements, loans, revenues, and utility bills."

The mention of lawyers jerked Amy into putting the engagement of her own personal lawyer at the top of her action list. "What is the hotel's website address?" Amy fumbled around for a pen and paper.

"I'll drop you an email once I've gotten off the line."

"Great. I'll log on straight away." Amy climbed out of bed.

"I brought my digital camera along. I'll wander back to the hotel, take a few shots and post them on an email to you, annotating the areas requiring remodeling."

"Fine. I'd like to say that it was a sound decision of yours to travel on a thirty day return. It's made a lot of sense," said Amy, switching on her lap top.

"Allowing the extra time prevents rash and untimely decision making. I know what I'm doing. Cascadia is about to be born," said Mike assuredly.

"Amazingly so," said Amy.

The Crystal Waters hotel's virtual tour images on the internet took Amy by surprise. She gasped at the humble lobby, suites and idyllic setting on the beach situated very close to crystal clear waters. Remodeling? Where? Amy thought, marveling at the images. Mike had set high standards. One of many qualities she adored about him. Once renovated, the hotel will be superb, Amy thought. Indulgently viewing the hotel's website, Amy opened each page and read everything from the restaurant menu to the range of accommodation prices with consumed interest. Slowly coming to terms with the incredible fact that she was now, in reality, a co-owner of the hotel, in partnership with Mike Brandleton and Planet Management, moved by this astonishing feat and the sheer luck of it all, reduced Amy to tears. It seemed almost impossible to believe in the realization of her dreams, her intimacy with Mike, enjoying the journey and all the unexpected benefits that came along with him. She'd held back on informing Mike of the possibility of joining him in a matter of weeks. Commitments and obligations surrounding the contract Amy hadn't yet met and, without a temporary successor fully on board, she couldn't come up with a specific date of travel. Pulling herself together, Amy logged out of her laptop, power showered and dressed quickly for the office. She had to put Vincent on notice as soon as possible and prepare to kick-off the marketing, advertising and media machines once the tentative agreement to purchase The Crystal Waters Hotel was firmly in place.

Vincent answered the telephone and spoke soothingly, "Good morning to you, Amy."

"Good morning Vincent. I've news for you on Project Cascadia. This'll only take five minutes."

"Good, because that's about all I have to spare, so fire away," said Vincent quickly.

"Mike Brandleton called me first thing. He's found a hotel and proposes to make an offer. It's an established concern called The Crystal Waters Hotel. The asking price is six point five million pounds. The seller is open to offers and

Mike plans to negotiate a reduction on the asking price. The amount the seller would be prepared to accept? Your guess is as good as mine."

"Stefan's anticipative move in conducting the necessary checks ahead of time has resulted in us receiving a clean and clear cut report on the hotelier's business transactions," Vincent informed Amy.

"Oh … right, you are. I shouldn't be surprised, learning that you have received advanced information on this?" said Amy, speculatively.

"No. You shouldn't be. Develop the business acumen behind our four c's motto. Both you and Stefan are right in keeping me informed of events as and when they occur. Mike Brandleton is the lead investor here. However, with reasonable levels of communication and the expertise of my project staff, the business can only go from strength to strength in our concerted efforts to remain steps ahead, wherever possible, during our business activities."

"You're quite right, Vincent. Finally, I'll not hesitate in kicking-off the marketing strategy once the agreed information on the purchase has been announced and duly circulated within the company."

"Continue to keep me informed every step of the way, would you?"

"Of course, Vincent."

"If there's nothing further to discuss, I must get a move on," Vincent insisted.

"I've appreciated your time," Amy said hanging up. "Richard? Please get one of the secretaries to forward contact details of key personnel in our marketing and media department. We may receive a purchase announcement later today on Project Cascadia."

"Splendid," said Richard, "I'll get one of the secretaries to wing that round to you in a few minutes."

Amy estimated that Mike's emails would appear in her inbox around early lunchtime. Locating the sheet of paper housing the scribbled list of potential candidates, Amy called the head of human resources requesting their details. On receipt, she'd select the best of three for interview. Wishing her life away, impatiently waiting for the afternoon to descend upon her, Amy spent the remainder of the morning dedicating her unequivocal efforts to the asset management contract.

"I'm popping out for a sandwich," Richard announced.

Amy's face lit up. "Good heavens! Is it lunch time already? How time flies," she said.

Richard sighed and smiled. "Late lunch. Two thirty," he said.

Amy checked her inbox. There were three emails from Mike. Adrenalin flowing, Amy opened the first email. This man will never, ever cease to amaze me, Amy thought, reading in sheer undulating astonishment Mike's expression of thanks, appreciation and recognition of her efforts. She sentimentally read each phrase repeatedly. Recomposing a professional stance, Amy viewed the photographs attached to the second email depicting areas in need of remodeling. He's incredibly meticulous, Amy thought, as she studied the images. Not having the educated eye or knowledge to identify all the areas Mike had earmarked for refurbishments, Amy couldn't offer comment on most. Zooming in on the shots, Amy noted the odd cracked tiles around the pool area and clearly agreed the need for a complete re-tile. Mike stated the need to replace the current pool loungers with brand new ones. Amy closely scrutinized the photographs and opined that the current pool loungers were in an adequate state. Frustrated, she hoped, in time, that she'd develop an instinctive sense and an eye for detail. The final paragraph of Mike's email stated that phased refurbishments to the penthouse suites, lobby, breakfast rooms, balconies and other areas yet to be identified would be a definite consideration. Amy opened the final email. Mike had copied Vincent, Stefan, Rory, the legal counsel department of Planet Management and his personal lawyer in a statement that read:

> Project Cascadia. In a small joint venture initiative, Mike Brandleton and officials of Planet Management, including Rory Gibson based in the Caribbean and Stefan Regis of the London office, successfully negotiated a tentative agreement for the purchase of The Crystal Waters Hotel, to be renamed Cascadia, in the sum of six million GBP. The sale is subject to a mutually agreed, signed sales and purchase agreement. Project Cascadia enjoys the initiate injection of a total of six point five million GBP of private investor funds. Planet Management contributed two million GBP from its Planet Management Investment Fund (PMIF) bringing the total investment to eight point five million GBP, approximately in the region of US$15 million. The Crystal Waters Hotel is based at Providenciales in the Turks and Caicos.

Vincent's response appeared in Amy's inbox. Without delay, Amy opened it and read Vincent's few short lines, congratulating them on their expertise that led to the tentative success of the purchase, his direction that a bulletin be circulated throughout the company upon the final purchase agreement, followed by the usual confidentiality stipulations in conclusion. Bursting with delight and pride, Amy picked up the telephone and called Mike's cell-phone.

"Hi, you've read my emails."

"Yes. They're all direct and to the point. Mike, you've conducted the preliminary purchase transactions saving half a million pounds in a few hours after having spoken to me. That's brilliant."

"Thank you. There's no point dilly-dallying so, at midnight, we agreed to meet at seven o'clock this morning. We're mortgage free and available funds of two and half million pounds sits in the pot. I've run an estimate on operating results for the next three years which looks promisingly profitable."

"You're an absolute genius, Mike."

"I wouldn't go to that extreme. We've a lot of work ahead. I intend to fly back to the UK in a matter of days purely to sign the necessary documentation and to tie-up a few other things and, as soon as we are the legal owners, after our celebrations, I will return to the Turks without delay."

Hardly able to contend with the fact of having Mike back in a matter of days, Amy coughed and stumbled at Mike's intimations of we, our and after our celebrations. Aroused, she desperately wanted him in her arms. She yearned for his touch. She missed being under his influence, engaged in long, love making sessions at his palatial settings in Hampstead. She missed the times they'd shared in over-indulgence where they'd drank bottle loads of champagne. Champagne hadn't trickled on her lips since Mike had left for the Turks "Where will you reside when you return to the Turks?"

"In Cascadia, of course, in one of our penthouse suites," he said.

"I'll be joining you sooner than you think," said Amy.

CHAPTER 24

Amy inscribed her signature on the final series of legal documents, confirming her part-ownership of Cascadia, in the cramped offices of her unwittingly disorganized but reasonably dependable, personal lawyer she'd only just recently engaged based in London, King's Cross.

"You now possess a legal share of the said property based on the Caribbean island of Providenciales, Turks and Caicos, plot number …"

Amy listened to the notarization. "Noted," she said, struggling to apprehend the meanings and implications behind the legal jargon and terminology. "I'll take a complete set of duplicates away with me."

"Certainly, Miss Scott. Please wait a few minutes. I'll instruct my assistant to package a duplicate set for you," said the lawyer, shuffling to an adjacent office.

Amy remained seated in the only available chair in the cramped offices. An overflow of dusty law books, folders and papers were stacked high on the remaining three chairs. Five minutes later, the lawyer came shuffling back and handed Amy a large sealed brown envelope.

"Please, Miss Scott, do not hesitate to contact me should you have any further questions or uncertainties. Litigation of the deeds, documents and processes on both sides of the water is bona fide," said the lawyer, assuredly.

Amy put the envelope in her briefcase and rose out of the chair. "Thank you. It has been a pleasure working with you. Thank you for agreeing to take on my legal matters at such short notice," said Amy, emotionally relieved and grateful that the legalities were now in order.

"My pleasure, Miss Scott," said the lawyer, distractedly delving into a large file on his desk.

Amy walked over to the main door, opened it, hovered and turned to the lawyer saying, "Please, call me, Amy."

The lawyer looked up at Amy, nodded and smiled. "Thank you for the invitation," he said. "I have the Power of Attorney for Mrs. Cartwright. Get her on the phone. And Mr. Benson's documents are ready to go. Arrange a courier. Premium same day service," he shouted across his office to his assistant sitting in the adjacent room.

Clutching her briefcase, fully confident that the distribution of the originals and the safekeeping of an additional set of duplicated documents were safely in the capable hands of her lawyer, Amy vacated the King's Cross offices and took a taxi back to Planet Management where she'd arranged to meet with Mike and members of the marketing and media team. Fingers crossed, Amy hoped to obtain budget approval and final sign-off on the editorial material that afternoon. The marketing and media staff worked dedicatedly around the clock, to produce the centre page spread in time for the quarterly issue of the online subscription only publication, HospitalityNews.com.

"Very impressive. Excellent. They've been back three times for tweaking and I can safely say that they are now bordering on perfect," Amy critiqued, closely examining the final proofs.

Cocking his head at the light-box, intensively scrutinizing the digital images, Mike discussed the final airbrushing with a couple of young, hip, male graphic designers. "They're great. The backdrop of tropical foliage and the clever lighting technique used in the foyer renders an irresistibly inviting appeal of the images," Mike commented.

Amy quickly ran her eyes over the images again and nodded. "Agreed. The photographer has done an excellent job on the shots and angles," she said, gathering spare copies of the images from the studio counter for further scrutiny. "Please, get them signed-off. We've one hour. We're just in time to meet the editorial deadline cut-off for this quarter. Thank you for your time and patience guys," Amy shouted to the marketing team as she sauntered out of the studio.

Mike followed Amy out of the studio and along the corridor to the elevator. Lagging deliberately a few short paces behind her, Mike locked his eyes on Amy's petite waist. Churning, his solar plexus stiffened at the movement of her firm buttocks, the subtle sway of her hips. The feline contours of her shapely calves on every step she took made his eyes water. He stirred silently. He couldn't resist the temptation to get closer to her, run his fingers up and down her spine. He raised his right hand then, changed his mind.

Amy stopped at the elevator, oblivious to what had been going on behind her.

"Can we reach an agreement on the next steps?" Mike asked, recomposing himself.

Smiling curiously, Amy said, "Certainly. What did you have in mind?"

"That we fly to the Turks in the next four weeks?"

Amy deliberated that four weeks would be far too soon. There is far too much to accomplish in that time, Amy thought. "Well, yes. Pending, of course, on Vincent's agreement to my release date and the surety that my temporary successor of five days now, is fully on board and abreast of all aspects of the asset management contract by then," said Amy, stepping into the elevator.

"I'm fully confident that you'll have everything in place and that we'll be flying out to the Turks together. I need you out there with me, Amy," Mike muttered in the crowded elevator.

Amy's heart quickened and her blood rushed to her cheeks. "I'll do my best," she said, stoically.

They rode the elevator to the ground floor and Amy escorted Mike as far as the revolving, reinforced glass doors leading out to the main street. "Well, I must be getting on, Mike, if I'm going to work on flying out with you in a month from now." Amy mentally ran over a multitude of things yet to be executed.

"I'll touch base with you in a couple of days, shall I?"

"As you wish," said Amy.

Mike halted a few paces away from the revolving doors. Moving slowly, he turned to Amy, leaned forward, placed his hands on her hips and pecked her left cheek.

Blushing, Amy drew back and looked round about her. "Please, no body contact. You must act formally towards me on business premises."

"You're acting over-cautiously now. It was merely a peck on the cheek," Mike challenged.

Amy was dismissive. "We must practice professionalism at all times. We'd agreed to this, Mike. I'd like to keep our intimacy under wraps, for the time being, at least."

"As you wish," said Mike aloofly. He turned on his heels, walked out through the revolving doors and immediately hailed a taxi. He climbed in and closed the door, without looking back.

Amy watched through the revolving doors as the taxi moved away and joined the slow moving traffic. Maddened by their cold, abrupt and unceremo-

, parting, Amy turned on her heels and headed back to the elevator. Back at her desk, she re-admired the glossy images and re-read the editorial. The exercise brought the thrill back. Quivering, Amy smiled in elated anticipation, regardless of whether Mike had gone off in a huff or not. He's easily remedied, she thought. She looked across the office at her temporary successor, Juliana de Freitas-Alexandria, seated at a desk alongside Richard, studiously reading through the contracts and documentation materials. Working enthusiastically, Juliana was grasping the role and responsibilities with admirable ease. Vincent highly approved of Juliana. He accepted her wholeheartedly on her suitability for the role, her skills, experiential track record, charming personality, general willingness and can do attitude. Aged twenty nine, Juliana was fairly pretty. Unusually attractive. Petite. Her green eyes were possibly contact lens. Her skin tone, a natural olive hue. Possibly of Latin descent, Amy had no idea. She'd bypassed the ethnicity pages of Juliana's resume. Her ethnicity mattered not. Amy preferred to read through the information that crucially mattered attributing to Juliana's strengths, achievements, qualifications, abilities and viable experience. There was a lot to plough through. Juliana's attractiveness also served as one of a number of fundamental attributes amid the aestheticism of collective consciousness of Planet Management. Vincent appreciated beauty and, as such, surrounded himself in beauty, and that included his entire complement, men as well as women, from the janitor, up. On observance, Amy hadn't identified an unattractive person throughout the company's UK organization, although that was open to personal taste opinion. Proud of her apt choice, Amy wandered over to Juliana. "How are you getting on?"

Juliana pushed the incentivisation agreement, aside momentarily and cupped her hands elegantly on her lap. "Getting there," she said, oozing confidence.

"Brilliant," said Amy. She pulled up a chair and sat down facing Juliana. "I'd like to go over a few items with you, if I may?"

"Sure," said Juliana.

"Over the next three consecutive weekends, we'll be working quite closely together to gain an understanding of the core competencies relating to specific items, contracts and relationships, the investment and management processes and, corporate governance practices following global standards. You're still agreeable and available for all this?"

"Yes, of course. I am indeed, Amy."

"In a month, I intend to fly out to the Turks."

"I understand. My intention is to become reasonably and practicably conversant in the role by then."

"Great. Obviously, we'll be maintaining a degree of regular contact whilst I'm away.

"Yes, we must seek to maintain that."

Satisfied, Amy smiled warmly at Juliana. "I'll let you get on. You look rather busy."

"There is a lot to take in," said Juliana, inclining her head, returning to the incentivisation agreement.

Amy got up and walked over to her desk. She retrieved the editorial materials from her desk and walked over to Richard. "Take a look at the editorial and digital images on Project Cascadia," she said, neatly laying out the materials on Richard's desk. Her telephone rang. Amy rushed over to her desk and picked it up. "Amy Scott."

"Amy, we have the final sign-off and are ready to roll on this," said the marketing and media manager.

"Well done. Please go right ahead," said Amy, hanging up.

"Very nice. Has Juliana seen these?" Richard asked quietly, gesturing his head in Juliana's direction, nursing his dented ego, coming to terms with the disappointing fact that he hadn't been included in the selection process as temporary successor to manage the asset management contract. Although recently promoted and enjoying the privilege of having clout and his own assistant, Amy was fully aware that Richard had been quietly pissed-off by the Board's decision to offer the position of temporary successor to someone other than himself. He took it as a punch on the chin and had been handling the disappointing situation pretty well so far, Amy thought.

"No. That won't be necessary. I deem that idea as tenuous for the present. There'll be room for that later. I'd rather Juliana concentrated her efforts on matters of a more pressing nature," Amy explained.

Overhearing the conversation, Juliana looked up at Amy and Richard and smiled understandingly at them.

Amy returned to her desk and pressed on solidly through to midnight.

A few days later, a small team of call centre operatives stemmed the steady influx of calls ranging from people in the hotel and tourism industry, investment bankers, venture capitalists, management consultants flaggingly competing with Planet Management, and multi-media journalists. A handful of anonymously assumably wealthy individuals offered funds and hinted their interests to be considered to participate in the current, future as well as conceptual investments. Carelessly speculating enquirers, probing further information on the Brandleton and Planet Management partnership, were also keen to obtain knowledge of private investor information. Most of the information sought was legally classified as strictly confidential and therefore, undisclosed to the public and private sectors. Call centre operatives strictly adhered to the carefully worded script aimed at protecting the identity of investors and the securitization of the deal. The marketing and media manager ensured that Vincent, Stefan and Amy were kept up to date on the news and inflow of statistical data generated from the influx of enquiries. The partnership was generating an unexpectedly huge amount of international interest that Amy had to break the news of her exploit to her parents before the news filtered its way to them by contrary means. She'd not contacted them in quite some time. A catch-up call was long overdue.

Saturday morning, Amy awoke to the late September sun glowing through her apartment. She got out of bed and showered. Wrapped in a white bath robe, Amy poured herself a full glass of fresh organic orange juice, brought the glass into the lounge, curled up on the couch and mentally went over the grueling work schedule planned for the weekend. Her thoughts shifted to her parents. Amy checked the time. At seven thirty-five, she figured that her mother would either be breakfasting, washing, ironing or undoubtedly engaged in some form of housework. Whatever, the case, Amy called her mother.

"Amy? Is that you, young lady?" "Where have you been?" "We haven't heard from you in ages." "Are you taking care of yourself?" "Are you eating properly?" "Getting enough sleep?"

Amy gleamed from ear to ear at the sound of her mother's voice and the fuss she made. "Yes, Mother." "I've been so tied-up." "I know." "I'm perfectly fine." "Honestly, Mother. I'm fine" "Yes, Mother."

"I'll hand the 'phone over to your father. He wants a quick word."

"Thanks, Mother."

"Amy?"

"Hi, Dad."

"I'd begun to wonder whether you'd left the country!"

"That's rather an uncanny statement, Father. That's precisely one of the reasons why I've called."

"Let's not go into it now over the telephone. If it's not too short notice, why don't you come over for Sunday lunch tomorrow?"

Amy needed some time to come to a decision. There was the walk through with Juliana tomorrow which she couldn't cancel. Amy shrugged. "Yes. I can easily manage that. At what time?" she said, preoccupied with thoughts on what to do about Juliana tomorrow.

"Lunch will be served at two. But, get here before then, if you can, so that we can all have a good old chat. I'll invite your sisters along."

"Good idea, Dad. I'll see you all tomorrow," said Amy, hanging up. Shame on you for not maintaining regular contact, Amy thought. Amy strolled into her bedroom and engaged in the ritual of moisturizing her skin with rosemary scented, pure vitamin E body oil. She pulled on a pair of denim jeans, a white v-neck sweater, slipped on a pair of black leather Italian loafers, ran her slender fingers through her hair, gathered her handbag, keys and cell-phone, applied a touch of lip gloss and left for the office. On arrival, at approximately eight-forty, Amy wandered absentmindedly over to her desk.

"Bright morning," Juliana commented.

"It certainly is," said Amy, slightly startled. "How long have you been here?" Amy put her handbag on Richard's desk

"An hour. I've read quite a lot in that time." Juliana pointed at sheets of paper and contracts blanketing the desk.

Good," said Amy. "There'll be a slight variation to our work schedule tomorrow."

"Oh?"

Smiling, Amy waved her beautiful hand in the air expressively. "It's nothing to worry about. We'll work the morning only and be out of here by one o'clock. Something's cropped up at the last minute which necessitates me having to leave earlier."

"Why not leave something with me to work on. I'd be quite happy to and, have no objections or qualms about working alone all day tomorrow," said Juliana, conscientiously enthusiastic.

"I'll think about it. By tonight, you'll probably change your mind," said Amy, deliberating the idea of grafting heavily through to midnight, possibly later. "Let's go over the corporate governance practices now, shall we?"

"Certainly," said Juliana.

The captivatingly delicious aroma of home cooking wafted from the kitchen out to the street, tantalizing Amy's taste buds. Using her set of keys she'd kept and never parted with since moving out of the nest, Amy let herself into her parents' house and crept down the hallway. Her mother knew someone had entered her house and rushed out of the kitchen. Screeching in sheer delight, she grabbed and kissed Amy on both cheeks. Amy's sisters, Helen and Emily, came running down the stairs. Her father emerged from the living room. They all converged on her at once.

Emily, twenty two, the youngest, gawked wide-eyed at Amy. "My God, Amy, you've lost an awful lot of weight."

Helen, twenty five, came to Amy's defense. "Leave her alone. You look smashing, Amy. You're all toned. Come here, give us a hug," she said, edging closer to Amy, nudging Emily out of her way in the process.

"There's not an ounce of fat on you," cried Emily, to the back of Helen's head.

"Like the hair cut. It suits you," said Helen.

"Goes with her face," her mother said.

"I like the new image," said Helen.

"How's the new job?" Emily asked.

"Nice jeans. Can I borrow them?" Helen joked.

"Wishful thinking. You'll never get into them. You've gotta lose more weight first and you can start with working on that fat butt," said Emily, in friendly banter.

They all prodded and poked Amy, and spoke simultaneously. The excitement over and greetings in order, Amy slipped off her loafers and placed them neatly in the shoe cupboard, switched off her cell-phone and dropped it in her handbag which she hung on the coat hook. Amy's hunger pangs raging, she dashed into the kitchen, washed her hands and assisted her mother in preparing the Sunday lunch.

"We've heard nothing from you in weeks. What's the reasoning behind this?" Amy's father chomped a hot and crispy golden brown roasted potato.

Amy popped a succulent morsel of spicy roast chicken into her mouth and, appreciative of her mother's home cooking, openly relished the taste. "Delicious … This is so yummy. I'm sorry Dad," she said, between chewing, "it's just that, I've been so busy." Amy's father sighed discontentedly. Amy licked her lips. "And before you say anything further, Dad, I admit that I am the first to agree that my excuse is not an acceptable one, I know," Amy added apologetically, crunching a mouthful of grated raw carrots she'd scooped out of the large, round wooden salad bowl using the wooden serving spoon.

"The most important thing is that, she's here now. Let's not go on at her, dear," her mother said sheepishly.

"It's since she's moved companies," said her father.

"You're right, Dad. My present role has been more grueli the previous one and warrants a huge amount of my time. I put in ver, hours. There's been so much to do and learn," Amy rationalized.

"You've something to tell us about leaving the country. Are you leaving the country?" asked her father, wearing a slight frown.

Amy situated her knife and fork on either side of her plate and gently dabbed her lips with the pretty, white cotton, laced trimmed table napkin her mother normally reserved for guests and special occasions. "No. It's a business trip. I've just recently gone into business with an acquaintance of mine. I'll be gone for a couple of months or so to the Turks and Caicos Islands in the Caribbean. I'm working on leaving in about a month's time."

"How fantastic," Helen gushed.

"Will you be back in time for Christmas?" asked her mother.

"Yes, Mother. Well … that's my aim."

"This is what I've always wanted for you, Amy. You running your own show, pushing your own buttons," said her father

"Thanks, Dad. I do remember you saying something in the past along those lines."

"What exactly is the nature of this new business?" asked her father.

"An acquaintance and I, along with investment from my employer, have acquired The Crystal Waters Hotel in the Turks which we've renamed Cascadia."

"A hotel! That's big business. I hope you haven't gotten yourself into a lot of bad debt?"

Amy shifted uncomfortably in her seat. "I've invested a small amount in the hotel, Dad. It's a good investment and a rare opportunity. Opportunities are scarce commodities and, as this opportunity has come my way, I've taken a stab at it and I've every ounce of faith that this business will succeed, Dad," said Amy defensibly.

"Well, you've always been a gutsy, clever girl. I suppose you know what you're doing," he said, biting into a roast chicken drum stick.

"I most certainly believe in this, Dad. I'm giving it all I've got."

"I congratulate you," her father said, scooping a mountainous helping of roasted chestnut and parsnips out of the serving bowl and onto his plate.

"Are you open?" asked Helen.

"Yes, we're open. We've bought an ongoing concern and plan to take over complete operations shortly."

"What dates would you recommend for a vacation out there? Spring or summer season?" Helen asked.

"I've a better idea. Why not join me during my stay? You'll meet my business associate, Mike Brandleton. In fact, you're all welcome to join me."

"It's a bit close, but I'll see what I can do. As soon as I get into the office tomorrow, I'll book some provisional dates," said Helen excitedly.

"Me too. What's the room rate?" said Emily.

"Emily. Don't be absurd!" said Amy alarmingly. "There'll be no charge. Provide me with your dates and I'll arrange to forward the relevant details to you regarding flights and so forth." Amy looked across the table questioningly. "Mother? Are you coming? I don't intend to rule anyone out. I'm not wickedly selfish, you're all welcome," said Amy benevolently, having no idea where she was going to put them all.

"You've always had a good, clean and kind heart, Amy. There's not a wicked bone in your body. You know, I don't like flying, Amy. Your father and I are too old to fly. You girls go out there and enjoy yourselves. Go on. I'll stay here with your father. Promise to tell us all about it when you get back and take lots of photos," said her mother resignedly.

"I understand. The offer will always be open should you ever change your mind."

"What's it like out there? I don't recall you ever having mentioned visiting that place on your travels. I've not heard of the place, it's got to be a worthy location, otherwise your company wouldn't have got involved."

"You're absolutely right about that, Emily. I've not been there. However, tourism is the main industry and the off-shore finance sector continues to grow due to the favorable laws which facilitate international business transactions. There's no wealth or inheritance tax and the Turks operate under a modern corporate law with the backing of a professional infrastructure."

Helen dropped her cutlery on her plate, waved her hands in the air and giggled nervously. "Wow, you're speaking a whole different language. I didn't understand a single word of that."

"Me neither," said Emily.

"Sorry, I didn't mean to lose you. It wasn't my intention," said Amy.

"That's OK, Sis. Provided there's sun, sea and sand, that'll do me just fine. I can hardly wait to get out there. I need a vacation, believe me," said Helen.

"You'll get ample sun, sea and sand, I can assure you," Amy concluded. After tucking into two helpings of fresh fruit salad and fresh cream, Amy helped with clearing the table and stacking the dishwasher, before challenging Helen and Emily to a game of scrabble. Her father retired on the couch with the Sunday newspaper. His head bobbed up and down as he fought off sleep during his read until he eventually nodded off, snoring contentedly quiet. Her mother, clutching a silver, slim-lined remote control, planted herself in her favorite armchair, feasted her eyes and ears on the thirty-two inch TV screen and flicked through soap opera channels. After beating her sisters twice at scrabble, effectively the bored winner, Amy suggested they wrap up for the evening. "Time I was heading home," she said.

"I'll call a cab," said Emily.

Amy retrieved her loafers and handbag, fished out her cell-phone and switched it on. There'd been no missed calls or voicemail messages from Mike. Wondering what type of day Mike had had resting on her mind, Amy walked into the lounge and knelt on the floor at her mother's feet. Amy said nothing as her mother watched the last ten minutes of the Omnibus edition of her favorite soap opera.

Emily cocked her head around the door. "The cab's here," she called.

"I know. I heard it pull up," said Amy rising to her feet, brushing herself off, although there was nothing to brush off, her mother kept the home spotlessly clean, one could lick the floors.

"It's been great having you around today, Amy. Promise me that you'll contact us more often," said her mother, rising to her feet.

"I promise." Amy pecked her mother on both cheeks and embraced her lingeringly.

"Mind how you go," said her father, pecking her lightly on her forehead.

"Thanks, Dad," said Amy. "You too, Dad."

Helen opened her arms to embrace Amy. "Come here, you. Give me a hug." Amy obliged.

Emily, never the demonstrative type, jokingly yelped and retreated to the kitchen shouting, "See you soon, Amy."

"See you soon," Amy shouted. Amy got into the cab and waved to her family huddled closely together at the main door frantically waving at her, minus Emily. As the cab moved away, relaxed, Amy ran through a mental checklist to call Mike, Rochelle and Katie in that order and her lawyer, in the morning, to go over the management of her personal affairs during her stay in the Caribbean.

CHAPTER 25

"Hello, Mr. Brandleton."

Mike had trouble attaching the almost unrecognizable, sexually dulcet tones to a name. "Belinda?"

"Yes! Bulls-eye! It's been a long time, Mike. How are you?" Belinda purred teasingly.

Sitting at the Edwardian Mahogany Davenport bureau, studying a report on the previous fiscal year of The Crystal Waters hotel, Mike suppressed his surprise. "I am well. Very well indeed. And you?" "Divine. Just divine." *newline*

Mike was growing impatient. "What is the nature of your call, Belinda?"

"You hardly sound pleased to hear from me, Mike! I'll get straight to the point, then," Belinda breathed. "As I'm an online subscriber to the Hospitality News, I've read an interesting article?"

"Really?" said Mike frostily, pushing the report aside.

"Yes. Really, Mike. Don't you see? I want to do business with you," Belinda petitioned sharply.

"And so do a lot of other people," Mike scoffed.

"I'm not a lot of other people, Mike. Look, I haven't called for a fight."

Mike paused. "Then?"

"My interest is in the area of the beauty business. Have you forgotten that I'm in the beauty business?"

Mike said nothing.

Belinda went on. "The article stated that you're looking for franchisees knowledgeably experienced in the state-of-the-art spa and beauty salon business? I would like to be considered and welcome a meeting with you."

"That can be arranged," said Mike. Fatigued, he got out of the Edwardian Mahogany elbow chair, paced around the drawing room and rubbed the back of his neck.

Belinda coughed. "Planet Management? Would that be the company Amy Scott is associated with? The woman who'd attended the workshop?"

"You're perfectly right."

"What a clever move!"

"Correction. Strategic."

"OK, strategic."

"When shall we meet?"

"Are you available sometime in the afternoon say, lunch time tomorrow would be perfect? That's the only time I've freely available. Otherwise, I'm fully booked out the entire week," said Belinda.

"Where shall we meet?"

"At my London offices, Omega Marketing on Maddox Street. You're aware of the location, right?"

"Yes. In the Regent Street area. That's easily located. At what time?"

"Twelve noon. We can have a thirty to forty minute discussion in my office, followed by lunch?"

"I'll accept the meeting. The lunch, I'll have to decline."

"Wonderful. A meeting it is," said Belinda, slightly disappointed.

"See you then," said Mike clicking off. He tossed his tiny cell-phone in his top shirt pocket, picked up the report and resumed study of the figures. Distracted, Mike's concentration levels were totally diminished now. He'd reached the point of no return and found it impossible to resume study of the report. Slinging the report on the bureau, Mike sat back in the chair and placing his hands on the back of his head, pushing back, gently tilting the chair onto its hind legs, Mike began rocking steadily. Smiling wryly, Mike closed his eyes and allowed his thoughts to drift back to the fun he'd had during Belinda's contribution to the boardroom role-play, which he'd personally viewed as a sweet tease, hot, raucous and enjoyably outrageous.

CHAPTER 26

Amy called Mike. His cell-phone was busy. She left a warm voicemail message promising that she'd call back. In keeping with the pecking order, Rochelle was next in line. Conversation was kept short and sweet as always. Rochelle congratulated Amy on her new business venture and accepted the invitation to fly out to the Turks. Katie was positively amazed on learning the true extent of the business venture now that Amy felt comfortable going into more detail, discussing matters more in-depth.

"Bloody hell!" yelled Katie, sitting in a local bar in Benidorn on her cell-phone, "You're in with the big boys!" Good old Katie, Amy thought, giggling amusedly. "I suppose our weekend in Barcelona gets the boot?"

"No. Not necessarily. There's always next year," Amy replied.

"That settles it, then."

"Come out to the Turks whilst I'm out there."

"That depends."

"On?"

"I've a possible venture in the pipeline myself."

"Have you? I'm pleased to hear it. Doing what?"

"Similar to what I've been doing in the UK but on a self-employed basis. I've made influential contacts in the last couple of years and I'm also equipped to fill in the loop-holes I'd identified ages ago but had kept quiet about, that nothing will stop me once I get going."

"You've discovered your niche. You've been busy. I'm glad to hear it. What stage have you reached?"

"I'm at a reasonably promising stage, there's nothing concrete to report yet," replied Katie vaguely.

"I totally get your point," said Amy. "Sorry to be abrupt, but it's time I pushed on. I've another call to make."

"Oh! Touch base with me before you set-off for the Caribbean, won't you? You won't forget, I hope?"

"No, I won't," said Amy rushing off her cell-phone. She wandered into the kitchen, swung the refrigerator door wide open, pulled out a bottle of Chardonnay, uncorked it, poured herself a full glass and took a large sip. She walked steadily back into the lounge and, nestling on the couch, dialed Mike's cell-phone again and beamed up at the ceiling, praying that he'd answer.

"Mike Brandleton."

On hearing his voice, Amy grew sick with instant desire. They hadn't been alone together since his return to the UK. Amy had counted that Mike had been back nine days, and admittedly, they'd both been totally stretched. "Mike. How are you?" Amy enthused.

"I'm well, considering I haven't seen the light of day having spent it all working in the drawing room with the drapes shut."

"Tell me about it, I know the feeling."

"Our ad has generated some intriguing responses to date."

"Precisely. Somewhat unprecedented. I don't recall there having been such interest on a project of this size."

"Size matters. It's less risky. The chance to join ranks with Planet Management, that's where the main attraction lies. The fundamentality of accelerating profitable growth cost effectively, expansion and lucrative diversification are speculatively high, that investors are keen to come in at a reasonably early stage and, at a reasonable expense to get intimately involved during the formation."

"You're not planning to accept additional investment are you, Mike?"

"Not at this stage. Later perhaps. Ideally, once we're better placed, established in growth and strength, I propose to take the business to new dimensions, where the inflow of private investor funds would be injected and enjoyed as a surplus to our requirements as opposed to a requirement."

"Sounds like you have some very ambitious aims tucked under your belt?"

"I most certainly do. By the way, have you given any further thought to flying out to the Turks? Only, I'm informing you now of my plan to be there either by the end of this month or during the first Friday in October at the very latest."

Feeling slightly put under duress, Amy knew she couldn't hold back on making a commitment.

"The first week in October should be OK," she said stoically.

"Good. We either fly out together or take separate flights."

"A month would be my maximum stay. During that time, I'll be working quite closely with Juliana, my temporary successor so, Mike, I'm asking you now to please be patient with me on this?"

"I understand your position and things will improve as time goes by. What are your plans for tonight?"

Weary, Amy looked at her watch. It was approaching eight forty-five.

"Working from home. Nothing pressing. Other than that single fact, I'm free otherwise."

"Come over. I'm sending a taxi to collect you in an hour. Would an hour be sufficient?"

"Sooner would be better," she said.

CHAPTER 27

"Take a seat Mr. Brandleton. Miss Mitchell will be with you shortly," said the young receptionist. She walked out of the room and closed the door behind her. The air conditioner humming whisperingly, distributed cool air evenly around the spacious rosewood wall paneled boardroom. In the centre, stood a lacquered rosewood table surrounded by twelve white organza upholstered, generously padded lacquered rosewood chairs. To the right, double-glazed windows draped heavy Arabian gold and blue brocade. Ostentatious. An over-kill, Mike thought. To his left, bottled water, fresh orange juice, tea, coffee, biscuits and Danish pastries were neatly arranged on a silver service catering trolley. Mike walked the few paces over to the trolley and poured himself a glass of sparkling spring bottled water.

Belinda entered the boardroom and closed the door behind her. She sashayed over to Mike. Heavily tanned, she wore a low-cut, white laced, buttoned down blouse. Swathed in a pink, calf length, wrap-over summer skirt, the ensemble was stunningly put together and modeled in true Belinda style.

"Ah, Mike. I'm pleased you could make it. It's great to see you," she cooed, extending her hand.

Mike sipped his water and set his glass on the trolley. He turned to Belinda, nodded, smiled genteelly and shook her hand. "Likewise."

Belinda eased forward. "First things first," she intimated whisperingly, embracing him.

Buckling, unable to trust himself, Mike fumbled a casual embrace. Looking directly into Mike's eyes, Belinda ran her finger tips along the back of Mike's neck and bringing her lips prominently close, she kissed him tenderly. Without resistance, Mike closed his eyes. Lost in blind ecstasy, mindless lust churned ped through every muscle in his body. Belinda's kisses intensifying, stinctually wanting more, pulled her close and kissed her, feeding her prog sive hunger. Belinda moaned and uttered on Mike's lips, "I'm all yours." She ran her tongue along his chin. "Yours." Her hand clamped firmly on the back of his neck, Mike jerked his head away and stood back in reproach. Visions of Amy's captivating smile impressing his mind haunted him.

"No," he said sharply.

Belinda smiled, unbuttoned her blouse, stepped forward and pressed her naked breasts firmly on his chest. Weakened, Mike groaned, cupped her shoulders and drew her closer to him. Her breasts were unusually cold and hard, felt through the fabric of his tailored cotton shirt. Her nipples lacked protrusion, sweet warmth and tender suppleness. Too skinny, her hips jarred him. She was incompatible and not fitting him right. To look at, Belinda was irresistibly breathtaking and had brought out his animalistic urges but, to his astonishment, he wasn't actually enjoying her in that inescapably, uncontrollably, undeniably and mindlessly deep erotic sensual way he thought would have been the natural inevitability, quite like what he'd been experiencing with Amy. Besides, Amy had used up virtually all his energies the night before and during the early hours of that morning. Belinda. Belinda. She's trouble. She's all wrong. This won't do, Mike thought. His heart and pulses racing rapidly, resisting his consuming animalistic desires, fraught with confusion and anxiety, pulling back, Mike grabbed Belinda by her wrists and yanked them down firmly at her sides. "Stop," he ordered. Belinda looked deeply into his eyes, searchingly, bewilderingly. Mike released her wrists, turned his back and took a couple of paces forward, saying, "Redo your buttons, would you?" His ears hissing to the sound of their breathless panting, Mike pulled a neatly folded, bright white, fine cotton handkerchief out of his pants pocket and wiped his face, neck and hands. He looked at Belinda's pink lipstick smudged on his handkerchief, scrunched it up and shoved it back in his pants pocket.

"You want me. There's no point denying it. Why deny it? You can't resist me and you know it. No man has ever turned me away, Mike? Please? Let's get it over with? Just this once? What are you afraid of?" Belinda pleaded in a voice contorted with anger, frustration, pain and rejection.

Mike spun round. His eyes fell on her odd but perfectly round breasts. Mike blinked hard. Implants? he thought. "I might have known. You've invited me here under false pretences—under the auspices of wanting to discuss the franchise," he said sardonically.

"In all seriousness, Mike, yes, I do want to discuss the franchise and reach an agreement with you—today." Belinda re-buttoned her blouse fumblingly. "I just thought that, perhaps, we could, put things to the test, remember? I thought you'd enjoyed that little escapade we had? It's never left my mind. And you?" Belinda raised her eyebrows questioningly and suggestively.

Mike brought his hands behind his back and clenched his fist. "Sorry to disappoint you, but you're entertaining the wrong idea entirely." Belinda stepped forward. Mike stepped back "Look, Belinda, it's no use, I won't do it. Let's forget this … the whole thing … the franchise. I'm not prepared to go ahead with it."

"Get out," Belinda yelled ragingly.

"With utmost pleasure. And please, do not call me again," said Mike. He coolly turned and walked out of the Omega Marketing boardroom, leaving the door wide open.

CHAPTER 28

"There's a call for you, Amy," said Richard.

"Thanks. Just give me a moment," said Amy hesitantly, inserting her ear-piece. Amy had booked a conference room to go over with Juliana, and with-out interruption, the research and style of Planet Management's business inquisition of the asset management acquirement. "Who is it, by the way? Any-one of importance? Take a message for me will you, Richard?"

"It's Mike Brandleton?"

"Put him through, thanks." Amy stood up behind the conference table. "Give me a moment please, Mike," she said, pushing the hold button on her cell-phone. "Would you excuse me, Juliana? I need to take this call. Please con-tinue going over the documentation," she ordered, stepping out of the confer-ence room. Amy walked a few paces along the corridor and released the hold button. "Mike? You've caught me in the middle of something. What can I do for you?" she said anxiously, her body a little fatigued from their recent strenu-ous lovemaking.

"So far, you've done more than I could ever wish for."

Amy said nothing. She proceeded to the elevator and looked at her watch. One forty-five. Time I stopped for a bite to eat. I'm sure Juliana could use some lunch, Amy thought. Frazzled by Mike's statement, Amy decided to play along. "Really! Such as?"

"Ah ha!" returned Mike.

"I'm not about to guess. Keep it to yourself," she said, stepping into the ele-vator.

"Dinner. This coming Saturday, at eight. I've hired Isuko Oki, the Japanese company to take care of the cuisine and wonderful entertainment for the evening in the form of, no other than, a Japanese magician."

"Sounds fantastic! Where shall we meet?"

"It's all happening at my place. It's our celebratory night and my thank you to you."

Tears welling, a lump forming at the back of her throat, Amy said, "I've work planned over the weekend." Realizing her response, Amy retracted. "Forget what I've just said. This is so wonderful of you, Mike. I'll be there at eight sharp," she said stepping out of the elevator on the ground floor.

"Good. See you then," said Mike, clicking off. Amy's thoughts drifted; mesmerized by the way they'd made love recently; they appreciated, explored and were tender to each other like never before. Superb, Amy thought. She stepped back into the elevator and returned to the conference room.

"Let's break for lunch. We'll dine in the staff restaurant."

"Sure," said Juliana, reaching for her handbag on the floor under her chair.

"I ought to inform you of the fact that we've a very hectic week ahead. We'll be working until midnight most evenings. On Saturday, I've a pressing engagement, so we'll work a half day, wrapping up around noonish, taking Sunday off." said Amy, standing in the doorway.

"Whatever you say, Amy," said Juliana, getting out of her chair.

Fingers crossed, Amy banked on Juliana having the mental agility and physical stamina that would enable her to keep up with the tough and grueling pace looming ahead. "There's only one way to find out," Amy murmured as she walked along the corridor with Juliana to the elevator.

"Excuse me?" said Juliana.

"Oh. It's nothing important," said Amy.

CHAPTER 29

"I'll not forget this magical night. Thank you," said Amy dreamily, pecking Mike on the cheek, running her fingers along his chest as they lay nude in his bed. Amy turned to her right, looked down at the floor and smiled. Exquisite silk lingerie, adorned with 18 carat gold beading, lay strewn on the floor, a surprise gift from Mike he'd purchased when he'd wandered around Piccadilly on the day of the farcical meeting with Belinda. He'd not informed Amy about that event, nor had he any intentions of doing so. Amy closed her eyes and relived the moment Mike had lingeringly, gently, sensuously and slowly peeled each item of lingerie off her body.

"Glad you'd enjoyed the Sushi and the magician," said Mike. "We've a lot to organize on the launch party in the Turks when the tourist season's over say—towards the end of November or the beginning of December." Amy sighed but said nothing. Mike peered down at her. "It's past midnight. You're tired. Get some sleep. You've an early start tomorrow. We can talk about this some other time."

With her eyes shut, Amy nodded saying, "I want to remain awake for a little while longer."

"I love your strength," said Mike.

"You'd stated earlier that you're booking your flight on Monday?" enquired Amy, seeking reconfirmation.

"Yes. I hope to arrive the first Friday in October at the very latest and I also hope that you'll be accompanying me then."

Amy fidgeted on the rose scented, cotton sheets. "I'll do my best," she said. "I've invited family members and an acquaintance along."

"Good idea. It'll be a pleasure to meet them all. I've arranged to start work as soon as I get there and interview a number of interior designers specializing in Penthouse suites."

"I love your expediency."

Mike turned to Amy, smiled and ran his thumb along her forehead. Amy opened her eyes. "I'll formally meet the hotel staff and have the head chef rustle up a few dishes for sampling. The menu requires a complete overhaul that, with his creative input, we should come up with a fitting menu."

"Will there be anything left for me to do once I get there?"

"There is a great deal to learn, hands on … a very great deal." Mike fondled her breasts and responded by letting out an ecstatic moan to their sweet warmth and tenderness, her nipples hardening and protruding. Amy moaned. Mike felt a cold chill as the image of Belinda flashed before him for a split second. Shuddering, he managed to block her out of his mind, instantaneously. "We've our private celebration to look forward to after the launch before the real hard grime and testing ground kicks off," Mike whispered.

"Looking forward to it," said Amy, stroking Mike's erection.

"You greedy little cat," Mike joked.

Amy giggled anticipatively.

CHAPTER 30

Monday morning at ten o'clock, Vincent ordered Amy into his office. She hadn't closed his office door when he'd tossed a sheet of paper across his desk at her. Startled, Amy looked at Vincent then looked at the sheet of paper landing on his desk.

"Explain this to me!" he demanded.

Amy walked over, looked at Vincent again, reached forward and picked up the sheet of paper. Her hand shook. It was a typed letter signed by Carlson Brandleton on company letterhead. Her legs suddenly weakened, so Amy pulled up a chair, sat down and read an account of defamatory details relating to Mike Brandleton, the disgraced and ousted son, alleging that Mike had dishonored the family, embezzled and misappropriated private equity and company funds, strongly urging Planet Management to immediately terminate all business relations with Mike. And, last, but not least, the letter ended on the note that Mike was a drug abuser, followed by "… please do not hesitate to contact me should you require further information …" Shocked, but dubious, about the contents, in need of time to think things through and not wanting to incriminate herself, Amy said nothing. The information was difficult to fathom. Her world was beginning to crumble, come crashing down at her feet. Success is like clay, it can all but crumble at any time, Amy thought. A mental aberration, she couldn't remember where she'd read those words, but they'd somehow resurfaced from the deep recesses of her mind. A Fortune Cookie, read way in the past maybe? She couldn't quite recall exactly.

"Well?" uttered Vincent icily. Amy sensed the disgust and disappointment in Vincent's tone and manner. He turned his back to her, stood behind his desk and faced the window. Something he often did when making crucial decisions.

Amy stood up and placed the letter on Vincent's desk. "I'll look into it. I'll get some answers. Vincent? I'd like to state that … not everything one reads is entirely based on fact—I don't know what else to say really."

"I don't believe that you're in a position to make such a statement, said Vincent scathingly. "And might I ask you, are you aware of any of this?"

"Vaguely. I had no idea it would come to this, to be honest."

"Vaguely?" said Vincent in disgust. "What is the true nature of your relationship with this business associate of yours … this man—Mike Brandleton?" His voice was firm but calmer now. He had spun around and was staring coldly into Amy's eyes. His eyes were like fish. No expression, just a cold, glassy, penetrating glare.

Amy breathed hard and inclined her head ashamedly. "We're intimate," she answered hoarsely.

Vincent said nothing and turned to the window. "You have one week to come back with something … something that would convince me from canning the project and taking legal action."

Amy clenched her fists, the tips of her French manicure dug into her palms. "Vincent? You'd had Mike checked out. Everything came back clean. No criminal record. No disputes. No courts. No debts. No adverse information. Nothing."

"His father simply hadn't pressed charges but chose the option to oust him, leaving him to prey on the likes of you and me. Who knows what else he may have scheming out there. Furthermore, you were not born yesterday, you are learnedly and totally aware of the untold numbers of scams and fraudulent activities taking place every minute of the day across the globe, from false identities to paying an insider to wipe government computers clean of incriminating records, the buying and selling of information etcetera, etcetera."

Stunned, Amy stared down blankly at the letter. "I'd like a photocopy of this, if I may?"

"Go ahead." Vincent waved his hand swiftly in the air and pointed at his personal photocopier.

Amy stood up and walked over to the photocopier situated next to the shredder. The water dispenser was situated at the far side of the photocopier. Water, Amy thought. Her throat was parched and her lips were dry. She couldn't bring herself to ask Vincent for a cup of water, he'd given her more than enough, she couldn't ask for anything more. Gliding her parched tongue along her lips, Amy photocopied the letter. She returned to Vincent, placed the original letter on his desk and folded the photocopied sheet in half.

"One week from today," Vincent warned. Dejected, Amy walked out of the office without further utterance and strolled back to her desk.

"Richard, I'd like you and Juliana to jointly take over for me. I have to suddenly leave the office. I should be back sometime this afternoon. Not sure of the precise time." She coughed attempting to ease the discomfort of a dry throat.

"Sure. Anything specific you'd like us to do now?" asked Richard. Juliana wandered over and parked next to Richard.

"No. Just business as usual for the moment," said Amy. She fixed her gaze on Juliana saying, "You've done remarkably well and come a long way that I'm confident you're quite capably ready to take over most of the role with your eyes closed." Juliana smiled and nodded. Amy turned her back, blinked away her threatening tears, picked up her handbag and walked to the elevator.

"Gosh. What was that all about?" Richard whispered.

Juliana slid into Amy's chair and settled herself comfortably at Amy's desk. "Don't concern yourself. I'm going into her email inbox now to see what requires immediate action?"

Richard said nothing.

Baffled, Amy held back on making immediate contact with Mike. She drifted into Cino's, ordered a hot rum liqueur coffee at the counter, sat at her usual table and watched the pedestrian flow. Feeling alone and uncertain in the world, Amy wondered how many of the pedestrians were truly happy, what they were all going through, facing up to or running away from in their daily lives. She laid the letter flat on the table and read it over, dissecting every word and nuance.. A waiter brought her coffee over and placed it on the table. She thanked him and took a few sips. Strong and delicious, Amy thought. She stared out of the window, tried to recall everything Mike had told her about his family feud, including Erica. A myriad of images reeled through her mind, from the day she'd first laid eyes on Mike, his excessively calm demeanor, the websites, the clothing, the secret codes he'd used at Candies, the clothes in Amsterdam to the drugs in the compartmentalized box. She grew suspicious about the cost of his luxurious lifestyle; the fact that he'd quite casually and comfortably invested five million pounds in his new business, his plans to practically live offshore, in the Turks, one of a number of hideouts popular with embezzlers and crooked CEO's, she thought. She wondered where she figured in Mike's life and, Vincent, her boss, the man she'd esteemed and highly regarded to date was now threatening to take legal action. Emotionally fraught, confused and in pain, Amy began to doubt her own intelligence. She couldn't deny the fact that she was infatuated with Mike and infuriated at allowing herself to be taken for a ride. Nauseated, Amy stopped herself from throwing up. She beckoned one of the waiters over. "Flag down a taxi outside right away, please?" she said, stuffing the letter in her handbag.

"Yes, Madam," said the young waiter, speeding off.

Amy stood up, left money on the table and went out front to wait for her taxi. She was desperate to take a shower, she suddenly felt soiled, filthy and overwhelmingly dirty.

Amy entered her apartment and slammed the door. Livid, she marched into her bedroom, undressed and tossed her clothes haphazardly on the floor. She grabbed a bath robe and threw it over her shoulders. Slumped in a heap on her bed, Amy wondered whether to call Mike or take a shower. Indecisive, she got up and paced her apartment. She retrieved her cell-phone out of her handbag and proceeded to the kitchen, telling herself that it would be better to call Mike before taking a shower. To calm her frazzled nerves, Amy opened a bottle of red wine, poured herself a glass, sat down at her kitchen table and sipped at it, melancholically. It was another ten minutes before Amy finally got up. After taking a long, hot shower and time spent recuperating on her couch, Amy called Mike. "I've bad news for you." Mike remained silent. "Mike? Can you hear me?"

"Yes. What is it?"

"I have, in my possession, a copy of a letter sent to Vincent from your father," said Amy, trembling furiously with rage.

"You do, do you? Well. What does it state? Read it to me."

Amy read the entire letter out loud, slowly and clearly.

Mike remained compellingly controlled. "Fabrications. All fabrications. I'd suspected he'd be viciously gunning for me to prove his ruthlessness. I'd mentioned to you that I'd be prepared to fight his every intransigence." Amy had recalled the conversation. "I'd suspected that he'd have inevitably learned about my new business due to the advertisement posted on the internet which I've noted is presently featured in a number of industry and travel websites. With this move, I've, no doubt, become a competitor and a threat to him."

Amy sighed. "Knowing what your father is capable of doing, surely, you could have traded under some other name!"

"I understand your concerns. In time, the company will effectively be known as The Brandleton Group. With a little fishing and digging around, my father would eventually learn about my set up sooner or later, regardless of the company name."

Mike's calmed approach frustrated and infuriated Amy. "A reputational risk, the letter is quite damming that Vincent has threatened to pull the plug on the venture and take legal action should this fiasco not get cleared up within a week. And where do I figure in all of this, Mike? I could lose my livelihood and—this is just awful—bloody, fucking ludicrous," she said in a voice wearied with stress.

"I'll talk to Vincent," said Mike.

"I'd rather you do so now and resolve this—fucking nightmare." Her pulses quickening, Amy stiffened. "I trusted you, Mike. I thought you were the best thing that has ever happened to me."

"You've no reason to mistrust me, Amy. In fact, I'm a changed man, for the better, thanks to you."

Amy swallowed hard. Anger and resentment shot through her veins. "What the fuck is that supposed to mean?" she returned implacably. "What about the drug abuse!" she screamed.

"I've nothing to hide, Amy. You've seen what I take. Admittedly, I dabble a little here and a little there, without dependency. I've nothing to hide. I'm no abuser, far from it. I can simply discard the lot now without the need for further indulgence." Amy said nothing. "Listen to me, Amy?" Mike pleaded, "I'd normally do this much better, face to face but, under the circumstances … put it this way … I'm not very good at the emotional stuff and would normally have put an end to this conversation from the onset. However, you've given me a new lease of life. Apart from the odd associate here and there, you are the only genuine person in my life. I love you, Amy. I mean every word. Take it or leave it."

Confused and uncertain, Amy couldn't concentrate. She loved him too. Resentful, ambivalent, her chest tightening, she couldn't bring herself to repeat those words, not right now. Numbed by Mike's statement, Amy couldn't reciprocate. It was difficult. She didn't know what to believe. But, her love for Mike influenced her decision to warrant him a chance to resolve matters. Action speaks louder than words, she thought. "I've taken the day off to think things through," she said. Her head pounding, she felt all life was slowly draining out of her.

"I'll get onto Vincent now and, if it's any consolation to you, legal action will be sought should my father persist in this madness. Granted, things could get a little untidy, turn into an ugly picture, but he's left me with no other choice."

From that point, Amy began to rekindle a little faith in Mike. "Report back to me once you've talked to Vincent."

"Of course. And I aim to allay all your fears, Amy."

Heaving herself off the couch, strolled into the kitchen to pour herself another glass of wine. She had to keep a clear head, so she opened a half liter bottle of spring water, brought it to her lips and gulped the entire contents. Slightly refreshed, Amy called Juliana.

"Everything's under control," said Juliana

"Good. Good. I'll be back in the morning. Please, leave early today. No need to work to midnight tonight. Richard'll hold the fort."

"Thank you, Amy. In that case, I'll depart within the hour."

"Fine. You do that. Put Richard on for me, would you?"

"He's in a meeting, due back between one thirty and one forty-five."

"Fine. Please update him for me," said Amy, clicking off. She returned to her bedroom, picked up her clothes and worked on getting her bedroom ship-shape again. Activity is the key, she muttered, too stunned to shed a tear.

CHAPTER 31

Vincent placed Carlson Brandleton's letter on his desk and looked at it, expressionlessly. "I've news to report regarding this letter," he said. He put his elbows on the desk and formed a pyramid shape with his hands. Tensed, filled with a combination of fear, the determination to stand by Mike and fight for her dreams, Amy held her breath, crossed her legs, leant forward in her seat and waited, attentively, for Vincent to spill the perilous news. Vincent looked at Amy and twitched a rare smile at her saying, "After a lengthy discussion, very late last night here, in my office, Mike Brandleton duly furnished me with an acceptable rationale behind his father's cause to draft up such a letter and, after discussing the way forward, Project Cascadia will continue to go ahead as planned."

Amy nodded and exhaled slowly. "This is good news," she said quietly, wanting to collapse on the floor in a heap in sheer relief.

Vincent turned the letter over, placed it face down on his desk and scribbled a few words on the back. "No doubt, Mike Brandleton will furnish you with the facts also," he said. "In the meantime, I'll retain the letter and ask you not to breathe a word of this to anyone."

Amy uncrossed her legs. "Of course. My lips are sealed, Vincent" she said.

Vincent shifted in his chair. "Amy, it would not be wise to withhold any information with the propensity to adversely put the project in jeopardy or disrepute. For instance, how solid is this … intimacy … between you and Mike Brandleton?"

Tensed, Amy searched for a fitting response. "We're seriously focused on our shared business aims that, in futurity, I'm confident our intimacy will not adversely affect the project. Anything worthy of report outside of that, I grant that you'll be first to know, Vincent."

Vincent elevated his eyebrows saying, "Good. Although, we're both aware that you've chosen to refrain from answering my question, for the sake of professionalism, may I ask you to eschew making your intimacy common knowledge?"

Amy smiled tightly. "Mike Brandleton and I have addressed that area to our mutual understanding in order to avoid any negativity impacting the project."

"Good observance of you both. I still have absolute faith in you, Amy, and, apart from that, there's nothing further of due importance to state, unless, of course, you wish to add more to this discussion?"

"Yes, I do have a question, Vincent? Are there any steps being taken to prevent any possible further disruptions to the project on the part of yourself or Mike Brandleton?"

"I've left that up to Mike Brandleton to take care of where his father is concerned. Having said that, I'll personally not hesitate to take appropriate action, should an untoward situation present itself."

"I sincerely hope we've seen the end to this and that we can continue to do business on excellent terms," said Amy earnestly.

Vincent nodded and turned to his computer screen. "Would there be anything else?"

Amy rose from her seat and moved away. "No."

"Good," said Vincent.

Not guilty, Amy thought, as she walked out of Vincent's office, closing the door quietly behind her.

Amy returned to her desk gloriously relieved at the positive outcome of the discussion with Vincent. Quiescently optimistic, Amy decided to call Mike before throwing herself into her work. Desperately craving for a private celebratory cappuccino at Cino's, Amy checked her watch. It was seven forty-six. Richard and Juliana were due to arrive at any moment. Amy picked up her cell-phone and logged on her computer. Juliana, stepping out of the elevator, pre-empted Amy's call to Mike. Vowing to call Mike during her coffee break, Amy replaced her cell-phone on her desk and worked solidly for approximately an hour, delegating heavily to Juliana.

"Problem solved," said Mike triumphantly.

"Saved by the bell. You've managed to come up with a solution. Well done, Mike."

"Only just. You were right. Vincent was seconds away from terminating the contract. It took some convincing. He's a hard man. I'd offered an affidavit, a costly get-out clause to form as part of the contract, a promissory note, everything and anything in mitigation. Risky business. My father would have had great difficulty coming up with hard facts and viable evidence to fully support his allegations." Mike hissed. "Risky. Loopholes could crop up. I'm prepared to do anything, anything to uphold my integrity and credibility."

"What a relief. Going forward, how confident are you at keeping your father at bay?"

"The answer to that is, not very confident at all, to be truthful, but I'll have to come up with something to stop him in his tracks."

"What do you have in mind?"

"Plan A, I'll have my lawyer write to him, threaten legal action, defamation of character, that sort of thing, see what transpires. Hopefully, that should work where I won't be forced to go into Plan B. I'm wildly guessing that his game plan was that Planet Management would've pulled out of the deal for fear of bad publicity and the resultant knock-on effects but, little does he know, Planet Management has not gone running scared, nor I, most importantly, which leaves me still in the game, willingly battling on."

Amy sipped her cappuccino. "Well said. What's next?"

"To get out to the Turks as soon as. My plan would be to book the flight sometime today now that I've cleared things with Vincent. I'll forward my itinerary to you by email should you want to get on the same flight—I could hold a seat for you."

Amy breathed and sipped more cappuccino. "No. Please, that won't be necessary. Once I've completed the official handover to my team, I'll book a flight and email the particulars to you."

"Splendid. I do hope that you'll be close behind me."

"That's what I have in mind."

Mike coughed, discomfortingly. "Our affair ... our ... our secret's out, I'm afraid," said Mike, hesitantly apologetic. "It couldn't be helped. Vincent had a way of weeding it out of me."

Amy laughed.

"What's so amusing about that?" asked Mike, unsurely.

"Not only had he suspected, he rooted it out of me too, indirectly, of course," said Amy, laughing. "Sorry, Mike, I'd forgotten to mention it." Mike laughed. "Joking aside, we are expected to continue as we are Mike ... *discreetly* that is?" Amy emphasized.

"How on earth are we going to manage that, sleeping together in the Penthouse suite of our own hotel for goodness sakes?" exclaimed Mike, coolly.

Amy shrugged. "We'll devise a plan. No-one would suspect us unless, of course, we're being watched and, as the hotel would be effectively ours that entitles us to sleep in our Penthouse suite without openly flaunting our affair. How does that sound?"

"Painful. The hotel staff won't be fooled that easily. They're a ubiquitous lot, knowledgeable about most of what goes on, clandestinely. They're guilty of it themselves," said Mike laughingly.

"I'm more concerned with Rory and anyone else associated with Planet Management and other officials we'll be communicating ..."

"You're getting paranoid again. Let's cross all those bridges when we come to them, shall we?" Mike broke in.

"Agreed."

"Stefan's expertise would be required again."

"That's fine. He's on standby, working solely on this project."

"Splendid," said Mike.

Amy's cell-phone bleeped its call waiting signal. Could be Vincent, Amy thought. "Mike, I've got to dash off. I've a call waiting. Sorry!" she said, reluctantly cutting Mike off, pushing the call waiting button.

"Ten minutes before the signing ceremony commences," announced Richard promptly.

Amy drank her cappuccino hurriedly. "Thanks. I'll be there in five." Sunlight flooding her immediate area, Amy pulled out her make-up bag and mirror and swiftly applied a light touch of crystal shimmer lip gloss, strokes of blusher and a light patting of silk translucent powder. She dabbed Creed's Spring Flower perfumed scent behind each ear and gently combed her finger tips through her hair. She had to look her best. It was her first signing ceremony. A handful of financial press photographers and journalists were attending the planned publicizing of Planet Management's recent acquirement of a boutique investment management company. Lifting herself, Amy vacated the table. The waiters gawked at her strutting out of Cino's and heading down the street back to the office building. She entered the conference room punctually and was ushered to her designated spot at the signing table. The briefing discussions, announcements, signing ceremony and group photo sessions went smoothly. Vincent and the CEO of the boutique investment management company held a brief press conference, to which Amy was not required to participate. She dashed off to complete the handover with Richard and Juliana, delegating the onus of the asset management project to Juliana with Richard providing support as and when necessary, as well as assuming the remainder of Amy's responsibilities during her absence. Richard proudly glistens at the concept of assuming the better half of Amy's responsibilities, boosting his once thwarted ego. Amy then emailed Mike requesting him to book her a thirty day return on his departure flight.

Amy opened her eyes and smiled at Mike, peacefully asleep, snuggled closely to her in the large, round, white rotating bed. Her eyes roamed the unfamiliar surroundings of the luxuriously palatial master bedroom in the Penthouse suite of their newly acquired hotel. Light flickered through the white wooden plantation styled shutters. The intoxicative perfumed scents of tropical flowers flooded the room. Items of elegant rattan furniture were appealingly appointed around the master bedroom. International artwork graced the white-washed walls. A Plasma TV, CD and DVD player were fixed juxtaposition along the wall facing her. Jet-lagged and disorientated, Amy had lost track of time. They'd arrived on the Providenciales Island, Turks and Caicos mid Saturday morning, at around eleven forty with Stefan due to arrive the following morning. Rory had kept the meet and greet session of the former hotel owner and the hotel's top tier management intuitively short prior to expediently whisking them off to their Penthouse suite by one fifteen, sharp. Mike displayed the "DO NOT DISTURB" sign on the door, swept Amy into his arms and carried her into the master bedroom. They made love speechlessly, slowly and quietly. Two hours later, Amy awoke. Thirsting, she got out of bed and embarked upon a search for water. Spotting two sets of toweling bathrobes and slippers nicely presented on the rattan couch, Amy shuffled wearily over, slipped on a set and quietly crept out of the master bedroom into the sophisticated lounge with its modern décor, ottomans and Italian styled couches. She walked over to the impressively styled open-plan kitchen, appointed at the far end of the lounge. A digital clock inset on the door of the aluminum refrigerator displayed the late afternoon time of three seventeen. She fetched a half liter bottle of water out of the well stocked refrigerator, drank the entire contents and set the empty bottle on the aluminum and oak wood breakfast bar. Turning round and walking to the window, Amy flipped opened the wooden shutters. The tropical sunlight flooded the lounge. Wearisome, in need of more sleep and slumber, Amy crept back into the master bedroom. She stepped out of the slippers, let the bathrobe fall at her feet and exhaustively crawled back into the bed.

Mike stirred and turned to her. Squinting, he reached up and pecked her on her cheek. "Good morning. I'm famished. Breakfast?" he whispered croakily.

Amy chuckled wearily. "It's around three-thirty in the afternoon, Turks time that is."

Mike raised his right arm, checked his watch and said, "We've dinner, tonight at the Grace Bay, Blue Ocean Club. I took the liberty of asking Rory to reserve a table for two at the oceanfront restaurant. Are you free at eight o'clock?"

Amy giggled. "I'll have to check my diary," she joked, paradoxically relishing in the idea of a weekend spent in paradisiacal orientation of thirty days on the lush Caribbean island, its people, the hotel, interrupted by periodic checking of her Blackberry and cell-phone and, on Monday, focus her attentions on learning, hands on, the ramifications of running a hotel, touching base with Vincent and Juliana on the asset management project and any other business in between.

"Rory has arranged a series of dining appointments." Mike propped himself up on his elbow and gazed at Amy. "Lunch tomorrow with the former owner of this hotel, his wife, plus the proprietor of the real estate company followed by dinner with the launch party organizers on the same day. Rory and Stefan will be joining us at both."

"My word," exclaimed Amy stretching her arms. "That's a heavy eating schedule."

Mike yawned. "It's all part of the package."

"Rory has worked out the launch party budget, no doubt?"

"Yes. During my initial visit, we'd selectively identified the most advantageously beneficial offers and opted for this particular company who are also public relations professionals skilled in knowing really important ways to generate attention. Be warned. Expect a dizzying affair of the island's media, celebrities, dignitaries and business people all to be present. There'll be a pre-opening exclusive that Vincent has expressed an interest in coming along to."

Amy raised an eyebrow. "Vincent?" she exclaimed.

Mike nodded. "Yes, he'd expressed his interest in coming along after we'd cleared up the problem of my father and ended our discussion running over a few points related to the hotel business and launches."

"Excellent."

"A dinner with the Penthouse designer specialists has been scheduled to be held on Monday."

"Brill," said Amy headily, impressed with Mike's accurate recall of appointments. "And the spa?"

"Yes, the spa," murmured Mike. "I've left that in the hands of Rory and Stefan to come up with the most appropriately thrift company with proven ability to build unique, state-of-the-art, deluxe spa facilities on the grounds as well as in the Penthouse suites, offering the most ultimately luxurious therapies from hydrotherapy, thalassotherapy, to ayurvedic, complete with relaxation rooms, fitness studios and certified personnel," said Mike, suppressing the memory of Belinda, "We've got to get it right first time."

"I agree," said Amy, astounded by Mike's extensive spa requirements.

Mike threw back the Egyptian cotton sheets and got out of bed. "Coffee?" he asked, throwing on the remaining bathrobe and shoving his feet in the slippers.

"Bottled water would be fine."

"Coming right up."

Amy looked around the room and pinched herself. "No, I'm not dreaming, this is real. It's all real," she whispered.

Mike returned with two opened bottles of water, walked over to Amy and handed her a bottle. Amy drank gratefully. Mike gulped his water thirstily, placed the empty bottle on the bedside table and removed his bathrobe, tossing it on the floor alongside Amy's.

Amy gasped at the beauty of his nakedness. "Adonis," she whispered cooingly, placing her bottle on the table.

Mike smiled, climbed onto the bed and straddled her.

Nestling at the candlelit dinner table, Amy daintily sipped fine, white wine that had complemented their gourmet cuisine, perfectly. Lapping up the surroundings and breathtaking views of the oceanfront restaurant, Amy bade her admiration to the beauty of the lush gardens and the colorful array of tropical flowers generously emitting their delicate night perfumery. Her eyes fell on Mike seated opposite her, they were saying, "*I love you.*" Amy hoped he'd read them accurately. Her cell-phone bleeped, vibrated on the table and flashed its intermittent glow of fluorescent green. Blood rushed to her cheeks at the sight of Jenson's name and number. She cleared her throat, pushed the accept button and spoke coolly. "Hallo?"

"Hey! Amy! It's been a long time. Where are you? You're cell has tripped over to an overseas ring tone!"

"The Caribbean?"

"Wow, woman! There's no stopping you. Let me guess. Antigua?"

"No. The Turks," she said, perturbed. "What can I do for you? I'm in the middle of something right now."

"Just wanted to touch base with you … find out how you've been getting on … that sort of thing."

Amy looked at Mike. Mike smiled and waved his hand in the air majestically, gesturing Amy to take all the time she needed.

She peered into her wine glass. "Busy as usual," she said, bluntly.

"You're still mad at me. I know. I can hear it," said Jenson, reproachfully.

"I'd rather not go into that, thank you." Amy's frustration was beginning to show, she lifted her head and looked at Mike. Mike looked back frowningly at her.

"I wanted to invite you to a wine bar or a quick coffee but, as you're out of the country and …"

"It's over." Amy still looked at Mike.

"Yeah. Don't I know it," said Jenson, sarcastically. "I believed that we stood the chance of remaining on friendly terms, at the very least."

"Move on. Emigration may be on the cards for me," said Amy, threateningly.

"Congratulations to you. I'll be sorry to see you go. You're one of a kind, Amy. I'll never forget you."

Amy blinked. "Thank you for your kind sentiments."

"Look, putting our past aside, I want you to know that I'll always be here for you and if you ever get stuck or need a helping hand, an ear or whatever, I'll be here for you."

Quivering at the unbearable thought of ever having to call on Jenson for help, Amy leant back in her chair and smiled sweetly, promisingly and reassuringly at Mike. "Thanks again," she said, softly, "Bye, bye," clicking off her cellphone. She lifted her wine glass, brought it to her lips and sipped her wine in plausible silence. Leaning forward, Amy put her wine glass on the table, turned towards the ocean boasting its impeccable shade of night sky blue waters, lit by the placid moon. The ocean's waves delicately splashed and sprayed the talcum powdered textured sand, beckoning lovers taking a nighttime stroll along the beach to feel the water.

"Let me see. An old flame?"

Amy cleared her throat. "An old admire. He's not one to worry about. I'll not accept any further calls from him. That way, he'll eventually get the message and delete my cell-phone number in due course," she said, pained in having to taint her magical night explaining Jenson away.

Mike nodded and beamed at Amy searchingly. "It's flattering that I am the beau of a sought after woman," he said, neatly folding his used linen napkin, placing it on the table. "I'm rudely impelled to make an enquiry overhearing the statement about emigration?"

Amy smiled nervously, outstretched her arms gracefully in the air, looked left and right and said, "Here, with you, of course."

"Delighted to hear it," said Mike.

"Fancy a stroll along the beach front?"

"Certainly," said Mike.

Sunday lunch was enjoyably relaxing; the guests were quite informally jolly, pleasant and entertaining. Later that evening, during the sumptuous dinner with the launch party officials, Amy learned the intricacies and differential facets of staging a launch party from pre-launch publications, pre-opening exclusives, ribbon cutting ceremonies, media tours, guest screenings, types and suitability of entertainment, whether to have a lavish soiree or an exquisitely tasteful affair, party sponsors to budgets; all quite heady, but an interesting and welcomed insight. Amy was conscious of the fact that it was evidently common knowledge among the staff, including Rory and Stefan that she had been residing with Mike in one of the Penthouse suites. No-one had acted suspiciously or untoward. They were treated with the utmost servility and respect by all with no questions asked.

The weekend sped past in a mist of pleasant memories. A full and relentless Monday morning tour of the hotel grounds, an inspection of virtually every floor, guest room and Penthouse suite, inevitably took its physical and mental toll on Amy. She rubbed her aching hands together, hurting from the aftermath of endless handshakes with everyone she'd met including the full complement of house-keeping staff during the morning line-up introductory session. Her cheek bones ached from wearing a fixed smile. Her head pounded, overloaded with heaps of internalized information on hotel jargon.

Monday afternoon, a sit down, champagne lunch by the pool with Mike and a few incumbents of the hotel management, openly voicing undiluted and inordinate views during their intensive discussions, aided in alleviating Amy of her discomfitures regarding her ability to become a positive force and asset to the venture. Analytical, Amy identified the undeniably attractive benefits and business potential in Cascadia—the hotel industry in general. After lunch, Amy shut herself away in her ground floor, fully equipped, air conditioned luxurious office suite and eased herself comfortably on the high-backed, black leather reclining chair behind her desk, directly facing the ocean. She looked at the computer screen and expediently responded to Vincent's demanding emails that kept flooding in fast and furiously. Amy felt that Vincent's demands and expectations of her were bordering on the unreasonable that she was almost tempted to remind him of the fact that he'd agreed and signed to her relinquishment of the majority of her responsibilities handed over to Richard with the onus of the sensitive asset management contract being handled by Juliana. But she thought better to conduct silent discretion, mobilizing Richard to instruct the teams to urgently furnish Vincent's demands; discussing the expected percentage returns on Planet Management's investments with Juliana and telephone conferencing-in Vincent to participate in the discussions. Amy noted that Richard had impressively sailed through all tasks with ease making time spent with him on the telephone a minimal one. At five o'clock, Amy logged off the computer and sauntered out of the office to the hotel lobby. She spotted Mike behind the reception desk observing the staff at work. Unsure of whether to make an approach, Amy strolled over to the spa and booked a nine-thirty massage for that evening. She returned to the lobby, took a deep breath and wandered over to Mike. "Excuse me for interrupting," she said.

Mike turned to Amy and smiled. "We're partners, you couldn't possibly interrupt me," he said cheerfully.

"At nine-thirty I'll be in the spa having a massage. Would there be anything you'd like to go over with me before then?"

Mike thought silently then he said, "I've nothing further today. The final and second leg of the tour of the hotel takes place tomorrow. I'll have a better idea on conclusion of the tour."

"Splendid," said Amy stoically, depleted of energy.

"Dinner?" asked Mike.

"Sure, we have an appointment, do we not?" enquired Amy.

"Yes. We've dinner at seven with the Penthouse interior designers. The restaurant's a couple of miles away. We'll drive out there in one of the hotel's fleet of cars and, should discussions overrun, I'll arrange to have you brought back here in time for your massage. How does that sound?" Mike put it to Amy.

"Perfect." she said.

CHAPTER 32

Dinner was superbly set in the unobtrusively, charming shack styled restaurant in the less affluent tourist area. Ignorant of the subject, Amy found the discussions on the technicalities of interior design very informative, if not educational. She listened astutely to Mike's renditions, knowledgeably putting forward his ideas and specifications from square footages, gleaming stainless-steel spa tubs, walnut floors to his and hers dressing rooms. Whilst Mike spent the night at the restaurant in continued discussions, Amy indulged in the head to toe massage which proved to be a fitting end to a hectic day and served as a mental preparation for the second leg of tours around the hotel complex scheduled for the following morning. At ten fifty, Amy returned to the Penthouse suite from the spa, collapsed on the master bed and stole a peaceful snooze. She was prematurely awakened by her cell-phone. Reaching up, Amy whipped her cell-phone off the round glass bedside table and thrillingly read a text message from Rochelle stating that she'd be arriving on the island that coming Saturday morning. Amy immediately responded *"Meet you at the airport."* She climbed off the bed, strolled over to the rattan dresser, bent forward slightly and jotted down Rochelle's flight details on a Post-it note. Eagerly awaiting news from Helen and Emily, Amy vowed to keep her cell-phone switched on at all times. Mike walked in quietly as she was on her way back to bed.

"It's late. I thought you'd be asleep by now," he said, adorning a weary smile.

"No. I've not long returned from the spa, a few minutes ahead of you. Besides, my cell-phone got me out of bed."

Mike began to undress. "Switch it off," he said, crossing the floor to the shower room.

Amy darted her eyes at her cell-phone. "It's around six o
evening in the UK. People may still want to get in touch with me," she said
loudly.

"You'll be far too busy to take any calls once I've emerged from the shower,"
said Mike audibly, over the power jet sprays.

Amy picked up her cell-phone and promptly switched it off.

Rochelle pinched and nudged Amy in the airport as they strolled together, side
by side, a safe distance behind Mike on their way to the car park.

"What a lucky scoop you've made, Amy. He's a scrumptious dish and a real
gentleman," Rochelle whispered under her breath, as she watched Mike load
her heavy suitcases inside the silver Mercedes people carrier with manly ease.

"At times, I can hardly believe it myself," said Amy quietly.

Waiting patiently, modeling his tan, looking healthy and undeniably handsome, Mike held the passenger door opened for them.

Rochelle, the first to arrive, climbed into the vehicle. "Thank you, Mr.
Brandleton," she said courteously.

Mike smiled at her behind his Cartier sunglasses. "Please, call me, Mike," he
said, discretely patting and rubbing Amy's butt as she climbed into the vehicle.

Mellow jazz music playing, Mike drove leisurely along the scenic route to
the hotel. Amy and Rochelle talked non stop, sitting comfortably relaxed in the
back.

"I'm so looking forward to our diving expeditions," said Rochelle.

"We could go tomorrow morning if you like. The hotel has a boat leaving at
eight or, we could go out one of our Hobie Cats," Amy suggested.

"Let's do that." exclaimed Rochelle excitedly, battling sleeplessness and jet-
lag as she peered out of the window at the tropical waters, streaking the edge of
the powdery sands with contrasting white waves, the locals strolling idly by,
individual tourists jogging clinically on the beach along the water's edge, local
fishermen returning from their catch, basking in the sun, busily tightening and
reinforcing their fishing nets in preparation for the next fishing trip.

"Great. Meet me in the lobby at seven for breakfast. By seven forty-five,
we'll set off for the harbor," said Amy, pausing unsurely. "On second thoughts,
would it not be a better idea to give it a day or two before diving having just
flown in an altitude of thirty-five thousand feet?"

Rochelle turned to Amy and gazed at her thoughtfully. "You have a point,
there. Perhaps you're right. Instead of diving, I think I'll opt for sailing and a
long swim in the ocean with a bit of snorkeling thrown in."

"Brilliant," said Amy.

"Have you decided on a date for the launch party? Where can I shop on the island for that special outfit?"

"It's a long way off yet. We're hoping to stage the launch, in January, during the off season. Who knows we may stage it earlier, in six weeks, who knows? Looks like you'll have to return to the island, I'm afraid."

"Oh! In six weeks at the earliest! That far away will give me time to shed some of this weight." Rochelle made a poor attempt of sucking in her stomach.

"My sentiments entirely, speaking of weight loss," said Amy.

"Why, Amy? You look wonderful. This is the best I've seen you."

Blood rushed to Amy's cheeks in the cool, air conditioned vehicle. "Rubbish," said Amy. "You look wonderful too."

Rochelle shrugged her shoulders. "I disagree."

"It's your prerogative," Amy returned.

Mike pulled up at the main entrance of the hotel. Two bell boys came rushing forward. One opened the doors and the other loaded Rochelle's suitcases onto the high brass, luggage cage and wheeled it away to a secure holding area, out of sight, adopting one of Mike's numerous changes, processes and procedures recently put in place. Luggage lying around the lobby was one of Mike's pet hates. A bell boy waited, obsequiously, at the vehicle. Mike tossed the fob device at him. Catching it, his eyes beaming with excitement, the bell boy took the prestige vehicle on a careful joy ride to the car pound and parked it alongside the hotel's fleet of cars.

"Enjoy your stay with us, Rochelle. You're in perfect hands," said Mike, nodding at Amy, beckoning the staff to fetch them all a glass of freshly made tropical fruit juice.

"It's a charming place, beautifully tucked away in seclusion. Stylish, quiet, homely and peaceful," remarked Rochelle impressively, looking around everywhere as she followed Mike and Amy to an intimate lounging area.

"Thanks. We plan to renovate the entire hotel, working from the top floor," said Amy, confidently proud.

"Renovate? Ouch! I don't envy you. There's nothing wrong with the place. It's gorgeous," said Rochelle, flopping herself into an armchair.

A barman swiftly entered the lounge and placed his tray of three glasses of fresh tropical juice at the centre of the table between them.

Amy looked at Mike. "Actually, it's all Mike's idea. I'm quite looking forward to the challenge."

Mike handed Amy and Rochelle their tropical fruit juices, lifting the long-stemmed glasses off the barman's tray. "I'll leave you ladies alone, if I may," said Mike, taking his glass, excusing himself.

"Makes sense I suppose putting the Cascadia signature—your personal touch on the establishment," said Rochelle.

Amy observed that Rochelle had trouble stifling a yawn. "Precisely," said Amy, nodding profusely. She sipped her juice. "Let's head to your room." Amy left her glass on the table and sauntered out of the lounge, along the corridor and let herself into Rochelle's deluxe room. Her luggage had been delivered. "Would you like me to arrange the luggage unpacking and ironing service for you?

"No. I'll unpack them later." Rochelle rushed over to the sliding glass patio doors that opened out onto the landscaped gardens with the beach a few paces away. "This is just too much. Divine!" she gasped.

"I'm glad you like it. I suspect you'll want to take a shower, a nap or whatever. I'll be in my office for a couple of hours. Call me on my office extension, number ten, should you need me. The front desk, they'll be happy to locate me if I've wandered off somewhere. By the way, Mike and I would like you to join us for dinner tonight at eight." Amy idled in the doorway.

Rochelle unlocked one of her suitcases and started to unpack. "Work! On a Saturday! You drive a hard bargain," she said, placing her underwear in the lilac scented drawer of the rattan dresser.

"It's purely my choice. There's so much to learn about the industry that, whenever the opportunity presents itself, I tend to cram in as much as possible"

"I understand and, quite right you are too. With that attitude, you'll be a great success."

"That's my intention. Thank you," said Amy flippantly. "Well?—Dinner?"

Rochelle smiled widely. "I couldn't possibly refuse."

"Meet me in the lobby, by the front desk at five minutes to."

"I'll be there," said Rochelle.

Amy closed the door quietly behind her and headed to her office. Shaking her head at how busy she was going to be over the coming weeks, contemplating work, entertainment and relationship demands set upon her, she thought she'd make the effort to grab a massage, a steam or sauna, a swim, a relaxing lunch or dinner in between. She entered her office, poured herself a tall glass of freshly squeezed orange juice, sank in her black leather chair and marveled at the Atlantic. The island growing on her, Amy would discuss the extension of her stay of a further thirty days with Mike and Vincent. And, after that, she'd take a surreptitious look into the pros and cons of emigrating.

It was the last Saturday in January, an early evening and the island of Provo had basked in the relentlessly hot sun. A faint breeze traveling through the tropical gardens flurried around the eclectic array of guests. The launch party consultants exceeded their expectations by delivering their impressive expertise to precision. Vincent attended the pre-launch soiree and ribbon-cutting ceremony alongside the island's local celebrities, mayor, government representatives, business and public officials. Impressed with the smart, new renovations, carried out with minimal disruption to customers and staff and, Mike revealing his ambitious strategic plans to expand within the industry, Vincent discretely expressed his probable interest in Mike's business aims, by making a verbal and tentative offer to inject additional funds with continued Planet Management backing and support.

"Let's discuss this more pragmatically when the excitement's over." said Vincent, lightheartedly debating the hotel and real estate business over a glass of vintage champagne in Mike's office.

Mike discussed Vincent's offer of additional investment with Amy and his personal lawyer. All were in agreement and Mike planned to return to the UK in March to pursue the matter. The main launch was held during the late afternoon of the last Saturday in February. Arriving at the main doors of Cascadia were select members of the island's local press, business and industry magazines, visitor bureaus, TV and radio, all influentially lured by the launch consultants' captivatingly coercive coverage of Cascadia's unique facilities and ambience. A number of hotels opening and launching on the islands were not all enjoying the same level of success as experienced by Cascadia. They were launching to only a handful of guests, experiencing a decline in guests failing to make their appearance owing to the unappealingly ordinary advertising suited to ordinary hotels, poor public relational know-how and weak contact listings. The consultants hired jointly by Mike and Rory popularized Cascadia's few weekend giveaways and featured an interesting and impressive story on branding, service and quality in industry publications, newsletters and on travel websites. The local radio broadcasted both launches live from the hotel lobby.

"You've really gone up in the world, Sis!" said Helen in the crowded Roman themed reception room, amid the live performance of the islands' prominent Caribbean steel band. "And as for Mike, what a hunk!"

Amy smiled wearily. "Please, let me be the one to break the news to Mu.
and Dad about my relationship with Mike?"

"Of course, Sis. Don't worry I'll warn Emily, although she doesn't seem to
give two hoots about you and Mike." Helen laughed.

"Thanks, Helen. Warn Emily, anyway."

"Will do."

"By the way, where is she? Any ideas?" Amy scanned the crowds.

"She's in your office, surfing the net."

"That's fine, but she ought to come out and mingle. As hostess, I've got to
be seen to be circulating. Enjoy. I'll catch you later." Amy weaved her way over
to Katie who had drastically altered her image, for the better. Shedding a few
pounds and ridding herself of the French plait, Katie wore her Auburn hair
shoulder length. Surprised at Katie's strict eating and exercise regime, now a
fully fledged vegetarian, a week spent on the island, Amy observed that Katie
ate an assortment of fresh fruits, vegetables, beans and a carefully measured
handful of nuts. She'd jog daily along the beachfront, followed through with a
strenuous work out in the gym, without one day going amiss.

"Amy!" Katie showered Amy with boisterous hugs and continental kisses.
"It's such a wonderful launch party. And the renovations are amazing. The
entire hotel's magnificent, but the Penthouse suites, they're just magical. I
adored the Rain Room with the option to select a sauna, steam and laconium
as well as special lighting and music by the touch of a button. The glass swimming pools on the roof, the rainbow colored water falls in the bathrooms and
all the remote controls and gadgetries without losing that personal touch and
comfort have been brilliantly put together. You've done remarkably well, Amy."
Katie gushed discernibly.

"Thanks, Katie. All the credit ought to go to Mike as they're all his dreams
and concepts coming true," Amy philosophized.

"You deserve to take some of the credit too, Amy. Don't take anything away
from yourself. Remember, behind every successful man, there is a woman.
Don't forget that. I can bet your bottom dollar, Mike couldn't have done it so
well without you."

"I guess ... you could be right," said Amy.

"Hey, seriously speaking, I like the island so much, I'm tempted to hang
around and perhaps, drum up some business," speculated Katie.

Pleased and surprised, Amy blinked hard and sipped her champagne. "I'd
like that very much indeed, Katie. Accommodation at my hotel would be available to you, at a preferentially discounted rate, of course," said Amy, pinching

ly believe that she'd actually landed exceedingly well, sur-
...ations.

...nd considerate of you, Amy," Katie shrieked.

this more in-depth tomorrow."

"Great... ...er know, we could be doing business together, you and me?"
Katie giggled nervously and winked at Amy.

"I might like that very much, Katie. The concept is worth considering. Let's talk about it tomorrow." Aghast at the potentiality and probability of going into business with Katie and having Katie with her on the island, Amy considered a very welcoming and pleasing idea. She looked around the room and smiled warmly at a number of guests who'd made eye contact with her. "My feet ache. I need a five minute breather," she said, tired of mingling.

"Feel free. Go right on ahead," said Katie.

"This young lady can tell a great gag. They're absolutely hilarious. Hello again, Katie. We met earlier?" A distinguished looking, middle-aged man, had edged his way through the crowd towards Amy and Katie. Smiling widely he extended his hand to Katie.

Amy recognized the man as the editor-in-chief of a consortium of industrial publications. Moving away, Amy smiled and raised her eyebrows teasingly at Katie. "I'll leave you to it," she said. She rode the private elevator to her suite, entered the lounge, looked around and, hardly able to contain herself, Amy smiled blissfully. Never in my wildest dreams had I ever imagined that my life would have come to this! she thought. Wearing an elegant, pure silk ivory cocktail dress adorned with sequins, Amy was a breathless picture. The sun's fluorescent glow illuminated the luxuriousness of the cool, air-conditioned suite. Amy slipped her petite feet out of her sequined leather ivory sandals and, settling back on the rich cerise, leather chaise-longue, picked up an incoming call on the private business line. "Hotel Cascadia, Amy Scott speaking," she warbled, bringing her knees up to her chin and rubbing her aching feet.

"Mike Brandleton. Is he there?"

"He's heavily commitment at present that it'll take me a few minutes to locate him. Would you care to leave your name and number?"

"Tell him it's Carlson Brandleton on the phone. I'll hold on, thank you."

"Yes. Of course, of course." Outraged and trembling, disguising her shock, Amy put Carlson on hold, swung her legs off the chaise-longue and pressed the button that automatically connected her to the front desk. The head receptionist answered after four rings. "Would you locate Mike Brandleton straight away, please? Ask him to come to the suite. I've Carlson Brandleton on the line holding for him."

"Right away, madam."

Amy returned the telephone to its cage, settled back on the chaise-longue and waited anxiously for Mike to arrive.

The head receptionist located Mike in the reception room conversing with a group of guests, called him aside and relayed Amy's message. Concealing his anger, ambivalently curious, settling to hear what Carlson had to say, Mike returned to his guests, apologized for his brief and untimely absence, promising his return and without drawing undue attention, quickly made his exit.

Amy nervously checked her watch. It was approaching five o'clock. Approximately six minutes had flown by since she'd taken the call.

Mike marched into the lounge and, without saying a word to Amy, swiped the cordless telephone from its cage. "Hello?" he howled, marching out onto the balcony.

With Mike out of earshot, conversing on the balcony, Amy panicked. She feared the conversation could result in her losing Mike, her hopes, dreams and all she'd worked for. Threatened, confused and angry, her thoughts deliriously clouded, her heart thumping, Amy got on her feet, slipped on her sequined leather ivory sandals and hobbled tremblingly and awkwardly slow out onto the balcony hoping to catch the odd word or phrase that would give her some form of an insight. She stood behind Mike's normally strong and athletic frame. His back was now hunched and his shoulders tensed. Stricken, Amy inhaled and exhaled slowly, raised her hands and placed them gently and lovingly on Mike's shoulders. In an attempt to sooth his tension away, Amy started massaging and rubbing his shoulders. Mike ended the call, turned around and looked at Amy with cold and expressionless eyes. Her heart slipped a beat and her stomach lurched. Numbed, Amy looked coldly into Mike's eyes. "What is it, Mike? Is there something wrong?"

"It's. It's, Erica," he said.

"What about her?" Amy's lips quivered slightly.

"The bitch has taken an overdose."

Filled with mixed emotions, remorse, devastation and guilt, Amy looked away. "Fatal?—

I mean, has she died?"

"No. She was discovered on time, got rushed to hospital and had her stomach pumped. She's making a good recovery now." Mike inhaled deeply and braced his back and shoulders.

"What else … did he say?" Amy probed nervously

Mike exhaled slowly. "With regard to the letter, he's apologized, congratulated me on Cascadia and has asked that I return to London, owed to the fact that his intentions are to make amends … reconcile."

Discouraged and afraid, Amy gazed searchingly at Mike. "Father has actually apologized." Mike gazed at Amy. She was now witnessing his muddled expressions of shock, confusion and disbelief etched on his face.

"What are you going to do?"

Mike looked up at the sky. "Return to our guests and enjoy the rest of the party."

This is totally unacceptable. Senseless, Amy thought. She was convinced that Mike had gone into a state of shock, some sort or delayed reaction. She wrapped her arms lovingly around him in an attempt to prevent him from leaving the balcony, stalling him. Mike gazed into her eyes and began kissing her passionately. The sound of rapturous applause, cheers and wolf whistles were heard from the guests, watching from the tropical gardens below. Caught off guard, Mike and Amy burst into nervous laughter.

"Our secret's out," said Mike, laughingly.

"Now what do we do?" exclaimed Amy, smiling widely.

Mike took Amy by the hand and led her back into their Penthouse suite.

THE END

978-0-595-42199-2
0-595-42199-7

Printed in the United Kingdom
by Lightning Source UK Ltd.
120417UK00001B/79-96